Reluctant pilgrim

The Lost Book of
Margery Kempe's Maidservant

ffiona perigrinor

Reluctant pilgrim

The Lost Book of
Margery Kempe's Maidservant

with illustrations by
Michael Gabriel

Anglepoise
Books

Anglepoise
Books

Anglepoise Books
46 Hayfield Road, Oxford, OX2 6TU www.oxfordfolio.co.uk

Cover design and typesetting by Kate Kunac

Set in 11.5/15 pt Baskerville

Illustrations © Michael Gabriel, 2021

Printed by Biddles Books Ltd., King's Lynn, Norfolk, England

ISBN: 9781916309951
British Library Cataloguing-in-Publication Data

A catalogue record for this book is available from the British Library

10 9 8 7 6 5 4 3 2 1
www.perigrinor.co.uk

Solvitur Ambulando

… Long is the way
And hard, that out of Hell leads into light.

John Milton: Paradise Lost

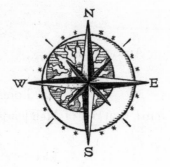

Travels & Travails ...

1 *'my lady is dead'* – Bishop's Lynn, June 16th, 1439   9

2 *'it's now that my life begins to change'* – Norfolk, 1373-1393   22

3 *'torn between silk & sackcloth'* – Bishop's Lynn, 1393-1413   74

4 *'I shall pilgrim to the holy places'* – York, Canterbury,
Lincoln, London, Bishop's Lynn, Zierickzee, 1413   124

5 *'you good pilgrims are bound to love one another in the name of
our Lord'* – To The Holy Land, 1413-1414   163

6 *'at last I see you for who you truly are'* – Rome, Bishop's Lynn,
Bristol, Compostela, 1414-1417   207

7 *'many swore we'd burn'* – Leicester, Lincoln, York, Beverley,
Bishop's Lynn, 1417-1431   245

8 *'I thanked God for his kindness'* – Bishop's Lynn, Danzig,
Calais, Bishop's Lynn, 1431-July 1441   294

9 *'...some safe harbour...'* – Bishop's Lynn,
July 29th, 1443   328

AFTERWORD   333

1

Bishops Lynn, June 16th, 1439

'My lady is dead now, dead and buried'

I come back one last time and sit in the room where she took her last breath as the sun sets and darkness draws in. The little screech owls in the copse beyond the orchard begin calling to one another, the last sheep cough as they settle close together, and the bats fly down from the eaves as they always do in the half light which is neither day nor night, harbingers of the day's end. I watch their intricate dances on their familiar invisible paths and think about our journeys all those years ago, the terrible perils we faced, and the threat of being burnt alive in this life or the life hereafter.

Just as the church bells begin to chime for the last service of the day, the candles start spluttering, their wicks grown thick, tallow spilling onto the boards. A sharp chill seeps into the room and it isn't that kind of a chill that arises sometimes when the tide is out or there's about to be a storm at sea, but rather a clammy cold that reeks of the grave, and something stirring within it. Yet it has been warm all day and still, like the stillness we knew waiting for a wind to carry us over the seas or back home again.

I sit, shivering.

Suddenly the casements rattle, the door flies open, the candles flicker, go out, then flare up again, casting dread shadows on the opposite wall. I see a wretched multitude of poor people there, struggling and straining against the gale, such pain and despair, such groaning and gasping like *the grim figures in the Doom paintings at St Margaret's when the Bad are taken from the Good and harrowed into the jaws of hell – those poor, wasted souls, haunted, tortured, burning, lost.*

Dogs howl in the lane outside, a horse paws on the cobbles in the stable yard, hooves rasping on stone. Somewhere in the distance a babe starts to cry, that sudden sob of instant pain or a bad dream, feeling herself alone, then just as suddenly she ceases, settling back into the comfort of sleep.

Just one long moment ...

Then stillness once more and a warm silence, sweetness almost. And I think about my lady talking of the sweetness of Our Lord.

While the bells are still chiming the candles start to burn steadily again, the air is balmy and the cheerful cries of the owls herald the night once more. Yes my lady is dead and at peace now I reckon, finally at rest after all her journeying, her soul released from the bonds of evil and pain and free to meet whatever there is to meet beyond, on the other side.

I get up, open the chest at the end of her bed and take out the bundle of parchment, which is wrapped in the last piece of silk she bought from the slant-eyed maiden in Bethlehem. At the bottom there is an old leather pouch, which I hadn't noticed before. Several small phials tumble out, as well as various pilgrim emblems, the palm of Jerusalem, scallop-shell of Compostela, Aachen mirror, Danzig sailing-vessel and many more. I hold them in my hand awhile, then take them into the yard and let them fall slowly one by one into the well, listening as they splash into the water. It's fitting they too should have a burial. Then, once again, silence.

There's nothing here for me anymore. These past three days have been so full that I am tired to the bone, yet it's only two weeks since my lady first suffered from fever. She refused to see the physic or be purged, though Spryngolde came to sit with her each morning. Once again, as in those early days, she was plagued by visions of demons crawling from under her bed and fighting with the angels above. She ate little by day, was wracked by an endless cough and so pained and restless at night that I quit our bed and slept on the rushes in the chamber next door. At times I heard her calling for the sin-eater, then the sound of something thumping the bedposts, and I thought of her poor head. But she would not let me come in to her.

That night she raged throughout the darkness. I remembered the time so many years ago when they called me to her and how we'd struggled together until the skies lightened and then both slept, her head on my shoulder. This time she fought alone. When dawn came she let me feed her some warmed wine and bread soaked in gruel, and was peaceful until the coughing started again. All that next night she coughed and coughed though uttered not a single complaint until daybreak when she bid me fetch her confessor and the clerk.

I could not leave her alone with the bright light of death in her eyes and called out to the yard-boy,

"Go Thomas, go quickly and tell Spryngolde your mistress is dying. Call Jane, then rouse our neighbours, tell them to come straightway and help me attend to her. Ask one of them to go to the Guildhall, then summon Richard the clerk, and bid Roger come too that he may take my messages."

And he, crossing himself with tears in his eyes, stumbled swiftly away.

Widow Joan came first with a crucifix, which she held in front of my lady's face urging her to confess her sins lest she die like a hellhound in her bed. But that she would not do until her priest came. To keep Joan at a distance I lit a candle and helped my lady hold it so that she might have a light to gaze on in her fading moments, locking her frail fingers round it and binding her weak clasp with cloth to stop it from slipping. More neighbours came and soon the gossiping began.

"A saint, a holy woman, a saint, a true saint ..."
    "Stuck up and full of pride ..."
"Poor man, cast off like that ..."
    "Herring and pike..."
"A wise woman, a good pious soul ..."
    "And her father ..."
"Yes, and all those poor children, that son, her eldest son ..."
    "Blessed Lady, intercede for us ..."
"Praying and pilgrimaging ..."
    "Her writing ... that book, her book."
"Those trials, those Lollers ..."
    "A saint, a saint ..."

Then Richard arrived with his servant and writing materials and the whispering ceased while everyone crept forward to hear the details of her last will as she said them, not faltering once. First was the list of her debts as she recalled them. She named me one of her executors and charged me with overseeing the arrangements for her funeral, as she'd already explained and made me swear to observe, and she asked that her other executors, Richard and her confessor, distribute alms on her behalf. Then she told the long list of prayers she wanted said in all the churches in Lynn and at the annual Mass at the Holy Trinity chapel for as long as there was money left from the sale of her chattels and house.

Her coughing started once more and she gasped pitifully for breath. When she was able to breathe again, she named the sum she wished to be set aside for a candle to be burnt forever in her memory in the Trinity chapel, then she whispered that the rest of her property was to be sold and the funds divided between the Black, White and Grey Friars to pray for her, her father and all the departed.

But she said nothing about the monies she'd promised to bequeath for the clothing and dowries of two motherless maidens, and I did not press her.

All this effort weakened her and she started choking. I went to her and rubbed her back. Joan and some of the other women started their harassment again, shouting at her to confess her sins before the demons came to snatch her soul away, pinching her arms whenever her eyes glazed over. Those who truly loved her were now weeping and shuffled closer on their knees. A few reached out to touch her as if she were already some holy relic. Others stood with folded arms, whispering out of pursed lips. Slowly her gasps receded and she was silent. I took the candle from her hands, helped her lie down and stayed by her side.

Robert Spryngolde arrived soon after with several other priests who were her friends. They pushed the crowd back and circled round her bed in their black and white robes, chanting prayers. Spryngolde moved even closer, bending his ear to her lips. There was silence now as she began to make her last confession, then a rumble in the lane outside, an echo of footsteps, the ringing of a hand-bell and someone calling out,

"Here we are, we are here." An elderly priest came in bearing a lantern, behind him another carried the sacrament in a chalice, with several members of the Trinity Guild following after. They placed the Nunc Dimittis candles at the four corners of her bed and lit them. The chamber was now full of the crowd, murmuring and muttering, until Spryngolde bid them all hush and humble themselves and get down on their knees.

He gave her the sacred host, anointed her with oil, held his crucifix before her face and began to sing a verse from one of the psalms.

> *'Hear me when I call, O God*
> *I will lay me down in peace and sleep*
> *For thou maketh me dwell in safety ...'*

Most everyone joined in and now there was much weeping. And before the chanting had come to an end Margery was gone, peacefully, without a roar or shout or even an ordinary death rattle. It was as if she had finally come home.

Slowly the crowd drifted away and the priests and guild members left too with Richard who took the deeds I gave him from my lady's chest. Priest Spryngolde stayed awhile, smoothing down her eyelids. She'd died with his image in her eyes, and he too had her last living look in his. Apart from me, he had perhaps spent more time with her than any other soul on earth, but I was glad when he was gone and only Jane and I, the boy and the girl, remained there with her.

Thomas's crooked body was even more twisted than usual with his sobs, and the girl was blubbing too.

"Come Thomas, what would your lady say now she's gone to her rest and joined the host of angels? Remember, she was always wont to tell you how merry it is in heaven so be joyful now she's there. And you wench there's no need for tears for all her suffering's over. I beg you, cease the two of you. I need

14

water to wash her, go take the big pitchers and draw some from the well, then light the fire that we may heat it. And make haste – there's much work to do."

Jane went home to fetch her great copper pan while I told Roger to send news of Margery's death to the churches and convents further afield beyond the town. Then we filled the pan with water and set it on the fire. The boy went back into the yard and gathered some fallen rose petals and rosemary, bay and lavender too which he threw into the basin. Thomas had been simple from birth, but always loved my lady.

She still had the warmth of life in her when we washed her but was now just a withered tree, her belly sunk to a void, dugs shrunken and dry. As I bathed her, as I had so often after childbirth, I remembered the many babes she had borne, a dozen or more, and who were now all departed. And I thought they were as much my children as hers. Finally I wept, but in truth it was as much for them and especially for little Mary as for her and my tears were soon spent.

We dressed her in the white kirtle and gown she'd kept for this special occasion and which she had permission to be buried in rather than the common shroud that us ordinary folk are sewn into at the end. I pulled out a thread from the hem of my tunic, hung her ring on it and placed it around her neck. She used to wear it on her marriage finger, but her hands were too shrunken now from the ravages of those final days. It was the only ring she had left, the one she'd had made long ago and treasured more than all her fine jewels. It was engraved with the words 'Jesus est amor meus', though the letters were now very faint.

Jane put a silver penny on each of her eyelids. I placed a stone on her tongue and bound her jaw. Then we heard the ox cart in the lane outside and two apprentices came in carrying the coffin. I laid sackcloth and ash on the bottom as Margery had told me, wanting repentance even after death. Then they helped us lower her into it; she was lighter now and already beginning to stiffen. I covered her face with a piece of white silk and lit more candles. It was growing dark, the church bells were tolling and the criers were proclaiming her death in the streets outside. They passed along our lane bearing torches, casting shadows on the chamber wall, but I left the shutters open so the mourners could come in.

I sat by the coffin as the neighbours arrived. This was the night watch, and I recalled how often I'd sat and watched before especially at the vigils of her husband and eldest son. It's hard to watch at the first vigil because you can sense the life that's ebbing away. Later on you know you're just sitting with a corpse. And of course it had usually been Margery who led the prayers.

Now I was glad of Joan's zealous prayers and no-one noticed as I slipped out into the night. I walked down to the river and found comfort as I often do, listening to the sound of the water lapping against the quay. The tide had passed the turn and soon all the debris of the day, the flotsam and jetsam of life, would be carried out to sea. I stayed until the moon began to set, then went back to join the mourners. They had all finished their gossip and were kneeling silently around the coffin with their memories, and I alone with mine.

The clerks returned at first light with the Trinity banner and the great black, velvet coffin-cloth, which Margery had donated to the guild. It had once born the inscription '*Orate pro anima*

Isabella Brunham', evoking prayers for Margery's mother after her death. When her father died she'd asked me to add his name, which I did reluctantly. It now bore the emblem of the Holy Trinity, Margery's new parents.

The boys carried her coffin, covered by this pall, to the cart outside and set off for the Guildhall with I alone, following. We soon arrived and most of the guild members had already assembled there. The bannermen who'd been out since the lifting of the curfew, distributing cloaks and candles to lepers and paupers, came to stand by the cart with their banners and flags. Many of the criers who'd also set out at daybreak, going beyond the town walls and over the river to West Lynn, were just returning. They were followed by a multitude of poor people who always relish a funeral for the food that is distributed afterwards.

By now a great crowd of priests, friars, and townsfolk had gathered. The criers took up their bells to play the funeral chimes, as the coffin-cart started to make the circuit of the town to all the churches and chapels where Margery had worshipped. First we went north to the church of St Nicholas and the Hospital of St John, then south to the St James chapel, past Greyfriars Tower and across Bever's Bridge to All Saints, and finally over Ladybridge before coming to rest at St Margaret's.

It was well past noon when we reached the church in a blazing heat. Eight friars carried the coffin inside and set it down before the high altar on the great iron hearse, with the banners bearing the heraldic devices of the Lynn guilds and Margery's family draped on the bottom rung and candles lit on the layers above. Priest Spryngolde stood in front and held up his arms for silence. And so the first Mass began.

The church was packed with a great crowd, women who'd not

17

been permitted to join the procession, more guild members, and those paupers greedy for alms. Some of my lady's enemies were there too, though there've been fewer of those in recent years for she'd rarely quarrelled or upset others as she had in earlier days. I was surprised to see so many young people there, folk who could only have known her through gossip and the stories of her adventures and journeyings: nothing like that had ever happened in our town before. Most people left when Evensong was over, except those who loved her and stayed through the night. They shuffled closer to the altar and knelt around the coffin, and were soon joined by several nuns from Denny Abbey and other nunneries further afield, as well as some hermits from town.

The second vigil is always more peaceful than the first, the body has been washed and dressed and the gossips have all had their say. After the turmoil of the procession, clamour of mourners, thunder of drum rolls, ceremonies and prayers in all the churches visited along the way, weariness sets in. I've learnt to sit and wait. This night, tired from the tumult of my lady's last illness, I was content to let memories come and go, memories of nights spent sheltering in churches or inns waiting for fair weather or suitable travelling companions, memories of coming home again, and remembrances of betrayals.

I am used to death. You don't get to my age without it being an almost daily occurrence, and anyhow I knew death from the day I was born. Yet this was the one death I knew would be the hardest, in part because my lady had long ago sworn me to secrecy if she were to die before me. And there was the other matter that had not been settled between us. In my heart of hearts there is much I still find hard to forgive, and I do not think she forgave me either, even at her last hour, as if it were I who had been responsible for her many torments.

Yet perhaps I am at fault for I cannot say with complete confidence that I've learnt to judge right and wrong, good and bad, as she said she could. That we saw things differently is not so troublesome any more. I've learnt to accept other people's reality even when it's completely at odds with my own. No, hers was rather the sin of omission, not what she did, but what she did not do, though I can understand the cause of that as well.

I must have slept with the muddle of my thoughts, for soon the sky started lightening in the eastern window and the stars were fading. Most of those around the coffin were still, asleep perhaps on their knees. I got up and walked out into the graveyard through the maze of wooden crosses, avoiding the open pits of the common graves. That is my destiny, not my lady's. She was to be buried in the church next to her father beneath the statue of Mary Magdalene, and the slabs had already been moved so her body could be laid to rest by his side.

It was fresh and sweet outside with the gay dawn song of the blackbird and the moist stillness of the early morning. I sat under the yew tree until I saw Spryngolde coming through the western gate and the bells started tolling again, summoning us back to church. He asked that I come and witness the burial at the end of the service and make my farewell, but I pleaded weariness and said her two servants would go for me instead for this last stage of her pilgrimage. I knew it would take more than her interment for me to say goodbye.

When the last Mass was over, it was time to leave for the Guildhall. Thomas and the girl stood with Spryngolde and the clerks waiting to close the coffin and bear my lady to her final resting place. I stayed a moment and took one last look at her. She seemed to have shrunk during the night, appearing like a ghostly wraith in her white gown with the white kerchief over her face. In life we'd been nearly the same height and shared the same birthday, almost twins you might say. Yet now I am three days older than Margery and feel more dead than she, with no kin in this world, while she will join her family. She has left her heritage. I shall leave none. Dust unto dust, memories like the tiny specks dancing in the shafts of light streaming in through the east window. As I turned to leave, the light dulled under a passing cloud and I felt myself alone in the darkening church, my eyes stinging from tiredness and the smoke of candles wafting up to the roof, together with the echo of the many prayers.

The wake meal had already begun when I arrived at the hall. There was plenty to eat and drink and it was as if the gloom of the morning had passed and we were celebrating. Perhaps we were. Death unites us in our common fate but eating together draws us back to life and binds us close again. I talked to few people, most are used to my silence though I was not always so. Long custom and a sense of being invisible, especially when in the company of Margery, have almost muted me. I spoke to Agnes and arranged to come to her in a day or two after I had gathered my belongings and taken the key of my lady's house to the Guildhall. There were some neighbours who asked me about her last days, and the young ones who wanted to know about her travels. I told them it was a long time ago, that it was her story, not mine. I left as the shadows were lengthening, and now here I am with my few chattels and the prospect of a new life in yet another home. Thankfully Agnes is almost as solitary as am I, and I know I won't have any problems looking after her.

But there is one more thing left to do.

I get up, close the shutters, secure the door, take another

candle from the candle-box and light it. I sit on the stool with the candle in the bracket beside me and the bundle of parchment on my lap. The white silk is soft and as I smooth my face with it, I am taken back to that moment at the end of our first long voyage, back again on the *San Raffaello* with the scent of pine trees wafting in on a warm breeze, the gentle rocking of our vessel finally at anchor and the cries of the boys as they swim out to greet us. Some of our company toss coins into the water and it is so clear and still that they glisten like gold as they tumble down to rest on the sandy sea bottom. I watch as the boys dive into the surf and I can still hear the laughter of one of them as he emerges into the sunlight, clutching a sparkling coin in his small fist.

I see it now glimmering brightly, as the shafts of light start to unlock more memories of many years ago.

2

Norfolk, 1373–1393

'it's now that my life begins to change'

I have very few memories of my childhood, but there is one which comes to me again and again. I am about three years old. I am sitting on a stone step. It's probably the step up to the dwelling where I live. It's a warm day but I have bare buttocks and the stone feels hard and cold beneath me. It's very quiet and there is no one nearby. I have a toy in my hand. I think it's something my uncle made for me, a spinning top perhaps or a little cart with wheels; I just remember something circular, but it is broken. I don't cry because I already know something much bigger has been broken, something that can never be mended again.

Mostly I'm looked after by an old woman called Nanna. There are two little boys in our family, Aldwin who's the same age as me and Erwan who's much younger. I sometimes rock baby Erwan to sleep in his cradle by the fire. They are my first friends. My uncle is often away and my aunt is busy too, though we eat together at mid-day and she sometimes takes me on her lap and sings to me and smooths my hair. I sleep with Nanna and the boys and she makes us pottage in the morning and sups with us in the evening. Every day I watch the chickens in case the fox comes. If there's an orphaned lamb I help to feed it and when the servant is busy I sweep the floors and gather kindling for the fire and acorns for the pig.

When I'm a little older I take the pots down to the stream and scour them with rushes until they shine bright and help churn milk to make butter, or I go with my aunt to the fields when she brings bread and ale to the workers. Sometimes, as a special treat, she takes me to a market to buy spices or a new calf. Once I remember helping her collect reeds to mend the thatch roof. I call her Aunt because that's what I'm told to do, though the boys call her Mother.

Often visitors come to our home. Women come to gossip with Nanna and they all cook together if there's to be a feast, or borrow the large pan when they need to make ale. Men come too and talk with my uncle and sometimes they set up a board outside, and one of them sits there and writes what my uncle tells him, then reads it back to him. I like to watch him do this and think he must have magic in his hands to be able to make those different marks on the parchment, and even more magic in his eyes to be able to tell all those stories again by looking at the pictures he's made.

Sometimes I play a game of making these magic signs in the dirt with my finger or a stick. Nanna and my aunt laugh but don't stop me. I tell them I'm writing about how many sheep there are in the fields, how much grain is in the barns and the sort of things I hear my uncle telling the man who writes. One day he shows me how to make the numbers from one to ten, then from ten to a hundred. I practice this often and ask my aunt to tell me some numbers and draw them for her in the earth. I try and show Aldwin how to do them, but he says it's silly stuff and runs away to chase the chicks and torment the mother hen.

One day when I'm playing outside making numbers in the yard, a gentleman comes on a horse with a servant. He draws CXXXVII in the dirt and I tell him it's one hundred and thirty-seven, then he shows me how to add the numbers and take them away, and says I'm to practice doing sums and show him what I've learnt when he comes again. He gives money to my uncle, but takes nothing away with him. He also brings cloth, which my aunt makes into clothes for me and he gives me comfits, which I share with the boys.

The next time he comes I'm able to do all the sums he asks. He teaches me a song which begins A-B-C and gives me a parchment book with the alphabet letters, bound together between horn boards. He tells me it belonged to his daughter but she doesn't need it any more. Another time he comes with a little girl. She's about the same age as me and wears beautiful clothes. He asks if I've learnt my letters and I tell him all the ones he points at, and he says to the pretty girl:

"There Margery, you see it's just as I told you. It's easy to learn numbers and letters if you really want to."

She just laughs, tosses her head in the air and rubs out the sums we've been doing in the earth with her soft leather boots.

It's now that my life begins to change. When we go to church on Sundays, Nanna takes me to the priest, gives him a farthing and leaves me there with some of the older children from the village nearby. The priest tells us stories from the Bible and teaches us how to read simple words. At home my aunt takes me to collect herbs and berries, explains how to make poultices and powders and what recipes are best for which ailments. She shows me how to make candles from sheep fat and how to spin yarn and she says when I'm a little older I shall go and live with the nuns in their convent. She says this is a great privilege and honour and she's very pleased for me; it will be better than staying at the farm and I'll be safe from temptation. I don't know what she means and the memory of the broken toy comes to my mind, but I don't tell her I don't want to leave her and Nanna and the boys.

One Sunday night when I'm in bed with the boys, Aldwin asks what I did with the priest that day.

"Oh, important things like numbers and letters, which you call silly stuff because you're silly stuff yourself."

"What makes you think you're so clever," he says kicking me.

"Well, the fine gentleman who comes sometimes thinks I'm clever and he doesn't give you anything, only me."

"If you're so clever then why are you living with us instead of with your own parents? Perhaps you weren't clever enough for them and they gave you away. You don't belong here and my dad said it'll be good riddance when you leave us and get shut up with the nuns."

He kicks me again and I grab his hair and bite him and we fight each other and roll over and over and Erwan tumbles out of bed and yells.

Nanna comes in, soothes Erwan and puts him back to bed, slaps us both hard and then Aldwin says he wants to piss and goes out. I'm shaking and in tears and she hushes me, sits me on her lap and asks what we were fighting about.

"Aldwin says I don't belong here and should be with my own parents. Where are they Nanna? Why did they give me away?"

"Hush now, little creature. Your parents didn't give you away. They both died of the pestilence, God save their souls, soon after you were born, so we gave you a home. But you must be good now and tomorrow I'll make a straw mattress for Aldwin so he can sleep on the floor, and you're not to quarrel anymore or the goblins will come and eat you both up. We'll never speak of this again or you'll have to sleep on your own too."

I feel very worried after this, but I don't have much time to think about it because everything starts to go wrong. The summer never comes and it rains continually. My aunt is unhappy and doesn't take me on her lap anymore. It's difficult to keep the floors clean because there's mud everywhere. Once I fall into the stream as I'm washing the pots and am almost swept away by the torrent, but a man pulls me out and takes me home. It's cold all the time; the corn cannot ripen and there's little hay for the cattle or grain for the fowl. We no longer have much to eat and forage in the forest for nuts and berries. Many of our neighbours die of the sickness, which comes back again, or from lack of food.

My aunt says it will get better next year, but it doesn't. It continues to rain, more people die, the animals weaken, the firewood is never dry and there is even less food than the year before. I'm always hungry and my aunt's new babe dies, then she sickens too. She dies one winter night and I sit on the cold step outside, wishing the clouds would go so I could see the stars. Now I've even more to do helping in our home, but I work very hard, hoping I'll no longer be sent away to live with the nuns.

Everything is different after this. I miss my aunt, but no one pays much attention to me. Aldwin and I don't fight anymore because he has to help his father on the farm. The fields are mostly empty as there are few men left to work. My uncle often goes away and Nanna looks vexed and doesn't speak much. Then he's gone for several days and comes back late one night with many men. They bang hard on the door and when Nanna gets up to let them in, I wake too and tiptoe behind her. They are soiled from travel and I hear them telling Nanna strange stories, which I don't understand at first.

"Yes, it's true, it's just like we heard," says my uncle. "The people followed Wat Tyler, rampaged through London town, murdered the King's chancellor, killed many others and did much damage."

"Aye," says another, "and at first our boy-king was affrighted and promised to free us from our landlords and abolish the poll tax and we were cheered, but the next day he broke his word and betrayed us, and his soldiers killed poor Wat …"

"And without a leader," interrupts my uncle, "no-one had the stomach for a fight. But we couldn't be stopped for long and now there's burning and bloodshed in the country nearby."

I want to hear more and hide in the shadows so they won't find me and send me back to bed. They go on talking and it must be very late because I fall asleep. Then I'm woken by a noise and someone comes rushing in. It's Robyn from the ale-house. His face is filthy, his tunic spattered with blood and one of the sleeves is torn. Nanna helps him take it off and there's a deep cut on his arm. She gets a basin of water to wash it and though he grimaces with pain that doesn't stop him talking.

"We've lost," he says, "lost everything. Jack Littlestar led us to Norwich and we burnt many buildings and went on to Yarmouth and destroyed all the records and legal bonds we could find. We did the same in Bishop's Lynn, but Bishop Henry gathered a great force and followed us to Walsham Heath, you know where I mean, we've had good poaching there in the past. Then Littlestar was captured and beheaded right there and many others were killed as they fled to the woods. I caught the tip of a soldier's sword, stabbed through my arm I was, but rolled into a ditch and lay as still as a corpse till they went away."

Then everyone starts talking at once.

"Are we still bound to our masters and the land for just a few coins though there're fewer men left to work in the fields? We should be paid more."

"What about the tax we have to pay? If the records are lost does that mean we're free, free to live and work where we want for fair wages?"

"Yeah, and free from all those wealthy priests who demand we pay the tithes though we don't have enough for ourselves?"

Nanna interrupts them with an urgent question,

"Has the fighting stopped, is the countryside safe?"

I want to hear what Robyn has to say and creep out of my hiding place, but knock over the basin and Nanna scolds me and takes me to bed.

"There's nothing to fear girling, it's all over now. The people were angry and wanted to choose where to live and earn more money for food, because they're hungry. They didn't want to pay the new taxes so they burnt the records, because without those no one can make them work for a pittance. They want to better themselves. Just like you. If you must go to the convent, may the good Lord help us, you might learn to read as well as doing sums. You'd have a safe life as a nun."

I start to protest but she shushes me and draws the covers over me.

Now my uncle often stays at home. Then one evening at supper he tells Nanna he's going to marry again, a widow from the town.

"I don't want to work on the farm, there're better opportunities in the town. Edwina's husband had a bakery, and I'll soon learn the business and maybe open a pie-shop too. As the girl's future is settled, I don't have to stay here anymore. I want the boys to learn some trade and can pay for them to be apprenticed."

Then he turns to me and says,

28

"See you're ready to leave by Michaelmas, we've looked after you long enough."

Nanna reaches out and holds my hand,

"But couldn't she live with you and the boys? She'd be lonely in the convent. She's a clever girl and could help you in the bakery. You could find her a husband and then she'd have a family of her own, rather than being shut away with the nuns."

"No, I don't want that little hussy on my hands a moment longer. She's growing up and I won't take responsibility for her when she gets up to mischief like you know who. Good riddance, is what I say."

I don't really know what he means but it seems he does not care for me at all.

In the next few weeks Nanna gives me lots of extra work, helping to sew new shifts and the cobbler comes and makes me some boots. I try to tell her I want to stay with her, but she gets grumpy and finds fault with whatever I'm doing if I start to speak to her, so I never have the chance. Then one morning the fine gentleman comes again and I'm lifted up onto his horse.

Nanna passes me a bundle of clothes and some bedding and tells me I'm to be a good girl and pray for her. She puts one of the hens in a sack, ties it onto the saddle and tells me to give it to the nuns and so we leave and I don't let her see how fearful and sad I am.

It's a long ride through the countryside and already late afternoon when we reach the convent. It's surrounded by fields and a high mound, with a pond, windmill, barns, cookhouse, dovecote and gardens, and the main building with its stone cloisters and chapel are clustered together in the middle. I'm taken to meet the Prioress and the gentleman gives me a pewter goblet, spoon and bowl. Dame Cecilia is very old but she has bright eyes that look straight into mine. He tells her I know my letters and numbers and he wants me to continue learning. Then they ask me to say the paternoster, and she rings a bell and another nun comes and leads me away. I go with this nun, who's called Sister Margaret to the dorter where the other nuns sleep and she introduces me to three older girls called Matilda, Amice and Joan whom I'm to share a bed with. Then she takes me downstairs to eat in the refectory, before going to the chapel to say prayers, and then to bed.

Those are all of my childhood memories. I suppose it was a happy time especially in those early years playing with the boys, the blossoming of spring, the thrill of the harvest and the dark winter nights sitting at the hearth and listening to Nanna's stories. After the years of famine, sickness and the rains and then my aunt's death, it was quiet in our home and sadness seeped into the pit of my stomach. But I still enjoyed the farm, the birdsong, the rhythm of the days and seasons and when I wasn't helping Nanna, I had freedom to roam.

There were no children of my age nearby apart from Aldwin, but I had many friends in the hedgerows and in the little shelter I made in the copse beyond the sheep pens. And I had the doll my aunt sewed for me from scraps of fabric. I called her Marion. She was my little sister, my most trustworthy friend and a very good listener to the many tales I had to tell. Even now I marvel I had so much to talk about when I rarely ventured further than the village on the other side of the hills.

Often now this childhood I comes to visit me in my dreams. She seems so real that I no longer know how true those memories are, because I've told them to myself so many times they've become stories. Stories are true, but like memories can also lie. Yes, there was always Nanna, reliable and kind, and I no longer feel she blamed me for my final cruelty to her, my aunt too and the boys, especially little Erwan. And sometimes when I see a morning mist shrouding the land at an early summer's dawn, the first star of the evening that comes to greet the dark, hear the blackbird singing good-night to the day, or watch a hare erect and upright jumping here and there seeking refuge in the undergrowth, I hold my breath and feel I could leap in delight, just as I did all those years ago. Yet I wonder why I remembered so little, why I asked so few questions and if I really had been such a sad solitary child, because I do recall some happiness in the quiet safety of those days.

I must have been nine or ten when I was sent to the convent. To start with it was hard to live that strange new life, ruled by bells, the long periods of silence and frequent services in the chapel. It was easier for us children who boarded there; we didn't have to get up in the middle of the night to go to the chapel like the nuns. Our day started at first light with prayers and breakfast, then we stayed with one of the nuns, spinning or doing embroidery, making ointments, distilling herbs, and learning to sing the church anthems. We were shown how to treat wounds and when the great feasts came, we made confections and sweet smelling balms for the guests.

Once or twice a week, Matilda, Amice, Joan and I spent the morning with the boys and chaplain when he visited, learning sums and reading. Before our mid-day meal we went to the noonday Mass, then were busy helping in the dairy, fetching eels from the millpond, working in the gardens, feeding the livestock, preparing produce for the market and also for the great Garlic Fair which was held every year at the end of the summer. Then we had supper, went to Mass again and so to bed.

I found it very hard to begin with. I missed my home and hated the rule of silence. During the day we were not permitted to speak unless we needed to ask for something. We could only talk freely when we had lessons or at bedtime before the candles were snuffed out, but in the first few weeks I was so tired and sad that I often cried myself to sleep. So it was some time before I really talked to my bedmates, and when I did they just started boasting about the convent.

"O you ninny do stop whining. You don't know how lucky you are to be here," they told me. "Most nunneries are dreadfully poor, but ours is rich for we have a farm and rents from two manors as well as the mill."

"There's the guesthouse too for travelling friars, and sometimes a great lady comes to stay with her horses, pets and maids and pays much money for it."

"And a few old folk give us their land in return for board and lodging."

"So we're the best and most important convent in the land," they all chorused together.

Then they told me their stories.

"My father's a merchant," said Matilda. She was by far the prettiest and had nicer boots than the rest of us. "When I'm a little older I shall marry Robert, another merchant's son. I'll have a big household and many servants and scores of fine gowns. And we'll have many parties and much business, so that's why I'm here, to understand sums. And I expect I shall have lots of children and ..."

But Amice, who wasn't pretty at all and had a very big nose, interrupted her,

"My parents were very wealthy, much richer than yours Matilda. My mother didn't need to read or do boring sums as we had a steward and a scribe and I had my own maid who attended to my every need. I was going to marry a nobleman, much more important than a stupid merchant. But then the plague came and all my family died and the steward stole our gold and my uncle, who was a bishop, God rest his soul for he is dead now too, said I'd been spared for a very special reason and paid a dowry to the convent that I might become a nun. And for sure I shall be Prioress one day and rule over you all and everyone else as well."

Joan said only that she'd longed to be a nun since the day she was born. I liked Joan best. Though she was plain, she was kind and gentle. Then they asked why I'd been sent there and I said I didn't know, only that my aunt had spoken of it before she died.

"Well, who were your mother and father then and what's your aunt got to do with it?"

"I don't know, I think I'm an orphan just like you Amice. I suppose my parents died of the plague when I was born as I don't have any memories of them."

"Suppose, suppose … they must have been somebody, though they obviously weren't as important as mine."

"I don't know, I know nothing about them."

"If you don't know anything about them, perhaps they just gave you away. Or maybe you're a changeling and that's why you're always snivelling and are so secretive. Did you ever have any real parents? Who were they then?"

"My aunt and uncle, I suppose," I said, before I'd even thought what I was saying, just wanting her to stop.

"Then you must be both a fool and a bastard," said Amice, pinching me hard and she and Matilda laughed and I hit out at them, screaming loudly. Sister Margaret came to ask why we were quarrelling. Joan told her and Margaret bid us be silent and blew our candle out. I lay awake for hours after that feeling very confused and was thankful for the rule of silence so at least no one could ask me any more questions that night. Why, I wondered, had I never thought who my real parents were? But that is the way it sometimes is with children, either they are too trusting to ask questions, or else too wise and know when not to ask.

The next morning when we were having our lessons, Sister Margaret came and sat with us. I was learning fast, reading and calculating well, better even than the boys. I still had that bright memory of the clerk and the magic of those signs I used to trace in the earth. Margaret watched us and when the lesson was over told me to follow her.

We went to the Prioress' chambers. She had her own suite of rooms and a little dog and her own servant too who cooked for her. She told her maid to set the table for three and started talking to Sister Margaret about plans for a new barn. I saw how they spoke together with deep affection and was surprised. It was so unlike the refectory where no one showed any warmth, where we all ate in silence, holding up different fingers to indicate if we wanted salt or ale or bread. Sister Margaret answered all Cecilia's questions, then said she had a special request. Although I was still young, she saw I had a talent for numbers and was already able to read. She wanted to have special care of me and asked permission that I assist her in her work as sub-prioress.

"Of course she may," said Dame Cecilia. "You could do with some help and if she's as clever as you say that will certainly lighten your burden."

Then she turned to me and asked,

"And what say you: is that your wish too?"

I was thrilled and took her hand and kissed her ring as we had been taught.

And so the days, weeks and months passed. In the first few years my uncle sent a cart so I could visit my old home again for the New Year festivities, at the end of the harvest and finally to help nurse Nanna when she became gravely ill. He had moved to town by then with the boys and his new wife, so she was living alone with a wench from the village. I had leave to stay with her until she died.

She had become very frail and was unable to eat solid food, so I fed her pottage in the morning and soup in the evenings, just as she had me when I was a child. I brought potions from the convent, which relieved some of her pain, but she grew weaker and weaker. I wanted to discover the secret of my birth, yet I was also fearful and much too shy to ask what I really longed to know. Then one day the man who had taken me to the convent came again and I took him to her bedside. As he was leaving he said he'd call the priest as he feared she wouldn't last the night. Then he asked if I was content at the convent. I had not thought I might say otherwise.

Nanna's eyes were closed when I went back to her. She was suddenly so much weaker and I knew that once the priest came I wouldn't be able to talk to her alone, so I held her hand and found the courage to ask her my simple question.

"Nanna, who were my real parents?"

Her hand was like a little claw in mine.

"No, no don't ask … I won't, I can't tell you that," she whispered, turning away from me.

I took her head in my hands and turned it towards mine so she had to look at me.

"Then tell me, why did I come to live with you, and who were those people I called aunt and uncle?"

I did not let her go and watched as she struggled to say the words.

"The woman you called aunt was my daughter. She was your wet-nurse. Your mother died giving birth to you and your father couldn't look after you so we offered to take care of you."

"Is he still alive then? You told me both my parents died of the plague and now you talk of my father. Why can't he look after me?"

She closed her eyes but I knew she'd heard me.

"Nanna, please answer me. Where is my father, who is he?" As she tried to pull away, a door clattered and we heard the priest outside.

"Who is he?" I asked again.

She opened her eyes, looked at me, then struggled to turn her head to the wall. I knew then I'd never know my father's name. I hated her for her stubborn silence and left the room without saying goodbye, left her alone and sent the servant in to be her only companion at her end.

With Nanna's death the convent became my only family and home. Although I had been there for about four years, I'd always hoped I might go back one day and live at the farm. That dream was over and I dreaded my return, but Margaret immediately made me welcome and having much to do softened the blow of all my losses.

As sub-prioress she provisioned for the convent and checked the produce that was brought in from the farm. At the end of each year she distributed shoes to the nuns and cloth for their habits. She noted what was used in the kitchens, what given for alms, and what was sent out to be sold. She collected the gifts and tithes and decided when to reduce the rents if the tenants were too poor to pay. I followed her every day as she checked the stores, and wrote the numbers down on the roll I carried.

She also travelled frequently with the convent bailiff to different markets to sell surplus produce and buy goods, which the convent farm couldn't provide. I often journeyed with her, and sometimes we went to a monastery to deliver an embroidered cope, which we had sewn, or took calfskins from our stock to the workshops in the town. I enjoyed these outings because I often found the cloister life tiresome and dull.

A year after Nanna's death, Amice and Joan became novices and Matilda went to join the household of the man she was to marry. The boys we'd studied with left and new girls and boys arrived. Slowly I began to forget those early days of my childhood and became accustomed to the daily rule of work and prayer, high days and holy days, chapel services and silences, all marked by the tolling of the bells. Day followed day with little variation.

In time I stopped having lessons with the chaplain, but Dame Cecilia asked me to read to her most days. Her eyes were worn and she said she preferred to hear God's words spoken out loud. She had a copy of the Bible, which had been newly translated into English and given her by her brother who was a noble lord. I read a few verses at a time, and if she wanted to ponder them, I read them again at my next visit. Sister Margaret usually came for the mid-day meal and I often stayed to eat with them.

Now it happened one day I'd just finished reading, when Sister Margaret arrived. I remember it was the story of the talents and the faithful and unfaithful servants, how God rewarded those who took the coins he gave them, traded them and returned with a great profit, while he cursed the one who'd buried his money for safety in the earth. The story puzzled me because we were told it was good to be poor.

I wanted to ask the true meaning but Margaret bid me fetch some balm from the store cupboard for Dame Cecilia who was suffering from a stiffness in her bones. It was only when I was walking through the cloister that I remembered I'd forgotten to ask for the key. As I returned and was about to knock, I saw the door was slightly ajar and heard voices within.

" … and she reads really well. So tell me, has she expressed a wish to be professed and join our community as a nun?"

"No," answered Margaret, "she's never once talked about taking the vows, but always busies herself with whatever task has to be done."

"The problem is she couldn't succeed you as sub-prioress when the next elections come if she were still only a lay Sister. You know how much I'd like to surrender my authority here. I'm tired and want to pass my last days in peace and prayer. I'm sure you'll have sufficient support to be elected as the new prioress. The convent has flourished so well under your careful housekeeping, but you'll need help from someone who is familiar with sums and able to read."

"Then I'll ask her to think about becoming a postulant," said Margaret. "She's old enough now and we've received money well in excess of her keep so she wouldn't even need a dowry. She may not have a true vocation but there're many ways of serving God."

I lifted my hand to knock.

"Of course there's the problem of her mother," said Dame Cecilia.

I froze and held my breath.

"Bastardy is a bar to taking vows," she continued, "but I'm sure the Bishop would give her dispensation if we asked."

I did not wait to hear more but fled to the cloister and walked round and round with fearful thoughts in my head and black dread in my guts. Now, finally, I'd heard something about my mother, but it was terrible news. I knew I'd be damned for her sin and even if I wished to become a nun, being a bastard would always stain my soul. I'd wanted so much to find out something about my mother but this was shocking. And I hated her.

The following day Sister Margaret bid me come into town with her. I was so ashamed after what I'd heard, but dared not disobey. The bailiff came with us and Thomasine too who worked in the dairy. She was to accompany me to the parchment-makers to deliver some calfskins and then we'd go to the market to meet Margaret.

There was a large crowd of men at the workshop, tanners visiting from another town, but the master was out delivering goods and only he could settle the account. Thomasine wanted to visit her cousin who had a stall nearby, and said she'd be back before he returned, so I sat down to wait in a dark corner behind a pile of skins. The men went on talking, thinking I suppose, I'd left with Thomasine. Then one pulled something out from his jerkin and started to read. It was the same story I'd read to Dame Cecilia just the day before.

When he'd finished, the others all began talking.

"The way it is, is like this," said one. "Those who increased their money are like our priests who are meant to be God's servants, but just profit from his word at our expense. And there're the others who don't want to share any treasure but keep it all for themselves, like the one who hid his coins in the earth. That's like the friars who grow wealthy from the alms we give them, but give us nothing in return, except to tell us what we may think and what we may not. The story tells that God rewards those who increase his gifts, but how can we do so when we're kept ignorant of the truth and forbidden to read for ourselves?"

"Yes," said another, "that's the true meaning." Then he added, "If I could read, I wouldn't need a priest any more. I'd just learn from the Bible stories and find out for myself what's good and what's bad."

They all started cursing the meanness of the priests and the falseness of their teachings.

"Yes Jack, and all those prayers they say are nothing better that the mooing of my goodwife's milk-cow and the grunting of her pig."

"Or the crowing of my grand-dam's prize cockerel, strutting here and there and showing off to his hens."
Everyone laughed and another said,

"And what about that bibull buball they mutter and mumble when they say the Lord's prayer in that Latin language?"

"You're right again Jack, they should speak our good English. I believe it's more important to keep God's commandments than be a friar who sermonises all day long but never keeps his vows. As for venerating the saints, well that has to be wrong, worshipping statues made of wood and clay ..."

"Yeah, and they tell us to bow down to them as if they were real, but if they really are real then why can't the Virgin Mary blow the cobwebs off her face?"

There were chuckles again and someone else said:

"Anyone would think we were sheep to be fleeced, but I warrant the good Lord would rather we were let free to graze in his pastures than be herded and shorn."

Then the man who'd read said his master spoke of a learned

cleric called Wycliffe who believed anyone who had a truly righteous heart had authority that came directly from God, while those in the Church were often sinful and didn't have the right to rule over ordinary folk. It was this man who'd translated the Bible into English so that everyone could read it.

"But you need to be mighty careful for the priests don't like it and condemn anyone who reads."

I thought of Dame Cecilia and was alarmed. I'd never heard talk like this before, but it ended abruptly with the sound of people talking outside and the master came in with Thomasine. And so we finished our business and left.

However hard I try, I cannot see that young woman clearly as she follows Thomasine through the bustling streets to meet Sister Margaret. Did I say young woman? No, she's really still a girl, she hasn't even started her monthly bleeding yet though she's well passed the usual age. She would of course be wearing the homespun tunic that all the convent boarders wore. That clothing dictated a certain type of behaviour, a meekness and reserve, but I knew she wore another habit beneath that quiet kindness brimming with humility, which hid her frustration at being cloistered, hid her longing for the tumult and excitement of the town, to be like the carefree young women at their market stalls, flirting with the men, laughing and cursing each other. And hid her anger too, because she'd had no choice in the matter since those she'd once believed to be her family had given her away.

With my adult eye I see her climbing onto the cart, sitting between Sister Margaret and Thomasine as the bailiff flicks the reins and the wheels start rumbling out of town. I imagine there is a bitter cold, a hoar frost still clinging to the trees, the sky a pale February yellow slowly deepening into dusk. Thomasine will be chattering about her cousin and Sister Margaret will be smiling for she always had an open ear for the tales of ordinary people and the rule of silence was not observed beyond the convent walls.

The bailiff too will be telling the latest news he'd heard about young King Richard, he who'd some years before betrayed Wat Tyler and the peasants. I see her nodding gravely at the latter and laughing with the former, and asking Sister Margaret if she'd been able to buy all the necessaries for the Lenten diet. So how I wonder did she bear that inner ice of shame and the numbness of her doubt? Or did she remain cheerful and attentive all the way back, as if the only two worlds she'd ever known had not fallen apart within the space of just one day?

Just as I cannot really recall the journey back, so I have little clear remembrance of the next few weeks, though one day is etched deeply into my heart. I know for sure it was during the season of Lent. This was always a difficult time after the rigours of winter, with only sparse food during those forty days of fasting, no meat, eggs or cheese for the midday meal and no supper either except bread and ale. Even though there was no farm work to be done, there were the long services to attend and the weaving and making of clothes. We all hated those mean lean days and especially we hated the hunger, which created an appetite not only for food but for so much else the body desired.

I do remember it was a very hard winter with heavy snow, and many of the nuns were sick. We also often nursed the elderly who lived alone and had no one to care for them. Many came seeking succour during these bitter months and the infirmary was full. Then Maud who'd been helping Sister Anne fell ill, so I offered to take her place and spent all day and night there.

I didn't read to Dame Cecilia or help Sister Margaret, yet it seemed neither noticed and I was content to be free from their attention for a while, as I was still confused by everything I'd overheard. Yet it was a heavy task and I felt more weary than ever at the dawning of each new day. It was at this time too that I started my monthly bleeding, but told no one so wasn't able to have the day of rest and sustaining food that was prescribed for those woman days.

Some several weeks passed and we were nearly half way through Lent, though thick snow still lay on the ground. One day a villager came, Edmund was his name, a man who sometimes helped in the dairy. His mother was ill to death but he said he couldn't care for her, so we took her in. He brought her on his back; she was a poor scrap of a creature and held onto him as he tried to leave, but he turned his back and walked away.

Even though I wasn't then so familiar with death, I said I would keep vigil at her bedside though Sister Anne made me promise to tell her if the old lady worsened. I offered her some broth but she would have none. She lay with the covers up to her chin, then fumbling in the bedcovers asked me to hold her hand. Her grasp was tight and the memory of Nanna came back and I wanted to pull away, but she held on fast. She slept awhile, but whenever I tried to free myself her eyes opened and she clung on.

"I've something to tell you," she suddenly whispered, still holding tight. "I have sinned and don't want to carry this sin to my grave."

"Then I'll call Sister Anne to fetch the priest."

"No, I'd never tell a priest," she answered, then said no more. I watched her gasping for breath, but there was still strength in her hand like a little child who's fearful to let go.

I heard the chimes of the Matins bell that rung deep in the

night. The next Mass was three hours later, the first of the morning. Death usually comes in those dark hours, but if the dying live till the dawning, they often last another day. I tried to free my hand again but she would not let go, so I closed my eyes and was soon asleep. I don't know what woke me, but then saw the old lady's eyes were wide open and she was staring at me. She looked very alive and was licking her lips. She pulled me towards her, panting and dribbling.

"Listen," she mumbled, "what I want to tell you is not a sin. Now, as I'm dying, I know at last it is true and good, and what is true and good cannot be a sin. It's my story, the story of my life."

It was silent in the infirmary and dark. The last candle had burnt out as I slept. Moonlight, shining through the windows and brightened by the snow outside, shimmered down onto her face. Perhaps it was a trick of the light but she seemed young again and almost beautiful. I wiped her lips and she took some water. Then she started talking, her voice now clear and firm.

"There was a boy I loved when I was a child and loved even more in my maidenhood. We grew up together, but my father said he should marry Hawise, as she was the eldest. I was wed to a man from another village and we had two girl children. Sometimes he was harsh with me, and I with him, that is often the way of marriage. Then my sister died in childbed and Edmund came and said we could now be together. It was midsummer and we were working in the fields. I lay in his arms in the hay. He was soft and tender, and to be with him was to be like a bird flying free.

We met every day and sometimes we met at night and lay under the starlight. Soon I was with child, but knew we could never have a life together and I didn't want him to suffer, so I sent him away to find a new wife. That was many years ago. There were often times I felt I'd done wrong, but to have told my husband would have caused pain and causing pain is evil. So he never knew he was not father to my son, nor does my son know. No one knows. I called him Edmund after my one true love, to remind myself of those sweet summer days."

She started coughing and I gave her some more water.

"You're young and have chosen your life. But I had to tell someone, for those moments in his arms were the most wondrous thing that ever happened to me and I've kept this love close to my heart. Even if it was wrong I've hurt no one. Love is a gift from God and I don't want it to be buried with me to rot in the cold earth. I don't want blame, I don't want to confess to a priest and call it a sin. I only want to tell my story. It belongs to the world of the living."

Then she let go of my hand. There was nothing I could say. I knew she was ready to die but it seemed she was now at peace, so I did not call Sister Anne. I just sat there with her in the moonlight, with all the sleepers around me, marvelling at her story. I thought about my mother, wondering if she too had known this tender love, and I no longer wanted to blame her or condemn myself. And I wondered why the priests called this gentle love a sin.

I must have fallen asleep as I recalled the old woman's tale and relived those moments I imagined in the hay, because suddenly I was woken by the tolling of the Lauds bell and Sister Anne shouting at me. Certainly much time had passed for I saw the poor creature was dead, her eyes open and mouth aghast as if in her last living moment she'd seen the Devil. I had slept while death came and took her away.

"You thoughtless, ungood, Godless churl of a thing," snapped

Sister Anne, "Go at once and tell Edmund of his mother's death, that he might take her away. And in the morning present your worthless self to Dame Cecilia, admit your disobedience, ask for a penance and make sure it's a hard one and do not come back. I don't need you anymore."

It was dark outside with fresh snow falling, but there was a glimmer of light in the barn. Edmund would already be there seeing to the cows. I was cold and tired but excited too, proud of my secret and curious to see this lovechild. And I thought of my mother again, and hoped I too had been such a special babe.

My memories of what happened next are coloured, visual and physical, like those paintings on the chapel wall that tell of Christ's Crucifixion and the Last Judgment. I leave the infirmary by the outer staircase, the crunch of my footsteps on the snow the only sound in the night. I cross the courtyard and open the gate to the farmyard. It is stiff with ice. The moon is white and low in the sky. Clouds race past it and put it out.

My hands are frozen blue, my cheeks red from the cold, and the bright light beckons ahead. I open the barn door breathlessly, for the wind is bitter in the yard, to the warmth and smell of the beasts. Edmund has his head against the flank of a cow, his hands on her udder. All I hear is the beating of my heart and the squirt of the milk as it hits the pail. I walk up to him and see the creamy whiteness in the bucket between his legs. His face is marked and blotched, his dark eyes narrow and his nostrils flaring as if I'd brought in a bad smell.

"Is the old woman dead yet?" he asks. I nod and make the sign of the cross. "And you've come to tell me on your own?" I nod again.

He gets up and knocks over the pail and I watch as the milk

streams along the ground, seeping into the filth. He comes close to me, panting and there's a nasty smell on his breath. I stand still, wondering when his tears will come. He comes even closer and I wait to see his sorrow. Then he staggers and falls against me, knocking me down and is on top of me, his knees by my head.

He pulls down his breeches and thrusts something into my mouth. I cannot scream. I think I will suffocate for there is slime in my throat, my arms are numb and I cannot move. He gets up laughing, pulls up his breeches and walks away. My hand is lying in something wet and warm, I know it is the milk from the overturned pail.

"Don't think about telling anyone, they won't believe you. Go back to your nunnery and say I'll come as soon as my work is finished, and take the old hag away."

I don't know how long it takes me to get up. I see myself from afar lying with grime and straw around my mouth, my arms out to the side. He is sitting on the stool again and I hear the milk streaming into the bucket. My legs will not move. I want to retch. I am terrified of making a sound. Then I am outside and the snow is coming down in great whirls like the lashing of a whip. It is as cold and friendless as death. The latch on the barn door has not caught and bangs in the wind. I hear footsteps coming towards it and will my feet to hurry. As I run the earth slips beneath me and I fall and bury my face, my mouth, in the snow.

Perhaps it is the swineherd who finds me, or one of the sisters coming to collect the milk. I am back in the infirmary and Sister Anne is scolding me and someone says Edmund has come to take his mother away. After that I remember nothing.

I must suppose, since I do not remember, that I had a fever after my fall. The warmth and good food of the infirmary would soon have restored the hurt flesh, but not the torture of the mind. When I left the infirmary I went to one of the solitary cells. I still had a heavy cold and didn't want to infect anyone else. I do recall I went to Dame Cecilia and told her I wished to do penance as Sister Anne had instructed. She listened carefully and suggested I ask my conscience what punishment I deserved. I told her I would not read to her, nor help Sister Margaret until after Easter as I'd become too proud of my accomplishments. I said I would clean the cloisters and refectory instead, and do the laundry and empty the latrine buckets for the rest of the Lenten period.

She looked at me curiously.

"Are you sure you committed such a grievous fault?" she asked. "You were tired and have suffered enough after your fall in the snow."

For a moment I wanted to tell her everything but had no words to say it. Besides I felt too much shame.

"Yes, I am to blame. I should not have let the poor woman die alone in her sin without sending for the priest to hear her confession and ease her way into the next world. That was my Christian duty."

"So be it. But mind you are not too hard on yourself. Never forget that charity starts at home."

So I set myself a punishing task. I know now that mortifying the flesh also crucifies the mind, but I was too young then and knew no better. I went about my self-imposed penance with that mask of humility I'd learnt so well. Whenever in later years I've succumbed to a feeling of smug self-righteousness, I remember this time with both anger and disgust.

I barely recall the routine I set myself, scrubbing flagstones, polishing the tables, wringing laundry with open blisters on my hands, carrying the latrine buckets to the cesspits, anything which would tire me out so I could sleep at night and avoid my guilty feelings. My humiliation was a running sore, for Sister Anne took pleasure in finding fault with everything I did, setting me constant new tasks with her callous ways, walking with her garden clogs in the cloisters just after I'd washed the flagstones, and sending back the infirmary laundry with complaints that it was still stained. Her sweetness and patience was the habit she wore, while underneath lay a cruel shift. I've come to know that well, there is a heavy price to pay for too much kindness. Yet as I look back now I see some wisdom in those punishing tasks, they were an anchor for my mind.

Then Easter came. Although I'd shunned everyone during the latter part of Lent, I could not miss the Great Week cele-brations. All the rituals and vigils passed in a fog until the dark night of Holy Saturday. Joining the silent line as we crept bare-foot into the chapel, I tried to make myself invisible, but now and then an arm brushed mine, a Sister I was fond of or one of the younger boarders who was in my care. Nor could I avoid meeting the eyes of Dame Cecilia and Sister Margaret before bowing to them, as I was required to do.

And so the services continued and I felt increasing fearful that everyone would notice the putrid smell which hung about me. As I knelt in the choir stalls I was sure they were all turn-ing away from me. What was it, my stale breath, rancid milk, the odour of the latrines? I recalled the instruction I'd received when I was still pure and innocent and tried to focus on every word sung and spoken. Do I remember when Holy Saturday dawned to Easter Sunday? It seemed one long, dark endless night. Then I heard the joyful jubilation, 'Christ is risen'. I watch my feet as they step over the flagstones, barely able to bear my weight. I feel my arms trembling in my sleeves. There is fire in my eyes, a twisted rope round my head. We are facing the altar and about to sing. Suddenly I hear myself screaming, but no sound comes from my throat for it is tight and numb and I cannot breath. And then nothing.

They say all madness comes from the Devil. An affliction of the mind is a personal disorder, a blemished soul, a wrongness of the heart. Physical illness is sent to test our faith and remind us of the suffering of Jesus on the cross. Madness is an individual's responsibility, a human failure, while bodily disease is sent to encourage us to transcend the human condition. They say too the Devil is not God-given but belongs to humankind, a legacy of the sin of Eve. Even now, in my old age, I see the sympathy for those suffering from physical disablement is rarely extended to those who have lost their minds. It is as if the flesh held more value than the human spirit, though the spirit can be blighted just as much as the flesh. But the body is visible and we witness its infirmity, while the injured mind is hidden behind our daily platitudes.

In church paintings multitudes are shown with boils and pustules, leprous skin, deformed limbs - a myriad of visible disorders. But there's nothing that speaks of the rank wounds of diseased thoughts, running sores of conscience, bilious vomit of guilt, stomach cramp of despair. Madness must be purged with foul emetics and terrifying exorcisms. Those who've lost their wits are left to rot in a maze they cannot master, while the sick are comforted and cosseted as a mother hen clucks to her chicks. The sick may complain of her ailments and have her brow smoothed and palate teased. The mad had better keep her nightmares to herself. No one wishes to know the frailty of the human spirit.

What happened then? As I learnt later, memory can remain locked and hidden until someone else's passion opens the gates to that agony which could not be borne before. Shock is often greater than pain and helps freeze body and mind, and the will to live carries us to a place, which seems like safety but is only a false refuge where hidden doors may open at any time and startle us with further terrors. I was like a little hedgehog curled up against the bitter cold, unable to move or find nourishment.

It was not until midsummer that I rejoined the community, yet I remember little of how those months passed after that Easter Sunday. I know I was sent back to the infirmary. The Leech came to bleed me and I was allowed much rest. But what rest could there be for that tormented soul, fighting those demons and the trinity of her despair, her mother's sin, the blasphemy at the parchment-maker's and that outrage in the barn? In all this I feel for that young girl who had no one to turn to and had to bear her grief entirely on her own. That was the cruellest demon of them all.

Without memory there is no story, and without story there is no meaning. I tell it now. Physically she recovers, but the burden of guilt is one no Leech or diet can cure. She leaves the infirmary and is once again in the solitary cell, alone, for many days. The pain is endless and after the pain she is numb, then occasionally she is neither numb nor pained, and that is even worse.

Dame Cecilia visits once in a while. Sister Margaret comes and tells Bible stories, the one about Lazarus who was raised from the dead, and says there is always hope, sickness passes.

She talks of the virgins who hid their lights under a haystack so did not see the bridegroom coming and fortune passing by. And once it is the story again of the Lord, his servants and the gifts, which one of them hid, while the others invested wisely and were enriched. And she asks her to get well and come back to help with the accounting because it is a hard task doing it all on her own.

She drifts into the comfort of sleep even before Sister Margaret has left, then wakes in the dark. She is rested and content and sees herself reading to Dame Cecilia again and walking with Sister Margaret noting down numbers – this many bushels of wheat, those many cades of dried fish, these ounces of pepper, that many gallons of milk. Then suddenly she is wide-awake, tense and frightened. She tosses and turns and seeks for sleep, but sleep does not come. Turns and tosses, tries to lie straight and then curls up, but the more she looks for sleep the more awake she becomes.

She cannot stop the thoughts that hammer in her head and writhe in her belly. What is worse, the real calamity, she discovers she has doubts about God's goodness and mercy. She finds herself standing in her shift on the cold flagstones. She kneels and tries to pray, but no prayers come. She hits her head with her fists and thinks of the buried talents. Again she seeks sleep, again she seeks prayer and again she hits her head until finally she is worn out and sleeps fitfully on the floor.

So what was it that finally brought me back to life, even if it were still a fragile existence? The news that Edmund no longer worked at the convent farm and had gone to live in the town, that helped. And life itself and all that I'd once enjoyed, stories, songs, the smell of blossom after summer rain and memories of letters written in the sand. But more than anything, necessity.

I recalled what Dame Cecilia had said about charity starting at home and knew I could depend on no one. It was up to me alone to learn to live again.

Little changed over the next three years. Dame Cecilia did not relinquish her position as prioress. A bad storm one winter meant major repairs to the chapel and she decided she should serve another term. I continued to read to her and helped Sister Margaret with the accounts and even learnt to write a little, though it was many years before I truly mastered it.

In the first year nothing was said about starting my noviciate. I knew I was being watched to see if the madness would return. But the next Easter passed serenely and occasionally I was asked to help those in distress, a duty I found increasingly rewarding and managed with some small success. To have suffered oneself makes it easier to treat with someone else's suffering. For some months I had the care of a young imbecile, the daughter of a noble lord, who'd been brought to board with us, and though she was simple I found her often wise, with that wisdom of children who see directly. I knew she would never leave the convent and when death took her in her first winter I was glad for her.

Two years later Sister Margaret asked me if I was ready to take my vows and I promised to answer her soon. I began to see there was little hope for any other life, and knew how fortunate I was to be in this convent and have her support. Although I knew I did not have a vocation, I appreciated the daily routine of work, chapel, silence and rest, despite those nights when black thoughts came to torment me. Mostly I was too busy and beginning to feel if not truly content, at least more at ease. And yes, it's true, the Devil makes work for idle hands, but I'd never learnt to be idle.

Since I was not yet a nun, I was still permitted to help in the convent fields, gathering rushes or weeding the gardens, and on occasion I brought bread and ale to the harvesters or the coopers who had come to repair vessels and kill the beasts. Sometimes I listened to them discussing those strange new ideas I'd heard about at the parchment makers' workshop some years before. I began to think them less threatening now and more true, especially since reading had given me the opportunity to think for myself.

I also came to know that neither Margaret nor the Prioress judged me for my mother's sin, and though I heard no more of it, Dame Cecilia often told me the story of Mary Magdalene, the fallen woman whom Jesus loved. Yet whenever I thought to say I was ready to become a nun, something held me back. I hadn't chosen life in a convent as Joan had, nor did I have a rich, merchant father like Matilda who just wanted her to have an education, and I knew I'd never be able to find work beyond the convent walls. I just was like plain, mean Amice, an orphan who had no choice.

I never forgot the name of the man associated with the talk I'd heard at the workshop. I heard his name again when the Bishop came on his annual visitation, to check the Rule was being correctly observed and ensure the accounts were in order. I'd been reading to Dame Cecilia that morning and we were about to eat when he was announced. He noticed the English Bible lying open on the chest, the moment he came in.

"Ah, I see you have the Wycliffe Bible. Since his death many people have been interested in his ideas, not only the townsfolk but the peasants too, but reading it would give them too much power. They're like sheep who must be sheltered by their shepherds. I dread to think what would happen if the common folk started to read. It's better we give them images to look at and sermons to instruct them, than let them have their own thoughts. Can they be trusted to interpret the Scriptures correctly? I doubt it. We must be on guard and protect them from themselves."

"Quite so, my Lord Bishop, quite so," Dame Cecilia remonstrated. "But I need to instruct my daughters in a language they understand, or they'll fall into the trough of accidie, of spiritual sloth, and their boredom will lead to malice and fits of temper. There are some here who are not so resolute, but when I give them clear instruction in their own tongue, their minds are challenged, the noonday demons have no power over them and they spend less time in spiteful chatter."

"No, no, my dear Dame Cecilia, I do not think that wise, and surely you know that Wycliffe has been condemned. You must put the English Bible aside …"

And before he'd finished speaking, she waved her hand to dismiss me.

But I could delay my decision no longer. This was a time of both anticipation and apprehension. I knew as a nun I could continue learning, and hoped I might grow in wisdom. If I worked hard I might rise to a position of power like Sister Margaret or Dame Cecilia. At the same time there was so much unlived life I would never enjoy. Never to have babies – that urge was strong in me, a thorn in my flesh. Never to lie in the fields with a man, the old woman's story was a constant daydream though poisoned by the child she bore. Never to gossip like the young women who came to glean at harvest-time, or wear pretty tunics and bind ribbons in my hair. Never to lie abed late or choose to stay up at night and chatter to the stars. But in truth I had nowhere else to go, no home, no family, no choice.

It happened then, when finally I'd resolved to tell Dame Cecilia I was ready to take my vows, that she summoned me. And she had a visitor.

"This," she said, "is John Brunham, a worshipful burger of Lynn. He's come with a request. His daughter has been plagued by an anguish of the soul for many months. Leeches have attended her and the best doctors of physic in town, but they cannot help. She says devils torment her and though her confessor came once she refuses to see him again. She's young and newly wed and sometime since was in childbed. Brunham heard you were once afflicted and since then have helped others who were suffering. He asks that you leave now and attend his daughter and hopes you may bring her some peace."

"You are not," she continued, "bound by any vows to our convent, but it's my hope that once you have brought comfort to Mistress Kempe, you'll come back to us. I know you will behave with modesty and be mindful of all you've learnt here. You're required immediately and I've given permission for you to go to Lynn for six weeks. You'll depart first thing to-morrow morning."

With that she made a sign I was to leave. It was dark in the room and her visitor had his back to the light. I sensed he was looking at me, but did not lift my eyes, though as I bowed to kiss Dame Cecilia's ring, he turned towards the window and in that moment I glimpsed his face. It was the man who'd visited my childhood home long ago and who'd brought me to the convent some nine or ten years before.

I was much perturbed when I closed the door. Dame Cecilia had been unusually curt and although a part of me yearned to live in the real world with ordinary folk, I had little experience of that world and there was no one I might turn to, no one to show me the way. The convent for all its limitations was home to me, mother, father and all the family I knew. Now, suddenly, I was to leave. After supper, I knocked on Sister Margaret's door. I needed at least to say farewell.

"So, you are leaving us for awhile," she said.

"Yes, and I am fearful and have many questions."

"Well, I don't know what I may tell you. Finally the answer lies in your own heart. What else could bring you closer to God?"

This was always her way, sometimes focussing on the inner life as if there were no other world out there. Yet she moved serenely between the two, doing the convent's business in town, watchful of the young who came to stay, diligent in her work of the convent's accounts, yet also often deep in meditation in either chapel or cloister.

"Dame Cecilia told me I'm asked to look after John Brun-ham's daughter. I recognised him today yet know nothing about him, except he's the man who brought me here. He came a few times to my childhood home and it was he who encouraged me to learn the letters and numbers."

"Yes, he was always ambitious and values book learning, but I doubt he's a true friend of the Church and most likely prefers the wealth of Mammon to the riches of Heaven."

"Who is he then?" I asked.

"He's a merchant from Bishop's Lynn, a full day's journey from here, a port on the river Ouse, a noble town with many fine buildings and much larger and busier than the one you've visited with me. The Lynn merchants are rich and powerful. Many ships dock there and do much trade with different parts of our country, as well as other towns that belong to the Hanseatic League, a great trading fellowship over the seas. The largest church is St Margaret's and her priests are friendly to our convent. There are many other churches and friaries ..."

"But," I insisted, "who is he?"

She seemed annoyed at my interruption, but I carried on ...

"He's the man who brought me here and now he wants to take me away, but I don't know who he is."

"I cannot tell you much about him," she answered. "I only met him twice, first when you came here and later when he visited with money for your lodging, which he paid out of charity. I remember being told he trades in fish, cloth and lumber and was several times mayor, a member of the King's parliaments and has held other high offices in Lynn. All his family are engaged in this export and import business.

I've heard his daughter is married to John Kempe, the son of another wealthy merchant. I think she's probably close in age to you. They say her mother died many years ago. I don't know what causes this anguish, but let's think of some draughts and balms that might lessen her distress. Perhaps rue, hops or John's wort will help and maybe Sister Anne has some other suggestions. Quickgrass has good qualities and wormwood too often helps after childbirth, or you could try ... "

"Please, Sister Margaret, please tell me who he is. He left me here years ago and now he's taking me away and it seems both you and Dame Cecilia just accept his wishes. What am I to him, what is he to me? How does he know about me and why are you letting me go so easily?"

I have always known Sister Margaret to be composed and calm, yet now she was strangely flustered.

"We're not happy to let you go," she said sharply, "but we had no choice. You hadn't said you intended to take the vows, so you are free to leave."

"Well, now I'm not so sure – perhaps I should stay."

"It's too late. The first thing he asked was whether you had made a commitment to take your vows."

"Then tell me please," I begged, "what am I to him?"
She gave me a strangely mournful look, then said,

"I will tell you because I think you have a right to know, but you must never divulge it to any other person. It is indeed a sad story. What we were told and what I have heard was not given in sworn confidence, and at the time I doubt anyone thought you might ever be associated with him. But I fear we may never meet again, so I'll tell you. It concerns your mother. First you must give me your oath that you will say no more of this to anyone."

"My mother, something about my mother? Tell me, tell me …"

"You swear …"

"Yes, yes, I give you my oath."
And then she told me, though she warned there was much she didn't know.

"Your mother was from Danzig, a Hanseatic trading post on the Baltic coast. She was the daughter of one of Brunham's acquaintances, a merchant he did business with over the seas. I heard tell she and her brother came to his household for a year, she to be maidservant to his lady and learn the English language, and he to learn the trade. Then Brunham's lady discovered her young companion was far advanced in pregnancy, it seems she'd hidden it well. Her brother had left some weeks earlier on a commission but had then fallen ill, so returned to his own country to be nursed by his family."

"Brunham didn't know what to do, for he was responsible for her. Both he and his lady thought it best she marry but she refused to name the father. He offered to give her away with a large dowry, and there were several men who would have taken her for she was very fair, but she would have none of them. Most important was to avoid a scandal, so they gave word she'd fallen sick and kept her hidden in her chamber.

Now it happened Brunham's wife was also pregnant, and they both started labour on the same night. Mistress Brunham had given birth many times before but always to stillborn or sickly babes who died soon after, so there was great fear for her. This time however her baby thrived, a little girl they called Margery. But your mother died giving birth to you and Brunham decided, in thanksgiving for the gift of his own daughter, to take responsibility for you. So he sent you to the country, to be nursed by the wife of one of his bailiffs. Then, when he learnt you were good at numbers, he paid for you to come here and now he has other plans for you."

I was astonished and confused, happy and sad, surprised and shocked, but that was all Margaret could tell me despite my many questions. It was late and although I had nothing to prepare, no possessions to pack, the idea of this journey upset me for it was a disruption to the sheltered life I knew. I also worried whether I'd be able to help Mistress Kempe in her distress, and now that I knew my birth story, most fearful of meeting John Brunham again.

The Matins bells started to ring and it was time for us to make our farewells.

"Yes, it will be hard for you, but you're a clever young woman and if you listen to your heart you will know what to do. I know you will behave well, at the same time try not to be too trusting, that's a fault I have often observed in you. I also see you're a careful listener and when you speak it is always plain and forthright. But be mindful for few have clear hearts and do not like to hear the naked truth. And I doubt anyone has told you this but you are exceeding comely, so be wary. Never forget that beneath the charm of many men there lies lasciviousness and lust.

Michael, who is a member of Brunham's household will ride with you tomorrow. I've met him a few times when he brought coinage for your keep and you should be safe with him, may the Virgin protect you. He's old enough to be your father. Fare you well now my daughter and embrace this chance God has given you."

She held me in her arms and hugged me, and I fought hard to contain my tears.

It seemed she thought we'd never meet again, though she was wrong on that score. In many ways she'd been mother to me, happy to teach even if that sometimes meant a challenge or rebuke, while at the same time encouraging me to find my own way. But I knew the gift of her love and I felt much gratitude.

I remember the morning I left as if it were only yesterday, and wonder why that memory is so clear while others fade and blur. I think it not only because I've recalled it so often, but also because each new beginning has a freshness which repeats itself again and again, as if all hope were eternal. And this was truly a new beginning, for now I knew something more about my mother and Sister Margaret had uttered no word of judgment against her.

I woke to the chimes of bells. It was no longer dark, there was that early morning light that hovers between night and day with a moment of birdsong then silence again, the false dawn. It was time to get up. In that instance I knew I was being watched. A woman was standing near the window wearing my clothes and although I couldn't see her clearly, I felt her malevolence. She looked sternly down at me and I waited for her to speak, but she said nothing only continuing to stare. I wondered why she'd come and what it was she had to tell me.

As the darkness faded, so her image grew less distinct, dissolving slowly. And then I understood she was the spirit of my past life. I blinked and she was gone and there by the casement I saw my convent habit hanging on a peg and a new blue tunic, mantle and cloak lay folded on the stool. I dressed quickly and went to the entrance parlour where Michael was waiting.

I was anxious about being alone with any man and frightened too about going out into the world without a single friend. I stayed awhile in the shadows so I might observe him. I thought him most noble and handsome and that enchanted me. I began to relish the prospect of travelling with him to Lynn. I stepped into the light and he turned to greet me.

"Good morrow, mistress and well met. Let us leave now. I have bread, cheese and a flagon of ale, and we'll stop and breakfast on our way."

His horse was already saddled and there was a mule for me. Michael assured me the beast was docile and helped me mount. And at that moment, astride my mule, I felt strong and proud and more sure of myself than I had ever been. I followed him across the courtyard, hooves echoing on cobblestones. Then the great wooden gates closed behind us, and we took the road out through the village and away, with the convent bells ringing in the distance for all eternity.

Lynn was everything Margaret had said and more. When I'd accompanied her to our nearby town, I kept my eyes down as we were taught, but here in Lynn I held my head up and dared look all around. It was early evening when finally we entered by the south gate, crossing the Mill fleet into the precincts of St Margaret's Priory and beyond to the great square, where hawkers and stall-holders were packing up their market goods. I'd never seen so much bustle, so many buildings and so many people.

There was a confusion and patchwork of churches and friaries, dwellings of wood, stone and flint, taverns and ale-houses, allotments and orchards, streams, bridges, dykes and ditches, animal enclosures, ovens, foundries, workshops and stalls, lanes thick with the debris of urban life, the square thronging with priests, sailors, merchants, farmers, old ladies squabbling over market remnants, young women with toddlers riding on their hips, children scampering here and there chasing dogs and cats, lepers and beggars with hungry eyes, and yells and shouts in many languages. By the quays were the warehouses, and the rigging, masts, flags and pennants of fleets of ships anchored, far across to the riverbank on the other side with the marsh beyond. Everywhere there was a hint of the salt of the sea, and the smell of tar and rotting fish.

I'd never seen such a wide river before and so much water flowing into it. Later, I saw how foul it was. Many dwellings were built beside the fleets or on top of the bridges and all the refuse and filth of the latrines emptied into them, flowed to the river and out to sea. When the tide was out and the fleets dry, much muck lay in the mud and rats scampered everywhere. Children clambered into them with little pails seeking treasure, for to a child any shell, bone or strangely shaped scrap has value.

And there were lots of children, mostly unfathered, for sailors came and went, leaving behind pregnant maidens who'd been beguiled by their foreign looks and traveller's tales. I did not judge these women or their children, mindful of my own lack of a father. Over the years I often looked at the faces of those seafaring men, searching for someone of my own blood, but never saw any with the same strangely mismatched eyes as I. At least not for now.

It was growing dark when we arrived at the Kempe household in Fincham Street. Michael made a swift farewell. He'd spoken little on our journey except to answer my questions for I was delighted with everything I saw, and he'd laughed at me once saying,

"By all the saints you are a lovely young woman and so full of fancies."

I'd felt a great blush rising to my cheeks and was hushed for a moment until I saw something afresh to marvel at and comment on.

I was taken to the pantry and told I would meet Margery on the morrow. The household servants crowded round but the steward sent all away but two, Adam and Betty. And though I was greatly wearied, I wanted to hear everything they could tell me about their mistress. Betty spoke first. She was the new babe's wet nurse, a plump young woman with sparkling eyes and a pronounced pout.

"I've never known a woman make such a fuss of birthing as this one, and I've seen aplenty, my ma's had a round dozen, I was there for the last six and they just slipped out of her like eels through a net. As for me, I sang anthems all the time I was labouring at mine. But Mistress Margery, she yelped day and night like a fox in a trap and wouldn't let it out. You'd have thought it were some monster asking to be born. What a fuss that was …"

"Aye, indeed it was," this from pasty-faced old Adam, the fat pastry-cook.

"The rafters and beams, casements and doorframes, everything shook with her yelling and helling. But finally, long after the good Lord willed to be sure, there he was, the sweetest little creature you ever did see. But when the midwife had washed and swaddled him, cradled and cuddled him, then handed him to her, she just closed her eyes and turned her face to the wall. That was very strange indeed."

"Indeed, it were," nodded Adam.

"And that was six months ago now and I've had care of little Johnnie ever since as she refuses even to hold him. Can you imagine that?"

"Imagine that, not wanting to hold your own babe."

"Yes and then it grew stranger still. Soon after the birth she was tormented by nightmares and woke the whole household with her shrieking and screaming, roaring and cawing. We were all quite frightened …"

"Quite frightened, indeed."

" … then her husband, that blessed man who worships the ground she walks on, bought her a precious coral pendant to keep under her pillow, for coral keeps the night demons away."

"Aye, they cannot abide the coral."

"But she'd have none of it. Then they thought she was going to die and summoned her priest …"

"But you forgot the Virgin's milk …"

"Indeed, I did. Her father sent alms to the Walsingham shrine, for a little bottle of holy water from one of the healing wells to be mixed with a drop of the Virgin's milk, which flows from her image there, blessed be the Virgin. It must have cost him a pretty penny …"

"A very pretty penny …"

"But she wouldn't accept that either. Then after the priest's visit she became really crazed, refusing to see her goodman or have the infant anywhere near. Now she's abandoned her prayers and won't go to church. Sometimes she screams that devils are coming and at other times she throws her food on the floor …"

"All my fine pies and pastries …"

" … or smears them in her hair. She yells rudities and crudities, claws at her flesh and once bit her hand so hard you can still see the mark. Oftentimes she soils herself, or is silent and stares at whoever comes to attend her. I did once and was truly terrified."

"You were indeed and came to my kitchen as ghostly white as my best flour."

"At other times she sings nonsense rhymes and dances round her chamber with lewd gestures and foul words. We've no idea how to help her …"

"And sometimes they've bid me bind her to the bed so she doesn't harm herself. Tis very strange."

"Very strange indeed," said Betty.

"And," said Adam, "we all put our faith in you, Missie, because otherwise we see no end of it. Her husband and father are much distressed and worry she's possessed. I've known her since she were a child and she was most docile so long as someone paid her attention, and if they did not, well then there were almighty tantrums. But this is sad and dire indeed and I include her in my prayers every night."

Then he made the sign of the cross and Betty took me to her chamber, for it was late and I was to share her bed. I lay awake all night, listening to the unfamiliar noises, remembering the long ride and everything I'd seen, thinking about my mother and how charming and gentle Michael had been and wondering what the next day would bring.

I was taken to Margery the following morning, to a chamber that smelt of the rankness of fear. I know this smell well, it is the odour of madness. I was told she was quiet, given a candle and warned not to open the shutters, for she could not abide the light of day. Of course I was curious to meet this woman whom I'd seen just once as a child. I wondered if she might remember me or have any idea who I was, the strange connection we had sharing the same birthday, and how her life had dictated my fate. But I doubted she would.

Secrets give you power. This secret gave me confidence too for otherwise I'd have been very unsure of myself. I knew if I could help her I might be able to stay in her household, though I already judged her for her wealth and all the fine gowns I imagined hanging in the alcove closet at the side of her chamber. I'd had no need to feel envious before, since we were more or less the same at the convent but now it gnawed at my guts like rats at a sack of good corn. Yet I was not worried about her madness for I knew that isolation is often the larger part of grief.

When I entered her room, she was sitting on her bed in her shift. I greeted her, took out the balms I'd brought and offered to rub her head and shoulders. She assented, was silent for a while, then said:

"They told me a new servant was coming, a woman from a convent, yet you're not wearing a monastic habit. So what are you?"

I gave her my name and said I'd not yet taken the vows. She asked what I did so I explained the routine of the convent day. Then she wanted to know who my parents were and I said I was an orphan. After some silence she asked if I knew any stories and I related the tale of Joseph and his wonderful coat, the envy of his brothers, how they wanted to kill him but then sold him into slavery, how he became an important officer in the land of Egypt, was slandered and imprisoned, became a great interpreter of dreams, foremost minister to the Pharaoh and finally reconciled with his family and saved them all from famine.

The way I told the story pleased her and she asked for more. She was like a child hungry for tales at eventide, as if a story could hold back the darkness. I started then to speak of Moses and his mother who'd hidden him in a basket of bulrushes, but she grew agitated and I knew I had to find another tale lest she slip into a craze. So I recounted the legend of Saint Sitha, the young maidservant who suffered much abuse but was meek and humble and proclaimed that housework was her penance.

Then the servants brought refreshments and she invited me to eat with her. Later, when they came to take the vessels away we heard the thin cry of a babe outside. And suddenly she lashed out, upsetting the bowls and spilling wine on the floor.

"Take that brat away," she shrieked, "I want none of him."

She chased the servant out and slammed the door. Then she turned to me and started screaming, arms flaying out to hit me. I remained still and sheltered my head with my arms. Her eyes glazed over and she began beating herself, hitting her head with her clenched fists. I knew that feeling and knew too what would have stopped me beating myself. I took her in my arms and held her tight, though she fought like a drowning cat, and I soothed her as I would a frightened child until she was quiet. Her body shook with pitiful sobs and then I was sobbing too, as all the agony of my own distress rose up from the pool of my memory and flooded into me. And so the two of us stood there together, arms around each other, joined in our unspoken misery.

Later we lay on her bed and slept, she drained by her violent outburst and I wasted from witnessing her terrible suffering and the release of my own pent up grief. When we woke I massaged her head again and asked what ailed her.

"O, you wouldn't understand, leading the life you do. You wouldn't even know what I was talking about."

"Is it about a man?" I asked, for I'd learnt from the chatter in the convent fields that this is what concerns most young women.

"Well yes, it might be," said she, "and what if it is, what could you tell me?"

She said no more. I remembered they'd said her sickness began after the priest's visit and wondered if she'd spoken of some sin and had been judged harshly for it, just as I'd always judged myself.

"Have you told anyone the reason for your grief?" I asked, "for often a secret borne alone is too much to bear."

"No, there's no one I can trust."

"Then why not tell me, for I will not gossip and will swear an oath if that helps," and I held her in my arms again and stroked her hair with all the longing of that young woman I had been, alone and friendless.

"Perhaps you're right, after all you are a nobody and when you return to your convent who will you have to tell?"

And so she made me swear. As I said she was greedy for stories, but now it was she who relished telling her tale as if all the light shone on her.

"It was soon after I was newly wed and mistress of my household and my husband was very proud of me, delighted by the way I welcomed his associates and said none of the other merchants' wives were as merry and gay as I. And I wanted more than anything to succeed, for my honour and the worshipful name of my kin. Then it happened I had occasion to give hospitality to a foreigner while John was away on business. He was a great flatterer and we contrived to lie together before he sailed back to his country on the next tide. Soon after I found I was with child and didn't know whether it was his or John's and was tormented throughout my pregnancy. When I gave birth I wished the babe might die, but he thrived and I cannot bear to look at him in case he wears the stranger's face. I was ill for many days, then they called the priest to my bedside.

I didn't want to tell him my fears about the brat's father, so I spoke only of my sexual temptation, but he was very sharp with me. He told me to repent and make a public act of contrition. But that I can and will not do. I refuse to be seen by the townsfolk and jeered at. And now I dread I will be damned forever."

I was astounded and the memory of the old lady and Edmund came back to me. I thought how a cuckoo in the nest is fledged with wickedness and for her sin and frivolity she would surely be cursed into eternity. Then I remembered what Sister Margaret had said about unwelcome plain speaking and was quiet for a while, because I knew I wanted to stay in her household. I had no wish to return to the convent but reside in the world of the living, find out who my father was, and travel perhaps in one of those tall ships to the country of my mother. And if I were to succeed then I needed to be cunning and help

Mistress Kempe in her distress.

We lay side by side on her bed, her head on my shoulder,

"Mistress, what has passed has passed. Now be wise and wary. Everyone in your household is shocked you have no love for your babe. That's a path that must lead to danger. They all know you're his mother and there's no reason for them to think more about it. Betty will care for him, but he's still your son, so you should show him some affection, even if you have to live with doubt about his true father for the rest of your life. That's the price of your fault and cost of your contrition. Now, steady yourself, grasp the pikestaff of penance, leave this sinful past behind and go forward."

She was silent a while, her face turned towards mine.

"And surely, you'll have more children, so why should anyone question the fatherhood of your first-born, and you so newly wed? No one is going to look at his face and ask whom he most resembles. I've often observed at the convent when infants are brought for baptism, people always say how like the father the child looks, even when he does not. That's nature's way of keeping husbands happy and wives too perhaps. If you're contrite then God will forgive you. It was a foolish mistake that belonged to your youth, but now you're a mother and must learn to repent and bear the burden of your sin on your own."

She started to protest, kicking and struggling, mad with guilt and rage, but I took her in my arms again, stroked her brow and reminded her that the sum of her sin would be the loneliness of her guilt, and though I knew her secret I did not judge her, and her repentance would be the path to salvation. Still she fought and hit me, but I held her close until she quieted.

Again we slept and again she woke full of anguish and remorse, weeping all those tears, which I could not.

"Mistress, don't distress yourself so. Don't forget the love Mother Mary has for all who are truly repentant. Remember also the love of her son who never forsakes those who turn to him. And he loved the fallen woman Magdalene too."

Everything else I told her that night was what I'd liked to have heard myself, had I found the courage to speak of my own great grief. And soon she grew more and more at ease, then she suddenly sat up in the bed laughing quietly.

"Look there, look, do you see him? There is the Lord Jesus just beside me, so noble and comely, clad in a mantle of purple silk. He's smiling at me, forgiving me. Do you see him?"

I looked and saw nothing but the shadows on the wall.

"And listen, he speaks. He tells me, 'Daughter, why have you forsaken me for I will never forsake you.' And now he's going, ascending to heaven on a brilliant ray of bright light."

She seemed entranced, fell on her knees and said now she was at peace and would sleep, and on the morrow would take charge of her household again and be reunited with her husband and the babe. And then she slept.

But I could find no rest and began to feel a great bitterness, like a crabbed fruit, jealous of her fortune. Silently, as the hours passed, I railed against God who had given her so much and me so little, she with her husband, wealth and newly confident faith, and I only with tortuous memories for family and none I could call my own.

In later years I came to understand how sour and cruel was the fruit of my bitterness, how it compelled me sometimes to spite and punish her, harking back to her sin whenever she was joyful, blaming her for my own dark fate. These sharp pricks of unjust meanness brought me much turmoil, since at times I loved her dearly, enchanted by her childlike candour.

Finally I also slept and when the morning dawned Margery woke before me and said I was to be her maidservant, and that she would keep me close and we should be friends forever.

3

Bishop's Lynn, 1393-1413

'torn between silk & sackcloth'

I doubt anyone from the convent would have known me had we met a year later. I didn't go back, and though I sent messages I never heard a word. Everyone believed Margery's recovery was a miracle which perhaps it was, though I now know that talking to a stranger is as good as a plenitude of prayer or any physic's potion. Be that as it may, soon after Brunham sent word I was to wait on him. I was worried as I didn't know what he might have to tell me, whether he'd say anything about sending me to the convent then arranging for me to leave, and of course there was much I wanted to ask him but was bound by my oath. Besides I was much too shy.

I was taken to his warehouse and once my eyes were accustomed to the gloom, I saw it was packed with bales of yarn, rolls of cloth, fish barrels and crates. Brunham was standing behind a table covered in parchment rolls. He greeted me courteously as if we were strangers, gestured to a bench and bade me sit. I gave him my mistress's greetings, and was going to tell him about the babe when he interrupted me.

"Yes, yes. I'm grateful that my daughter has recovered her wits, and body and soul are restored to health, thanks be to God. I hear she's taken responsibility for her household again, and am pleased my confidence in you has not been misplaced."

Had he let me speak I would have told him her recovery was not my doing, but he continued,

"And it seems she's well pleased with you too, for I hear you're engaged as her new maidservant. So now we'll write to Dame Cecilia and tell her you won't be returning …"

I felt a moment's irritation that he did not even think to ask if this was what I wanted.

"… and you may of course send messages to your companions."

He beckoned to a man I hadn't noticed before. As quickly as the message was dictated, the words were written, then Brunham brought the letter to me.

"Would you like to make your mark?"

"No," I said, without any thought.

He was startled but it had not been my intention to be so curt and he could not have understood, I was not objecting.

"I shall write my name."

The clerk gave me the quill and I steadied my hand. Of course I knew the letters of my name, for I'd drawn them over and over in the sands of my memory but had never had need to write them before. I sensed Brunham looking at me, but I did not falter. When I finished he took the parchment, stared at it, then told the scribe to attach his seal. While we waited two people emerged from the shadows. One was Michael, whom I hadn't seen since our ride to Lynn. He smiled, bowed his head and said nothing. Brunham introduced the other as Ralph, John Kempe's valet, though we had not yet met. He was a tall, handsome man but thin, as thin as a caged rook.

Then he waved his hand to dismiss me and as I reached the door he said:

"I trust you will continue to exercise a good influence on Margery and be as kind as kin to her."

Strange words, I thought. I was after all, just her maidservant and could never be as grand as she.

As I sit here now I understand that writing my name had sealed my fate. No one had called me that since I left my childhood home and was given a new name by the nuns. But at that time I was so full of anger, guilt and shame that I resolved never to think of my former life again and put the convent and all that it stood for, good and bad, out of my mind. I felt ready to accept whatever new adventure life would bring, and believed it was simple to sever the bonds of the past, change my name once more, forget all that had happened and who I had been.

As I said, no one from the convent would have known me in my new role at Fincham Street. Being Margery's handmaid was not arduous and the variety pleased me for it was a busy household with frequent comings and goings. My day started when she summoned me to help her dress, arrange her hair and assist with her washing. She was always most particular about cleanliness and could never abide any mote of dirt. She also expected me to plan the daily menus, although Ralph did much of the household provisioning.

Often she'd ask me to tell any stories I knew and I said I'd be happy to teach her to read if she wished. But that she did not, for soon she was pregnant again and lay abed late, calling me to attend her in her chamber or the solar when her friends were visiting. They usually brought sewing with them, as well as their gossips, and there was always more time expended on the latter than the former. And Margery never finished her needlework, but made up for that lack by the skilful stitching of her stories, sometimes the very same ones I'd related earlier in the day. But just as she relished the telling of her tales, so I found occasional fulfilment in embroidering my own fantasies, especially about finding my true father.

When a new shipment arrived from over the seas, we went to the quays to watch the men unload their cargoes and the merchants bargaining for goods, especially when it was cloth. Margery was very partial to colourful silks and fine brocades and her husband was always indulgent and could never tell her no. So I frequently had new tunics to sew and my work was much admired. On rare occasions, she let me have one of her old garments but always made it clear that I was to refashion it into something plain and simple.

Sometimes a monk came from St Margaret's Priory or a priest from one of the other churches in Lynn and read from the Scriptures. These clerics had several holy books besides the Bible, all in Latin, which they translated for us. I recalled my talks with Dame Cecilia and was, at first, bold enough to ask questions and say what I thought. But I soon became mindful that they preferred to tell us the meanings, and didn't welcome anyone who had her own ideas. There were other times when we visited some of Margery's neighbours and heard very different tales, in particular at Katherine's home, whose husband owned several books and also employed a scribe.

This scribe read not only the sacred texts but also stories, like the legends and romances of King Arthur's knights and their quests of chivalry. I enjoyed these tales, which told of real people, their lives and adventures. Some were in Latin and French, but these he was able to speak in English too. The one I cherished most was the story of St George who saved the maiden from the dragon and told her to throw her girdle around its neck. Then the monster followed meekly behind them to her father's court, like a dog on a leash, where it was killed and all rejoiced. I wished there'd been such a knight to save me from that beast in the barn, and marvelled that gentleness might overcome evil and terror.

The months of Margery's pregnancy passed quickly. Everyone wondered if she would show any signs of her former sickness, but she was cheerful and carefree, amusing herself during the day with her friends, games and good works, and at night with her husband and their acquaintances. She revelled in the attention and was gentle and kind, but never played with little John, pleading the delicacy of her condition. As he grew older and was weaned, I became as if his true mother, until many years later when she paid him unwelcome attention.

Her friends had many suggestions to soothe her during her pregnancy. Mabel lent her a little amulet to wear around her neck, with a magic formula rolled up inside which had given her relief in her own childbearing. Katherine spoke of special charms that had lessened her labour pains, and another friend told of the girdle that was kept in the sanctuary at St Margaret's and was known to be most beneficial for pregnant women. Margery sent alms to the Prior that she might have the loan of it to ease her toil when her time came.

I procured chamomile and valerian for infusions and pastes to rub on her belly to bring comfort for the unborn creature. And Sybile, the new midwife Margery had engaged - for she would have none of the first one blaming her for her distress - this new midwife advised her to wear a little bell under her gown, letting it dangle between her legs, so the babe might turn his head down to hear the chimes as she walked, ensuring a safe and easy delivery.

As I'd never witnessed childbirth and was to assist Margery when her labour started, Sybile requested I attend a birth with her to learn what was necessary. Though we hadn't yet met I was fearful of Sybile as were the others in the household, for they said she had many strange ways and the townsfolk held her in great awe. Perhaps her frequent presence at the mysteries of birth put her beyond ordinary understanding.

Her man came one early evening and took me to the Purfleet Bridge where I found her watching the river.

"Look," she said "and tell me, what's happening to the tide." I turned to answer and was surprised to see so young a face unlined by cares and years, yet long wisps of white hair escaped from inside her hood.

"It doesn't move, it's slack and at its lowest and must soon turn."

"Yes, and so this babe will be born before the night is out for that is the way of life. Babies arrive with the flow of the tide just as death comes on the ebb. I see from your eyes you are no stranger to birth and death and so am happy to teach you, and you will learn well from me. Now come, let us make haste. "

And she hurried away with her crimson cloak billowing behind her and her man at her heels carrying the birthing stool.

The chamber was hot when we arrived, crowded with women, young and old, relatives and neighbours of the woman we were attending. There was much noise and chattering, which did not cease despite the loud moans coming from the bed. They said she'd already had a show of blood, her waters had spilled and they'd given her an infusion of poppy juice to ease the pain.

Sybile went to the young woman, lifted her shift placing the palms of her hands gently on her belly, and called for hot water and clean cloths. Then she guided her to the birthing-stool and asked me to stand behind, holding her whenever she willed. She was a small woman yet heavy in my arms. At times she lay back on the stool, then crouched on all fours while I supported her. Often she gave a great bellow like a wild beast, which I felt deep inside me. Sybile told her how and when to breath and push, and whenever she howled the women counted, for they said the babe would be born by the sum of twenty. With each yell I became tense and tight as I tried to provide relief for this labouring woman, willing her do what had to be done.

"Fourteen ... fifteen ... sixteen ..." everyone shouted, and still the babe was not born. Suddenly there was much activity in the chamber – one woman unlatched the casement shutters, another opened the closet door, a third unlocked the chest at the bottom of the bed and several women started untying the knots in their girdles, as Sybile urged her on ...

"seventeen ... eighteen ... nineteen ..."

and then we both roared. And as our roars faded there was a small wail and everyone clapped and made the sign of the cross.

The young mother was soon resting on her bed again with all her friends congratulating her, smoothing her brow and rubbing her belly with a salve of rose petals. When she was dressed in a clean gown and cuddling her son, her husband was called in and messages sent to the godparents to meet for the baptism the following morning.

I've never forgotten that birth. Over the years I helped Margery many times in all her labours, which were always hard for her, but that first birth was something wondrous that I never felt again. Though that young mother was unknown to me, there was an ease of trust between us and we were as one in our work of giving birth together. When she screamed in pain and effort I sensed her pain deep within me and also outside, as if there were someone telling a story about the miracle of birth and we were just little children listening and watching. But if there were something distant, there was also something very close. As I felt her roars and as I finally roared myself, I knew what it was to be both a woman and a creature. And more than that, what it was to be the vessel, the bearer of new life.

Margery's time came a month after this. Once she started her labour all her women friends gathered round, and while we waited for Sybile I left the chamber on a pretext to go to the river and watch the tide. The ebb had passed and the Ouse was on the flow, so I had great hopes for Margery. But her babe did not come on that tide but with the next when we had long given up counting. Childbirth was always very hard for her. She was a little scrap of a babe, a girl child, but Margery was happy and took her in her arms.

That was the first of Margery's many labours I attended and she was content with me, saying I should be her maidservant for always. Her sickness did not recur after Isobel's birth, but soon another wet nurse was engaged as she did not have time for this babe either. She said she needed to busy herself with her household and friends, give hospitality to her husband's associates and mind the apprentices. No doubt she was much relieved the demons hadn't come back to torture her - it seemed she had them banished from her mind.

What concerned her now was that people should think well of her, for many had called her feeble-minded and wondered why John hadn't taken the stick to her during her months of madness. I know there were some neighbours who were disappointed she hadn't lost her wits again – envy often gives birth to thoughtless cruelty. But feeble-minded? No, that she was not, rather single-minded, seeing herself at the centre of the world, accountable to no one.

But the gossip was gall to her and she soon thought of a way to remedy it. She'd been too sick to attend the Purification rites after the birth of her firstborn, but well enough after Isobel's birth to be churched and show herself to the townsfolk. Some three or four weeks later she called me to her chamber. Stored in the chest at the end of her bed was a roll of gold brocade, which she'd acquired a few months before at great expense. As I came in she'd taken it out and was holding it by the window, its rich hue shimmering in the sunlight.

"Look you, see how beautiful it is. I knew I'd need it soon and now I have a merry idea. We shall cut it and sew it for my Churching, as I've no other decent gown to wear. We only have a couple of weeks but you're cunning with the needle and will make beautiful work of it and there will be time enough for I'll excuse you all your other tasks."

"But mistress …"

"There's no need to thank me for my compliments. And I've an idea for a new headdress to match it, with piping and gold cloth. So go to the market and purchase some wires and then you can practice with my hair. "

"But Margery, do you not think a simple kirtle would be more seemly – that is the custom I have observed and …"

"No, no, no," she interrupted. "Simple clothes are for simple folk who have no need to display the honour of their household and their kin."

"But don't you remember your friend Katherine who wore a plain blue gown and simple white veil when she was churched, and you said the humble garments suited her and she looked just like the Blessed Virgin."

She was still toying with the brocade by the casement window, wrapping it around her as it sparkled in the light. Then, pulling off her headdress she shook out her hair so her golden curls blazed in the sunbeams. She did indeed look radiant, and I turned away.

"Yes," she retorted, "they did suit her. And she's very plain."

"Well, perhaps you could cover your hair with the fringed, damask cloth that the Prior sends to those coming for the

Purification, as your other neighbours do. Or you could wear one of your own silken veils."

"No," she answered sharply "and who, and what are you to tell me how I am to dress? You forget how worshipful my family is and cannot know what is proper for someone of my blood."

I might have paused and bit my tongue, but did not.

"But consider Margery what your neighbours will say if you ignore the custom. You know some have called you half-witted, and if you go to church decked out from head to foot in glitter and gold they'll have good reason to call you vainglorious as well as mad. They'll be watching carefully, ready to find fault if you try to better them. Rivalry will stir them up and they'll continue their slanders."

"So what do you know about honour?" she said, stuffing the brocade back into the chest. "I don't need you to tell me what is fitting and though you were orphaned as a babe, your father can never have been as worthy as mine. So go to the market, look for wires and gold cloth, then come back and start work on my gown."

I felt a cold rage rising inside me. I had not disclosed the truth of my birth to her and she knew nothing of the deep heartache I felt through not knowing who my father was.

As I stood in the doorway I answered her back:

"Remember Margery the townsfolk don't know the true reason for your madness - only you and I know that."

And so I left. I'd never crossed Margery before, but I wasn't worried that she'd dismiss me, for we were bound by her secret. Nevertheless I stitched my eyes and fingers sore for the next two weeks to make that golden gown, though finally she wore a modest tunic instead.

Those first years in Lynn are the ones I remember most clearly. Everything was new and exciting. In the convent there had been little to disturb the day's routine and the yearly festivals repeated themselves with a certain regularity. But in Lynn, even though tides ebbed and flowed, spring and neap, and ships docked and sailed away, nothing was predictable. Nothing perhaps except for Margery's pregnancies, which occurred almost every year. Yet almost as often as she gave birth a little one died while John, her firstborn, grew stronger and stronger, and she bore only one more girl child after Isobel.

Despite this yearly burden, Margery flourished and at times it seemed she shone like the brightest star in the firmament. I began to love her more and more, for she was always gay and merry until such time when a little one died and she came to share her loss with me. Then she was like a child herself and, taking her in my arms to comfort her, I found comfort for myself. But mostly she was released from the duties of motherhood, for now as well as being her maidservant I also helped the nursery maid. Margery never forgot her wish to outshine her neighbours and be mistress of the foremost household in Lynn, so I was always busy sewing new gowns and surcotes for her in the latest styles, which few of the other merchants' wives wore.

We had no reason at this time to disagree and I kept her secret, but then I had some secrets of my own. Of all the household servants apart from Betty, Adam was the one I felt most at ease with, and I learnt one morning that he had helped the roasting-cook in Brunham's household before he came to Fincham Street.

"Aye, I were just a boy then and those were merry days indeed with the daily banquets Brunham gave for the fine dignatories and noblatories of the town, as well as the members of the King's parliamentories. I was young and strong in them days, strong enough to turn the heavy spits and suffer the heat of the roasts we served, and you had to be full sturdy to carry those great joints to the boards for carving," he told me, pinching intricate patterns onto the pies he's preparing, with his chubby fingers. "That were a year or so after Mistress Margery was aborn."

" So, you knew her mother?"

"Aye, I knew Mistress Isabella. She were always busy with good works and playing the lute."

"Playing the lute?"

"Aye, and Michael came often to make music with her, for he were very fond of the music. They were occupied with it at all hours of the day – even when her little girlie wailed and wanted suckling."

He put the pies he's been making into the great oven, wiped his brow with his floury hands so his face was as white as almond milk, and poured himself a tankard of ale.

"Strange that were, and it were sad tunes she played. They told me she'd learnt them from a foreign missie who'd been in her household. But that were just before I came."

"A foreign missie?"

"Aye, but as I told you that were afore my time. Some said she were a pretty, young damsel and died all of a sudden of the fever. Then just as sudden a few years later Mistress Brunham died and her little boy too, and perhaps they're all up in the heavens now, God rest their souls, playing those sad tunes. Now move yourself wench I've work to do."

Adam never spoke of my mother again and I found out that none of Margery's other servants had worked with Brunham before or knew anything about his lady and her maidservant. But it gave me much pleasure to hear something more about my mother, and I resolved that when I had saved enough from my wages I would buy a lute and learn to play myself.

There was something else – I hadn't forgotten Sister Margaret's strange remark when we made our farewells. Since Michael was old enough to be my father and had accompanied Mistress Brunham in her lute playing, then he must have known my mother. I thought of this often and also how he stared at me sometimes. It had bothered me at first but now it held a happy mystery. I often puzzled at night before I fell asleep how I might speak with him and ask if he'd known Mistress Brunham's young companion, but could not imagine there'd ever be a time when I might meet with him alone.

Some months later Margery decided to give a great feast to celebrate her new daughter. I was braiding her hair one morning when she told John.

"Let's host the New Year Revelries this year, invite my father, his household, our neighbours and business associates. He's always held the feast, but now I'm mistress of my own household it's right that I should do so, and we'll have minstrels, mummeries and dancing, and I'll prepare the better banquet."

To my surprise John did not immediately agree.

"Margery dear heart, it is your father's privilege to honour his servants and guests. I don't think it wise to change the custom. Besides … "

"But it's always so dull. Now it's our turn and we need to show everyone I'm well again."

"But think of the expense …"

"O that's not a concern, the tradesmen will be happy to advance us credit. And we needn't even lay out funds for new attire as I've still not shown myself off in my golden gown …"

and taking the comb and ribbons from my hands she nodded my dismissal and moved towards John, unlacing her shift.

Then the day of Margery's banquet came. I sat at the end of the high table on the dais in the dining hall where she and her intimates were seated. I had little John to mind and Isobel's cradle by my side. Betty was with me and I worried how, when the dancing began, I might find a way to talk with Michael. But I needn't have fretted for as soon as the flute-player sounded the first note he came, took my hand and led me into the circle.

I was so happy he'd chosen to dance with me before all the fine ladies and knew for sure he had something important to tell me. Yet there was such a crush and so much noise with all the music that speech was impossible. And then I saw Betty waving at me, pointing at Isobel who wanted to suckle and little John who was demanding attention, so I bowed to him and made to leave. He held my hand tight, drew me away from the others and whispered.

"You lovely little creature, so full of mirth and such a dainty step, you remind me of someone I knew years ago, a dear young friend," then smiling, he let me go. Then little John was tugging at my sleeve and I did not even know how I had gotten back to him.

I didn't see Michael again that day, for the boy had eaten too much and vomited and had to be put to bed. I lay awake all night thinking of Michael and was determined to find a way to speak with him again, for now I was certain he'd known my mother and persuaded, more and more, that he was indeed my father. But no one in the household could tell me anything about him, and even old Adam had no new stories to share except what I already knew, that he was a member of Brunham's retinue.

Margery was delighted with the success of her New Year

celebrations and resolved to hold another for the Shrove Tuesday
feast, though John pleaded she invite only close kin. She was
pregnant again and he urged she not overburden herself.

"But we'll have the harper again," she said, "and get some
boys to help with the meats, and make a Frumenty with saffron
and the last of the milk and eggs before the Lenten fast. And
…" stroking her belly, "this time I will need a new gown …"

Of course John could not say no. We were all very busy, but
I was so excited at the prospect of seeing Michael again that I
paid no heed to the extra tasks. Betty complained that I tossed
all night and spoke in my sleep as if I were teasing the babes,
but in truth I was rehearsing what I might say to him. But when
Tuesday dawned at last, both little John and Isobel had fevers
and Betty too was sick, so I was forbidden to attend the feast.

Still I quelled my anguish and found the courage to ask
Margery that I might at least stay to see her guests arrive and
arrange the folds of her gown as she stood to greet them. And
so I contrived to welcome Michael when he came and was
very bold. I told him how sad I was to have been called away
when last we met, how I'd miss the chance of talking with him
again. He held my hand and whispered that he should like to
speak with me too and bade me meet him in the morning at the
Gesine chapel.

"Your mistress will be late abed I'm sure, and have no need
of you till the noontime Mass, so come early on the morrow."
And I knew then what it meant when they said that angels have
rainbow wings and fly to heaven in pure delight.

A heavy river-fog seeped into the dawn dimness when I
left Fincham Street, just after the bells rang to lift the curfew.
Though I willed my feet to hurry I had to mind my step along
the way for fear of treading into a ditch or pile of muck, which

had not yet been swept out of the lanes. The sea-damp wind pierced through my cloak, but I hastened forward and was soon in sight of St Margaret's. Some of the townsfolk were already there shuffling through the doors, for this was a special holy day, Ash Wednesday, the day of repentance. I rushed in, past the kneeling figures and those standing in line with bowed heads, waiting to be blessed with the ashes of contrition, away from the chancel candles and the high altar into the gloom of the Gesine chapel.

At first I could see nothing and no one, except the grey stone statues, the silent effigies lying on tombs, and shadows flickering on the wall. There was no sound of any footfall, only the muffled mumblings of the priest and "amen," "amen," as the kneeling figures stood up, crossed themselves and left. Slowly my eyes became accustomed to the darkness and I saw the outline of the Madonna statue with babe in arms, the dim colours of the Nativity painting and the glimmer of the golden haloes of the blessed mother and her child. And as I peered at them glowing through the shadows, I seemed to see the ghost of a man beside them, the Holy Father.

Then someone appeared from behind the columns, came towards me and laid his hand on my shoulder.

"God greet you, mistress," he said and I turned towards him, searching in his face to see if there were features there I knew to be my own. "God greet you again, I say." He held my face in his hands as if he too were seeking an answer. "And what is it that you want from me that we had to meet so early and in private?"

"I think you know me," I whispered in great awe of this secret that must now surely be revealed, "you knew me from the first time we met and brought me here to Lynn. Are we not two of a kind and ..."

He smiled and whispered, "You came alone?"

I nodded. And before I could say more he pushed me into the shadows, his hands fumbling between my legs, and brought his mouth to mine.

I was frozen in deathly agony, unable to move. How long it was I do not know, but suddenly I heard footsteps coming towards us, and kicked him hard and fled.

This was a long time ago and I forgive that young woman now for her folly, so great had been her eagerness to find her father, and I marvel at her kick. But I did not think so then and when I returned to Fincham Street, in a great tremble, I was ordered to bed as everyone thought I too now had the fever. I was there for many days, berating my fate and foolish fantasies, for forgetting Sister Margaret's warning to be mindful of the charm of men, and railing against God again that he never protected me. And that troubled me much, for as often as I tried to follow the rule of prayer and church rituals to assuage my guilty feelings, so I fell into doubt again.

Margery was most gentle on my return and sent me delicacies and messages that I might recover quickly. I kept to my bed for many days, worrying about meeting Michael again but was well satisfied by Adam's daily portion of chatter when finally I quit my bed.

"That Michael? Well would you know, he just upped and lefted the week after our Shrove Day feast, so they says, upped and left as swiftly slick as raw yolk leaves shell, went to distant kin in the north, and has now written he's found other employ and won't be back. His master's none too pleased I hear, and tis strange indeed."

I was relieved to hear of Michael's departure, and anyhow

soon distracted. Spurred on by her envy of others, the desire of maintaining a lifestyle she now gloried in and the constant acquisition of new clothes, led to continuous conflict for Margery's extravagance matched neither her husband's purse nor his aspirations. John was a mild, unambitious man unlike his older brother Simon who was one of the most successful merchants in Lynn. But whenever he remonstrated with her about her expenses, she tossed her head and snapped at him or enticed him with sweet talk and flattering words.

"Would you have me dress like a maidservant while Simon's wife is always richly attired and they have the grandest household in Lynn and all the foreign traders competing for his business? You forget how important my father is, so much more successful than yours. If we are to succeed as well as Simon then we need to make the greater display so we two can shine brighter than he."

John could find no answer to Margery's arguments, for he was dazzled by her. As the clothes she now desired to create this sumptuous spectacle and outdress her relatives and neighbours were beyond my skills, she engaged the best tailors in town to fashion new cloaks, which were slashed and underlaid with different coloured silks, gowns and tunics embroidered with golden thread, and silk and fur-lined hoods with intricate trimmings and tippets. Cobblers and tanners were commissioned to make belts studded with gems, and boots and gloves of the softest kid leather you could ever find with silver clasps and jewelled buttons.

But fine displays don't earn cash and as John's debts began to mount, Margery promised she would help, like the other merchants' wives who assisted their husbands in their ventures. But since she'd never learnt to read and keeping accounts bored her, she decided to increase the household brewing and sell the surplus ale for profit. Many were pleased to purchase from us for it was a tedious task having to make a fresh brew every few days. At first she was successful and we were always busy, not only with preparations for her dinners, new clothes and minding the babes, but also with the extra brewing, which truth to say was very hard work. Then it came to her to make a real business of it, expand the production and flavour the ale with different herbs. She employed more servants and told everyone she'd be the foremost alewife in town.

Though I attended her daily to help her dress and do her errands, we spoke little at this time for nothing was good enough for her and she demanded that we all assist her in her enterprise. But as often as we did so the ale soured or went flat, the servants were dismissed and new ones engaged. Finally after some two years she admitted defeat and assured John she'd mend her ways. The gossips were delighted.

"Look," mumbled one, "how she slouches around now like a minstrel's dog, after all that bragging and tongue wagging …"

"Hip wagging too, I'd say," grunted another, "forever flaunting that foolish finery."

" … wagging her tongue about being the best brewer in town."

"Pride it was, wasn't it that tarred the wings of angels."

"Sour puss, sour pout, sour ale," they all muttered together. I too was losing patience, for in her disappointment at her failure she sometimes treated me ill and I wondered if she cared for me at all.

During these years of constant entertaining, the work with the brewing and Margery's children, I began to spend more time with Ralph. He sometimes accompanied me to the markets and showed me who to trust and how to strike the best bargains. Sometimes when Margery and John were dining out, we shared the solar bench in mostly comfortable quietness, he with the household accounts, which had to be balanced every week and I with my sewing. He rarely spoke and I was silent too. But as the months went by, I felt less shy and came to trust his calm company.

One evening as we sat together at our duties, I saw him vexed and offered to help. He was surprised when he saw how good I was at calculation.

"Where did you learn that," he asked, "for you have a rare skill?"

"In the convent where I was sent as a young girl. I helped the sub-prioress who kept the accounts and so had many years of practice."

"What else did you learn there?'"

"To read."

"What did you read?"

"The Prioress had a copy of the Bible written in the English tongue. Most days I read to her and learnt much from the Scriptures."

He was silent for a long while and I watched as his comely features took a twist and turn and his face became scarred with scorn.

"And what think you now, now you are free to think and see how it is in the world beyond those convent walls?"

I told him then of the wild talk I'd overheard, my growing distrust of priests who seemed only guardians but not messengers of the faith, my many doubts and my sadness at having no one to share my thoughts with. He showed no shock or surprise, and now that he had something to say was no longer silent either.

"There're many who think like those tanners you heard and despise those churchmen who want to be keepers of our consciences and tell us what we should think. I warrant that beneath their fine embroidered vestments, their cassocks, copes and chasubles, their maniples and tunicles and most especially underneath their preaching stoles, there lurks a multitude of sins. And the monks and friars are no better, despite their humble habits, black, grey, brown, white, whate'er you will."

He paused a moment, then said:

"I observe you often ask but keep your own counsel. Can I trust you?"

I nodded, and he continued:

"I meet with certain tradesmen in the town and some craftswomen too and talk and read of these matters and you'd be welcome to join us. I say nothing of this to anyone in the household; here I'm just John Kempe's servant and grateful for that, for he's a kind man. But I have a secret and a double life."

He paused again and I wondered what else lay hidden behind his gentle countenance.

"The man I later knew to be my own blood father, may the Devil keep him, was forged of the basest metal. He fought in the Great Rising hereabouts when I was a boy, and often prattled proudly of how he'd faced the riff-raff rebels with Bishop Despenser on Walsham Heath and seen them all dispatched. He couldn't accept that those common folk, peasants as he called them though many were in trade and free men and women, could think for themselves and wanted freedom, fair treatment and honest leaders. The True Commons they called themselves for they wanted self-governance and I was angry whenever he spoke of it and even angrier now, though my mother bids me hush for she was once much beholden to him.

She had been his Lady's maid, as you to Margery are. He bedded her and when she was with child, with me, he married her to one of his servants and gave them money to set up a dairy business. They made out well enough and had children of their own, but I no longer lived with them for he, having no other son, desired I should have an education. Although he never publicly acknowledged me, he paid for me to go as boarder to the Priory here, intending I find some position in the church. But soon after he fell ill and died and Kempe's father, who was a member of the same guild as he, took me to his household. But I would no longer study to be a priest and so came here to serve as John's valet.

I'm fortunate, I have a good position and will never starve, but I see how my poor mother struggles, for she is widowed now, with all her children. The good folk I talk with, we don't want rebellion, like those dreadful times that ended on the Heath. We don't want to take what is not ours and have not worked for. But when we read together we talk about charity and wish the priests would set a better example, so that they, the merchants and nobles would treat us more fairly. And most of all, we want to be able to think what we will, confess our sins in our hearts and find our own true faith for ourselves."

The candlelight burnt low and was soon entirely spent as we spoke on into the night. Before we parted he made me promise I'd keep his story close, and warned me,

"Watch yourself carefully with Mistress Kempe for I do not think she'll take it kindly if she sees we have a friendship. Though you may not know it she expects absolute loyalty from all her household and you more than anyone."

That was the first of many talks we had, and I was pleased to find a friend to read and talk with.

A year or so after Margery's failure at brewing, she decided on a new venture, bought two horses and hired a man to grind the people's corn. He'd been a successful miller before, but nothing he tried, whether spurs or carrots, would induce her horses to turn the grindstones. They wouldn't budge and if they did it was to trot backwards. This second failure rankled her greatly though she never admitted it publicly, only blaming the miller and the beasts. In her endless search for perfection she could never abide any setback or adversity, and we all felt her wrath. It was not long before new rumours crept around the town that the Devil had gotten into her beasts and some said it was a lesson sent by God to show her the wickedness of pride.

"Sins committed in pretty pelts still stink,"
said one, and "stinking pretty pelts" became the common jape in the lanes and alleyways, even after the miller was dismissed and Margery's project abandoned.

After that the household was swiftly silenced and I saw a look in Margery's face that reminded me of the young woman I'd met years earlier. Humiliated by her failures and stung by accusations of pride she set me a new task, making vests out of old sacking from the malt-drying kilns to sew inside her shifts. The work blistered my fingers dreadfully but only I knew for what they were intended. Yet despite these mortifications, she still wore her glorious gowns, and even now I shudder to think how she must have itched and suffered under her skin, on the inside, while to all the world around she glowed and dazzled like sunrise on a cloudless summer's morning.

As if that were not enough for penance, she sought another way to prove her worth and excel above her neighbours, spending more and more hours on her knees at St Margaret's or at home closeted with Priest Spyngolde, while her friends were often dismissed at the door. And while I continued to be busy looking after her, I started to notice how strangely divided her life had become, torn between silk and sackcloth, partying and praying. I also suffered constant anguish for her poor husband who smarted daily under the stings and arrows of her harsh words.

It was no secret that John Kempe thought his wife a bird of paradise, and as often as they would go cooing to bed together, there'd be shrill shrieks and coarse crowing in the morning when she swore she'd no longer share his bed. Despite her delight in night-time pleasures, she hankered every morning after chastity. She delighted even more in those hours in church at her devotions, while at the same time still revelling in her position in society, even if her poor husband was rarely good enough for her. Over the seven years or so I'd served Margery, I came to understand her better; her desire was split in two and her piety was as disturbing as her pride.

One of the preachers we often listened to was William Sawtre, who sometimes spoke of the same matters Ralph's friends talked about, though in a milder manner. Mostly he urged his congregation to neighbourly kindness, rather than worshipping at shrines and going on pilgrimage and especially he proclaimed the divinity of human nature. Then we were told he'd been forced to renounce his teachings. We went to hear him talk one fine May morning at St James's churchyard, just beyond the mill. A great crowd had gathered there, including many who'd once cheered when he preached he wouldn't bow down to the cross that was the death of Jesus, and cheered even louder when he declaimed he'd rather worship a man than any saint or angel.

But they were silent when the Bishop of Norwich demanded he abjure his teachings, and jeered and jibed when he did so. After that Sawtre moved to London where he continued to declare his beliefs. A year or so later he was examined again, sent to trial, condemned by Archbishop Arundel as heretic, taken to Smithfield and burnt. This shocked us all for we'd never heard of the burning of a priest before, and Sawtre had been a truly charitable man.

It was frightening news. Many of the common folk who'd censured the priests for their wealth, hypocrisy and lack of charity and talked amongst themselves about the true nature of their own beliefs, now did not dare do so openly. After the news of Sawtre's death, Ralph and I became more wary whenever we went to meet our friends. In the pulpits and marketplace a new word was being used for those who read, talked together and were believed to be followers of Wycliffe. They called them Lollards or Lollers, and it was not a name you wanted to be called in public.

❧

Ralph and I talked together of other matters too. I came to trust him more and more and slipped into sometime fantasy teasing myself that he would soon have me as wife. Indeed he grew increasing courteous, familiar and kind, though we had always to be on guard when Margery was near. But the more I sensed her watching me, so I began to watch her, and noticed that as often as she scorned and scowled at poor John Kempe, she smiled and smirked at other men.

Then came the time when we quarrelled again. One morning at Mass she became most fidgety, busily glancing here and there, smoothing her cheeks, pouting her lips, tossing her head and holding her hands up high in prayer so that her sleeves rolled down past her elbows, and she did indeed have dainty arms. Of course there were times when she posed and postured, petted and preened herself in private but never in a public place. At the end of the service she bid me wait outside while she finished her devotions. But I watched from the doorway and saw her whispering to a young man, playing the merry maid, and it was some long time before she came to join me, for all the world like a giddy young girl.

She went out again that evening to St Margaret's, or so she said, magnificently attired. I was busy with the babes when she returned but heard much commotion in the hall below. The next day as I was helping her dress, she suddenly turned on me.

"You're too often out and about in town with John's valet and no one else with you, or huddled in corners with him. People will talk and I do not wish the honour of my household be besmirched by such behaviour."

"But Margery, you yourself went out alone last night and surely that was not proper."

"Yes, so you told me, but it's not up to you to say what I should or should not do. Besides you were busy and couldn't come with me."

"But it was you who set me those tasks."

"Only because you've been slack of late, flirting with Ralph and not attending to your chores. Just know this, so long as you are my maidservant you'll have a roof over your head, and food and clothing as you require. But if you ever think of leaving me, I'll cast you out with not a single groat. Anyhow Ralph will soon be gone. He is dismissed. I've asked my father to procure a post for him in London since John no longer has need of him. Now go away and mind your business."

I felt a great rage, but bit by tongue and left to seek out Ralph, though he was nowhere to be found. So I went to the kitchens.

"Aye wench, he's gone, packed and gone, as slithery quick as I would toss a holy Tuesday pancake. Didn't say where he was going neither. There were a mighty row last evening when your mistress came back in, and a rare thing to hear her mild mannered man so angry. And then they called Ralph and now he's quit the household with not a crumb of a farewell nor message to nobody, though he did ask me to let you know. Some say he were a Loller and that's why he were dismissed, but I know nothing about that. Tis strange, most strange indeed."

I was sore upset that Ralph had left no message and truly angry with Margery, but she never gave me chance to speak of my grievances. And I was frightened too for I heard talk in the market that the Justices were hunting for Lollards and wondered if Ralph had fled so fast because he was in danger.

If she'd been cruel to me and Ralph then Margery was now even harsher on herself, forever swift to mortify her flesh the moment she felt the tickle of temptation. After her flirtation that day, she stopped inviting guests to dinner or seeing friends and thought no more of business ventures, young men or the latest fashions. And that was not the end of her self-imposed sufferings for she also stopped eating meat, though she'd much relished it in the past, and satisfied herself with a meagre diet. She became thinner and thinner, always denying herself the comfort of a good meal, assuring all she was nourished by the holy Eucharist. Her new enterprise was to be God's most faithful servant. She spent most of her daylight hours in church and engaged one of the White Friars to read to her, the life of Bridget, the holy maid from Sweden and the writings of Walter Hilton and Richard Rolle, two devout men from our own country. Master Alan he was called and they became good friends, though they were as contrary as curds and whey, she as garrulous as ever and he in contemplative silence.

Remembering all this now, I think those early years in Fincham Street were mostly happy until this time, and the years passed quickly while I was busy but comfortable enough in my role as maidservant and sometime mother to Margery's children. There were sad times too, for many of her little ones died and by the time she stopped bearing children only her firstborn John, his brothers, William and Godfrey, Isobel and Mary and Edward, her last baby, were still alive. Of her many children, only six survived.

John was now a young man, wayward, lazy and unwilling to learn. I thought often of the cuckoo in the nest and wondered whose son he really was. But for sure he was his mother's child, for like her he could appease us all with his charm as if to make up for some hidden blemish. Yet Margery never learnt to love him and asked her father to find an apprenticeship for him over the seas. I was sad to see him go as I felt a strange affinity with him for his unknown father. Sometimes there was talk he'd come back one day, but it seemed he was happier in those foreign parts.

Then troubles came to Lynn. Our soldiers were fighting the King's wars over the seas, many of the foreign ports were closed and trade was as slow as a slack tide. The guilds paid bribes to get preferential business terms, then increased the taxes to fund this expense while claiming the money was needed for the maintenance of the town walls and waterways, though that work was never done. There was little employment for the common folk and many had no labour at all. People complained and there were more beggars in the streets than ever before.

Both Margery's husband and father were members of the Trinity Guild, and the people became accustomed to wait for them as they went there about their business. They sometimes gave out small change but it was not enough to buy food to fill empty stomachs and as trade declined there were food riots in town. Some of those responsible for the disorders were the same tradesmen Ralph and I had once spoken with. It seemed they now talked of different matters and no longer criticized the priests, but fell foul of the town officials and the merchants instead. Now in truth they became rebellious and wanted to change the old ways.

While the poor starved, the officials continued to raise the taxes, creating further anger. Beyond the safety of Fincham Street the disturbances grew and the justices struggled to keep the peace. Finally the officials and the townsfolk agreed to meet. They soon reached agreement that the guild members had acted outside their jurisdiction and it was decreed that in future financial decisions had to be taken by all the members of the civic community. This calmed the commoners but also gave them a voice. One of the first commissions undertaken was to review the accounts of the past ten years.

Within a week they announced their findings. Two of the former mayors were accused of mishandling the finances and one of them was John Brunham. He was immediately discredited and Margery was sorely humbled, mocked not only for her failure at brewing and milling, but now for her father's disgrace. At the same time John's debts continued to mount and his business began to fail. No longer was I required to stitch and sew, but always to be ready to accompany Margery to church or on visits further afield to certain holy men and women from whom she sought counsel. It seemed they brought her comfort for soon her black moods passed and she was gay again now that she had a new circle of friends to charm and chat to.

Priests came to visit every day, and Margery was always ready to sermonize on matters sacred and godly. It was as if she inhabited a different realm to the rest of us, either overcome by fervent feelings as she stood at prayer, or all aglow in her contemplations of the divinity. Just as her father's sun started to set so hers began to rise and there were not a few neighbours who now looked up to her, praising her for piety. But when she told them of all her visions and how merry it was in heaven, many laughed at that and asked why she'd come back if she'd already been there.

The wheel of Fortune turns continually whether we see it or no. In a good summer when the harvest succeeds and overwhelms us with its bounty, we tell each other it's never been so glorious and forget that clouds and rain will surely come. And when the frosts are harsh, gales blow and the sea fog never lifts, we grumble and say we can't remember when a winter was so cruel, until the fine days of spring surprise us. In health we're never mindful of sickness, and when we ail we cannot recall what it is to be well. But the seasons of chance follow each other as surely as rain follows sun and if we're wise we remember that everything changes in time.

A few years after Brunham's disgrace winter came very early and was one of the coldest I remember. Even in Lynn so close to the sea, there were heavy snowfalls and the rigging of the ships was perpetually stiff with frost. The fleets and streams were frozen hard, shrouded by strange mists, and air bubbles beneath the ice startled us with eerie echoes. It was as if all life lay trapped under the surface, struggling for release. An uncanny silence settled all around except for the hoarse call of seagulls and crows crying their hunger. There was now little fresh food to be had unless someone had surplus eggs or milk, so I often left for market early to buy what I could before others came to shop.

That winter season was one I vividly recall, another memory I've traced over again and again. The market square was almost empty that bitter morning, though a few hucksters were already there putting out their sparse produce onto the boards. A ship had moored in the night and a crowd of men huddled together on the quayside, clutching bowls of steaming soup, which they'd cooked in a large iron pot.

The glowing embers of the fire lit up their faces and they seemed like ghosts, their caps and hair glistening ice-white in the freezing-fog. They spoke in the German tongue though I heard some English too, for a few of the hawkers had gone to join them and warm their hands. Then one of the strangers left the group and came towards me, his head shrouded in his hood. Despite his tall stature he was bowed and dragged a foot as he walked, a man well past his prime, I thought.

"God's greeting, mistress," he said. "I'm told you belong to the household of Margery Kempe who is daughter to John Brunham. Chance has brought me back to Lynn after many scores of years. It was a dark season when I left and I had not the heart to return. But now I am back, for our vessel was lost in fog last night and as fortune would have it we found safe harbour here. We'll leave on the next tide. Does Brunham still have the same warehouse, would you accompany me there, for I should like to know how he and his lady fare."

He spoke the English language well though must have left our shores a long time since, as he did not know Mistress Brunham was dead.

"Yes, and I'll take you to his home," I answered, "for he's more likely to be there at this early hour."

Mercer Row was only a short distance away and we walked in silence. Over the years I'd served Margery I'd seen her father countless times, though always felt uncomfortable in his presence. We rarely spoke and though I often sensed him watching me, I only ever wanted to talk about my mother but would never have dared to do so.

It was growing light when we reached Brunham's home. While we waited for the servant to unbolt the door, the stranger pushed back his hood. His face was pinched with cold and hollowed by age, and he blinked his eyes against the rising sun. But when he opened them it was as if I were looking at myself, for he had the same odd eyes as I - one blue, one brown.

Brunham was in the inner chamber and came out to greet his visitor. It seemed he did not know him until he said his name, but I was too startled to hear it. And even more startled when Brunham dismissed me brusquely,

" Go back to your mistress, she will have need of you," and he pushed me into the alleyway before the stranger even had time to look at me.

Fincham Street was not far away, but I took one wrong turn after another. I wanted to know what this man had to say to Brunham, for his eyes told me he was one of my own kind. When finally I did get back, Margery was waiting impatiently for me to accompany her to church. We left together but I did not hear a word she said, sorely shaken by this chance encounter.

As we walked through the square I saw the sailors were busy loading water onto the German ship. The sun was now up, there was a biting wind and the tide was on the turn. Soon they would be sailing away. My only thought was how to meet the stranger before he left. As soon as we were in church I made an excuse, did not even wait for Margery's response and hurried out into the daylight towards the quays.

The gangplank was still down and the captain standing beside it, waiting for the last of his company. Then I saw the stranger making his way between the market stalls and I went and stood in front of him, blocking his way.

"How was your meeting with Brunham?" I asked, "Did you get the news you wanted?"

He nodded and tried to pass, but I would not let him go.

"Look at me," I said, gripping his arm, "Look at my eyes. They are the same as yours." He saw me then, and gasped.

"Who are you? Where do you come from? They said you were maidservant to Brunham's daughter and he knows you. But now I see your face it looks familiar, like someone I knew long ago."

I was sure then that he was my father and led him to a quiet corner of the square. I knew I had to tell my story and it was quickly done. I was so eager for him to hear it, I hardly dared look up until I'd finished. And when I did I saw fury on his face, but he just stared at me and said nothing. There were shouts from the ship and the captain was waving urgently. He started to walk away, but I held him back.

"Did you know my mother? Are you my father?" I asked.

"No, no," he said, struggling to speak, "No, not that. I was told my sister died of a fever. I was away at the time and gravely ill myself. When Brunham's message came with the news, I didn't want to come back again. I thought there was nothing left for me in Lynn. He lied to us then and has held the truth from me now. He did not tell me she had borne a babe. We were twins and shared one heart."

He was silent, nor was I able to find any words so stunned was I by what he told me. Then the captain started shouting at him again.

"Listen, I have to return to my ship. I have business to attend to in my own country and we're already much delayed. Now I see you, I see my sister and miss her still. All this is so unexpected. Be patient, I'll return in the spring and take you home."

He bowed his head and walked away. I followed him to the quay and watched as he boarded the ship. He turned to look at me, raised his arm in farewell and disappeared. Then the crew cast off and steered into the flowing tide, the sails billowing in the wind as the ship headed out to sea.

I'd often seen women at the quayside staring downstream, watching as a ship departed, screwing up their eyes for one last sight of the vanishing sails, then closing them to hide their tears. At other times they'd stand gazing at the vacant waters, waiting for a sign of a ship coming home. I'd noticed grief on their faces as they scanned the horizon and seen their empty eyes, which come from too small a portion of hope. It had always seemed to me the sea was a place for the lonely and outcast, for those whose family and friends lived out of reach, far away beyond the water, never to return.

I'd had no reason to linger on the quays before but now, that morning, I could not leave. I too, in a single moment, had become one of those waiting, watching women. Yet the sea was no longer drear and desolate, but rather bathed in the promise of homeliness and safety. The noon bells had not yet rung but in that short time my world had changed completely. Now, suddenly, I had family and my true uncle would come and take me back, to the land of my mother, to the place where I belonged.

I no longer recall how the daylight hours passed, but woke in the night to hear the wind howling. A sudden thaw had set in and with it came a fierce storm and rain that fell in torrents. The gale continued all morning, then came an uneasy silence. The day was busy and although Margery was unusually sharp with me, I didn't mind her rebukes. Evening came and I was still wrapped in the warmth of happy anticipation. Then just as darkness fell the quiet was shattered by the tolling of the St Nicholas bell, which tells of shipwreck along the coast. I put on my cloak, went to the quays and asked if anyone knew what ship it was. They all said it was the German vessel that had moored there the day before. And I stayed there in the rain, staring out to sea at the empty horizon.

Fortune's wheel had spun too fast, and what had been suddenly, unexpectedly joyously up was in an instance, hopelessly, horribly down. Numbed by tears and the desolate seas, I had an overwhelming wish to speak of my pain and there was only one person I could turn to.

I had come to see that for all those who mocked Margery there were others who held her in high regard. Over the years of her changing fortune, it seemed she'd grown in sympathy and many sought her advice, for at times her words were salted with sense. The ridicule and contempt she'd had to face had strengthened her resolve to be open to suffering, though whether it was her own or others I cannot say. But she was sometimes able to listen, and to be heard is balm for open sores.

Margery was at home that evening, when I returned from my bleak vigil of the seas. I went to her where she sat in the solar and told her the sad story of my birth, my meeting with the stranger, my true uncle, my own flesh and blood, and now the news of the shipwreck. She listened and reached out to hold my hand. My tears came then. But when I told her what my uncle had said about her father's deceit, she unleashed her anger.

"He lied in order to save you further hurt and pain. What else would you have had him do?"

"But when someone lies to you, they overlook you, diminish you, dismiss you. I had family over the seas who would have welcomed me. Instead your father sent me away to be cared for by strangers, then took me from them and put me in the convent, then brought me here to serve you. And all the while my uncle did not even know of my existence. Now I am even more alone than I've ever been."

"No," she said, "you are not alone, you are part of my household, part of my family. My father gave you a childhood and an education. You have shelter, work and food to eat. What more do you want? Would you rather have been an unfathered child begging in the streets and later, as you grew up, one of those women who sell themselves on the quays for a morsel of bread? Instead of judging my father, consider what your mother did, then failed to do. Had she named the man she sinned with or agreed to a marriage to conceal her disgrace, then you would have had a father. But she was stubborn and had no thought for you."

I was too shocked to say anything. And she continued:

"Our Lord provides and takes away. Come with me now to church and I'll pray you might find some comfort and learn to accept your suffering, just as you need to accept God's will. Indeed you might pray for even more suffering for that will bring you closer to God, and when you have cleansed the evil from your soul, he will fill you with his love and grace," and letting go of my hand she moved away and stood smiling by the casement.

The kindness she offered with one hand, she took away

with the other, forgetful of her own transgressions. I could not stomach her pious sentiments and righteous fervour, for I had sin enough to bear without blaming my mother. And in the face of her blind belief I wondered again if there really were a just God, since he continued to punish me with undeserved sorrows. As for praying for more suffering, it comes unbidden whether we will it or no. But Margery bade me come to church and I could not disobey.

I was sick for many days after that, tormented by anger and despair. At times I found myself slipping into the craziness I'd suffered in the convent. Finally, craving a safe place to mourn the heartbreak of loss and betrayal, I begged a small alcove to sleep in, in the roof of the dwelling with only rats and bats for company. At least they did not preach so I was not troubled on that score. Margery did not visit and left me quite alone. Only Betty attended me, bringing food twice a day. But I shunned her company and sent away the delicacies, which came from Brunham's household.

Day and night I wept without cease and came to know the most dreadful truth of all my losses, my loss of faith. I'd tried to follow Margery in her devotions to rekindle my belief, but now I distrusted her. What did she know of suffering in her smug sanctimony? But to lose faith meant damnation for all eternity. At times I asked myself, if I'm in agony now then is this purgatory in the present time and not in the hereafter? That brought me scant comfort, I was indeed in hell.

I do not know how long I might have mouldered there in fury and grief, had I not had the one little visitor I could not say no to – little Mary, Margery's youngest daughter. By chance she found her way to my refuge and with that clarity of heart that is a quality of childhood, she told me not to be distressed by the bleak, black days of winter for soon gentle spring would come, then I'd smile again and be her friend. And she pleaded that I come back and join the household.

She came later that day with a message.

"My father begs he might speak with you. Please let him come for he is distressed and you've always soothed away my troubles."

In all the years I'd been Margery's maidservant, near twenty as I reckon, I'd never been close to John Kempe. He was always somewhat bemused and in the shadows as we all were, like moons revolving around Margery's bright and dazzling presence. I could not think what he might have to say to me, but had not the heart to deny his little messenger and her calm trust in this meeting between her mother's maidservant and her father. I agreed and he came at once.

"God greet you, my good lady," said he.

I waited, curious to know what he wanted.

"Margery is at church with neighbours. We are alone."

Had he a secret to tell me? I could not imagine anyone might have a secret from Margery, except the ones we shared. He seemed more hunched and bowed than usual.

"I can't tell what causes your distress and why you've taken yourself from us. I know Margery is sometimes harsh and have oftentimes observed how you meet her rebukes with patience and forbearance. I fear she has treated you mercilessly, though don't know the cause of her complaints and it's not for me to pry. I do not beg forgiveness on her behalf nor make excuses, but ask understanding from you and charity, if not for her then for us, for myself and the children."

I still had no idea what he wanted and told him so. Margery

did not require my service and there were servants enough to cater for his and the children's needs.

"I do not seek your help in the household nor with my brood," he replied, "but have much to tell you and would be glad of your counsel. When first you came here Margery said only you understood the secrets of her heart for I was never privy to her innermost thoughts. Now I'm much at home and she talks in astonishing ways."

"Is she out of her wits again?"

"No, rather God is in her soul, not the Devil. Mostly she is calm and ever since she was near crushed to death by the beam, it is as if she floats on air and her feet do not touch the ground."

"Crushed to death by a beam? Is she hurt? What beam? When? Where?"

"Some several days ago it was when she was at prayer at St Margaret's, and suddenly a great stone and part of a rafter fell from aloft right on to her back. But she bore not a single wound despite its great size, and walked away with no hurt or pain at all. Nor has she felt any since. Everyone was amazed and as always there's double talk in town, some saying God protected her, while others hold it is the work of Satan, a sign of wrath rather than a mark of favour."

"Were you there with her, was anyone else hurt?"

"No, a neighbour was nearby but did not see it fall until it hit the ground with a great bang and heard her shriek. Master Alan said the beam and stone together weighed nigh on six pounds and proclaimed it a great miracle. I'm only a merchant and know nothing of such matters, but what do you think?"

"I don't know John, but you must be grateful she is safe."

"I am, I am, and I sometimes wonder if indeed she is one of God's favourites and I a poor sinner for judging her a mere mortal woman. And now she's vowed to go on pilgrimage to give thanks for her deliverance and has asked me to accompany her. I'd rather stay at home yet dearly wish to be in her favour again, for she no longer dines with me, nor lets me lie close to her and I miss our intercourse."

He paused and I waited.

"It's said old King Henry is dying and his son, Prince Hal they call him, has let it be known he'll not tolerate the teachings of Wycliffe and those Loller heretics. There's been much trouble throughout the land, more arrests and trials, especially hereabouts and some folk are whispering that Margery's a Lollard for she doesn't desist from preaching. The people here are used to her but if we travel the country I fear she'll attract attention and be judged heretic. If you came with us she might heed your cautions."

I doubted that. In my days of solitude, I'd had time to consider my future. Now Margery knew my birth story I felt more bound to her than ever before. At the same time I didn't much care if she were taken as a Lollard, in fact to tell the truth, I would have been happy to see her dead. But I did not think for one moment I could influence her in any way. Just as I was going to speak John continued:

"Her father is unwell. The day you retreated to the attic, he took to his bed. His servants thought perhaps he'd had a fall, but in truth he's not been well since he was found guilty of meddling with the taxes. Now he grows worse. Physics visit him daily but report no change. It seems a heavy burden lies on his soul. Margery went to see him and says his mind is wandering.

She's even more disturbed these two nights past when she saw visions of him on his deathbed and Satan hovering above to catch his soul. That vision repeated itself again this morning and she's determined he's possessed by some evil. You know how much store she sets on her visions. We shall not leave to go on pilgrimage until Brunham is in better health, God willing, or is dead."

"And what would you have me do?"

"Tell Margery you'll take care of him. You drove her fiends out many years ago, but now she's troubled and will hound her father to a hellish end with her talk of devils and demons, prayers and purifications. He's always indulged her, but has told his servants she's no longer welcome until she stops meddling by his sickbed and preaching his salvation. He's no longer young and perhaps his time has come. But if you went to nurse him, she'll cease her nagging and both our households may have some peace."

I felt only malice in my heart, had no wish to bring comfort to Brunham and thought there was much truth in Margery's visions for his wickedness of hiding me from my family. But just as I was about to say I would not nurse him, I paused and wondered if this might be a chance to find out more about my mother. If Brunham's mind were wandering he might slip into a dotage and I'd be wise to question him before he was lost in a fog of forgetfulness. I'd missed my chance with Nanna and blamed him for that, for had he not sent for the priest as I sat at her deathbed, she might have told me more.

And to be truthful, for it is to serve the truth that I write this now, though I was still bound to Margery for the present and could see no way out of that, I wanted my revenge on John Brunham.

So finally I quit my attic to tend Brunham from dawn to dusk and did so for several days. When first I entered his chamber the air was stifling, foul and putrid, the stench of iniquity. The barber-surgeons attending him had studied his urine and stools, consulted their astrological charts and proclaimed he was suffering from an excess of black bile. They gave him potions and applied leeches to bring better balance to his bodily humours, but still found him too cold and dry and argued about how next to treat him.

One advocated spicy food but he would have none of it. Another prescribed a dish of bitter herbs and this too was rejected. The third called for minstrels to play joyous music but he sent them away. The last prepared a paste made from the heads of seven fat bats to spread on his head, which he'd used before with some success. They covered his bed with furs and feather quilts to heat him up, but when I touched his forehead it was as cold as ice and his eyes were glazed over like those of a stale fish. He did not seem to recognize me. I feared his wits were already dulled and I might never be able to question him.

I stayed for two more days, but he remained the same and never acknowledged me. On the third day Margery gave me an infusion of betony steeped in holy water and bunches of rosemary which her hermit had blessed, but instead of taking them to him I dumped them in a ditch on my way to Mercer Street. I wanted him both alive and dead and did not mind if the devils came to torture him. Yet that day there was a change. He became feverish and had a constant gurgle in his throat. His attendants said they'd successfully treated his melancholia, and he was now suffering from a surfeit of yellow bile and phlegm, which was the most complicated humour to shift.

It seemed to me that apart from a common ague, he was also plagued by guilt. His eyelids were no longer crusted with angry pus, and a constant stream of tears fell upon his cheeks. I knew he now recognized me, yet he said nothing as he lay listless upon his pillows. I thought then to offer to tend him through the small hours, hoping once his physics left I might speak with him privately.

He slept long into the night until I opened the casement window to wake him from his slumbers. Then he stirred and started to cough so I gave him water to sip. When I saw he knew me I asked if there was anything he needed, and helped him sit up. I warmed some gruel and fed it to him spoon by spoon. His breathing eased and I thought the time had come to confront him. Yet I knew it better to be gentle first, so he was not on his guard.

"Margery's children are worried about you," I said, "and asking how you are. Godfrey and William practice their letters daily and say they'll write to you. Isobel rose early this morning to accompany Margery to the first Mass, dear little Mary has said prayers and lit a candle that soon you might be well, and the little boy thrives."

He stared at me blankly and there was no response.

"You remember Mary, don't you? Mary, Margery's youngest daughter."

"Mary, Margery, Margery, Mary, " he mumbled. "Mary, Margery, Martha … where are they?"

I hesitated but did not answer.

"Martha …" he repeated with an empty look on his face and a voidness in his eyes. Then his lids shut out the light, he started wheezing and was soon asleep. I shook him hard but he would not wake, so I cursed him and was minded to pull back the covers and let him freeze to death. Instead I waited until dawn and when his physicians arrived I left to return to Fincham Street.

But I did not go there directly. Instead I went to Sybile. Over the years I'd assisted her with many births and had been thinking what I might do so I could leave Margery's household and I thought to set up as midwife, when I'd saved enough money from my service to rent a room for a year or so in town, though that was not the reason I sought Sybile out. She was known to be skilled in the art of simples and was wise in all manner of ailments and afflictions. I wanted to know the most beneficial recipe for restoring memory.

"So whose memory are you planning to plunder? I doubt it's your own," she continued sharply, "and you've no right to steal from another's."

I was surprised by her response and struggled to answer.

"It's John Brunham's. He's ill and I've been helping to nurse him. The fever has now broken and he's on the mend in his bodily nature, but it seems he's lost his wits and cannot even recall the names of his grandchildren."

"What is it you want him to recall? Sometimes forgetting is Nature's way and it's not for us to meddle. He's an old man now and has lived his life, though these last few years have not been especially memorable and he's no longer respected in town. When we face death it is good if we can remember our past with pride, but not everyone is able to do so. Let him be. The greater wisdom is to live in the present. There's always pain and regret in the past and that often leads to bitterness. Memory serves us well when we learn forgiveness, otherwise it sours us."

I looked away, not wanting to meet her eye.

"Yes, but I thought he was struggling to tell me something."

"Or were you struggling to ask? I've often wondered what Brunham is to you and you to him. I've observed you over the years as you helped so many mothers in their labours and it

117

always seemed to me you watched them with both tenderness and sorrow as if you had an unasked question, something you wanted to know, something about motherhood that they could not tell you."

She looked straight at me but I had nothing to say and bowed my head.

"I cannot help you unlock Brunham's memory, but I can give you something to ease his discomfort. I have a potion here made from black hellebore, which will be good for his complaint. Two drops in water twice a day is enough but mind you don't give him a drop more than that. In large doses it is toxic even for the strong, and deadly for those who are weak. This will serve him for seven days, then you may come for more," and she took a flask from her cupboard, pressed it into my hand and ushered me out.

I am an old lady now and all this was a long time ago, but recalling those days I still feel the blemish of my infamy. I do not make excuses though understand how it came about. It was as if in the shock of finding my uncle then losing him, I lost part of myself, that part which belongs to common humanity. I no longer cared for myself or the safety of my soul, and so I did not care for anyone else nor considered the evil deed I intended. In truth, charity starts at home.

I see this now, having met it again since, that when we are at our most vulnerable the demons of power rise up to tempt us. They promise us the world when we do not even feel we have the right to stand on our own small plot of earth. They present themselves as our saviours, whereas they serve only as jailors and send us spiralling down to even greater evil and despair. But I did not know this then.

I spent another week with Brunham watching by his bedside as he grew weaker and weaker while his doctors argued amongst themselves, some saying his astrological chart presaged a cure, while others predicted his end was near. Since the first night I'd stayed with him he'd not spoken a single word, yet would only accept sustenance from me.

I tended him carefully and never left his side, ever wishful that he would regain his wits, but I could not induce him to talk. Margery visited every morning, Brunham's servants no longer forbad her access but he did not seem to know her, though once when she came with her priest he grew querulous and they had to leave. He had voice then, but only to whine, not to make meaning.

I kept all of Sybile's potion close by, waiting for a time I might administer it. Finally one night when we were alone, I started to talk. I decided to be direct, so told him I knew my birth story and wanted to know more, whether he had any idea who my father was, and especially about my mother, her family name, what she looked like and where she was buried.

He stared at me with vacant eyes, like a beast in the field who knows but cannot say. I asked again, looking directly at him, and he did not even blink. Yet when I got up to fetch some water, he was keenly alert, his eyes following my every move. I spoke once more and his answer was yet another blank stare. Then I turned my back, took out the flask and emptied every potent drop of it into his goblet. He drank it without a flutter, then shut his eyes and was soon asleep.

I was so very weary but dared not close my eyes. As the candle burnt low so I swiftly lit another, fearful of being alone in the dark with this dying man despite the gleam of the waning moon outside. Time dragged and the silence was heavy, broken only by the scurrying of rats on the rafters above, the tramp of the Watch's boots outside and the tap of his stick on the cobbles, like a blind man feeling his way. Then came the howling of Brunham's hounds, and a yell from the hall as one of the household admonished them, and was answered by a more dismal barking. Then silence again. So silent I could barely hear Brunham breathe except for an occasional small and easy sigh as if he were contentedly at rest.

That was one of the longest nights I've ever known and I've known many. I shook him several times to rouse him from his slumbers but he never opened his eyes or uttered a murmur of protest, just sank back into the safety of his bedding. Infinitely slowly the sky began to lighten and the bells started to toll for the lifting of the curfew. Suddenly he awoke, white-eyed and staring and began to shout, choking and dribbling, was dumb and tight-lipped for a moment as he voided his bowels and then screeched and yelled again. His servants came running and he spoke to them directly asking that Margery be fetched forthwith, and demanded fresh linen be brought with a basin of water that I might clean and dress him.

When Margery arrived his eyes were clouding over again and his voice was faint, but he greeted her by name and seemed fully restored to his senses. As soon as a stool was brought for her and put by his bedside, he dismissed the servants. I followed them to the door but he called me back.

"I am sick to death and will not last this day," he said. "I am old and my time has come. I am at peace. My council and executors know the terms of my will and I have told my chaplain how I wish my obsequies to be observed. Some of my chattels will be sold to meet the expense of my funeral and sums set aside for the poor. The rest will go to you Margery, you are well provided for."

She nodded, but said nothing.

"I would advise you to use some of the monies to discharge your husband's debts. John was never that successful, but he's a good husband, times are hard and we do not have the influence we once had. I beg you be mindful of your duty to him."

Again a nod, though it might also have been a toss of the head. We three were stilled into silence until Margery rose, saying she would summon his chaplain.

"Wait, there is one more thing I have to say to the two of you before I am shriven." His voice was so low that we had to bend down to hear him.

"And you must both swear an oath never to tell another soul." He paused and we looked at each other, wondering what he had to say. He started coughing and I rubbed his back until his breathing eased. We both nodded and crossed ourselves. Then he spoke again.

"Long ago I committed an indiscretion which I never acknowledged. It would not have been fit to do so then and later it was too late. Such matters do not sit well with the honour of our name and the roles we are obliged to bear, so that the common folk may learn by our example. And what has been done cannot be undone. What I ask now Margery is that you provide sustenance to an impoverished worthy woman, treat her kindly as your sister for the span of her lifetime and see she's comfortable at her end. As well as that I ask you for my penance and in my memory to pay for the livelihood and dowries of two little orphaned girls in Lynn. Do this, I pray you, in memory of my youthful transgression, and as an example of the charity of our kin."

Margery began to say something but he raised his hand to silence her and whispered he was ready for his chaplain. Then, looking at me he said,

"You have heard me tell Margery she must take good care of you. Now you may go," and Margery ushered me to the door.

Troubled though I was I could not return to Fincham Street and went instead to the quays to watch the tide. It was on the turn and would soon start to ebb. I wondered why I had been so blind and never thought that Brunham was my father, but now the scales had fallen from my eyes and it all made sense. I raged that having at last found a father, he was a man I could always only hate. I thought of what Sybile had said and wished I could let the bitter ghosts of the past flow out into the sea.

I do not know how long I stood there, but was frozen cold and started to shake. I drew my cloak around me and felt the weight of my purse dangling against my legs – that empty flask was a heavy load, like a millstone round my neck. I reached inside to throw it into the waters but could not move my arm for the weight of a hand on it, and a crimson shadow unfurling in the wind.

"So are you still seeking to understand the past and would you try to halt the tide?" Sybil asked. "Live in the present and when you learn to forgive you will be happy to forget. Seek to hate evil less and love the good more. Never act without thought and always think of who you really are, that will guide you."

I had no answer.

"I hear John Brunham is on his deathbed," she continued, "and wondered why you had not come back for some more of my potion. I had wanted to tell you that strangely I was mistaken and gave you a tincture of the white hellebore instead of the black. But it would have done him no harm and may indeed have brought him much comfort at the end." And before I could answer, she was gone.

The next three days were busy with the funeral ceremonies

and there was much to do. Margery did not speak about that last morning and anyhow I was silenced by my thoughts. They say death pays all debts but I felt that despite the great sum I owed, there was an even greater debt owing to me. Those thoughts continued to haunt me for a long time.

4

York, Canterbury, Lincoln, London, Bishop's Lynn, Zierickzee 1413

'I shall pilgrim to the holy places'

We left Lynn a few months later, in gentle weather after the pitiless cold of that winter season, and though I felt numb inside I reminded myself daily of Sybile's words and resolved not to dwell on the past. And as it was all in the household were busy planning our travels for Margery opened her home once again to gaiety and guests, offering hospitality to anyone who'd been to the places where she wished to worship. There was never a moment when I had not some task to fulfil, and was thankful to be so tired at the end of the day that I fell quickly into dreamless sleep.

This pilgrimage, so Margery told everyone, was to render thanks for her deliverance from the falling beam, as well as the fulfilment of her vow to pray for the people in Lynn in memory of her father and for the liberation of his soul, and she said she'd be seeking succour and salvation from the saints she venerated along the way. We had hardly spoken together since the funeral as she avoided being alone with me until a few days before we left, and then she immediately insisted we never talk about what had been said the morning of Brunham's death.

"My dear father suffered much at the end and I'm grateful for your care. But the terrible torment of those last painful days afflicted his mind and his wits wandered wildly into crazy, untrue fantasies. He was a good and honourable man and would never have committed any such gross sin, it was only the musings of a poor, old, suffering soul. So take note, Missie, we shall not speak of this ever again."

I started to protest but she would brook no interruption and just went on talking.

"As I said, we shall never speak of this again, and now there's much to think about and I leave it to you to make all the arrangements. My friends the friars, wayfarers and other good folk who've eaten at our table have told me where to go and how to proceed. But there's another matter I want you to know so that you may support and sustain me should I suffer derision or disdain."

Then she told me there was more to this pilgrimage than she'd disclosed. She desired to meet with certain devout men and women and share her visions with them. Later she intended to travel further afield to Jerusalem, Rome and Compostela, the holiest places in all Christendom. And there was even more.

"You should know my true intention is to take a vow of chastity. I cannot do so without John's agreement, though I haven't spoken of this to him yet. And mind you do not do so either. But that is why he must come with us, to see how determined I am when we visit the shrines, and hear how the holy hermits I confer with approve and applaud my decision to give up this life of sex and sin.

I shall pray to God to help him know this is right, then we'll go to our bishop and he shall sanctify our vow. As you know John isn't keen on journeying but I've promised we'll visit York to see the Mystery pageants, which all say are much more splendid that those in Lynn. When our friends spoke of all the wondrous devices, the music, masquerades and guildsmen acting the stories from Creation to Doom, he was much delighted. And so I hope to beguile him, and once he's had his enjoyment and sees that it means not a glittering gem nor a bolt of fine cloth to me, then I'll win his agreement, live forever more as a maid and never share his bed again."

I was shocked and thinking how much John worshipped the ground she walked upon knew he'd be loath to live apart from her. But she just spoke on.

"There've been other women before me like the holy Bridget who died the year I was born. You remember her story, don't you, how she was kin to royalty, married young as I did, gave birth to many babes as I have, then travelled with her husband on pilgrimage to Spain. On his death she founded an order of nuns and lived in Rome in great poverty, caring for the destitute and suffering much censure. That is part of the trial of the truly saintly life, as I've often told you. Later she went to Jerusalem and died soon after. And I shall pilgrim to those holy places, and be forever chaste like her and you shall be my handmaid and take good care of me."

And she folded her hands in her lap, and looked at me with a bright and piercing stare.

"But Margery remember, the blessed Bridget didn't throw her man aside. Even though she followed the maiden path, they lived together until he died. Is that really what you want, to cast John off after all the enjoyment the two of you have shared?

Could you not still serve God as wife? John's always let you do what you will and only recently spoke to me with much awe of your spiritual endeavours."

"No," she answered swiftly. "I can no longer bear to be his wife and enjoy the lust of his body, that is now abominable to me. At night my only desire is to lie as still and cool as a virgin, listening to God's words. And he has promised he'll slay John's sexual desire. Maidenhood is the purer state ..."

"So it is said, but pray tell me why should God love virgins more than wives? Remember all the pain you bore in the trials of childbirth. Surely that is reason for him to love you more rather than less... for you, like other wives, have laboured hard at his work of creation. And does he really need the love of maidens all for himself, can he not share them with mortal men for whom they were created?"

"O, you simple soul, have you learnt nothing in all the years you've served me? In my visions every night now I listen to the secrets God tells me, and in the daytime to those holy folk who shut themselves away from the world so as not to be tempted by the body's beastly craving. I've sworn to make this sacrifice though it will be a very great trial for me. Now go, there's much to do."

And she turned her back on me.

I was astonished when I heard her speak of her resolve. Though I'd vowed never to forgive her for denying our father's sin, I wondered if I had misjudged her and failed to understand the true depth of her devotions. I'd perceived her through the narrowness of my own eyes, blinded by her extravagant display and her single-minded pursuit of sanctity to which I'd been audience for years. Truly it is easier to see the dust in your neighbour's eye than the blot in your own.

But when she spoke of a pilgrimage to Jerusalem something came alive in me, joy at the prospect of travelling over the seas and having new adventures and a vain hope that the Holy City might be somewhere near Danzig and we could go there too.

That summer pilgrimage was the first of many journeys I made with Margery, but it remains bright in my memory for it opened doors to yet another reality. In my childhood, my view of the world had been etched by the ploughing of the furrows, tilling of the soil, sowing and harvesting of crops, and my ramblings along the footpaths, which gave access to the common land then led me back home again. My place on earth had been marked by the rotation of the seasons, by the rising and setting of the sun and the waxing and waning of the moon.

In the convent the horizon broadened and my days were further marked by the calendar of feasts, rule of church bells, keeping of accounts and visits of the travelling clergy. In Lynn, tide and trade rose and fell, merchants and tradesmen came from far and near, Margery gave birth and little ones died, clothes were worn and torn, store cupboards stocked and emptied. But now, on pilgrimage, we slept in different places every night, spoke with different people every day and the countryside changed constantly. It was like dropping pebbles into still waters and watching the ripples as they unfolded into ever widening circles.

We set off in the merry month of May, Mary's month, the season of mirth and pilgrimage and the most beautiful time of the year. The bitter winter had been slow to release its grip, but now the land warmed with the lengthening of the days. There was always something new to see, and the changing light and landscape, sights and sounds, voices and views, smells and scenes helped to loosen the bonds of my despair, and I resolved to put dark thoughts aside.

Everywhere along our route the tender green of the hedgerows was wreathed in white, shrouded with delicate, lacy keck, pungent wild garlic, sweet-smelling hawthorn, plum, sloe and crab apple blossom. Mostly we set out at dawn when the morning mist was rising, and each time I remembered the child in me who had so loved telling tales to her playmate Marion. I used to say the chaste white blooms were images of the Virgin's purity and later, when the bluebells, cranesbill and cornflower blossomed and the morning sky was a heavenly blue, I said they were the colour of Mary's mantle. It seemed the simplicity of faith was beginning to bloom in me again.

First we travelled to York, sometimes walking alone, at other times with any pilgrims we met along the way, by water occasionally or, when tired and footsore as we often were, on horseback. Every day we passed many men and women on their pilgrimages, young and old, some fettered with heavy chains as penance and struggling sore, others with shaven heads or barefoot and bound to a companion, ankle to ankle, arm to arm. There were also the sick and dying, carried or pushed in barrows by hopeful friends and grieving families. And sometimes we saw other pilgrim folk, lithe and carefree in gay attire, dancing and singing, happy to be released from the bonds of their daily toil and delighted to play and wander at will.

Most of all I enjoyed it when we rode. Margery and John were accustomed to horseback, and he would ride alone and I with her. I loved the peace of these rides, for we rarely spoke as we ambled along, Margery mostly deep in contemplation and John softly singing the carols and love songs of his youth or reciting poems and ballads of ancient times. The days passed joyously with the gentle rhythm of the beasts, the freshness of young green leaves and hedgerows bursting with the bounty of spring.

I recalled the comfortable days of my childhood and the peace of the convent cloisters, and started to feel some tenderness for Margery again as I rested my back against her warm bosom and she with her arms around me while she held the reins so I would not fall. At nightfall we lodged in inns along the way and spoke with fellow travellers though Margery, pleading weariness, would seek her rest early, saying she'd lie with me that I might feel safe, or so she told John. He had to sleep on a trestle at the foot of our bed, and when he protested she always hushed him and told him to wait until we reached York.

I had marvelled all those years ago when first I arrived in Lynn, but was even more amazed when we came to York. The river there was much greater than the Ouse, but far from the sea so there was no tide to flush away the muck of the people and the filth of their industry. The lanes and alleyways were more crowded and noisier than ours and there were markets every day. There were many magnificent guildhalls and churches too, and rising high above them was the Minster with its two square towers.

Margery insisted we visit it the moment we arrived, for a friar had spoken of the painted glass windows, which sparkled like jewels in the morning light. Yet it was not the great East window she rushed to see, but the St William window that was just then being composed. She cajoled the craftsmen to let us view their work and found the one she sought with a great shriek. It was indeed a wonder, for depicted there was the image of a sleeping man hit by a stone falling from the church roof and then showed him walking away healthy and unharmed, just as she'd been when the great timber fell down on her in St Margaret's. A crowd drew near and she told them of her miraculous escape, and they knelt with her and cried, "Praise be the Lord." And I knelt too, for who was I to judge?

There were many hermits living in York, housed in their own singular cells attached to the walls of different churches, anchorholds they called them. John and I accompanied Margery early each morning and often sat together while she talked with them. Days passed and he grew restless and I watched the way he looked at her and sometimes at me, as men of all ages look at womenfolk especially in the summer months, for all the world is fecund then with an insatiable appetite, thrusting to create. Even the most moderate of men grow frivolous at this time as their minds turn to pleasure, and I did not like that lewd look in John Kempe's eye. So I wished the day of the Mystery Plays might come and he would be distracted and hoped that Margery might be too, for she was ever changeable like a field of corn blowing in the wind.

But finally we did not see the plays, for our plans changed suddenly. A man came to our inn one morning with a message from a very great lady, Joan Beaufort, Countess of Westmoreland. It threw us into turmoil.

"Who is she Margery, what does she want from you?"

"I don't know John, except she's kin of one of the most worshipful households in our realm. Her father was John of Gaunt, the great Duke of Lancaster, so she's also cousin to the King. And now she desires to speak with me."

"How does she know you're here? Have you met her before?"

"No I have not, but the hermits I've been visiting may have spoken of me and my devotions. In truth I no longer relish the company of nobles who are too worldly for my tastes, but we cannot refuse such a summons."

I did wonder at that. Had she really changed so much?

We went soon after to the Westmoreland residence. Lady Beaufort's steward received us kindly and lodged us in a sumptuous chamber for our own. He said the Countess would send for Margery later that day so she went to the Lady's chapel, while John strode into the park, which was well stocked with game. I sought out the maidservants for I wished to learn why Margery had been summoned there.

"Our lady is a powerful woman," they told me. "She has eight children and is great with child just now. She's strong and determined, has opinions of her own and doesn't hold that any woman should be ruled by men. But her eldest daughter, who's staying here just now is not so valiant and often comes for shelter. Her husband treats her ill and beats her on occasion. Perhaps that's what she wants to talk about."

Margery did not tell us what discussions she had with the two women, though later there were others who demanded we speak of them. Now she was colder to John than ever, insisting yet again I sleep with her and he take the trestle bed. He protested loudly, but she would have none of it and silenced him into submission. And she also spoke of a new destination.

"Lady Beaufort suggested I attend the feast day of John Twenge, a holy man of Bridlington, some three days journeying from here. He died a few years since and is now declared a saint for the many miracles that have come to pass after the common folk prayed to him. Many knew and loved him and especially William Sleightholme who dwells there, so he will serve me too and I shall confess to him."

When John complained again, she hushed him.

We left the Countess's household at first light so we might travel in the cool of the morning as the summer heat had grown intense since our departure from Lynn. The freshness of those late spring days had already begun to wilt under the great glare of the sun, and the hedgerows and fields were parched and dry. There was no sea breeze thereabouts to temper the heat of the land, and by midday all the creatures of the forest and birds in the air were stilled into quietness. Time seemed to have halted, yet it was as if a waiting storm lay hidden behind those cloudless skies.

That first day John hired horses, but the next day we set out early on foot, he and Margery walking ahead until the sun was at its summit. Later we sought shade and lay on the ground to rest. I slept awhile, then woke to hear voices nearby.

"So Margery, if a man came by right now and said if you refused to have sex with me he'd cut off my head, what would you do, lie with me or see me dead?"

"Why do you ask," she answered, "since we've lain together chaste these past eight weeks?"

"Because I want to know the truth of your heart."

"Truly John, I would rather see you dead than turn back to our uncleanness."

"Then you are no good wife to me," he shouted, reaching out to her, his arms around her waist, but she pushed him away and they walked on arguing fiercely as I traipsed behind. We left the cool of the trees and entered the fierce heat of the land again, and the quicker Margery walked, the swifter was John behind her.

We came then to a tall stone cross. John stood in front of it still shouting loudly and said he wouldn't budge, and if she wanted to continue her pilgrimage she'd have to bed with him again.

"Why can't you be like other wives and eat and drink and be merry with me?"

"You know I've vowed to keep the Friday fast and will not break my word."

"Then why won't you lie with me anymore and delight in our bodies as you used to? Doesn't it say in the good book that woman was created by God for man for his comfort and enjoyment and that a husband has dominion over his wife and her body? I've always abstained in Lent and on the feast days as the priests instructed us, even when you often wanted otherwise, so do not now forget your marriage vows and the marital debt you owe me."

He went over to her, put both his hands on her breasts, then clutched at her buttocks.

"You know I'm right and we shall lie together here now, right now," and he tore at her tunic, while she raised her hands to defend herself and hit out at him.

"Truly John I'd rather drink the muck in the gutter than fuck with you."

I watched them struggling and she began weeping piteously, pleading that first she might say her prayers. He let her go and stood apart as she knelt at the foot of the cross, and only then did he notice me and look away.

We three were still some long while. At last Margery stood up, her face aglow. She came to my side and bowing her head, all anger and scorn spent, lifted her eyes sweetly to John and said:

"If you please, you shall grant me my desire, and you shall have your desire."

For a moment I saw the light of hope on John's face, but it was snuffed out soon after, like a hound that leaps to greet his master but instead is severely chastised without so much as a friendly pat, because then she told him of her determination to dedicate her life to God, to live as a virgin and make a pilgrimage to Jerusalem. In return she promised to pay all his monetary debts.

"This," she said, "is God's true will revealed to me just now. And for a sign he also grants your wish that I feast with you every Friday and he asks that we seal this promise together with three paternosters."

She went over to him and he was about to say something then bit his lip and looked at her with awe, for he could find no answer to this absolute conviction. She started to say the prayers and so the matter was resolved. I wondered at the ease with which she got her way, though knew John to be so loyal and gentle he would never have dared compete with God for his wife's affections.

After the ceremonies in Bridlington, Margery urged us on to worship at the shrine of St Thomas Becket. Canterbury was to the south, a much further journey than we'd made so far, but the weather continued fair and the travelling easy. John was forlorn and no longer sang his love songs, but Margery was in fine spirits and full of speech. She had come out of her reverie and was bold and boisterous again. It was ever so, for she dawned like an April day, with moments of sunshine, cloudy skies, a tempest, then calm and brilliant sunlight again. She and Constancy would have made uneasy bedfellows. However, she was true to her word and feasted with us at the end of the day. But we were poor company for, like John, I too was stunned into silence.

Canterbury was the most popular shrine in all our land and

the streets abounded with pilgrims. We lodged with some of Margery's acquaintances and John went straightway to visit a merchant friend and get news from home. The townsfolk here he told us when he returned, were full of great cheer because old King Henry, who'd died at Eastertide, was to be buried in their cathedral and there'd be much work for many skilled craftsmen to fashion his tomb. There was praise too for his son, the new King who, it was said, wanted to make friends with old enemies.

"They say that young Prince Hal quarrelled in the past with Archbishop Arundel, the Lollard-hater who condemned and burned Sawtre, our priest from Lynn. But now he's king they're reconciled and friends again. They also say he's thrown off some of his old companions like Lord Cobham, whom others call Sir John Oldcastle, one of Wycliffe's supporters. The people here have no love for Lollers, and are ever watchful for any hint of heresy."

And he'd been told that all was well in Lynn, the household and children flourishing and his apprentice managing the small business that came to his warehouse.

While Margery rested that afternoon, John and I sought to dine in a nearby inn that was packed with pilgrims newly arrived from Southwark. There were a dozen or more eating and drinking in rowdy discussion and as we had little to say to each other, we were content at first to listen to their chatter.

"Well, what about that story the widow told, that women want mastery over men, more than anything else? Is that so of all maids, d'you think?"

It was a young yeoman who spoke, with a beaming nut-brown face. He was kitted out in handsome green and well armed with a bow, arrows fletched with peacock feathers, dirk in his belt and hunting-horn slung over his chest.

"Nay lad, I don't think so at all," answered a burly fellow with bulging eyes and a large wart on his nose. "When they comes to my mill with their grain, they wants a strong man to heave up their sacks and lift their petticoats too, and they don't mind if I take a little bit extra here and there neither. It's the other way round, women wants men to master them, to grind all day long from cockcrow to the night's end," and he waved his huge hands in the air, poured more ale into his tankard and drank it off in a single quaff.

"That might be so, but I warrant I can win any damsel with riches, flattery and gorgeous clothes, for it's wealth they desire most in the world though they may lie and cheat to get it," said an imposing gentleman with polished boots and the slick attire of a merchant. "Just give them that and you'll be their master and rule over them for all eternity. And what say you, if you ever take your nose out of your Oxford books and think about women?" Stroking his forked beard, he turned to the thin young man beside him who was staring morosely at his empty platter.

"What do I think?" replied the cleric. "I have no idea what women want, but a patient wife would be the most virtuous. Now, as to the matter of thinking, the Sceptics held Plato's ideas were wrong …"

"That weren't the question," roared the Miller, "and furthermore patience and women don't go together, you'd never find a wench in bed with virtue. Now I'll tell you a tale of a pretty young hussy who let me open her sack of fine ripe grain and…"

Next to him a shabby-looking parson sat between two prim nuns, who were most elegantly attired with finely pleated wimples and coral and garnet beads rippling at their wrists.

Each had a little dog on her lap, which she fed with morsels of bread dipped into a dish of milk. They both nudged him, he grimaced, then held up his hand as if to make a blessing.

"Not now Sir, not now, you told your tale a long way back. It's not your turn and I've a much more telling matter to discuss. It's about the widow in our fellowship, who spoke about her five husbands and in particular about the last one she favoured most who was much younger than she …"

"Yeah, in God's truth, that she did," interrupted a friar, who just then came to the table and set down two pitchers, his little eyes sparkling and chubby cheeks festooned with ale froth.

"And she quoted from the Scriptures and told how she'd been thrice to Jerusalem, Rome and Compostela, and often goes on pilgrimages. I've seen other women like her, gadding about the countryside, gushing and gabbing to all and everyone, preaching about not paying the marriage debt. Are they seeking God or adventures with young yeomen like you Robin, who they meet on the road? Is it lusty men they really desire while pretending to make pious prayers and pilgrimage?"

"That's my question too," said the parson. "And it smacks of Lollardy, that's what I think."

"Yeah, Yeah," they all chorused, banging their tankards on the boards, "those Lollers are a right pest. Women who read, travel on their own and talk of throwing off their husbands, they should all be burnt."

I looked at John. His face was ashen white.

"Hush, mind your manners, here she comes," the merchant whispered.

A jolly buxom woman of middling years waddled into the room, clad in the common pilgrim tunic that other folk wore, but on her legs she had tight scarlet hose, which she'd embellished with spurred riding boots of the palest leather. A generous mantle of azure silk billowed to her knees and at her head she flaunted a fine wimple of white embroidered linen, topped by the widest brimmed hat dangling with more pilgrim emblems than I'd ever seen. She waved and grinned at everyone.

"Welcome Alison, welcome," smirked the friar, "come and join us, have some ale, and tell us more about your pilgrimages and those good men of yours."

John stood up and I followed him out of the inn.

The following morning we went to the cathedral, to the shrine of St Thomas. His tomb was as magnificent as everyone had said, covered in silver and gold, with jasper and agate carvings, studded with emeralds, sapphires and diamonds and there was one ruby the size of a man's thumbnail, which glowed like blood in the morning light. The cathedral here was even finer than York Minster with many shrines and altars, coloured windows and painted walls telling the Bible stories, and as I looked at them I could see the words in my head that long ago I'd read to Dame Cecilia.

I accompanied Margery there again the next day and it was already thronging with people. We looked at the images on the walls and windows and when other pilgrims joined us she started telling the stories she saw depicted there, for everyone enjoys a story. But I knew the friars didn't like women talking in church, and one of the Black Friars came to shush her and moved the crowds away.

I cautioned her that night, reminding her what John had said about the people here, how they hated the Lollards and told her the clergy had seemed displeased with her. She grimaced stubbornly and would have none of it, saying she heard me but I doubt she really listened. The following day when she was there telling tales once again, two monks came and stood close by. One of them demanded to know what she, an ordinary woman, had to say about God. Margery answered him curtly.

"Sir, I'll speak of him if I wish, and hear him too."
He tried to interrupt, but she continued,

"And you of all people should respect God's servants, may God forgive you."

And he retorted:

"Nay mistress, it would be better if you became recluse and were walled up in an anchorhold than speak out loud like this, scattering the word and …"

But the younger monk stopped him and the crowd called out:

"Let her say what she wants, she tells good stories, explains the parables and paintings, and we want to hear more."

So Margery began a fable of her own.

"Good pilgrims, I do not fear to be chastened, so listen to my tale and you'll understand why. There was once a great sinner like me who, as a penance, was told to hire men for the price of good gold and silver to scold and scorn him for a year and a day, so he might suffer even more, and thus through his torment and shame would come to goodness. One day he was in a great crowd such as we are now, God bless you, and stood amongst them as I stand here now, and when the people started to revile him he welcomed their contempt with laughter. But when they asked why he did so, he said because that day he hadn't had to open his purse and pay a single penny to anyone to chide him. And nor have I today. You saw the only cost I've had to bear for speaking of God is censure and I promise you the greater slander you experience on this earth, the less misery you shall have at death, God save you all."

I was amazed that she would speak so in church to strangers with clerics standing by. The crowd cried out angrily.

"False Loller, preaching to us and mocking the monks."

"Let's get a cartful of thorns and take her away to be burnt."

They stood between us, pushing and shoving and jostled her out of the nave, taunting her with their threats. I struggled and tried to elbow my way to get near her but there were too many people and I lost her in the throng.

It was crowded outside but soon the mob was gone. I could not see Margery anywhere, so made my way back to our lodgings, and she was already there.

"So there you are, and where do you think you've been, deserting me like that?"

"But Margery, I couldn't get to you, they held me back and I was truly frightened."

"So you say but I was in terrible danger, yet you played false and left me on my own to face those crazy women."

"But it all happened so quickly – one moment they were loving your stories, then all of a sudden they turned on you. And don't you remember what John said last night, after that Black Friar told you to stop telling your stories, about how the people here have a fear of Lollers and ordinary folk preaching in public, and I warned you too."

John had been sitting nearby in the dark and when he heard me say his name he came out of the shadows.

Margery scowled and continued, "Well, I don't need your warnings. And since you don't protect me there's no point in you staying here with me. Go get your belongings and be ready to leave at first light."

"Nay lady," said John softly, "you must have a handmaid to look after you and care for your needs. You both had a shock

141

today but we leave for home tomorrow and can then find some peace." And he took her arm and led her to a corner of the chamber where they spoke awhile and then she came back and said that if I mended my manners I could continue to serve her and then, shrugging her shoulders, she dismissed me. But she did not call me for supper that night, though later she required me to share her bed as had become her custom.

We departed Canterbury the next day to return to Lynn, as soon as the Angelus bell rang, but no sooner there then Margery demanded we leave again. She was now resolved to have her vow of chastity ratified so she could make preparations for the pilgrimage overseas. Our own bishop had died not long before so Spryngolde advised her to go to Lincoln. She had grown distant and unfriendly since my rebuke at Canterbury but still required my service. When we arrived there, we were told Bishop Repyngdon was away and we'd have to wait until his return.

A few days later one of Bishop Repyngdon's household came with a message, summoning us to his palace. When we arrived, Margery went alone into his chamber, and much time passed. Then one of his servants came and told us to follow him. She was on her knees and the Bishop took John's hand, drew him close to her and asked:

"Is it your will that your wife take the mantle and ring and you live chaste the two of you, for evermore?"

And John knelt, with a stunned look on his face, placed his hands between the Bishop's and whispered, "Yes."

Then Bishop Philip blessed them both, invited them to dine a few days hence and sent us away. And before the week was out we were on the road again, this time for London. Margery was now resolved to meet with Archbishop Arundel, the most powerful churchman in all the land. Once again she was speaking to me and showed me the four golden coins Repyngdon had given her. Yet despite this generous gift she was in a sulk.

"Repyngdon listened to me but I do not trust him. When first I opened my heart to him I thought he believed in me, and he even said I should write down my thoughts and feelings for all posterity. You heard John agree that we live chastely, but finally he would not sanction my vow and said I should go to the Holy Land first. So we'll visit my Lord Arundel and get his approval for my Jerusalem journey," for now she really was determined to go there, whether as a vowess or not, and would see Thomas Arundel before that, come what may.

Our journey to London was swift for Margery was in great haste. It was the greatest city I had ever seen, like all the towns we'd visited jumbled up together, with another on top. The moated stone walls were higher than those around York, the city gates finer, the houses taller some with five storeys, the streets dirtier and crowded with livestock, the mansions along the Strand where the wealthy folk lived grander, a babble of a hundred foreign tongues, fountains with fresh water at all the street corners, the great river awash with barges and ships of all kinds, and smaller vessels and boats cluttering the quays and hithes along the river banks.

The townsfolk were all magnificently attired in brocades and silks of dazzling colours, guildsmen out and about dressed in fine liveries and workshops everywhere. Yet Margery didn't once lift her eyes to look but harried John to find the quickest way to Arundel's palace on the other side of the Thames. As the river was in full spate, the people advised us to take the great stone bridge over to Lambeth, but she did not tarry there either, neither to look at the Tower where prisoners and heretics were housed, nor at the walls where traitors' heads were displayed high on pikes, or at the great water wheels under the arches for grinding the people's corn, not even at the shops on top of the bridge, so set was she on meeting this great man.

There was a noisy crowd at the Archbishop's palace when we arrived, members of his household, supplicants, petitioners, hawkers and beggars seeking alms. There were more clerics than I had ever seen, swaggering and bragging, all so rowdy and opulently dressed. But Margery, having no mind for manners, went over to a group of them and scolded them for their rich clothes and brash language.

"And you should mind God's word and keep silence in awe of him ..."

They just stared at her and laughed but a woman next to me shouted out.

"Have you no respect for these good men of the church? You ought to be sent to Smithfield and I myself would bring a bundle of faggots to burn you."

John took Margery by the hand and led her to a corner of the hall, and I watched them as he whispered to her and she remained calm.

I gasped and the loud-mouthed lady grabbed my arm and muttered,

"If she's kin of yours, you should be careful. She might be decked out like a gentlewoman who should know better, but she sounds like one of those sneaky Loller tradeswomen who speak against our priests. When the Archbishop hears of her insults he'll send for her and test her faith, I'll be bound."

"That he will," agreed her companion. "He's got no patience

with Lollards. And I heard tell just now that yester-night he summoned Oldcastle to answer charges of heresy, but he got wind of it and fled to his lands in Kent taking some rabble with him. It'll bring bloodshed and rebellion just like the Great Rising, God help us."

"Aye but our clerics and Justices are more canny now and use informers too to sniff out rebels and heretics. They'll find the guilty ones. So what's her business here, anyways," she demanded, thrusting her face in mine, "and what's her name?"

I said she had come with a petition and quickly walked away.

Sometime later one of Arundel's priests came to say he was ready to meet us. We were led into a garden where he stood with some of his servants. We knelt to receive his blessing, then Margery told him she'd come with a petition. He gestured to a stone seat where I might sit with John, and took her off to another part of the garden. It was soon dark and the first stars were already appearing when she came back and said he'd granted her wish.

"The Archbishop has sanctioned my pilgrimage to the Holy Land and instructed one of his clerks to prepare a letter to take back to Lynn, but we must return in a week's time to collect it when it is signed and sealed."

For the next few days friends and strangers came to hear Margery as she spoke about her conversations with the great churchmen she'd met, but to my ears her pious prattling seemed only a different colour of all the boasts and blusters of earlier years. As she had little need of me, I was let free and grateful for that as I'd been thinking of Ralph and was minded to search him out after all these months. I had scant idea where to look but thought to go to the tanners' district since most of our friends in Lynn had been glovers and parchment-makers and connected with that trade.

I was directed to Cheapside which was a wretched place and asked at several workshops with no success. Then I came to one where an elderly woman was talking with some apprentices, and when I gave her Ralph's name she sent them away and looked at my curiously.

"Ralph ... Ralph from Bishop's Lynn do you mean?" she asked. I nodded and she drew me aside and whispered:

"So, what's your business and who is it asking for him?"
I was suddenly fearful. I'd no idea what trouble he might be in and so I lied,

"Mistress Kempe, I'm just an old acquaintance, passing through."

"Passing through, is it, and do you have a Christian name?"
I was about to tell her, then changed by mind and lied again,

"Marion."

"Marion, then, Mistress Marion Kempe and no, I don't know where he might be. A bit of a firebrand he was with his Loller ideas. Mayhap he's gone into Kent with that old man Castle he's met sometimes. I'll tell him if ever he comes back."

There was noise in the alleyway and a figure shrouded in grey emerged out of the gloom. She put a finger to her lips, turned me round, bid me be careful and pushed me away. I was shaken by her curt farewell and hastened back to Margery, and stayed there until we returned to Arundel's palace, collected his letter and left London.

That then was the summer of our first travels. We'd been on the road for some four or five months and now the pilgrimage season was over, the leaves beginning to turn and the days drawing in as we made our way back to Lynn. I felt a happiness to be returning to familiar surroundings and especially to the children.

This was a shorter journey than any we'd made so far and Margery had much to talk about to those we met along the way, stories of encounters with bishops and hermits and the Archbishop's great seal to show those who doubted her. What she did not speak of was the deal she'd made with John and I wondered what he felt. But he was ever courteous, talked of new trade ventures once his debts were paid and seemed to have closed his mind to the other side of the bargain. I envied him that, as I have others whose minds do not linger on matters that leave a sour taste in their mouths. And I wondered then, as I still do now, whether it is better to remember or forget and on which side madness lies.

We were less than a day's journey from home when we came to a settlement we hadn't visited before, a small community lying in the marshlands of the Fens. Margery insisted we leave the main thoroughfare to worship at the church there. Ahead of us was a square tower with a spire, but the way was blocked by water and a bridge with a rope slung tight across. By the side was a rough shelter fashioned out of branches. John called out and a creature emerged clothed in skins, a great hulk of a man with a straggly red beard, unkempt hair and empty eye sockets, or so it seemed until I saw his gaze was fixed beneath his upper eyelids. His feet were bare and in his calloused hands he held a club.

"Who shouts at me?" he bellowed, fixing his eyes down and glowering at us.

"God keep you, good Christian soul," said Margery. "We wish only to cross to the other side and worship at the church."

"Only the pure may cross and you're not pure," and turning to me with a wave of his club he continued, "I see wickedness on your face too, but the man may go and he shall give me a ha'penny for it, for I am the keeper of the bridge. Go then and leave these women behind for me to batter once they've said their prayers, for 'tis better they pray first than the Devil snatch them should they try to pass over straight away."

He stood firm and did not move, when a young woman came singing across the bridge, with a loaf of bread clutched to her bosom and a jug of milk in her other hand.

"Come now, Tom, let these strangers pass. D'you not see they are angels not devils and have no evil intentions?"

And hearing her voice his face glowed with welcome smiles, he unleashed the rope and guided John to the bridge.

"May God keep you," he said to Margery, and turning to me he broke off a crust of bread and pushed it into my hand.

"Evil harms she who thinks of evil, so turn your mind to pondering only of good. This is the bridge of good and evil, and I have a morsel of wisdom for you that will keep you safe. Out of the bitter root the most beautiful flowers may grow," and he lent his arm to steady me and helped me mount the bridge.

"And do not talk as you go," he called out after us, "lest Satan reach up and pull you down."

The young woman came back with us and said to have no fear of our return for Tom was always gentle despite his rough ways. He'd been crazed from childhood since the day his mother had tumbled off the bridge into the marsh and drowned. He was there when she fell and the priest had damned her, saying she'd thrown herself into the waters and refused to let her be buried in hallowed ground.

Most people in the village believed a demon had pushed her, for a bridge is always a place of peril, and many held Tom a holy man and full of good counsel. He fell into a frenzy on the few occasions when he remembered the past, but mostly he forgot. Yet he refused offers of a home in the village and paid for his victuals with the pennies he collected from keeping the bridge's pathways clear. And when we returned he'd woven flowers along the side of it and, giving me a posy, waved us on our way.

You never return to the same place that once you've left and when we got back, Lynn was strange and familiar, hostile and comforting. Mostly it was the smell of the sea that greeted me, the warmth of neighbours and the children, though that was tinged with sorrow for little Edward had sickened and died the day we left London. After all the sights we'd seen Lynn might have seemed dull, but for the ships moored along the quays - they now held the promise of adventure.

There were stories to tell and news to share but Margery had little time for either, and rushed off to see her priest to talk about her Jerusalem journey. On her return she charged me with making the arrangements and told John to introduce me to those of his acquaintances who'd been on pilgrimage there. I asked that first I might go to the convent to visit my friends and tell them of our plans. Margery did not deny me this, but insisted I attend to her business first.

"And I haven't yet decided that you'll accompany me. My priest warned me I shall have trouble with you and I'm minded to go alone or engage a younger woman."

Before I could protest John was firm with her, saying I knew her well, was familiar with her needs, a younger maidservant would be flighty and it wouldn't be safe or seemly for her to travel alone. I was grateful for this as I felt a fierce rage and might have let lose my anger for her slight. Despite her wish to cast him aside John always had a care for Margery and now it seemed for me too. But I wondered what Spryngolde held against me, it is not wise to make an enemy of a priest.

"Well, perhaps you may come," said she, "but first you must see to my comfort. Then I'll let you know whether you can attend me, and if there's time you may go to the convent and tell them of my great endeavours."

I was vexed by her unkindness, but reminded myself how much she always needed me and would need me even more once I'd completed the preparations.

John took me to meet with two men who'd been to the Holy Land and they talked of the different pilgrimage routes, of vagabonds and kidnappings, shipwrecks, pirates and tempests, about what money to take and which papers were needed. They spoke of the extortionate cost of travelling, the fees ferrymen charged, the tolls to be paid and about certain inns run by murderers where more than twenty corpses were disposed of each week.

Then one asked which fellowship we were joining and told me there was a priest in Norwich who was leading a pilgrimage to Jerusalem, and I realized I didn't have to arrange everything on my own. Over the years of serving Margery I'd never learnt to depend on others, but was now thankful for help and sent a message to the Norwich priest. Within a few days he came to Fincham Street and a clerk was with him. I was thankful Margery was not at home, for I knew she'd have no liking for either of them. Nor indeed had I, but to a hungry man even stale bread is good and I had an appetite for this adventure.

I recall Ralph once saying that clerics were either like ravens or doves. Sir William, for that is how he liked to be addressed, had the manners of a merchant and was clothed in the finest burnet cloth with fur-lined cuffs and collar and a jewelled cross dangling to his waist. This alone would not have marked him as a hypocrite, but for his friend Simon, a pardoner who sold indulgences. But while William was handsome, Simon was not. Indeed he was most ill favoured, with thin yellow hair as greasy as cheap candle wax, and pimples on his sallow cheeks and chin. And his voice was as shrill and strident as an aged goat.

Dame Cecilia had spoken long ago about such men. Pardoners she said were charlatans, and the indulgences they sold were false documents with their promises of forgiveness of sins and freedom from penance in purgatory. A true indulgence was meant to guide sinners to make amends to their neighbours or those they had hurt in this life, and lead them to kindness. Pardoners took money from simple folk, tricking them into believing they could buy forgiveness without ever having to admit remorse or the need to change their ways. She reminded me that simply saying sorry was an empty way of discharging the debt of guilt, for if there was no true understanding or contrition then it was easy to fall into evil and unkindness again.

Sir William said there were six or seven who'd be joining the fellowship but we'd meet with other groups along the way. He was planning to leave within the next few weeks, sailing from Great Yarmouth to Zeeland. Once there we'd join the pilgrimage route along the river Rhine to Constance, then across the mountains to Venice where we'd spend the winter until the spring winds came to carry us over the seas. He'd been advised of the hostels where we'd be welcome, said we should take ducats for our expenses and had a list of other essentials we would need.

"You can buy sea-chests in Venice to store on board the vessel, but for now I advise you to pack your belongings in a sack so nothing is spoiled while we journey overland. We'll hire mules to carry our baggage when we are not on the riverboats. I'm told you should take three sacks, one for food and clothes, another for patience and the last, and biggest of all, for money. We cannot rely on charity so the mouth of your pilgrim purse must always be open, but I warrant your mistress has no shortage of coinage now her father's dead and all his wealth is hers."

I didn't much care for his interest in Margery's money and did not say she had considerable debts to pay. There was little more to speak of, but I was anxious to know who else was coming and dismayed when he said Simon was.

Margery was pleased when I told her we could join a fellowship going from Norwich to the Holy Land. John had engaged an advocate to set out the details of her will and further the sale of some of her properties, so she had money to settle their debts as well as funding the expenses of the journey. She then told me her priest had prepared the licence for her to travel, together with another for her maidservant but had written no name on it. Yet she now entrusted me with her cash for the pilgrimage and didn't talk of abandoning me again. But it seemed there was less trust between us now than ever, even though we held each other's secrets in our hearts and since Brunham's death were yoked even closer together. All that had passed the morning of his death still remained unacknowledged, but I could not force her to talk of it. We were kin, shared the same blood, yet no one would believe me if I spoke of it. I was beholden to her for my livelihood, just as her good name was in my power.

With most matters settled she now asked me to see to her other requirements.

"Now, as for my clothes," she told me, "I had a vision last night, that our Lord desires me to wear white raiment as holy virgins do. I need everyone to know I've given my body to God and will be chaste for ever more."

I was minded to tell her she was not special white bread but just common wholemeal brown like the rest of us. Instead I said:

"Margery the priest told me all our fellowship should wear grey tunics with a red cross sewn on the front. He was most particular and we need to do as others do. Besides white will easily soil and I shan't be able to wash your garments while we're on the road. Wait till Venice or better still, until you've returned from the Holy Land and have fulfilled your vows. And there's still much to prepare before we leave."

She started to protest, then wavered and finally agreed. My purchases were soon made, tunics sewn, cloaks refashioned, new boots cobbled, sturdy staffs crafted, hats bought and two large leather satchels procured to hold money, trinkets, and papers. I bought pewter spoons and cups, water bottles and a little sheath knife that a sailor was selling in the market. I also visited the apothecary for potions and purgatives, balms and bandages, syrups and salves, and I spent the day with him as he noted down dosages and applications. I'd rather have gone to Sybile whose remedies I trusted, but had not the courage to see her after our last meeting.

As always people were divided when they heard Margery's plans. Some whispered that pride was wont to go before a fall and she'd surely die along the way, but there were others who gloried in her enterprise and gave her money that she might pray for them. And word soon got round that Spryngolde would be preaching from the pulpit that anyone who was owed a debt by Margery or her husband should go to Fincham Street and settle their claims with her. This too caused tittle-tattle and the men started gossiping as well, for they held it a scandal that any man should be beholden to a woman, and they would have been even more angry had they known Margery was paying off John's debts in order to buy a single bed for herself.

I did not go to St Margaret's that Sunday when Spryngolde made the formal announcement of our pilgrimage. Instead I fulfilled my plan to visit the convent. As I mounted the mule, which John out of kindness had procured for me, and rode through the town gates with Andrew from the household, I was stirred with both dread and delight. I was travelling back to the past to meet the young convent-girl who'd ridden towards her future and yearned I might regain some of the hope and wonder she'd felt at that time. But that girl had also been beset by shame and anger and it seemed she'd not been able to leave her troubles behind.

Since then I'd known further tribulations both of my own making and through the turn of Fortune's wheel. And although there was much to look forward to, I had no certainty of making this Jerusalem journey in the hopeful spirit of other pilgrims. I recalled those Doom paintings of torture and hellfire and wondered where they came from, for I knew they were also there inside me. But if hell raged within me, then why should heaven not blossom there too, and did I have to wait until I was clothed in a shroud to feel free and joyful? I could not speak of this to any priest. I'd been thinking too that if I died along the way, there'd be no one to mourn or pray for me and I had a deep desire that someone should know where I was in case I did not return. I put all my hope in Sister Margaret.

It was only a few weeks since we'd returned from London, but it was good to leave Lynn again, the busyness of preparations and sometime uneasy company of Margery. And beyond the comforting notion of returning to those I knew once loved me, I wanted to meet the innocent young girl again whose infinite world had once been her home at the farm. And as we came into the countryside I started to find solace in the familiar land and open skies, remembering my childhood prayers to the deity I once believed lived in the sun and moon and all of nature.

In time we passed some ploughmen working in the fields, the air resounding with the crack of their whips, their hoarse calls to the oxen and the sharp slap of the plough bats as the villeins, following behind, broke up the heavy clods of clay. The turned earth smelt full and rich. Leaves were falling in showers of russet, scarlet and gold, and acorns and chestnuts tumbled and bounced as they hit the ground. Swine snorted as they foraged in the undergrowth, while the swineherds thwacked their canes to drive them on to better harvest.

Squirrels scampered along the branches of trees collecting nuts, and clustering around the brambles pheasants strutted, feasting on the last of the blackberries. The season of abundance was drawing to a close. Then I saw a small girl-child, who was gathering acorns in her apron, creep out of the wood and stare up at me as we trotted past, and I held her look in mine. And in that moment it was as if we knew each other, past and future in the present moment. Then a gruff voice called out to her and she laughed and skipped away.

At noon we stopped at an inn to take refreshment. I sensed the convent-girl observing me as I sat with Andrew, sharing a flagon of ale and trencher of bread and herring. Some ploughmen were seated round the hearth talking of their labours, the keen new blade of their plough, the strength of their beasts and straightness of their furrows. They looked at me and I thought all they might see was a self-assured woman apparently at ease, a stranger from the town. Yet like the little girl gathering swine fodder, I knew these men and their daily toil and, despite our differences, I knew too we were composed of the same soil.

"And do you do an honest day's work, do you do well, do you try better, do you do your best?" they called out laughing, and did not wait for an answer so happy were they with themselves and their labours. As they left one came and asked whither we were bound, and when I named the convent he smiled and said:

"We have no need of travelling, our work is our pilgrimage and ..."

Then someone called out, "Come on Piers, come on, back to work," and he waved cheerily at us and left.

I still think of that ploughman and his earthy wisdom. It comes to me now as I tell it again that what I'd been searching for had always been there within my grasp, not in the convent, nor across the seas, but in the ordinary tasks of every day. Yet such thoughts shimmer fleetingly like the sheen of a crow's wings caught in sunlight until the moment when the bird turns and is a flat black again, all sparkle lost, just as the mind fades once more into daily dullness.

By the time we reached the convent it was already dusk and I thought my memory to be playing false. What had seemed to my youthful mind a magnificent castle, a homely haven, despite the later nightmares, was just a cluster of small decaying buildings, the great wooden gates open, the courtyard deserted and covered with leaves, the inner doors and casement shutters all closed.

Andrew took our animals to the stables for there was no yard boy there to help. Neglect was everywhere. I rang the bell and waited until a nun came shuffling out. The news was quickly told. Dame Cecilia was long dead, Margaret an invalid, and the new prioress away visiting relatives. I left Andrew in the parlour and climbed up to the infirmary. There too was disorder. I didn't recognize Margaret at first, for in my mind I saw her as the robust woman of twenty years before, but she knew me immediately and did not seem surprised I'd come. And she had much to tell.

"After you left there was no one to help with the accounts and then there was a fire and the tithe barn burnt to the ground together with some of the outbuildings, and all the monies we'd set aside for yearly costs and a secure future were needed for repairs. Several of our tenants fell on hard times and our income was much reduced. In the last year of Cecilia's term of office we had another visitation from the Bishop who spoke strongly once more against her rule and usage of the Wycliffe Bible. She argued again our Sisters had no care for Latin and would benefit from reading in their own language, but he was adamant she put it aside. It seemed we were no longer in his favour and without his favour our fortunes waned.

In time our elderly lodgers died and no new ones came. The guesthouse was often empty, few new children were sent to board with us, and those who did paid little. We had only two novices after you left and their dowries were so small they did nothing to replenish our coffers. Cecilia died shortly after she handed over to me, worn out with worries.

I found it hard to find money enough for our sustenance and for the care of the destitute, and even harder to keep discipline. I had to ensure we spent less money, had smaller meals and pittances, but the younger Sisters were not prepared to make sacrifices and no longer mindful of the observances of convent life. After six years I lost the election. Joan died at that time, a gentle soul, and Amice became the new prioress. She was never much committed and under her our fortunes have dwindled. At times I despaired and doubted God's goodness for having deserted us."

I was surprised to hear her talk so, then thought how simple I'd been expecting comfort and solace for my own troubled faith. I saw too that it must always have been a struggle to run the convent, though as a child those difficulties had been hidden in my confident belief that adults always had the answers and were never hurt by life's reversals and misfortunes.

"Despite that," she continued slowly, "I've come to know that all shall be well. I thank God too for my doubts, which strangely have strengthened my faith. I fell last winter and have not been able to walk since. I'm often tired and am ready to die. I've lived my life as best I can. I'm well cared for, the chaplain visits once a week, and sometimes I'm able to comfort the sick.

I learn more and more that there are two paths to heaven, those of Mary and of Martha, the silent path of contemplation and the equally demanding way of service in the world, as you know well. Neither is better than the other. I'm lucky to have travelled both ways. If I preach from my bed there is no one to hear me but those who care to listen. And I take pleasure in listening to my own sermons."

Then she asked for my news and I knew that what I'd wanted to talk about, my uncertain faith and faint hopes, I could no longer say. I had to learn to find my own answers. So I spoke of my life in Bishops Lynn, the many years of serving Margery, her plans to go to Jerusalem and I to accompany her. I told of her visions, her fervent and florid devotions, her never-ending, showy quest of godliness and her unkindness to me and others. Margaret hushed me, saying we should never judge or look too deeply into another's soul. And she wanted to know what I'd be seeking in the Holy Land, but I could not honestly answer her.

"Sometimes we have to go far away to know where home is. Patience is a friend to doubt and you'll need plenty of that. New life is the fruit of hard labour and I vouch you'll have to bear even more than you have so far, God help you," and she asked that I pray for her when I reached Jerusalem.

Our farewells were swiftly said. I turned at the stair to wave goodbye and still see her now, pale and shrunken, the ghost of the friend I'd known in my youth. She must have been younger then than I am now, but she seemed so old. Andrew and I had a meagre, silent meal with the nuns, were taken to the guest rooms and left at dawn. The way back was drear, no ploughmen in the fields, no swine in the forest, no little girl gathering nuts. I hadn't known till then how much the convent still meant to me and how much hope I'd had of my return.

The day of our departure drew close. Margery entrusted me with our papers, permissions for our travels and the like, confident I could read them, though we both knew I should only do so in secret. News had come from London that Oldcastle had been tried and convicted of heresy, though he'd escaped once again and was still at large. There was greater fear of Lollards than ever before and of any common folk who could read.

Soon after my return from the convent a message came from Sir William to ready ourselves to leave. Margery busied herself with her farewells and did not need me to accompany her to Master Alan's cell, nor to see Robert Spryngolde. John lent me a small chest to store my belongings though they were few indeed, my two good gowns, a winter cloak and boots, some shifts, shawls and other small clothes, a goblet, spoons and a few household things. I hid some of my savings in a glove, having spent much on gifts for Margery's children, for finally as the time came to leave, I realized we might never see each other again, either one of them or I might die.

Isobel had already left Lynn to serve in the household of one of Margery's acquaintances and would marry the following year. William and Godfrey were apprenticed in other parts of town and only young Mary stayed at home with her father. They were all the family I had and I didn't want them to forget me. At the last moment I went to a scribe and dictated a letter to young John, over the seas. Although we'd not heard from him for at least a twelve-month, he'd always felt like a son to me and I doubted Margery would think to let him know of our departure.

We left early in the morning, but even so many of the townsfolk were already out in the streets. Mostly it was the women who came to bid us safe return, but there were some men there as well and as always lots of children and poor folk too. We both wore our pilgrim's habit, with our satchels, staves and wide-brimmed hats, and as we made our way to Gaywood it happened several times that an arm reached out to touch me with a mistaken, earnest plea, "Pray for me, Margery, when you get to the Heavenly City." And looking at my lady, it came to me that attired as we both were in the same grey tunics, there was little difference between us, and nothing to show which one had been born into wealth and family and which one not. At that moment I understood that even though I had to serve her, this was my pilgrimage too, and that perhaps the good wishes in the crowd were also meant for me.

Once past the Hospital of St John, we came to the East Gate where Spryngolde stood to bless us. There were some men there with pipes and viols playing anthems and carols. A few in the crowd struggled to get close to us and press coins or votive offerings to take on our way, but there were others who stood apart and I even heard one mutter "Leave a pilgrim, return a whore." Not everyone was a well-wisher, and I knew there were some who wouldn't mourn if we didn't find our way home again. Then the church bells began to chime as we climbed onto the cart, which a neighbour had decorated with flowers, and so we left Lynn with John as well, for he wished to stay with us until we sailed.

It was growing dark when we reached Norwich, but Margery wanted to go straight to the cathedral. Sir William and the rest of our fellowship were already in Yarmouth, but left a message at our inn with the name of our vessel where we should meet on the morrow. It was late afternoon the next day when we took the riverboat to the quays where they were waiting for us. We greeted each other, but the priest quickly stopped any further prattle.

"Let us keep quiet on this first night together," he said, "and mind each of you set your intentions for your pilgrimage, and pray to all the saints for a safe journey. We shall keep this silence until dawn tomorrow."

I remember even now what a warm night it was with a steady gentle breeze. Mattresses had been laid out on deck, and our fellow travellers were soon lying down, shrouded in their cloaks. We waved farewell to John and went to find our places to sleep. Before we'd even settled ourselves, the last bales of wool and sacks of coal were stowed, ropes untied, sails unfurled and the cog cast off to sea. Margery lay still and I heard the mumble of her prayers, while I lay on my back and marvelled, once the sun set, at the starlight and later at the moon when it rose.

As I recall now it was as if I were awake all night, and the

161

more I looked up at the sky, the more I imagined I was looking down into an immense pool of darkness, pin-pricked here and there in intricate starry patterns. I wondered, as I had as a child when I used to lie outside on the grass at the day's end and peer into the darkness, if those little pricks of light were glimpses of the mysteries and possibilities of our lives, and whether God sat feasting there with all his saints bathed in light behind the black pall of the night sky. And though I'd never sailed before on the open seas I felt no fear, soothed by the kindly pitch and toss of our vessel. As for intentions or prayers I doubt I thought of any, so excited was I at this great adventure.

I do not know if I slept that night or whether it passed in a dream. As the light dimmed on one side, so it glowed on the other and soon I heard a whistle. Pulling myself up I saw by the glimmer of the dawn sky that we were sailing in a channel with sandbanks on either side. Ahead of us were two tall towers and the silhouette of a drawbridge. It was morning and we had arrived at Zierickzee.

5

To The Þoly Land 1413-1414

'you good pilgrims are bound to
love one another in the name of our Lord'

*Agnes has fallen and cannot walk far and her granddaughter has
a fever, so I have to go to the market in her stead. Since Margery's funeral
I've not once returned to Lynn but busied myself in my new home. As I'd
hoped, I'm comfortable enough and thankful that we share the household
tasks. I clean, wash and cook sometimes and help with the goats and fowl.
If a neighbour needs me to mind her livestock or watch a child, I'm content
to take whatever I'm given for my time, some grain, cheese or a fleece to spin
into yarn. Between us we manage well enough with the livestock, foraging
in season and wood aplenty from the forest for the fire. Agnes lets me use a
corner of the byre, which I've swept clean and secured from the beasts who
shelter there at night, and I have an old stool and can sit and look out over
the sea.*

*The sea always brings back memories and I marvel that it's become such
a constant friend when I recall the fields and forests of my childhood. They
used to bring me comfort before I'd sailed on ships. Now it's as if I always
knew the sea was the place I came from and belonged.*

*I delivered the eggs to the huckster and went to buy some cloth to make a
tunic for Hilda. She's a warm-hearted maiden and as her mother is dead
so it pleases me to do her favours. I notice now I'm old and no longer have
Margery to look after, my memory takes me back to the kindness of those
who looked after me. And it's good to have the company of the young for they*

view the world without the heaviness of the past and live in the freedom of the moment. But I cannot let go of what went before, not yet, not until I've set it all down.

After buying the cloth I went to the parchment-maker's shop. One of the young priests from the Trinity Guild, whom I recognised from Margery's funeral, was there, but he did not know me and anyhow I'm just another old woman. He was holding a piece of vellum up to the light and testing its quality.

"I must have several quires of this, all as good as good as this, the best, the very, very best," he intoned as if singing the psalms, stroking the parchment with his thin, long fingers on the board.

The parchment-maker grunted, gathered a bundle from the shelf and asked:

"Is it something special you're commissioned to write Master Salthouse? It's only a month since we sent your regular order."

"Why yes, yes, yes there is," he sang again. "I'm copying certain passages from the book of Mistress Kempe, praise be her name, praise her, praise her, for the brothers of my house. She was already bedridden when I came to Lynn, poor soul, but I hear tell she was devout and saintly, saintly and devout, and her meditations are most wonderful, wonder-ful and won-der-ful."

I did not wait to hear more in case the parchment-maker called me over. Not everyone had been impressed by Margery's book and many still judged her for vainglory. And I'd no wish to talk of her, for even after her death she continues to demand attention. As for buying more parchment, I still have a few old pieces and if I soak them in milk and oat bran, I can wipe them clean and use them again. Nor can I write every day as I do not want to worry Agnes with my work.

But I was troubled as I walked back. I haven't been able to write for several weeks since I've had Agnes to mind as well as our home, yet memories of our Jerusalem Journey continue to surface with increasing urgency and are so different to what Margery recorded in her book, which tells nothing of what we saw or where we went, but only what she felt and what others thought of her.

When I got home Agnes had made a pottage and Hilda's fever had abated so we sat outside and ate together. As darkness fell I rounded up the beasts and shut them in the byre. Then I stood and looked at the moonlight shimmering on the waters, and it was as still and shining as brightly as that night on the North Sea when we sailed all those years ago to Zeeland at the start of our pilgrimage.

It took time to get to know our fellowship. We were eleven in all. Sometimes we travelled with other groups, but Sir William was most particular we stay together, and though I found him meddlesome, he had to shepherd an unruly flock. I learnt to watch him carefully, for when we docked that first morning there was such a crowd calling out in a babble of tongues that I was swept away in the crush and lost sight of our companions. It was easy to be overwhelmed by the bustle of each new place, but I knew I couldn't expect Margery to know what to do and kept reminding myself that it was my duty to serve her. I soon found William again who was bargaining with one of the sailors to load our sacks onto a cart and take them to the nearest inn.

We stayed in Zierickzee for several days and though I wished to get better acquainted with our fellow pilgrims, Margery required me to accompany her to church every morning where she spent all day in earnest prayer. In the evenings, she spoke to no one in particular and everyone in general, recounting her visions and telling pious stories. Mostly they ignored her for they were still getting to know each other, and while William tried his best to speak with her, I worried that she would soon cause an upset.

They were mostly ordinary folk and though devout had not

so completely denied their senses that they did not also seek some pleasure and entertainment, hence they found her ways unsettling. As often happens when there is a stranger in our midst that may lead to fear, then from fear to unkindness. And I doubt any one of them would have known a creature as odd as Margery who would not take a sip of wine or even a morsel of meat. Despite the promises she made to John at the foot of the cross on Midsummer's eve, she'd not eaten much for many a month and continued to deny herself ordinary meals that the rest of us enjoyed.

Apart from William the priest and Simon the pardoner, there was Martin his clerk, a large timid man who nevertheless had a small mean look. There were other churchmen too. Matthew, the chaplain of a noble lord, was going to Jerusalem in his stead and acted as our treasurer. He was a boorish fellow with an unruly thatch of grey hair and a bushy beard. With him were Edwin and his cousin Robert, one tall and thin, the other short and fat, yeomen from the same estate, and both carried bows and arrows for our protection. They often found much saucy amusement with other young pilgrims they met and regaled us at mealtimes with tales of their adventures.

There was also a wandering friar whose curiosity had set him on the road. If Martin's tongue was sharp like the bark of a little dog, then Friar Godfrey's was lisping and silken sweet and I wondered where lay the sting that hid behind the honey. He was one of those Grey Friars who loved to sermonise and practice homilies and I knew he and Margery would quarrel one day. The last two were Hugh, an elderly apothecary, who had a long white beard and hair tied back at the nape of his neck, and Nicholas, his fresh-faced, taciturn apprentice, who was always by his side. They usually kept to themselves but became good friends.

Despite the unease at the Zierickzee inn we left in good spirits and for a few days Margery and I enjoyed much comfort on the ferry. There was a small cabin at the back of the riverboat, which we shared with two women, and it was good to have shelter for it rained much of the time. Margery was mostly deep in her meditations and didn't seem to notice much. Every morning and evening we joined our fellowship outside – they had only an awning to keep them dry – and sang hymns and said prayers together, then left and did not speak with them. Nor did we eat together, but took our meals inside with the other women. On occasion we tied up at the riverbank, went to a church or provisioned for the journey.

We did not, however, stay on the same boat for long. As we travelled south the scenery changed, the banks grew steeper and were covered in vineyards and looming above these were forts and castles. Each time we passed a new one we had to pay a toll, and one day we were stopped by a heavy chain which hung across the river and our boatman said he could not go further and would have us disembark.

From this point on we frequently changed vessels and Hugh explained that the hilltop castles belonged to different barons and each one exercised his right to tax those passing through his lands. He knew the river well, for in his youth he'd studied at the university of Heidelberg. Sometimes, he said, the Rhine was a raging torrent, yet now it flowed so gently. Even though the waters were calm, he told us not to be deceived for there was much enmity between those who lived on the west bank and those on the east and, as I saw, the waters were sometimes stained with blood.

Most of our ferries were small and laden with goods, which the local people brought on board, so we often stopped to unload or take on more, and then we ate and slept at an inn or, where there were monasteries, claimed the right as pilgrims to hospitality. Some in our fellowship knew Latin, the language of the clergy, and were able to translate the legends told of these parts, fables of valiant heroes and resourceful maidens, of fey and fickle water-nymphs, cunning giants and powerful black magicians, dwarfs and dragons and especially of the skilful smiths who forged wondrous ornaments from the river gold, which had been recovered by men in ancient times. I was thrilled by these stories.

And so we made our steady progress along the river. Whenever we stayed at a monastery there were new tales to hear and the different wines and cordials, which each house brewed, enlivened our evenings and always there was much to wonder at and talk about. But Margery grew ever more discontent, wanting only to speak of Jesus and angrily dismissive whenever refreshment was passed round. Though she knew it not, her discourse coming at the end of a sometimes trying day was like a damp log smouldering on a fire that stank and gave no heat.

At last the company could stand her no longer and I blame myself in part, for I should have warned her, but she was never mindful that others might not welcome her never-ending sacred sentiments. So it happened one frosty morning as we were embarking on yet another riverboat, that Godfrey handed round a stone jar of strong wine, which he had cajoled from one of the monks. We were all pleased to take a sip, but when he offered it to Margery she was sharp with him.

"What need have I of that to ease the cold, when I am warmed by the heavenly fire of divine love? And so should you be and all our fellowship on this holy journey."

"So was the love of your husband not hot enough for you?" lisped Godfrey. "Remember mistress you're no longer at home with him to preach and peck, nag and crow as no doubt you used to."

And she, standing boldly in front of him, put her hand on her heart and answered.

"Almighty God is my own true lord and he is as great a lord here as in England, may we all praise him, and I have as great a cause to love him here as there, blessed be his name," and pushing him aside she got into the boat.

Godfrey was furious and cursed her and she accused him of shaming her and ungodly unkindness, and so they argued back and forth like thunder bolts booming up and down the river, while the rest of us cowered in silence. I sat beside her but she ignored me, and when William started to sing the *Stella Splendens* no one joined in and we sat huddled and hushed throughout the long day.

That evening our boatmen tied up by a small inn, beyond which was a steep path leading to a monastery. Godfrey and Matthew had been whispering together, then Matthew came to Margery, gave her a coin and said she had to fend for herself that night for they found no cheer in her company. Then they pushed me in front of them and jostled me up the hill. I should have gone back, but was weary too of her complaints, though as I turned the corner and looked back I saw the innkeeper had come out and was holding her arm so I knew she'd have shelter for the night.

There was much gaiety that evening and we stayed up late until the Abbot came to bid us goodnight. He'd heard of our quarrel, for the inn belonged to the monastery and the cook had come to give account of it, and he took William and Godfrey aside and spoke with them. First there was laughter, then they were silenced and Hugh told me the Abbot was speaking of the holy fool who'd endured much mockery for the love of Jesus. Godfrey looked shamed because he was a follower of Francis, the humble saint who'd befriended birds and beasts and called the sun and moon his brother and sister. But the arrogance, which simmered beneath his modest mien, grew even greater after the Abbot's rebuke.

When we left the next morning, Margery was waiting with the Abbot. He wished us all Godspeed, then reminded us in the English tongue,

"Pray forget not, my dear brothers and sisters, that every act of charity is a stepping-stone to heaven and you good pilgrims are bound to love one another in the name of our Lord, who is love himself. So let peace be your hymn and may you sing it together every moment of your pilgrimage."

Hugh took Margery by the hand, brought her over to Godfrey, bid them be friends again and so we set off.

A hoar frost had visited in the night, the sharpest yet of the year, and the trees along the riverbank were shrouded white and stiff with it. As the sun rose, the branches on the western bank glistened, wept, then shook themselves free, while those on the east side, in the shadows, held on to the ice. I was with Margery, Hugh and Nicholas on the shady side of the boat with the villagers who were taking their wares to the town beyond, while the rest of our fellowship sat on the sunny side. Then we came to a bend in the river and suddenly we were all bathed in sunlight and warmed ourselves singing pilgrim songs.

The noon bells were ringing when we tied up at the next settlement where there was a festive air. This was the first large market we'd come to and there was much to see. Hugh invited

Margery and me to come with him and showed us what herbs and remedies they sold in those parts, told us the best bread to buy and spoke to the people who offered us cheese and berries to taste.

There were stalls selling cloth and embroidery, wooden ornaments and little trinkets made of straw and for a while Margery was distracted. Then we saw a great crowd and went over to join them, though we had to push our way to get to the front. We found Simon there with his bundle of relics spread out in front of him, pieces of cloth and bone and little phials with liquid inside. Martin was holding up each one and Simon told what it was, while a local man translated for him.

"Now see this holy mitten, my dear good gentlemen, I'm telling you it once belonged to a saint. Anyone who wears it for the sowing of his seed, wheat, barley or whate'er he will, will see his harvest increase a hundred-fold. And this little bone comes from the hand of that same holy man and no, it isn't a pig's bone you can take my word for it, it has more marvellous qualities than you'd ever imagine. I've seen its magic myself. Put it in a basin, then give the water to your sheep and they'll be cured of the scab and bear many healthy lambs. And all you lusty young rams here and even you older ones, yes you sir," he joked, pointing at a wizened old man clad in rags who sat dozing with his back against a tree, "you may drink it too and your jigglesticks will grow immense in vigour and you'll enjoy much delightful congress and beget a plenitude of pups."

The people laughed and Margery started to speak out, but Simon just carried on.

"Now ladies, harken to me. These scraps of cloth come from that same saint's cloak, the very last, and any one of you good women who's lucky enough to own a piece may put it under her pillow at night. And you shall sleep sweetly and wake knowing your children will always be healthy, your husband kind, your servants obedient and your home safe. And you will have a long and peaceful life and arrive at heaven's gate at the moment of your death. So, dig into your purses, bring out your money and speak your price."

There was much chattering and clinking of coins as people counted out their change.

I'd seen men like this before selling relics at the shrines we visited on our English pilgrimage and was often tempted to buy something, for it is hard not to be seduced by promises of grace and freedom from hurt and hell-fire that purchasing such charms invite. And I've known people's suffering to be much eased by such trifles if they believed they'd been touched by the hand of God. Faith and hope are powerful medicines which we should not judge or deny.

But Margery was incensed and cried out loudly again, saying what he did was no Christian charity and it would be better he gave money to the poor than sell them baubles. The people didn't understand a word she said, but were not pleased by the interruption, and crowed and laughed at her. Hugh led her away but not before Simon had seen who it was creating the disturbance.

Now she had two enemies and that evening as we were warming ourselves by the fire, Godfrey came to Margery and handed her a package.

"Well mistress, the Abbot reminded us last night of the holy fool and how that may be a path to heaven, and as we saw today the common folk recognized you too, so here's a humble garment for you to wear so that everyone shall know you and celebrate that simple purity you speak of all the time. They'll see you are indeed a holy fool and this will keep you safe," and unwrapping his gift, he brought out an apron of shaggy sackcloth embellished with badger's hair, which he threw over her head and fastened behind her. Simon brought a pair of scissors and cut the hem of her tunic so she did indeed look like an idiot. Then they led her to the table, sat her down at the end and left her alone.

Although I saw her pain I said nothing, for I found it very funny to see her wearing the garb of a slovenly servant and thought the apron suited her. Hugh and Nicholas sat either side of her and William rebuked Godfrey who bowed his head. But she was silent all evening and when we were alone that night, she said if need be she'd be a holy fool for God and was willing to suffer scorn for his sake.

We travelled south for many days, sometimes by water and occasionally walking along the riverbank. No one dared goad Margery again and she wore her indignity meekly. At mealtimes she took her place at the bottom of the table, still wearing her silly apron and since she did not care to join the merriment, she remained silent. I marvelled that she bore the mockery so patiently, but to my shame did nothing to ease her pain other than my usual service to her. I know I was full of resentment and believed her disgrace was merited, besides I had no wish to make enemies of our fellowship. Yet mostly I was ignored as well and left alone with her.

At last after several weeks of tiresome travelling, we came to Constance on a great lake. We were welcomed here as pilgrims, for the city was crowded with clerics and there was much talk about the great council of Ecclesiastics which was to meet the following year. First was the problem of the popes.

The churchmen of Italy and those of France had appointed their own popes, so now there were three and no one knew to whom they owed allegiance and their taxes. They'd confer too about the followers of Jan Hus, who proclaimed the same ideas as those Lollards in our country, and were causing much disturbance. There were also to be deliberations on the life and revelations of the holy Bridget, and whether she should be proclaimed a saint.

These topics were of much interest at the inn where we were staying some several days until William found a wagon to take us over the Alps, and I was glad of the rest. Margery was absent most of the day making her devotions at the cathedral, but returned early one evening with an English friar, who was also a papal legate. He asked if he might join us and everyone welcomed him, pleased to hear more about the Constance Council. As usual Margery would have no meat though Priest William sent a platter down to her, where she sat at the end of the table. When she refused it, he appealed to the legate to encourage her to eat to keep up her strength. But he would not and was curt, saying it was not his business to interfere with her vows, and even if a pilgrim declared she would fast and walk barefoot all the way to Jerusalem he would not stop her.

Then Simon spoke about how self-righteous she was, preaching and prattling ever since we left England. But the legate already knew of our quarrels and told us he'd take care of her and asked to be given her money so he could finance a guide for her journey onto Venice. When Matthew handed him the coins and she counted them, she complained she'd been cheated until William said he had paid extra for her comfort and was keeping some for my expenses as I'd be remaining with them. And Margery agreed, happy to let me go.

I might have spoken then had she not seemed so willing to abandon me, but went instead to pack her belongings. She was mistaken too about the money for some of it was mine that I'd saved over all the years of my service to her. And so she left with her new companion, suddenly the great lady again, and I marvelled at her knack of befriending the powerful and turning troubles to her advantage.

It was good to rest after the two months journeying and peaceful without Margery's lamentations and the squabbles of our fellowship, though I didn't doubt we'd soon meet again. Not long after William announced we'd leave the following day, so we gathered at dawn to travel to the foot of the Alps. It was a fair morning when we climbed into the oxcart and slowly began the ascent up a very steep path, the last stage of our travels before Venice.

By midday the skies had darkened and it grew increasing cold, with a fierce wind flurrying snow. I'd never seen such towering mountains before and found them most menacing. The oxen were soon slipping and no longer able to pull the cart, the wheels slithering backwards on the ice, so we had to get down and continue on foot. In no time at all I lagged behind and might have been lost in the blizzard had Hugh not stopped to call my name and taken my hand to lead the way.

It was a great comfort when finally we reached the inn at the summit, just after nightfall. The night was bitter though I shared a bed with two young women who worked at the inn, both full of warmth and laughter. When daylight came they'd already risen and there was a strange, soft silence in the chamber and an icy cold. A blazing fire warmed the hall below, where I met Hugh staring out of the casement at a wondrous white world. Heavy snow had fallen in the night and still continued. We were snowbound, but I was relieved to hear that an English lady had stayed there some nights before with a companion, and had left in good spirits with mules to make the descent in fair weather.

We remained at the inn for several days until a thaw set in. Then we descended into Italy and on to Bologna to the hostel where we'd been directed. Margery was already there, much to the irritation of most in our group. Hugh asked her to join us again, pleading only that she be more cheerful, and she agreed for her guide was returning to Constance, Venice was only a few days journey away, and then we would rest until spring and fair winds came for our voyage to Jerusalem.

When John had introduced me to those of his acquaintances who'd made this pilgrimage before, they'd spoken mostly of the Holy Land and all the relics and rituals, but one of them was most particular about the splendours of Venice. Even so I was overwhelmed when we arrived at this fabled city of a hundred islands, which seemed to float on water, with magnificent buildings, bridges of many intricate designs and marble palaces lining the canals, and those canals crowded with many people and different kinds of vessels.

There were churches everywhere, both small and large, and most marvellous was the one they called the Basilica of St Mark, or Church of Gold, which had great domes sparkling in the sunlight and brightly coloured arches of gold and azure mosaics, each piece the size of a silver penny. It was adorned with cunning stone carvings, and four great bronze horses pranced proudly over the main doors. Later I climbed to the top of the Campanile from where I could see the whole town, the churches, abbeys, monasteries, towers, palaces, castles and nearby villages as if all afloat in the sea. I'd never seen the like of this before, not even in my dreams.

This church stood in the Piazza San Marco, where the fashionable people came to parade, women in gowns of vibrant silks, cut so low that even their nipples were visible. Their faces were painted white, lips and cheeks coloured with vermilion and hair shaved back at the forehead, decorated with jewels and piled high on top of their heads in thick, abundant curls. I marvelled at this until I saw stalls selling tresses of hair, black, blond and even red, something you'd never find in our country.

The men appeared to dress more modestly, but beneath their sober tunics they displayed brightly coloured leggings. Both men and women seemed very tall and walked with a peculiar grace, until I saw they all wore pattens at least two hands high so that their shoes and garments didn't get soaked by the frequent flooding of the pavements. There were many beggars in this town too and peoples the like of whom I'd never seen before, some so black I thought them ill at first, and their manners and clothes were very different to ours.

We lodged at the St George, a German hostel. On our second evening, after dinner, William advised us that we'd have a long wait until the spring winds came, so we'd have adequate time to prepare body and soul for the coming voyage and to see the sights.

"There is much to see in Venice and lots to buy as it is a great trading city with goods coming from the East, especially silks and spices, so you'll be wanting to spend some of your money on merchandise to sell for profit when you go back home. I'm told the best shops are by the Rialto Bridge and the keeper of the hostel has agreed we can store our purchases here till we return. The guides in the Piazza, who speak English, will tell you when and where the markets are and direct you to where you may buy bedding and anything else you might need for the voyage."

Then turning to Margery he continued.

"They'll also tell you how to get to the churches, monasteries and shrines, and where to find the most holy relics. So be you all of good cheer, for the journey ahead will be much more rigorous and demanding than the one we've undertaken so far."

At first Margery and I were reconciled. We spoke about the coming journey and shared our fears of the sea and the danger of pirates, for word was there'd been many in recent times. I went with her to collect the Venetian ducats, which John had arranged with a silk-merchant to supply her, and accompanied her to various religious houses. There was one, a great convent with many nuns who were splendidly attired, and here she felt welcomed and resolved to visit every day. I was pleased to do errands for her and with the help of the guides soon purchased sheets, pillows, mattresses and quilts and marked all with our names.

I bought a cauldron and kettle, and ordered two strong chests in which to pack our belongings, as well as cheeses, preserved ginger to settle our stomachs, comfits for energy, silk shifts and comfortable leather boots. I also bought a small hencoop with three young hens, that we might have fresh eggs on the voyage, and a barrel of water and another of wine, all to be ready for the time of our departure. I had time to visit the many wonders of this great city, but as for purchasing curios as William had suggested, to sell once back at home, I had not the coinage for that.

For many weeks Margery held her peace. I knew how fervent her devotions were and though I could not share them,

I often joined her at the Zacharia convent and began to find some comfort there in the tranquillity I'd once enjoyed in my own convent years. She did not preach at table until one day something Godfrey said angered her, another great quarrel ensued and she retired to her chamber. I had no wish to coax her out of it as our meals were much more enjoyable without her so I left her alone, and there she stayed all day when not at the convent or at prayer.

I attended her morning and night, but still she accused me of abandoning her. This riled me for I never knew from one day to the next what humour she'd be in. Nor was I certain how much money we had left since she now kept all of it, so when William asked if I'd wash and cook for the fellowship I was happy to do so and earn some coins. Yet apart from Hugh I felt little friendship from the rest of them, tarred as I was by the same brush that had been sullied by my mistress's bright and singular piety.

The winter months passed and more pilgrims arrived. Still we had a long wait, though there was much to see. For several weeks there was a strange and gay festivity in the alleyways and along the canals. Near everyone I saw out and about wore masks which completely covered their faces, as well as long, hooded cloaks buttoned from chin to hem, so you could not tell who was man or woman, noble or commoner, mistress or maidservant. These masks were plain blank faces in white or gold and I often watched people having conversations in their borrowed roles and envied them the freedom to be who they truly were. Their masks did not hide them but rather let them reveal their true selves, and say and do what they really wanted.

On Shrove Tuesday there was a great feast, which was paid

for out of the civic purse. When the Mass was over and even before the church bells had ceased, a bull was slaughtered and put to the roast in the San Marco square, that everyone might gorge themselves before the lean Lenten days ahead. There were stalls selling trinkets, sweetmeats and curios. And it was the custom for young men to throw scented eggs, filled with rose water or other such fragrances at the lady of their choice, and I was showered with one, though think it was a poorly judged throw as I was standing next to Clara, one of the pretty young servants from our hostel.

It was Clara who pressed me to come to the dance that evening, which took place in the square. She lent me a tunic, mask and cloak and waited until I was free from attending Margery. As soon as I put on that golden mask, I believed myself to be a grand lady, wellborn and beautiful and free from fear. And so we went into the Piazza where music was playing, and a multitude had assembled. I was soon partnered and part of the dance. Sometimes we danced in the round and I think I danced with women as often as with men, and sometimes I danced on my own. I danced all night and felt much joy and love for everyone behind my mask, and wished Margery had been there that I might have danced with her too.

Lent came and went and then it was Eastertide. I walked out to the headland most days and longed for favourable winds and then we had word that we should ready ourselves to leave. The day after this, as if to bid us farewell, the people held one of their great yearly ceremonies, which they called 'the Wedding to the Sea'. This was so wonderful but whenever since I spoke of it, Margery said I was mistaken in many details and always making things up. Though how she knew I cannot tell, since she was yet again on her knees at St Zacharia and not there that day.

On this day a great procession left the Golden Church led by members of the city's guilds, all gloriously attired, carrying silken banners and accompanied by the music of silver trumpets and the chiming of church bells. They were followed by Council members in their glamorous robes and behind them was the Doge, the leader of the Venetian Republic, who was carried in a gilded throne, which was canopied in gold brocade, lined with blue silk and bespangled with golden stars. He wore a golden cap and had a little monkey on his lap, a green and golden parrot on his shoulder, and behind him a black man walked carrying his silver sword of state.

They processed to the landing stage where a golden ship was waiting. The Doge's throne was set on the top deck, which was furnished with many mirrors and windows of crystal glass, adorned with silken draperies hung with golden bells and plush crimson velvet. Hundreds of oarsmen, their brightly painted oars sparkling in the sunlight, rowed out into the lagoon. I'd never seen anything so wonderful before.

When the vessel returned, everyone was blessed and the Doge threw a golden ring into the waves as a sign that he was marrying the sea and would henceforth be her Lord and rule over her. The wealth of this great city came from both commerce and also dominion over various islands and territories along the way to the Holy Land. And so this marriage was intended to placate the waters and ensure continuing peace and profit. But I doubt any of our fellowship thought of trade and territories at this moment on the eve of our departure, but were minded instead to pray for a calm and peaceful voyage.

Then it was time to leave. I was thankful to have Hugh's help, in all the haste and hustle, to load our baggage onto the boat that rowed us to our galley, which was anchored far out in the lagoon. By the time we arrived there were many other small boats packed with pilgrims, bobbing up and down, crowding round the vessel, and it was a great scramble to get on board. Edwin helped to stow our bedding in the lower deck where the rest of our fellowship and scores of other pilgrims were to sleep, excepting Matthew and Hugh, who'd paid extra to bed in comfort on the upper deck.

No sooner had I heaved our mattresses into the cramped spaces that were chalked on the boards, when there was a great blast of trumpets. We climbed to the upper deck where two silken banners were unfurled, one with the pilgrim cross and the other bearing the red lion of St Mark. Then the captain appeared, to further trumpet-blasts, and stood beneath the banners. He was a most handsome man in his elegant uniform, his thick black hair braided with crimson ribbons, bows in his curly beard and he strutted back and forth until everyone was silenced. We all gathered close to Sir William to hear what he translated.

"Welcome good pilgrims, listen and take note of what I say, for I shall not tell it again. You've travelled from far and distant lands to make this sacred journey all and every one of you, but, as we know, man cannot live on spirit alone and we beseech the good Lord every day to give us our daily bread, so I'll talk about food first. We serve two delicious hot meals a day, cooked in the poop at the stern of the ship. A bugle will summon you to eat. You may make small meals there at other times but only under the guidance of the cooks, and never think of cooking in the hold. There are barrels of fresh water there too and you may help yourselves so long as it lasts."

"The wicker baskets hanging over the seas are the privies

182

for you to use at your convenience, but mind you do not miss your step and tumble into the sea for no one will fish you out. On the upper deck, near the main mast, a market will open every day at noon where you can buy or trade food and other small necessities. The rest of the time it will be a quiet place for prayer. Mass will be said there at dusk and you priests must agree amongst yourselves who and when you will do so. One priest, one Mass, once a day is what I say, I will not countenance competition between you holy men."

He paused, then walked up to several priests, looked them boldly in the face, nodded and moved on.

"You can stow your chests by the mast, but you must lash them firmly onto the deck in case of rough seas and lock them securely against thieves. We will at times anchor at some town along the coast to provision and get sweet water, and you may be permitted to go ashore and see the sights. We'll summon you back with a trumpet call and make sure you listen out for it, for if you play the laggard you'll be left behind. My crew will help you into the boats and when they do, remember your Christian charity and pay them for their service."

"If there's a storm or pirate attack you must all go down to the hold and stay there. There's never to be any drunkenness, quarrelling or thievery on my vessel, and I shall punish any such wrongdoing severely. When the bugle sounds at night that's the signal to go to bed. Those found on deck after dark will sleep forever in the sea. On board my word is law. The voyage usually takes six to eight weeks. And you must all learn patience for though I am master of the ship, the sea is my mistress not my wife. Unlike the Doge, I do not have dominion over her. True she may sometimes be gentle and kind, but she is fickle, her mood can change at any time, and then she is haughty and tempestuous. That's all you need to know, I won't answer any questions, so mark what I said and never forget, my word is the law."

Then he dismissed us and there was silence. The crew took to their oars, three men to each and suddenly one of the pilgrim groups burst into song. We all joined in with our own words. The breeze freshened as we started to leave the shelter of the islands. The sails were unfurled, the rowers shipped their oars, and in no time at all the mainsail was full of wind, as the sun set and the lights of the dwellings and churches along the coast flickered and faded away. And so, to the sound of hopeful jubilation we were finally on our way.

Had I known the hardship we were to endure I would not have been so eager to go. But it's often better not to know the trials we have to face in life or we might wish never to have been born. The nights, especially, were a torment. It was so crowded below and stifling, sleeping head to toe in the immense heat, with the stench of the bilge water, clammy sand of the ballast, reek of vomit, stink of rats' piss, and the melting pitch, which smeared our clothes and stuck to our skin and hair. The seas were mostly calm on our way over, but the lurching and rolling of the ship made many sick. It was always noisy at night even when no one was retching, squabbling, farting or snoring, with the endless creaking and groaning of timbers, the crashing and slamming of the waves against the hull and the stamping and snorting of the caged beasts that had been shipped to feed us.

The darkness was terrible, but dawn was just as bad for it was often damp and cold before sunrise. There was always a rush when the morning bugle sounded to hang our mattresses up on the hooks, and climb out of the hatches onto the deck into the fresh air. People scrambled and shoved to get to the privies first, though some of the men just pissed in the sea and you had to be careful where you stood. And there was a queue for the poop too, as there was not room enough for everyone to sit down so those who came last had to dine on the remnants, standing in the sun. The food, which was fresh and wholesome the first few days soon became foul, mostly salt-beef with onions and lentils with vinegar. The bread was black and hard, the water brackish. Soon many of us had swollen legs and blisters under our tongues, and could hardly eat or swallow.

The days were as troubling as the nights. Often it was too hot to stay on the deck unless there was room under the awning. The sun dazzled, the sea-spray dried and cracked our skin, fleas were a constant irritation. There was little space to walk, and that was often taken by the sailors for their recreation when they were not rowing. On occasion I joined small groups playing board games, telling stories and riddles or we sang together, but still the time passed slowly. If the wind dropped, the oarsmen had to row and we made little progress. Then people laid bets on when we'd reach the next port and gambled at cards, and often there were vicious brawls.

One evening I stayed on deck after the prayers, wrapped in my cloak against the breeze, and sat with my back against the mast watching the darkening skies and the blue-black sea. There were others there too, sitting in a circle and shrouded in their garments. Then one of them broke the silence and spoke in muffled tones.

"Where are you all from, and what brings you on such a perilous journey?"

"I come as a penitent from hell," one answered gruffly. "I've been a sinner all my life, withheld the tithes, stole from my neighbours, fornicated with their wives and blackened my friends' names. Then this past year my wife and children died and I sought repentance for my sins and my priest told me to make this pilgrimage as further atonement. I've suffered much hardship journeying here and now put all my trust in God that he will punish me no more, that I won't fall back into evil ways and suffer pain in the fires of the hereafter."

"My troubles are as dire as yours," spoke another. "I woke one morning to a great lameness in my legs and consulted many physicians, but they could find no cure. Then I beseeched St Anthony, offering him daily prayers and gifts but still can hardly walk. So I come to beg that I'll be healed, my luck will turn, and when I've seen the Holy City I might find heaven on earth."

"So," asked the man who'd spoken first, and I thought his voice familiar. "do you all seek freedom from chastisement, to win favours and find grace by risking your lives and making great sacrifice?"

"Curiosity makes me a palmer," mumbled a third. "I was a soldier for many years, fought in many wars, saw much cruelty and little kindness and now wander the world to see if peace can reign on earth."

"Well I come for adventure too, to see new sights, meet new women and ..."

"I pursue peace," interrupted his neighbour, "and journey to give thanks to the Blessed Virgin who banished all my sorrows whenever I sought her intercession. And I'll ask that she protect me from any ill and forgive all my past and future sins."

"We also come to worship her, for she is our mother," and all the heads turned to hear so slight a voice. I guessed it was one of the two nuns I'd seen, who always kept apart and slept on the upper deck. "And we have vowed to utter no word on this pilgrimage unless it is to speak of her. We shall sing her praises at her birthplace so she shall know us, and we'll walk where she walked in sacred silence." and she stood up and glided away.

"Yes," whispered another. "I too wish to walk in the footsteps of Our Lord, his mother and all the saints, that their goodness might be mine."

"I want to touch the sacred relics and be close to the saints so they will hear me, for when we travel from afar in dread discomfort away from friends and all that is familiar, then we can see our own lives more clearly and deepen our faith."

"That is my ardent w-w-wish too," stuttered the one who sat with his back to me. "I come in the hope that my faith m-m-might be rekindled for I suffer m-m-much doubt, and, and ..." he paused. "And there is a great emptiness in my soul."

"It matters not where I come from," said the man who'd spoken first, and now I knew it was Hugh. "I come on pilgrimage to lose and find myself. It is as if my life were mapped out from the moment of my birth, with duties to perform and roles to play, yet nothing ever changes. Then one day I woke and understood I was an exile here on earth. So now I seek my way back, through the mystery of unknowing."

Then suddenly the bugle sounded and everyone moved swiftly away, but Hugh caught sight of me and held my wrist.

"And you, what brings you here?" he asked.

"You know that Hugh; I come to look after Margery."

"And do you seek nothing for yourself, freedom from damnation, forgiveness of sins, greater understanding, a deepening of faith?"

"More faith? More understanding? I often think what a friend once told me, that charity starts at home, so I try to find my own truth within."

"Ah, my master at Heidelberg, the wise Marsilius, taught that there are only individual pilgrims and many different ways to the centre. But to travel your own path you need trust, fidelity, confident hope and the strength to withstand doubt."

Then the bugle sounded urgently once more and we parted and did not speak of such matters again till long after.

And so the days passed. Once we saw dolphins and the crew were happy saying it presaged good fortune. Another time a sailor told me he'd seen a fish with a huge beak that was sharp enough to drill holes in the hull, and which could only be driven away by looking deep into its eyes. That augured ill fortune, and soon after a call came from the crow's nest that a galley had been sighted which was not flying the Venetian flag and so believed to be a pirate ship. We were ordered below and stayed there all day in fear of our lives, unable to eat, drink, or use the privies. None of us knew what was happening.

Then we heard much shouting. It seemed we were moving swiftly, and a man said he'd heard a Venetian vessel had been attacked the day before, and bloody limbs had been seen floating in the water. Now the only sound below was fervent prayer. We were all much frightened. Finally at nightfall, the trumpet sounded and we were permitted to come up on deck. The captain told us he'd tricked the pirates, saying we had plague on board and had managed to outsail them. But we had no food that day.

When we needed fresh water and supplies we sailed into a harbour, and if we anchored far out we had to clamber down rope ladders into a boat and be rowed ashore. Each time we came to a new place Margery dragged me off to church so I never had time to explore, and the priests looked different to ours with tall hats and ornate robes. When it was time to return, trumpets sounded warning blasts and once I had to pull her away from her prayers so we weren't left behind. After that she did not come ashore again and I was weary too, as the next town looked much the same as the one before and charged even higher prices for food and water. Once I visited an island where giant cedars and chestnuts grew and I saw oranges growing on trees, but near all of us who'd been there that day returned with a fever, which soon became a bloody flux. One of the German pilgrims died and was buried at sea and I was sick and even more wearied. And so I lost count of the days. And there seemed no end to this cruel discomfort, restless seas, blazing sun and endless voyaging.

Then at dawn on the forty-first day since leaving Venice, so I was told, we dropped anchor and our vessel was still. I was on my mattress in the dark below decks, still weak from my ills when I heard loud cries and a chorus of hymns. As I clambered onto the deck I saw many of our company were on their knees in tears, while others stood at the rails crying out to disembark. And there was the sound of happy laughter from some little boys swimming in the surf, waving and calling out for coins. On the shore dark, bearded men sat on horseback, with great curved swords sheathed in sashes at their waists. We had arrived at the Holy Land.

Then the bugles sounded and some rushed to the poop then rushed back again, because this was not a call to breakfast. The silken banners were unfurled and our captain appeared in his fine regalia, but the bugles had to be blown many times before finally he could speak.

"So here we are at the start of your holy pilgrimage," he told us, "but none of you may disembark until the formalities are completed. We've sent messages to the officials and you must wait till everyone has been registered and papers written for each of you, which are your permits and promise of safe conduct. I and my crew, with some Saracens and Grey Friars will accompany you to all the holy sites, and no one of you may carry arms for we shall protect you. Your mattresses and sea chests are to remain on board, take only your sheets, bare necessities and monies to pay for your guides, mounts, entrance fees, offerings and to give tips. You have fifteen days for your visit. And make sure you attire yourselves in your simplest clothing since here you are all as one, yeoman and noble, servant and master.

You may want to bring wine ashore as the water is often foul, but mind you do so secretly for the Saracens do not permit it in their land. Once we are on our way we shall eat local food, so don't expect the kind of delicacies we've served on board. Remember to take your hats for the sun is fierce, and wear your good boots as there will be much walking, or bring bandages if you've vowed to go barefoot. But no matter how you're shod, you must keep up with us for we shall not wait for dawdlers. Take your sticks to beat off the thieves and dogs we'll meet along our way. And now to celebrate our safe arrival a fine meal is being prepared and you should eat your full, for after that there will be no more food today."

It was long past midday before the papers came and we were given leave to disembark. Some jumped out of the small boats before reaching the shore, and such was the excitement that several, including mine, overturned and so, soaked through I had to wade to land. Many knelt and kissed the sand, while others wandered on unsteady legs towards the undergrowth, where several stern men halted their progress. Then we were rounded up like cattle and driven to the end of the beach where we had to wait in the burning heat to receive our papers before being led into a cave.

Here was another unexpected horror; it was dark, dank and dripping, stinking of shit and buzzing with flies. The only way to sit down was to clear a space in the rubbish. Two oarsmen guarded the entrance and would let no one out. We kept close together and were most despondent except Martin, who argued with one of the sailors and learnt that for a groat we could go outside to relieve ourselves and purchase rushes to sleep on. He told us that on the morrow we might buy food and sweet smelling balsam, musk and attar of roses to calm our minds and mask the foul odours. So I went out with Hugh and bought some dried grasses, but slept fitfully all night long, my mind still rocking from the long days at sea, close by my mistress.

We stayed in this hellhole, St Peter's Cellars they called them, another day and night, waiting for the other pilgrim vessel and our Franciscan guides to arrive. I went out again at dawn and bought food, with Hugh helping me once more. There were some local folk on the beach, staring at us, and certainly we must have looked strange, all attired in pilgrim tunics and broad-brimmed hats. But it was good to be in the fresh air again as I bargained for my purchases, and watched the buffaloes standing up to their necks in the waters.

Then we were harried back into the darkness of the dreadful cave where Martin was telling the history of this place.

"Did you know it was here that Peter wrought his miracle and brought the saintly Tabitha back to life, who was so loved by her followers that they begged him to restore her. So too, God willing, shall we be renewed in this holy place. And nearby I've heard is Jaffa where Job once lived, and on the beach outside, right here, is where Jonah was spewn up after three days in the belly of the whale, so this really is a place of rebirth, praise be the Lord. And they've said that tomorrow at first light we'll leave for Ramleh where we'll find much solace and rest." He told us much more and we were comforted by his words.

But the second night was as distressing as the first and Hugh was asked to attend to a Frenchman who had a high fever. He died just before dawn and his friends carried him outside to bury him in the sand. We woke early but could not leave until our names were called, and were then herded to the end of the beach. It was a steep climb from there to where the beasts were waiting. Everyone pushed and scrambled and I lost Margery in the crush and was seized by a young man who grabbed my hand and shouted loudly at me as I fought to get away.

I called out in terror, but there was much noise and confusion and no way of being heard. Then I saw others around me were also being roughly handled and those in front were already mounted on asses and mules. So I let myself be lifted onto my beast and soon we were all moving, a crowd of two hundred or so, each with his own muleteer, the captain and crew in front with several Grey Friars leading the way. There were also some splendidly attired officials riding on great creatures they called camels, with small heads, humped backs and strangely soft feet that splayed out as they walked. A dozen or so soldiers followed behind us, trotting on bare feet and naked at the chest with only cloths wrapped round their loins.

I remember it well, that first ride in the Holy Land. Later my memories blurred together but this day, after the relentless monotony of the seas, there was much to behold. In parts the land was arid and dry with barely a tree and sand everywhere, until we came to a village where swathes of cotton and fields of corn grew. Most of the dwellings were of mud with small enclosures round them, where little children played, black and naked. The elderly folk sat on their heels staring blankly into the distance, and women in rags came running over to us like so many crows, cawing piteously. Some pilgrims threw coins and they fought for them in the dirt until one of the Saracens rode back, cracking a whip and growling at us.

It grew hotter and hotter and there were no trees to give us shade and the sun was so strong it hurt my eyes and made me dizzy. And so we continued for a long time until we saw buildings ahead and had to dismount and walk the rest of the way. Once through the great stone gates we assembled in a courtyard under an awning of many colours, and told to wait with our own countrymen. Then a Franciscan friar came and spoke in Latin while all around his words were translated into our own languages.

"God greet you all and welcome, good pilgrims, to the Holy Land and here to Ramleh. I'm sure you have already been sorely tested on the voyage over, but the real trials of your pilgrimage have only just begun. From now, you'll need truly penitent souls, to which you must add Christian forbearance, charity, tolerance and tact. And first let all of you be mindful of your personal property, make sure you leave nothing behind where'er we stop, for if you do so you'll never see it again.

Observe the local customs for you are guests here. None of you is to wear white for that is the traditional dress of the peoples of this land. Don't enter any mosque, which is their place of worship. Don't wander off alone. Don't carve your name on any monument or chip off pieces to take home. Don't purchase relics. Always be orderly and patient and do not rush to be first at a shrine. Avoid fights and arguments, for these are gentle people but misunderstandings do occur. Love, meekness and humility must be your rule. Pay all dues you are asked. And I beg you not to forget to include in your charity my poor brothers, the monks of Mount Sion."

Then he bid us get on our knees and started to sermonise, but I closed my ears and was soon asleep.

We bedded the next two nights in a hospice where they heated water for us over a fire and we were able to rest and wash off the filth of the sea voyage. But few of us slept because of the heat and anticipation of the journey ahead. We left Ramleh in the cool of an early evening for a place called Mount Joy, and were told to gather rushes and make our beds on the ground. Then we ate by starlight and watched the moon rise. At dawn we were woken early and saw below us in the distance the holy city, glowing in the sunrise. The descent there was rugged, stony and barren and we rode past many ruined castles, which had been built by the Crusaders, until we came to a valley with dry stone walls where olive trees grew and lemon groves, gardens of fruit and fig trees too. Then as darkness began to fall, we came into Jerusalem.

I felt great awe to be here as I recalled the Easter stories and, like the others, dismounted, took off my boots and walked barefoot into the town through the David Gate, along a dark, narrow street and into a great white courtyard paved with marble and all round it were flaming torches. Many pilgrims were on their knees, or staggering like blind men, weeping and wailing. I knelt by Margery who lay on the ground, silent for once, arms out-stretched in the likeness of a cross. I looked ahead and saw the church of the Holy Sepulchre. It was for this we had travelled so far and been so sorely tested. I lay like her too, and waited. In time we were led to the Hospital of St John for a late supper, and so to bed.

Margery remained silent throughout the next day and I stayed with her even when we were summoned to dine. At dusk we gathered again in the courtyard for the vigil at the Holy Sepulchre where we would spend all night and much of the following day. When the doors were opened at last, everyone surged forward, and we were pushed and shoved and in terror of being crushed, until suddenly we were stilled by a great shriek, and a woman's body was carried out over our heads. I do not know if she were alive or dead.

Slowly we moved forward and entered two by two, Margery and I together and then the doors were locked behind us. We were given tapers to carry, though it was difficult not to stumble, blinded as we were by the gloom and the smoke of a myriad of candles. We processed through this immense edifice up and down many flights of steps, magnificent in marble, with a multitude of columns, sculptures, altars and shrines. All around us the sounds of praying, whispering, weeping, singing, sighing and sobbing echoed from the vaulted roofs.

The guides explained each site as we came to it in many different tongues and they were truly marvellous. I saw the stone where an angel sat, the place where Adam our human father was created, where Joseph of Arimathea washed the body of Christ, where the soldiers gambled for his clothes, and another place where Mary his mother grieved, and many more. I stayed with Margery most of the time, though we were soon separated from our fellowship, and we made our way to the chapel on the rock of Mount Calvary and the hole where the cross had been planted. Then we went to the chapel of the Holy Sepulchre and here Margery fell to the ground with the candle still in her hand. Though I went to help her, she lay there groaning and would not heed me. Then she started to weep and I had never heard her cry so vehemently before.

I left her with others nearby also in great convulsions, knowing she would come to no harm. I could hear the guides still talking, but more and more pilgrims lagged behind, kissing relics, gathering little mounds of earth or squeezing fingers or a fragment of cloth through the iron bars to touch some holy object. At times there were urgent shouts as someone called that there was a column shedding tears and another that was flecked with blood, though not everyone jostled to witness these wonders. Some sat with their backs against a wall, admiring the mosaics or talking about the sculptures. I even saw two men playing chess, and not a few lay sleeping on the ground.

I did not join the crowd when they gathered for the midnight Mass, but went into other chapels where different priests called Nestorians, Copts and Armenians held services, which I thought most strange. Later I came to the chapel where Jesus first appeared to Mary Magdalene, ate some morsels I had in my satchel, then lay down and slept. It was late the next day when finally the doors were opened and I found Margery again. We had to struggle to get out into the fresh air and pushed hard to get past the hawkers who were pestering us to buy candles, relics and rosaries.

The next day Hugh bid me visit the town with him and paid a guide to take us. We were shown Pilate's house, the place where Jesus washed the feet of the apostles and the little school in an alley where Mary learnt her letters. We had time too to observe the people of this land all dressed in white, and the women wore breeches underneath their tunics and some had black veils covering their faces. We watched them going into the mosque, which was splendidly furnished with colourful carpets and lit by a thousand burning candles, saw them shedding their shoes and bathing their heads from an immense urn by the entrance, then filing quietly through the doors, not chatting loudly as so many do when going to church in our country. Later we went to a covered bazaar, tasted the food, pungent, sweet and spicy, but the people turned away and did not greet us. Whether this was from fear that we were strangers or out of hostility that we were in their country, I do not know.

From Jerusalem we went to many other places I knew from the Bible. In truth if you know the Bible then you know the Holy Land and I was much enchanted to see all those places I had read about. Sometimes we travelled at night and ate and slept outside, which was much more comfortable than in many of the hospices that were filthy and crawling with insects. Once we met a great cavalcade with an Emir, which is their name for a Lord, with his retinue, musicians and hunting-birds, and a magnificent covered cart in which, we were told, his four wives travelled. And though we all halted and our muleteers lay down with their faces in the dirt, he looked proudly ahead and passed us by.

Once we were stoned by villagers and another time were attacked by thieves though our guards beat them off, hacking ferociously. Occasionally we were beguiled by the kindness of strangers, and once a lass offered me a sweet, cool drink called sherbet. I had a great fondness for the youth who led my ass and stayed close by my side when the terrain was rough, and let me drink from his water bottle when mine was empty. I was soon accustomed to the heat, the gentle pace of my mount and the freedom to be with my own thoughts. But each time we stopped at a new place I was cross again, especially at eventide when everyone talked about their feelings and sensations much as street traders do when extolling the virtues of their wares.

Margery wept copiously at every shrine we visited, was full of complaints, suffering more and more, her back aching and feet sore especially on the path to the River Jordan. Our guides joked that the way there was perilously steep, frequented by robbers and as hot as hell so if we were not ready to go there yet, we should take a holy day of rest. But she was set on going, and as our companions refused to accompany us we befriended two friars, She did indeed look much fatigued when we arrived and grumbled that her feet were burning. So I loosed her boots and left her sitting on the riverbank bathing them in the mud, while I walked carefully into the river, mindful of the shifting sands and filled a wineskin with Jordan waters, which I'd bought for this very purpose for her to take back to Lynn.

On another day we rode to the Mount of Temptation, where Jesus was tempted for forty days but then our beasts needed rest so we had to make the ascent on foot. A wind had risen as we started up the narrow, winding path with loose stones underfoot and thorn bushes that held fast to our tunics and scratched our skin. At times we had to crawl up craggy precipices and though we could see the chapel ahead and the caves cut into the barren rock where hermits used to live, I was frightened and did not think we could go any further, neither forward or backwards and called out to our fellowship but no one would help us. Then a Saracen came and I gave him coins to take Margery up. When later she complained I had abandoned her on the hill I bit my tongue that I might not scold her. I remember this clearly now as I remember other things she forgot, or was not minded to mention.

All this was in a place some distance from Jerusalem and it was here we saw where John the Baptist was born, where Mary

Magdalene lived, where Mary and Martha shared a house and their brother Lazarus was raised from the dead. Twice we passed the ruined walls of Jericho, the hottest and most desolate place I'd ever seen, but where there were underground springs shady date palms and fragrant roses grew. Yet on many days we saw very little, as sometimes there were long waits for guides, or fellow pilgrims who were lost or slow to leave, and always there was so much talking, gossiping and complaining.

At last we came to Bethlehem, a gentle morning ride from Jerusalem, through olive groves and orchards, cypress trees and fountains flowing with cool fresh water. Everywhere along the way there was a story, and I was reminded of the Bible tales I used to tell to my Marion. Those three springs began to flow when the three kings first saw the star, there on that hillside was where the shepherds watched their flocks, here by that ruined tower was where Jacob wrestled with the angel, and there on that stone is where the Virgin sat that she and Joseph might rest.

Most of all I delighted in the church of the Nativity with its beautiful gold and blue mosaics, though the roof timbers were rotten. The descent to the grotto was so narrow that everyone had to wait their turn, and it was a place of great quiet and peace. Jesus's manger was crafted of polished marble and nearby was the stall of the ox and ass, and the air was fresh and fragrant not fetid from the stale smoke of candles.

We were shown other underground chapels too, the well into which they said the star of Bethlehem had fallen and nearby was a deep and dreadful vault where the bodies of the thousand holy Innocent babes were thrown. Here it was I wept, recalling my childhood innocence. And I found my heart was no longer made of stone.

So our travels came to an end, but not before another two

days in Ramleh. Our guides took us to various bazaars and workshops where jewellery was crafted and where we might purchase sandalwood rosary beads, painted cloths with images of all the monuments we'd visited, and maps of the Holy Land drawn on silk. I watched some pilgrims buying other curious trinkets, like a bottle which held the sound of the bells of Solomon's temple, a phial containing one of the Virgin's tears, and cedar boxes filled with the very same earth from which Adam was made. And many boasted later, as they compared their spoils, that they had bought the better bargain.

These workshops also had rooms at the back where people haggled over precious relics, and some returned to the hospice with heavy bags. A few, like Simon, hired another beast to carry their extra baggage. And Margery, despite her angry words at the market by the Rhine made some purchases too, but assured me they were offerings for religious houses in our country. Tempted though I was I'd no money for mementoes but had taken pebbles from all the places we visited as a remembrance. I put them in my boots to remind myself that all my sorrows might be stepping-stones to joy.

It was with some relief that we returned to Jaffa and saw our vessels riding at anchor, pennants dancing in the breeze and boats lined up to ferry us on board. The formalities were soon completed, though many of us were hushed when we looked back and saw the wooden crosses in the dunes marking the memory of those who'd died along the way. We boarded our ship, the bugles were blown, silken flags let down, and once we were all assembled the captain addressed us again.

"Now, good Christians, let me remind you I am your master and the seas my inconstant mistress. But you all know my rules, so I shan't waste breath telling them again. Just harken this. I advise you to practice that patience and fortitude you learnt on pilgrimage. You will need it, I promise you, for our voyage back will be much more arduous than the crossing over. The winds are now contrary so it will take much longer, we have fewer provisions on board and the season of storms is approaching."

He said much more but I was too tired to pay him attention. And in truth my spirits fell as soon as the oarsmen rowed out of the bay and the sails were set, for the roll and pitch of our ship was much more uncomfortable than the journey out, our mattresses damp and mildewed, the hold hotter and stinking, and I missed the fresh air and the gay chatter of the Saracens. Margery came out of her reverie for a while and was boisterous, assuring all that God had promised her we'd reach home safely, and though I wished it I was not minded to pay attention to her visions.

It took us a week to find our sea legs and when we reached our first anchorage only a few pilgrims went ashore. A lethargy overcame nearly everybody; we had little appetite and mostly lay on our mattresses. Then news came that one of the sailors had died. Baskets of stale bread and a barrel of water were lowered into the hold, and piss-pots too, and we were forbidden up on deck less we also catch the fever.

Next we heard several strange fish had been seen, the one we'd been told of before that could pierce through wood, and another that puffed up like a huge ball and spat out water which stained the seas red. The crew became angry, for according to their lore this presaged ill fortune, and they guessed some had brought Jordan water and relics on board, which was also deemed unlucky. They came one night and searched us roughly, emptied our water bottles and carried away much loot, though many hid their souvenirs in the ballast sand and retrieved them later.

No one else died of the sickness and a few days later we were allowed on deck again though many remained below, sick with the pitching of the vessel. There was no provisioning at the next town along the coast, for beacons had been lit on the harbour walls warning of pestilence. Now we had only one meal a day and a single flagon of water. The sailors had supplies of their own and if we were thirsty we had to buy from them at great expense. Our progress was slow, fighting against the winds and contrary seas. To keep their spirits up, people told each other of all the wonderful sights they'd seen, but more and more they lost their marvel and freshness as if shrouded in mist or like a distant dream. The days dragged endlessly by.

One evening we were suddenly becalmed, the seas scumming white and great flocks of birds following in our wake. It was even more difficult to sleep in this stillness than with the tossing and lurching we'd endured before. Then just before dawn the wind began to freshen. I'd climbed on deck to get some water when something started to sting my face. Little piles of sand, a fine red dust, was blowing along the timbers, like those spirit lights or will o' the wisps that dance above the marshes outside Lynn, beckoning you to your doom. Others joined me and a gale started to blow, and soon our vessel was climbing up huge waves and falling into troughs, with howling winds and skies growing increasing dark. Many were retching and of our fellowship Martin was the worst and Margery rushed to his side, offering comfort.

But he cringed and clung to the rail and was violently sick. When his vomiting was finished, he swore he'd not made this journey just to end at the bottom of the ocean. Margery seemed hardly to notice the wild winds and squalling seas and stayed close by, holding his arm, as our galley rose and fell between the waves which poured over the deck, soaking us all.

Then the captain ordered the mainsail be lowered lest it rip in the wind. Some sailors made their way over to us, and told us to draw scraps of paper from a bag. Each had the name of a saint on it, and they bade us swear an oath to have a Mass said in his name if ever we made safe return to Venice. They told us to start praying at once for they'd never known such a tempest. Then the rain came lashing down in swirls, daylight disappeared, people slithered along the deck and the captain ordered us all below. A great wave swept over us as we scrambled into the hold, and there were loud crashes and cries as people fought to get there first. Then the hatches were closed and we were left in utter darkness.

First there was near silence as everyone murmured earnest prayers, until someone started blathering noisily. It was Martin again. He, who had been so helpful when we were shut in those dreadful caves, he was now a whimpering child. Margery went over to him shouting against the gale and despite their mortal terror, everyone hushed to hear her words.

"Have faith Martin and quit this nonsense. Our Lord spoke to me and told me not to be afraid, for no one will die in any ship I sail in."

She continued to shout loudly that everyone would be safe in her company and they needed to trust her.

He did not take kindly to being singled out like this and yelled that he wished she were at the bottom of the sea like Jonah, blaming her for the storm.

"Yes," she shouted back, as the seas smashed savagely against the hull. "I was once like Jonah, just as you now are Martin.

When God ordered him to go to Nineveh and prophesy against it because of the wickedness of the people, he feared they wouldn't listen to him, so he took another ship sailing in the opposite direction. But when the seas grew wild, just as they are now, God save us, and the ship was about to break up, the sailors cast lots to find out who had brought this evil upon them. In truth he who does not have faith in our Lord is full of evil."

A great crack from the deck above startled us, and the vessel heaved to one side. We all slid one against another, then tipped the other way and we tumbled again, and still she continued.

"Yes, full of evil. Then Jonah understood he could not escape from God, and confessed his sin, was thrown overboard and swallowed up by a whale. There, in the great belly of Leviathan, he pleaded with God. After three days God, in his merciful goodness, heard his prayer and caused the whale to vomit him up, unharmed, onto dry land - we saw the place in Jaffa."

There were more eerie bangs and terrifying thumps above us, but this did not stop her.

"You remember what happened then, Martin. Jonah did go to Nineveh and warned the citizens that unless they repented, their city would be overthrown. And they did listen and the King proclaimed a fast and put on sackcloth and sat in ashes, and all the citizens were humbled. But still Jonah was faithless and forgot that God is full of charity and always spares those who repent."

Another great crash silenced her for just a moment, but not for long.

"So Martin," she called out triumphantly, "never forget, this is no foundering ship of fools and God is at the helm. Repent Martin, repent and you will be spared. Have faith, believe in me and we shall all be saved."

This is not what a man like Martin wants to hear in the teeth of a tempest, when he has cursed and made a fool of himself and is covered in vomit. He called her a Jonah again, puffed up with pride, and asked why God should favour only her with revelations. But she clung to him and continued to tell stories in that fearful darkness down in the hold, and he was too weak and fearful to move away.

At last he was quieted and everyone started praying again. The roar and tumult of the seas, the groans of the sick, moans of the fearful and those who'd been hurt in the scramble to get into the hold, were almost drowned by the murmur of confessions and prayer. It seemed as if Death had been chasing us from the moment we left the Holy Land. I've known storms that raged inside me and thought them hell. But this tempest was not of my making, and I found strange comfort in our common peril and the knowledge that I was not alone in my suffering.

In time the wind abated and the storm subsided. When finally the seas calmed, the hatches were opened and the men were at the oars. But there was much damage; the poop had been washed away and the mast split in two. The sailors had to row until we came to harbour, where we spent several days while the vessel was repaired. We were much chastened but cheered by fair weather and the promise of a safe return. Though we had been blown off course, the winds were now set fair and our captain assured us we would be back in Venice before the week was out.

6

Rome, Bishop's Lynn, Bristol, Compostela, 1414–1417

'at last I see you for who you truly are'

I awoke with much joy as a cry rang out from the crow's nest, and once on deck saw a sailor pointing to the islands around Venice, the dome of St Mark's glittering distantly in the dawn light. Most of our fellowship were already up and eager with anticipation like me. We'd suffered so much on the voyage back, but now were near land again, our vessel was still, sails furled, anchors dropped and the oarsmen at rest. And everyone joined in singing the *Te Deum* to give thanks for our safe return.

Small boats came skimming across the lagoon with fruit, bread, dried meats, cheese and sweet water. We lowered baskets and haggled over prices, the captain ordered the last barrel of wine be breeched and told the cooks to prepare an early dinner. There was a great feast with the food many had just bought and much revelry, with dancing to the music of trumpets and drums.

Margery too was overjoyed and greeted our companions but they turned their backs and snubbed her. They'd said not one word to each other during the last week of the voyage, she'd spent those days lying on her mattress in tearful prayer while they were worn out from the rigours of the storm. But I knew they'd be planning the journey on to Rome, then saw some of them talking and went over to join them.

"We have to make haste the moment we're back," William was saying, then saw me, nodded and continued, "so I don't think we can travel with you and Mistress Kempe to Rome."

"Or have any more meals with her," said Martin.

"And I," said Godfrey, "can't stomach any more of her preaching ..."

"And don't forget her visions," added Simon, "I warrant they come from the Devil, I wouldn't go with her even for a hundred pounds."

"Well, let us not be so unkind and unchristian," concluded William, looking at me again. "I'm sure Mistress Kempe will be pleased to have more time to rest after all our trials, then you can find a man to bring her to Rome. It's your responsibility to look after her and, as you just heard, none us want to travel with her anymore."

I was outraged that they planned to desert us and resolved to tell Margery that they were going to leave quickly and so make sure we went with them.

When the Venetian officials had come on board and were satisfied we carried no plague, the trumpets were blown and only when it was completely silent did our peacock captain appear one last time and gave us leave to disembark,

"... and don't forget how generously we've treated you and please return the complement," he said, passing round a large leather bag already clinking with coins.

People started heaving their sacks and mattresses onto the deck, pushing to get to the front of the line. I'd already prepared our belongings so we all left together and soon arrived, much wearied, at the St George. I'd asked Edwin to sell our bedding and he returned with the money the following evening. For sure they were impatient to leave, but Margery paid no heed to me, though I didn't tell her everything I'd heard.

"Tomorrow we'll collect the rest of the ducats Giovanni has in keeping for me, and ask him where to find a tailor to make my white vestments. Then we'll visit St Zacharia and tell them of my sweet meditations."

I'd no doubt the nuns would admire her new clothes fashioned in the latest Venetian style but this wasn't the time for making a display.

"Margery, please wait till we're in Rome. William is planning to leave very soon and you heard how the roads are thick with thieves, but Edwin and Robert have weapons and they'll hire a guide."

"And who gives you the right to say when I should travel and how I should dress? Now I've been to the Holy Land it is mete I wear white."

"I don't doubt that Margery, but we must be ready to go with the others."

"O you faithless wench. God will let me know when it's time to leave."

So despite my protests we left to meet Giovanni the next morning, and when we returned in the afternoon our fellowship was gone. I cursed myself for not taking greater precautions, Margery for her crazy presumptions and Priest William for his unkindness.

The old hunchback, with his long pinched face and ragged coat, was still sitting on the steps outside our inn, just as he had the day we arrived. I'd heard him salute William in Latin and wondered if he was a mendicant friar. Now Margery went over to him and asked him who he was.

"God be with yourselves," he said. "I'm from Ireland, my

back was broken in an illness and my name is Richard."

"Well met," she answered. "You're just the man I was waiting for and now you'll take me to Rome."

"No, that I shall not. I know your countrymen left you behind, though God knows why they'd do such a thing. I saw them rush off in a rare haste this morning, but they have a guard of archers while I have nothing, just this stick and my old patched cloak. The road is dangerous and I couldn't keep you safe."

"Good Richard," said Margery, "you'll have nothing to fear if you're with me. Before I left on pilgrimage a holy man decreed that when my friends deserted me I'd meet an old cripple who'd help me. No one will harm us, you looking so frail and the two of us with just our pilgrim clothes and small sacks of belongings. God will look after us and you'll be well paid."

When she mentioned the sum he quickly agreed and I was truly frightened. I thought her foolhardy, there was no one to vouch for him and we might be robbed along the way. But sometimes it was as if she really had a guardian angel and though the spirit had not warned her we'd be abandoned nor opened her ears to my cautions, she was confident the hunchback was waiting there just for her. So we arranged to leave the following day, as soon as he'd bought a pack animal to carry our belongings.

It was good to be on the road once more, my feet on the earth. Now that Margery had a new audience, she began to recount her daily liturgy of devotions and visions, but I didn't have to listen anymore. Then sometime past noon while we were resting in the shade, I heard voices coming along the track, and a gentlewoman with her maidservant and two Grey Friars appeared. One of the friars was leading an ass, loaded with bags and a carved chest like the ones we'd seen in the Ramleh bazaar.

They greeted us and spoke to Richard, who told me they

too had returned from the Holy Land a few weeks before and were on pilgrimage to Assisi for a celebratory Mass. Then the gentlewoman opened her chest and showed us a life-sized image of the baby Jesus and the moment Margery saw it, she shrieked and her body heaved and shook, and the friars were much startled. When Richard explained her sobs came from her compassion for the childhood of Jesus they were greatly moved and said we might travel with them, and they'd pay for our food and lodging too.

And so we set off, though Richard said he'd make his own way during the day and join us at nightfall. The friars did not rush us, the road was easy, we were well cared for, and as neither they nor the gentlewoman could understand Margery she ceased her storytelling. For the first time in many months I was able to be alone, without any pilgrim talk. I welcomed those quiet empty days as I find it is almost impossible, even now, to have my own true thoughts and think clearly when I'm in a crowd with everyone talking, judging and commenting, which I can when I'm in my own solitude. I felt fresher and at peace.

Whenever we came to a town or village the friars preached outside the church or in the market square. Then Lucia opened her chest and brought out the baby Jesus, and Margery would begin weeping, holding it in her arms to nurse it at her breast, as the womenfolk gathered round, stroking and kissing it and sometimes dressing it in a little smock, hoping that any child who wore it after would be free from sickness. Occasionally a young woman reached out and pressed it to her belly and I saw the pain of Sarah in her eyes, the bitterness of barrenness.

The more attention that was paid to the doll, the louder Margery's cries became while the friars continued to preach, and it was sometimes truly deafening. Lucia also had a carved wooden bowl, which she placed at the foot of the chest. They received large sums after each showing, and sometimes a little golden bracelet to put on the Jesus-doll's wrist, a rattle or silver teething-ring and once, a toy knight on horseback moulded out of clay. Everyone seemed content, even Margery though she had no one to talk to but me.

Richard joined us every evening. Sometimes he was already waiting when the babe was put on display, and seeing me apart from the crowd often drew me aside.

"God be with you, sister. So here's your mistress again with her fountain of tears. My, she is a queer one, and I've seen her lamentations many a day now. Is that a true thing she says, would you be telling me, that God speaks to her and she has a sweet dalliance with Jesus every day? I never did see such a queer one before.

Now I'm wondering what she is, for either she's a saint or has lost her wits. And what would you be saying, since you've served her for so many years? For if she be a true visionary and I condemn her as a mad woman, then by all the saints I'll surely burn in hell."

I said nothing, I had no answer to that.

"I'm sure you can tell that I am a priest and for a penance was commanded to beg my way to Rome which is why I make my own way rather than travel with you, though to be sure I don't like taking from the poor. As for pilgrimage and venerating the saints, well I'm full of doubts but that doesn't sit well for a man of the cloth, and I don't know whether it is God or the Devil who sends me these contrary thoughts."

He was so earnest, this bent-backed Richard with his need to talk.

"I'm thinking too, did you ever speak with any travellers you meet along the road? I hear tell there are others like me who have similar misgivings and are sometimes accused of following Wycliffe. I'm also told there are new laws in our country, and anyone found reading or talking together about such things are taken to the Justices and flogged, so I don't know what to think anymore."

I wondered why he told me this, I was after all just Margery's maidservant.

"For sure I'm much dismayed. The people hereabouts are even poorer than in Ireland. Everywhere there is riot, no one keeps order, not even in Rome. That's why the roads are so dangerous and brigands abound. But would you ever be believing this, on my way here and there I've met with so much generosity that my heart breaks. Though the common folk are poor, they give their last crust of bread to any stranger in need, while those who are rich bake every day and have more than they require but they keep it all to themselves.

Generosity is free, a gift of grace," he continued, his gaunt features softening into a wide smile, "it belongs to all of us. Possessions are entrusted to us so we may give them away. If you hold on to them, they own and imprison you. Share them and you grow wings …"

We travelled like this for many days and I had a growing sense of freedom. The days had a gentle rhythm of their own as we made our mostly silent journey, until we came to a settlement where the Jesus baby was displayed, the friars preached, money was collected and Margery groaned and wept. She had too little Italian to sermonize but could still show off her own treasures like her new rosary beads, which had the exact measurements of the Holy Sepulchre and had lain in the chapel during our vigil there. These were much admired and I noticed how the women looked at us with envy and respect.

They too would have liked to travel beyond the confines of their homes, see the world and learn for themselves. And sometimes, when there was only one bed where we were lodged at night, which Margery and Lucia shared, I bedded with Bettina, the maidservant, on a straw mattress on the floor. Then we'd talk about our adventures in the Holy Land, in the simple Italian I'd already learnt, and in the telling of them I came to appreciate my travels more.

One morning we woke to hear Margery in a great temper, something I hadn't heard for a long while. She was arguing with Lucia and the mistress of the house, and despite the shouts and muddle of languages it was easy to understand what had happened.

"Where's my ring, my special ring, where's it gone?"

"Your ring?" asked Lucia.

"Yes, my good ring, my marriage ring, my wedding ring to my own sweet Jesus, I cannot find it …"

"Your wedding to Jesus, married to Jesus?"

"Yes, yes, I had it last night. Now it's gone, someone must have taken it …"

Margery treasured this ring greatly. She'd commissioned it with some of the money Bishop Repyngdon had given her, and now of course it was twice as precious since it had lain all night on the Holy Sepulchre. She usually tied it to her purse string when she slept, the purse she always wore around her neck. It must have fallen off and she was determined it had been stolen. She'd done the same to me once when a favourite bracelet had gone astray, and had hit me hard before I was able to calm her.

We found the ring at last, as we had the trinket before: it was in a dark corner under the bed. But Margery? She sulked all day. It's hard for people like her who dedicate their lives to God, they're so single-minded they can never believe they're not as good as they wish and cannot accept they might occasionally be a little bit bad or wrong, just like the rest of us. When they fail, they judge themselves truly evil and find this unbearable. That's Margery with her boundless wish for penance and the endless sins she can never stop confessing, like a dog returning to eat its own vomit, though she often told me she'd been forgiven all her past transgressions long ago. In truth, those who strive to be angels have devils trailing in their shadows.

At least the ring was found, but it spoilt the friendship between us all, and there was no showing of the wooden doll that day.

Then happily Margery had something new to think about. We came to Assisi, a small walled town perched on top of a hill and once again we were among pilgrims with their different banners and songs, tunics and badges, so now she had new folk to talk to. We said goodbye to Lucia, Bettina and the two friars. Though I saw them here and there in a church or shrine along the way, they no longer wanted to know us.

It was still a few days short of the special Mass but there was much to see like Our Lady's veil, which we were told had been used to swaddle Jesus. I remembered then one of the Grey Friars in Lynn talking about it and he'd said for all the trials of childbirth, the Virgin had even greater sorrows to bear when her son was crucified. This was just after Margery's last son was born, weakling that he was. And she, hearing the story with little Edward lying in her lap, had unravelled part of his swaddling cloth and wiped her tears away. After that the cloth continued to unravel, for he died a few months later, like his brother Edmond before him. By then our tears were dry for any dead baby, we'd wept for so many of them.

Richard and I had more time to speak now Margery was busy on her knees. He was worried about reports of worsening perils on the road and didn't want to travel alone with us. We'd both seen a lady arrive in town with many knights and maids and one of them, a woman called Zita, understood my questions and told me her mistress's name was Lady Margaret Florentyne. They'd travelled from Rome for the Assisi Mass and were returning home soon after. Richard asked if we might join them, and since Margery spent all her time in church with the other pilgrims, I had the chance to be on my own once again, free from cares and concerns.

A little distance beyond the town walls, in the forest at the foot of the hill, was a small chapel where the townsfolk said angels sometimes sang. There were many simple huts there for those followers of St Francis who wished to live in peace away from the crowds. I was walking there one morning and saw Zita again with two other maidens. She called me over, laughing and waving, asked my name and Beatrice, who was the sweetest damsel I ever saw, showed me the coronet of roses she was weaving.

"Look you here" she said slowly so I could follow her meaning. "Look at these beautiful roses. They bloom throughout the year in any soil but have no thorns, and their fragrance is the perfume of Paradise."

"And that's why," explained Zita, "it's called the Paradise rose."

"Paradise may be, smelling of heaven and without a single prickle," added the other young woman, a smiling, buxom wench, "but it wasn't about Paradise the holy Francis was thinking of when he tore off all his clothes and jumped naked into the brambles. It was the thorn in his flesh, the temptation of his own prick he wanted to be rid of as well as his breeches."

"O Flora," said Beatrice blushing, "do you never stop thinking about men and their sex?"

We all laughed and Beatrice shyly handed me her wreath. It came to my mind then that a rose without thorns is a monstrosity as well as a marvel. We'd all like to have the blossom of joy without the prick of conscience, but life is seldom like that.

Zita took me to another place, a little monastery just outside the city walls, called San Damiano. It was the home of many nuns named the Poor Clares after their first abbess. We spent the afternoon there, helping in the kitchens and putting out herbs, lavender and marigold blossoms to dry in the sun. I was comforted by the modest industry of these simple women and thought that my long service to Margery had not been such a trial after all. But then as has happened before, I soon forgot.

Soon after the Assisi Mass we joined Lady Florentyne's party. Richard went ahead with Margery, Lady Margaret and her chaplain, and I heard him interpreting Margery's daily discourse. I travelled with the maidservants who were always full of mirth, and was thankful I could now speak their language fairly well. They often talked about Rome and the mansion they lived in, which was enclosed by a high wall and protected by fortified towers.

"And when you're there you'll surely come and visit us," said Flora. "We have beautiful gardens and fountains too. Many years ago it was a pagan palace and in our park there are statues of naked men and women, images of the gods of ancient times. They're covered in vines but I know where to find them and they're wonderful to behold. There's no shame in their nakedness, and when I look at them I feel like ripping off my clothes too just like the good man Francis."

"And I," added Zita, "will show you many palaces and monuments outside the walls. Our city was once the centre of the world and conquered many countries and our emperors were great heroes. But now we don't have stable governance and the roads and squares are littered and sometimes foul with excrement. You have to be careful where you go for wolves and vagabonds roam around even in daylight."

"O Zita, you give such a gloomy account of our city, but it's wondrous fair despite all that. And surely," said Beatrice turning to me, "you'll take your mistress to worship in our magnificent churches. It's true many are ruinous as there's no money to repair them, but still you'll see how noble and holy they are. And many have miraculous relics, like the arm of St Matthew, and there's St Peter's head and the finger of St Thomas too and no Flora, don't make a tease about Jesus's foreskin, even the blessed Bridget knew it to be true."

"Beatrice you know I don't care a fig for dead flesh," said Flora as she put an arm round me. "But I'll show you a real miracle, a lusty living man, and we'll also go and see the marble face of a huge grotesque, on one of the city walls, with his gaping grimacing mouth. You can poke your finger right into it and knowing you, you're bound to get it out again easily, though it snaps firmly shut if a liar tries that trick. That's where I take my men friends, to find out if their sweet-talk is true or not."

And so the days passed in idle, pleasant chatter. Sometimes I helped Zita with her tasks, for these people were not travelling as poor pilgrims but had brought tents to sleep in, mattresses, pillows and bed linen too. They had hunting dogs and falcons, and twice we rested while they took a day of recreation. I rarely saw Margery except when she required. She was often upset because she couldn't talk to Lady Florentyne on her own. She never had the knack for foreign tongues, and was surly and silent too when the company gathered round the fire in the evenings and took their pleasure, drinking, singing and dancing. I knew she was impatient and missed the daily spiritual discourse but she wouldn't have thought to join us, and I didn't ask her.

Writing this now, as I sit in the byre overlooking the sea, with only Agnes for company and she as silent as me that sometimes we do not speak for days, I remember those times with much joy. I'd never known such warm, kindly women and as we chatted about our lives and they came to know me, so I knew myself better. It was indeed a happy time and I was sad when we came to Rome and I had to exchange my gay new friends for the sober sentiments of my lady.

Richard led us through the city to the Hospice of St Thomas where we met our companions. They were surprised to see us in such good spirits. Certainly we must have had an easier journey than they. Margery did not scold them and even seemed pleased to see them again. Her spirits had lifted as soon as we neared Rome and she saw so many spires on the skyline and heard the pealing of church bells.

At first there was peace again amongst our fellowship. Margery's immediate concern was to find a tailor. She bid me ask Zita where she should go, and I no longer had reason to deny her. Richard came to show us the most important churches, so we were rarely in the hospice those first few days. Then came the first dinner when we all gathered together and Margery entered in her new white vestments. Everyone gasped, they were still wearing their pilgrim tunics, as was I.

We sat down to eat and share our adventures on the road to Rome. I wanted to tell them about Lady Florentyne and her company, but Margery had not yet had the chance to speak about Assisi and all the sacred relics. And the more she talked, the more self-righteous she became and the more her tears began to flow. One by one our companions left the table, and once again a pattern was established. Either they arrived early and talked boisterously together, while Margery had to sit at the end of the table and could not make herself heard, or, if they came in separately, they sat as far away as possible, turning their backs on her.

One night soon after, Priest William came to talk to me.

"God save you, mistress, fare you well? And Mistress Kempe, how is she? I have a serious matter to discuss but since she's not here, you may tell her for me."

I was sure he had some complaint, but could not imagine what it might be.

"As you know this hospice was founded in memory of the blessed Thomas Becket and is a refuge for poor English pilgrims, but we all know Mistress Kempe isn't poor. She has money enough to buy fine new clothes and I warrant she still has a pocketful of ducats. So rather than remain here and deprive a needy pilgrim of a bed, she must leave the hospice forthwith and find other living quarters."

"But Sir, any money my mistress has is for our journey home, and the hospice isn't full so we're not taking anyone's bed."

"Be that as it may, but more pilgrims will be arriving soon. And it was the Master of the hospice himself who decreed she should leave, even though I pleaded with him. So tell her immediately and help her make ready to leave."

I didn't believe him for a moment and hated him for his hypocrisy.

The next morning, as we were walking along the riverbank towards a church, I started to speak with her but she was not concerned when I repeated what William had said.

"Have you forgotten how often I've told you that I find him lacking in godliness, and what's more he refuses to hear my confessions every day, saying once a week is sufficient for an ordinary woman like me. I can't abide him and as we'll be staying in Rome till Easter, I've asked Richard to find me somewhere else to live."

As was usual now the more she faced rejection, the more she revelled in luxurious thoughts of salvation.

"But Margery, you already spend too much time on your own, you don't speak the language and you like having people to talk to."

"So what do you know about it," she snapped. "I have to have solitude for my sacred quest and don't need company anymore, especially not those who break their pilgrim vows and make merry all the time."

"Then don't speak to them, just let them be, and if you entrust your monies to Matthew as we did when first we left England, then you can truthfully claim to be a poor pilgrim and remain in comfort at the hospice."

"And who do you think you are to talk about my personal affairs and why should I need comfort when I think of the sufferings of Our Lord?" she raged.

"At least let me come with you and … "

But just then we saw Richard waving from the riverbank on other side and climbing into a small boat to cross over, and Margery hurried towards to him.

He greeted us and said he'd found new lodgings for her and also a confessor who promised to hear her confession every day, though he warned her he spoke no English. Margery was delighted, insisting we return instantly to pack her belongings and I realised she had no intention of letting me go with her. She was leaving me without any means of support or thought for my comfort.

Margery's hostess Maria was an elderly widow who spoke a little English and had a boy in service who would take Margery to whatever church she chose. Richard settled all the details about meals, rent and laundry and then we left her. He promised to visit her occasionally and let me know how she was. I was worried for her and more so for myself for she had left me almost penniless. But William came after dinner, once he'd heard that Margery had gone, and said the Master was looking for help with the provisioning and he'd recommended me. And I was grateful for that, so at least I had some occupation and money to pay for food and other small necessities.

Richard was true to his word. To begin with he came almost every day to tell me about Margery. Although I was usually busy at the hospice and she never sent for me, I sometimes walked past her lodgings and once heard great outcry in the street nearby and asked what was happening.

"Oh it's that foreign woman again, a woman just like you, from England isn't it? She often walks here up and down, staying at Maria's place so they tells me, walking up and down. Always in white clothes she is, a most holy woman though we don't understand a word she says, praying and weeping as she walks, seeing nothing and nobody, nor minding her way, like a blind woman she is ..."

"Tis true, she's often deep in her devotions but no, not blind, that she ain't," said another. "Why, if there's a boy playing in the street, then all of a flash she comes out of her daze, picks him up, hugs and kisses him and starts weeping and laughing."

"And many of us were afeared she'd steal our little boys away …"

"And not only our little boys …"

"Yes, what was that about your son, Elissa, that gave you such a fright?"

"That it did. It was when Bruno was talking with friends one day …"

"And you should see Bruno, he's the most handsomest young man in all of Rome, we'd all like to have a son like Bruno …"

"Talking to his friends he was, right here, and then this foreign woman comes by … I saw her smiling at him, as if love had struck her with one of his arrows."

"Elissa, that's not what you said, you said she had the evil eye …"

"Yes but that was before I spoke with her priest and he told me it was only for love of the manhood of Christ that she worshipped young men, so I'd no need to fret. So now we're used to her we pay no attention unless a new boy comes to our district."

It was silent again, but I worried what Margery might do next.

The fierce heat of the summer months began to diminish and it was peaceful in the hospice. One evening there was much excitement at our table, for on the morrow it was the vigil of the holy Bridget who'd lived close by. She'd died some thirty years before but her maidservant was still alive and Zita, whom I often saw at the market, knew her well and promised to take me to meet her. Although she was ancient, her memory was clear and she had many stories to tell about her mistress, how sweet and unassuming she was. Knowing how much Margery enjoyed these tales, I hurried to her lodgings, thinking how pleased she'd be when I offered to introduce her to Bridget's maid and translate for her.

But when she heard me, she was angry.

"So, now you deign to come and visit, but only to boast about yourself and other maidservants, having deserted me all these weeks, leaving me quite alone. Well, I shouldn't have expected anything better from you. My priest warned me about you and you never did look after me properly."

This was not the response I was expecting, but as always I had no time to protest.

"Well, you're only a servant so wouldn't know what it is to be dutiful. You've never had to bear the burden of the marriage debt and learn how to serve others. In truth you are neither a Mary nor a Martha, whatever you choose to call yourself, so how could you know what it really means to be a handmaid? I'd make a much better maidservant than you, for sure."

"But Margery, it was you who deserted me and left me alone at the hospice, and I did implore you not to spend so much time on your own."

"As I told you before, solitude is the saintly path. Anyhow you knew I was on my own so why didn't you come to me?"

"Because you never sent for me and made it clear you didn't want me. Of course I'd have come if you'd asked."

"So Missie, now you make excuses and preach to me, and tell me what to do." She narrowed her eyes and stared at me a long while.

Then she said:

"Dear God, at last I see you for who you truly are, perfidious wench. Not a handmaid at all but a false and wanton strumpet, just like your mother."

At that, all feeling drained from me, my head felt so empty as if my eyeballs were being sucked up into a whirling void, and I was blinded and could barely find my way out. I could not forgive her that, and resolved never to see her again.

Some weeks later, November time perhaps for it was wet and windy, Richard came to visit and was exceeding worried. He said Margery had been fasting for over a month and he'd recently found her in a swoon on the floor of the Church of the Apostles. She'd had one of her visions, she didn't tell him what, but it was as if she were full of air without any bodily flesh. She told him she'd been ravished by the fire of love, by heavenly perfumes and celestial music. And she asked to borrow more money as she'd spent everything he'd already lent her on offerings and candles. And he begged me again to go to her.

I didn't want to see her ever again after our last meeting and wished she might experience some dreadful suffering of her own, so I made no promises. But the next day I heard more news of her. Many of our fellowship had gone to view some ancient monuments and when they returned Hugh came to speak with me.

"We were just leaving the place when we saw a mob of womenfolk swaying in a circle, jeering and joking, and there was Margery standing in the centre. She was most dishevelled, dressed in her pilgrim garb and everyone was taunting her, calling out, 'White clothes, pilgrim clothes, dirty clothes, where's the maiden now … pilgrim clothes, dirty clothes, dirty old woman, so have you been robbed of your virginity too, as well as your fine white clothes?

I offered to help but she told me to go away and the crowd soon left, tired of their spiteful game. She didn't look well and I'm concerned about her. Do please go to see her and I'll give you a potion that may bring her to better balance. You cannot let her suffer so."

I was much disturbed by Hugh's earnest pleas and saw how uncharitable I had been, but when I went to her lodgings, she was not there. Maria said she'd now turned maidservant and was living in another part of the city. So I sought out Richard and begged him go and find her.

"I'd been thinking to visit her but didn't know where to look. Then I met her confessor and when he named the district I was shocked, for it's the meanest place in all of Rome. It's roaming with cutpurses, though that's hardly a problem for herself as I doubt she has a single grosso left. Wenceslas said he'd tasked her with serving an old woman for nigh on six weeks, though to be sure I don't know why. I'm thinking it would be a very harsh penance for she's not used to work or poverty.

Now would you ever be believing this, when I asked around everyone was talking about her? You know what people are like, whenever someone new arrives they gaggle up in a gang, especially if it's a foreign woman they can't understand and is always in tears. They sent me off to the old lady's place and there was your mistress in a filthy hovel with no bed to sleep on, just rushes on the earth, an excuse of a fire smouldering in the hearth, though you'd have to sit right in it to get any warmth, and a pot nearby where a rat was feasting.

The poor old lady was lying in a dark corner, may God preserve her. Margery was just going to collect water and firewood and told me to leave as she wanted to go begging on her own."

I was shocked to hear this and he had more to tell.

"I'm sorry for her and angry too since she's spent all the money I lent her, money I'd earned from guiding pilgrims round the city, and now she can't pay me back. And she was really filthy, with sores on her hands and lice crawling over her, her boots broken, her tunic torn and patched with grime, and she wasn't even steady on her feet. But would she ever listen to a word I said? No, that she would not, and I don't know what I might do for it isn't my business to look after her."

I felt both resentful and guilty. Serving her again would be a heavy price to pay for her cruelty to me but I knew it really was my duty to care for her. Richard also said he could no longer be of service to us as he was planning to leave Rome in the next few days. So he bid me farewell, and we did not meet again until some two years after.

Now there was no one to look after Margery and I could not let her starve.

Soon after this a new pilgrim arrived at the hospice, a noble lord travelling as a commoner in an act of humility. I told him about Margery and he gave me money to take to her so she could buy food for herself and the old lady. I spoke to Zita too who sent an invitation from her mistress's house, and after they met again Lady Florentyne sent Margery a hamper twice a week, as did one of her friends who was also inclined to charity. So all in all she was well cared for. The local people came to love her too, for she had a kindly nature when she was calm and at peace within herself.

When our fellowship heard of her popularity, they sent me with messages asking her to come back once her penance was over. Since I now had monies from my labours I agreed to meet half her costs if they paid the rest. She returned soon after Christmastide but I wouldn't work as her maidservant any more, only serve her as I did the other pilgrims. And soon she had something else to occupy her. Lawrence, a priest newly arrived from England, brought money from various of her acquaintances that she might pray for them, and to fund her journey back to Lynn.

She was even more in favour when our fellowship heard our countrymen held her in such high regard, and less fussed when she started wearing white again. In fact her piety enhanced the reputation of them all. But of course it was a peace that could not last. William remained angry and started to question the problem of her confessor. How, he asked, could a German priest understand an English woman when neither spoke the other's language?

Most had grown tired of William's goading. Margery rarely recounted pious stories at table anymore, since she now had a noble lord and another priest to charm. Yet she insisted that Wenceslas had been able to understand her confessions after just one week, and claimed it was a miracle. It was Priest Lawrence who proposed a solution, which satisfied everyone. The day before Ash Wednesday was a time of festivities and he suggested Wenceslas be invited to join our celebrations and Margery tell a story from Scripture in her own words and afterwards he could recount it in Latin.

There was much rejoicing and laughter as the company assembled for dinner that Fat Tuesday eve. Wenceslas didn't mingle with the rest of us but stayed with the other priests speaking Latin. After the sweetmeats were brought in and the minstrels had finished singing, the Master rapped on the table and turning to Margery asked her to tell her tale. And at that moment I saw the Mistress Kempe I'd known in Lynn, full of fire and wit. She stood up, looked to where the priests sat and bowed her head, then to our company, and then lifted her goblet to Priest William.

"Good sirs and fellow pilgrims, may God save you all. As you know there was once a time when all the peoples of this earth had just one language. It was after the great flood which God brought when he saw his people were full of wickedness. The descendants of Noah travelled east and settled there. Then they said to one another, 'Let us make bricks and build a tower so tall that it will reach up to the heavens.' And so they started their work.

But when God saw the tower his people were building, he was not pleased. 'Look' he said, 'they are one people and speak one language and this is only the beginning of what they will do. They will soon think that nothing they propose will be impossible for them.' And so he came down to earth and brought much confusion, scattering his people over the earth and making each one speak in different languages as we do now, though in truth there is only one language to speak for always and without end, and that is prayerful piety and humble penance. And that is the first meaning of the story. Mark you this well."

And she raised her goblet to William again.

"Now the other true meaning is this. When God heard his people speaking together, he found their talk meaningless empty chatter. He knew they did not really understand one another and did not accept the differences between them, between those who are truly pious and those who just make a playful pretence of it, so help me God. That is the second meaning. And when they started to build their tower up to the heavens, he knew they believed themselves to be on the same level as he. He saw they were bloated with pride and starved of wisdom. And that is the third meaning. Such people are called babblers, because they are not humble, talk too much and don't know their proper place on this earth."

There was silence as Margery sat down and then, after a while, Wenceslas stood up and spoke his story in Latin. It was much longer but ended with words we could all understand, *"Turris Babel."*

The next many weeks were exceeding tiring. It was the custom in Rome during the forty days of Lent to join the processions and go to Mass at a different parish church each day and Margery vowed to do so. These churches offered more pardons and grace than any other in all of Christendom and she demanded I accompany her. Despite this whenever it rained, and that it did frequently, then we did not go for she said God had excused her from her devotions during inclement weather. And I was grateful to benefit from his generosity as well.

William had let it be known our fellowship would leave after the Easter celebrations and I was pleased to be going home, since the six months in Rome had become wearisome. I still could not forgive Margery those insults about my mother, but nor could I leave her as I had nowhere else to live. I was ever silenced by her, while she revelled in the attention of Lawrence, who also wanted to come with us. So finally we all set off together in some trepidation, as there were continuing reports of brigands on the road. But it was a peaceful journey since William and the rest of the company ignored us, and Margery delighted in her new friend.

At last we arrived at the harbour at Middleburg where we met other pilgrims waiting for a vessel to cross over to England. Then news came one was ready to sail and the winds favourable, so with great rejoicing I hurried to prepare our baggages and went to find Margery who'd just returned from church. She was in the solar with the priest and some strangers, telling stories as usual. But when I spoke about the ship, she would have none of it.

"No, it is not my Lord's will that I should go so soon, nor is it fit to travel on a Sunday."

She wouldn't be persuaded and I was much troubled not to be leaving since our purse was near empty and I didn't know where we might find money for our sustenance. But still I went to the quays to bid farewell to our fellowship, and Hugh came over to speak with me.

"And did you find that faith and understanding you sought on pilgrimage?"

"Truly Hugh I do not know. In the Holy Land I did feel at times I was amongst holy people in sacred times, but in Rome it was all heroes and history. Wherever I went there were monuments and martyrs, like St Peter, and since he has the keys of heaven it seemed many pilgrims believed if they worshipped him they would already have a foot in the door. Like Margery, you know how much she relishes suffering and sacrifice, so Rome was paradise for her. But as for me, I'd rather suffer no more."

"So then, have you still not learnt that charity starts at home?"

I was muted for a moment: I had forgot our talk of many months before.

"I think perhaps I do not know what that really means, but do wonder at times that if I were a better servant and more forgiving I might come to goodness."

He looked at me and gently stroked my cheek.

"Well, each one of us must find the way on our own path, but please be wary that you don't expend too much charity on Margery. I've observed your kind service to her and beg you try to free yourself from blame for her single-minded conduct.

Steady your heart and don't forget you told me that truth lies within."

And as he walked away I thought I heard Sister Margaret's voice though could see her nowhere, then I hurried back to our inn.

We stayed in Middleburg for several days. Margery was always occupied talking to those who had not sailed, and would never to listen to me. Each morning I went to the harbour to search out a ship that was England-bound but there was none. One day in fair weather she led us all to the countryside, bid us sit down, began to give instruction about the holy laws and spoke sharply too, because she'd heard some people swear great oaths and broke the commandments that were given by God. The priest gazed at her like a love-struck youth and many of the others seemed to eat her words, but as for me I would have given much for a morsel of meat. We were now so short of coins that we only had enough for one meal a day, though that didn't bother Margery.

Then the skies grew sultry, steaming hot, and I became faint listening to her. It was if we were back in Fincham Street and she was declaiming the merits of some new damask she'd seen in the market. I marvelled that the priest let her preach so. And suddenly, there was a great roll of thunder and lightning too and we all rushed back to the inn, drenched by the rains. We were in great terror and I wondered if the storm was a sign of God's displeasure.

Soon after news came of a vessel that was sailing to England. I told Margery and we followed her to the harbour, where there was a mean looking ship, and the priest was sorely frightened.

"Mother, there is no proper ship here, that's only a little boat ..."
But she would have none of it.

"God," she declaimed, "is as mighty in a little boat as in a big ship and I will go in that vessel by God's leave."

And so we boarded in hope and sunshine but soon the weather changed, and there was strong wind and churning seas, much fear and many prayers, but at last we arrived at Yarmouth and all gave thanks to be safely back on land again.

By now there were only a few groats whimpering in our purse. I'd spent all my money and Margery's too, yet she would not let me send messages to John to come and fetch us. Two of her new friends were returning to Norwich and offered us hospitality. She was set on going to the cathedral there to give thanks for our safe return and also to visit an anchorite she knew from earlier days. So we journeyed together and she was ever gay, and we much heartened by the kindness of those we met along the road. But it was surprising to be treated as strangers, though we spoke the same language. Nothing was as I'd expected and after being away such a long while I saw everything anew with different eyes.

It was gentle weather, the month of May, and I recalled our travels only two years before when Margery first told me of her resolve to go to Jerusalem. So much had happened since and though I felt no change within myself, I was treated with courtesy and even awe when people knew I'd been to the Holy Land. But for sure my mistress had changed. Now when she began her holy discourse she spoke with such authority while I … all I knew was that I knew less than I thought I'd known before.

In time we came to Norwich and housed with friends of hers, though she made it clear I was to take my place with the household servants, while she alone talked about our pilgrimage. Once again I was mostly mute, but had occasion to send a message to John to tell him we were back. Margery continued to call on me for service and oftentimes as in the old days, to rile at slights, like the holy man she'd met before and had gone to see again. But he was no longer well disposed to her, having heard gossip that she'd borne a child while over the seas, and this grievously affronted her since she ever yearned to be thought of as a virgin.

But she still had friends and there was one who gave her money so she was not without means, though continued to have need to prove herself. One morning she had some new clothes delivered and summoned me to help her dress before church. And so she stepped out in her new white gown with a white kirtle, and a white hood and cloak and I dared not remonstrate though this show of spotless purity rankled more and more. Few of the good people in Norwich had known her in her earlier years but there was occasional mockery, which as was now her habit she gloried in.

We travelled back with John and I was saddened to see how old he looked, as if all the good life had left him. His business had not prospered, he'd worried about Margery and had not been able to bear such a long time on his own. Without her there had been no one left at home to love and enjoy, for Mary had gone to live with Isobel, who'd married whilst we were over the seas. I missed Mary for she was the most gentle of all Margery's children and I longed to see her again. Indeed our household held little cheer, even old Adam had left to find better employ.

While some of our neighbours did welcome us home, many judged Margery ill for leaving her husband, and their envy of her journeying to Jerusalem was not appeased by her white clothes. Her behaviour too caused much division. She wept vociferously, her fits were worse than ever and oftentimes she became rigid and turned purple. Some said her seizures came from the Devil, that she was surely possessed of demons as in her early years, and they cursed and some spat at her. Others whispered that she'd taken the habit of drinking too much wine. Those who aspired to piety themselves believed what her priest said, that her disorders came from the passion of her devotions and they praised her heartily, while the others shook their heads and turned away.

But she did not have to suffer their spite for long, for as the winter winds came she grew increasing feeble and took to her bed, and John was much afraid she'd die and once sent me running for the priest to minister the last rites, but she recovered before he came. I was sick too and we were very poor company. That was a hard season for all of us. Margery owed much money and the tradesmen were no longer so generous with their loans.

Since that day she had called my mother a strumpet I'd resolved to remind her of the promise she'd made to Brunham and demand she give me money so I could leave her. I even considered saying I would besmirch her name and tell of her great sin in the early days of her marriage, but then thought she was already so poorly judged and indeed so poor, I'd gain nothing from her except harshness. I felt trapped like a bird with a broken wing, seeking the skies but only able to hop on the ground and find shelter in the undergrowth. I sent messages to Aldwin and Erwan begging for money to set up a business, but had no response. So I held my tongue and continued to provide what little service I was asked.

The months passed and we both remained much weakened. But Margery was determined to fulfil her vow to visit the shrine of St James at Compostela once her purse was full again. When admirers in Lynn invited us to eat, she usually found tasks for me and I was left behind. No doubt she recounted all her deep devotions and spiritual adventures for they promised her money for this next pilgrimage. Yes, I thought, you are still John Brunham's daughter and know how to wheedle your way with your friends and procure what you want. And while we were often sick and had little to eat she never seemed to notice.

Our varying fortunes were of little account to Margery, yet I found her much changed since our return. After those months of tedious travel with never any ease of comfort and the endless need for vigilance in each new unfamiliar place, watchfulness and worry had worn us hard. And so like me, her face was etched and pinched by time, her eyes sunken and cheeks hollowed and, as can happen to people who live together, we often walked in step and even spoke alike.

There had been many changes in our country too since we left for the Holy Land, as I heard when marketing in town. In the spring of the year when we were in Rome, rebellion had flared in many parts of England, stirred up by Oldcastle who was still at large. Many feared the return of that terrible uprising and burning of buildings that frightened me when I was a child. Then some of his supporters and Lollard friends assembled in St Giles Field in London, with much riot and rebellion and a plot to kill the King but they were swiftly crushed, though Oldcastle escaped yet again.

After that our Parliament passed new laws and encouraged the common folk to denounce anyone they suspected of heresy, which was now judged as treason. No longer could someone who was accused recant before a bishop, as many had done in the past; they were taken instead for trial in the civil courts, and a guilty verdict meant death. The authorities were increasingly watchful of anyone who could read and wandered in the countryside, alone or in pairs, and spoke out or preached without a proper licence. Everyone was fearful. And then I heard whispers that one of those arrested and burnt in London after Oldcastle's rebellion was Ralph.

I was deeply sorrowed and went to seek out our former friends that we might mourn together. But they shunned me at the door and I was left to bear my grief alone.

The following year, in June, Margery announced she was now ready to go on pilgrimage to Spain, but John was not pleased to be left alone yet again and would not give her a letter sanctioning her departure. Yet finally he let her go, for go she would despite him but only on condition she take me, and I could not tell him no.

So we set off and journeyed safely to Bristol with a boy from the household, sometimes joining labourers along the highway, at other times paying for a ride in a cart. Once there we found lodgings in a pilgrim hospice where Richard, whom Margery had summoned before we left Lynn, was waiting. He'd sent many messages asking for repayment of the monies she owed him, but eaten bread is soon forgotten and she'd not paid him. Now she had silver again from her neighbours and settled her debt straightaway, then begged him to come with us. But once the coins were safely in his purse, he refused to be enticed and swiftly took his leave. As I accompanied him to the door, he turned to me sorrowfully.

"Would you ever be believing this, I've been thinking of your mistress and her tempests of tears since those first days we met for they were a great puzzlement to me. Like a banshee she was, drifting about in her white drapes with all those weird wailings, incessantly seeking to quit her body, searching for answers in penance and prayer and always making an almighty show of it, but never showing love or compassion for anyone else. I now believe she's truly troubled and mistaken. I thought about you too, your long service to her, your passive patience, that never-ending laundry and wondered when you too might cease your repentance.

And now I'm back from Rome, I've come to understand a true pilgrimage is simplicity, staying still, knowing yourself. As I have money again I shall leave the church, lose myself somewhere and dig the soil. I pray you too may find what you need. And God be with you sister, now and for always."

So he left and I was troubled by his words, but had no time to think of them for news came soon after that King Henry had requisitioned all the vessels in the port for his war in France. Some said there'd be a six-week wait before any ship sailed to Compostela and Margery demanded I go elsewhere and seek out another pilgrim ship. Happily I met a couple who were also in search of a passage and were going to Plymouth and other places along the coast. So, in return for my services, they said I might come with them. They were kindly folk and though we were disappointed in our quest, it was a welcome rest from Margery.

There was much excitement when we returned, and I was greatly distressed for Margery was nowhere to be found, but the gossips were quick to tell me the story.

"Aye, there was much trouble after you left, so many shriekings and roarings at church that we could never hear the sermons…"

"And then there was the great Corpus Christi procession which we all wanted to follow and of course she came too …"

"In those white clothes of hers, not in plain clothes like the rest of us …"

"But don't forget, she's been to the Holy Land and has seen and knows much more than we do …"

"And she wept and wailed and couldn't hold back her tears …"

"Poor woman, she feels so much more than us, moaning and groaning at the very thought of Christ's suffering, God save her …"

"Howling and sobbing, screaming and crying like a crazed beast. I think she puts it on …"

"O hold your tongue, she's a truly pious woman, and such devotion …"

"Then all of a sudden, she fell to the ground shouting loudly 'I am dying, I am dying,' but Thomas Marshall, God bless him, came quickly to her aid and took her back to the hospice …"

"And I went too so that she might have a woman with her …"

"Aye, so you did, but why wasn't she with her goodman as we are, to take charge of her, that's what I want to know…"

"And I, for one, don't want her on board any ship I take to Compostela. She preaches all the time, just like those Lollers. And if she does come I'd rather she fell into the sea and was swallowed by a whale than came along to worship with me."

As always the people were divided, and if there were some who relished her every word when she was tranquil enough to speechify and tell her stories, others couldn't abide her and named her heretic. And they told me she'd then left the hospice and moved to an inn where her new friends gave her hospitality.

Now it happened, the gossips continued, just two days later a pilgrim vessel anchored in the harbour and the captain let it be known he'd be sailing for Spain the following week. Then Thomas Marshall went to the ship to pay for Margery's passage and promised his servant Patrick would accompany her. But one of her enemies, a wealthy man who was also bound for Compostela, stirred up the town and said she couldn't be permitted to go, a frail woman on her own given to fits, with just a male servant to take care of her and no woman companion.

"Then there was a great quarrel, with your mistress preaching Jesus had no love for the rich unless they were meek and something about some a foreign beast being threaded through a needle, and he demanding to know why her husband wasn't with her or at least a maidservant."

"None of us knew where you'd gone until the hospice keeper told us …"

"And so they went on fighting and might still be at it now but for an urgent message from the Bishop of Worcester summoning her to his hall. And that was just yesterday and we haven't heard of her since."

"And who," I asked, "is the Bishop of Worcester?"

"Thomas Peverel's a pious man, an enemy of heretics. Some years ago when there was trouble in our town, he convicted a tailor of heresy, a Loller he was, a heretic and a traitor, and sentenced him to be burnt at the stake."

The moment I heard this I hurried to the Bishop's manor, which was only a short distance away. When I arrived his household were talking about Margery too, for as usual she'd scolded them for their lax speech and lavish attire but they thought no more of it than the foolish blather of a feeble-minded woman. I also heard one say that Peverel was much impressed when he heard she was bound for Compostela.

That evening the Bishop called me to him and told me he'd pay my fare so I might accompany Margery. So her critics were silenced and we lodged with the Bishop until word came that the vessel was ready and we boarded with about a hundred other pilgrims, sailed smoothly over the seas to Corunna, then took the road to the shrine of St James. It was an easy journey and we had nothing ever to fear.

I remember well the story of St James from some Spanish sailors I met at the quays in Lynn, and the Golden Legends book read to us by Margery's priest. He was much worshipped by the townsfolk there as it was said he liberated prisoners, rid the insane of their demons and once pulled a drowning man, weighed down by a cloak of cockleshells, from the sea. He was known as patron of pilgrims and was the first apostle to be buried far from home and, since I'd never known my mother or her country, I thought myself an exile just like him. So making a pilgrimage to his shrine felt like going to visit a friend.

And in truth the celebrations at Compostela were more joyous than any of our other pilgrimages despite the greater crush of people. Our travelling there was not at all arduous and since we had no particular fellowship, more peaceful too as Margery was able to find like-minded pilgrims to worship with and avoid those she judged impious. Besides, she had Patrick to talk to. So I left them at their prayers in the church and enjoyed myself with those who'd gathered in the courtyard in front of the northern door. Most had travelled on foot through France and across the mountains, yet were more cheerful than any of the pilgrims we'd journeyed with before.

In this courtyard there was a pond and a fountain, shaded by orange and lemon trees, large enough for a dozen or so people to bathe in and wash away the dust of their travelling. So I climbed in, cleansed myself and played like a child with other strangers, then let the warm breeze dry my garments. Small groups gathered round, all in the pilgrim garb of their particular fraternity and entertained us all day long with much kindness and friendship.

There were displays of magic and juggling, stilt walking and fire eating. Fortune-tellers set up booths, jesters played with diabolos, mummers acted out stories, acrobats leapt and capered, boys cart-wheeled, falconers flew hawks and wenches, dressed in all the colours of the rainbow, minced and mingled amongst the crowd whispering sweet nothings to all and everybody. In the evening, hawkers set up stalls selling bull's-horn cups, leather bags, beaded bracelets, spicy sausages, grilled fish, cheese, almond milk and hippocras, and small confections the like of which I had never tasted before. Several hucksters peddled fresh scallops, the holy food of St James, and I was told eating them would confer long life and a forgiveness of sins.

So I bought some to take inside for Margery and Patrick, who'd found a quiet place in one of the church galleries on the side of the nave. I wanted to go back and join the crowd, but Margery insisted I stay. And she judged right for soon more pilgrims came in, children and old people, mothers with babies, the injured and sick too, all pushing and shoving to find a place to spread out their cloaks and rest for the night.

I'd hoped to join the merriment the following day but when the cathedral doors were opened at first light, another crowd arrived and we were thrust against those in front and pressed by those behind. A few who were still sleeping on the ground were sorely hurt and many lost their belongings in the crush. The heat was intense, the stench as rank as herring rotting in the sun. Then some among the rabble began reciting the Pilgrim's Prayer and soon the chaos ceased, though we were still unable to move. Sometime later the great doors closed and the priests bid us kneel. We stayed there all day until the evening vigil, and many nearby cautioned us against falling asleep and said that if we did so we'd wake up blind.

During the night different groups sang songs to keep themselves awake. We were given tapers and it was as bright as day. A great censer hung from the roof swinging back and forth, sweetening the air with incense. Then the priests led us group by group to the small side chapels and behind the huge altar, where steps had been placed for those who wished to climb up and kiss the marble hood of St James. At times a great cry rose up, followed by whispers of miracles, a lame man able to walk again, a woman given back her sight after many blind years. But we were all much worn after the tumult and thankful when dawn came at last and we were let out into the balm of the morning air.

Sometime later we were escorted back in groups for the celebration Mass, though I was tired and soon asleep. We left Compostela the following day and took a cart to Corunna where our vessel was waiting. The voyage back was even swifter than the way out, the seas calm, the weather fair. In five days Margery, Patrick and I were back in Bristol where Thomas Marshall met us and, having finished his business, he offered to take us to Melton Mowbray, just two days journey from there to Lynn.

7

Leicester, Lincoln, York, Beverley, Lynn 1417-1431

'many swore we'd burn'

I had a dream last night which startled me. I woke in utter darkness and was fearful, not knowing where I was. I felt numb, then knew I was back in the convent, in the solitary cell where I'd spent those horrifying weeks many years ago. I forced myself out of bed, went to the window and saw a single star shining in the night sky. I realized where I was when I heard Agnes coughing and turning on the mattress, then settling down again with a comfortable sigh. Sleep is often fitful when you're old, but it was as if I'd journeyed back into the past and woken in a different time.

In my dream I'm sitting on a stool in the byre. It is growing dark and I see the slither of a waning moon. I have a bundle of parchment on my lap. Outside there are sheep huddled against the fence, bleating to come in. Half are white and half are black. They disappear and then there's a goat by my side. As I look down at his muzzle and unblinking yellow eyes, he stands on cloven hoofs, his horns unwind and straighten out in twisted spikes on top of his head and I see it is the Devil. I try to bury the parchment in the folds of my tunic, but cannot hide it all. Then I know the Beast has seen my writings and has power over me.

I slept no more that night and as soon as the sun rose busied myself in our home. Summer has passed and I've been gleaning in the fields, gathering nuts, collecting sheep's wool from the briar, salting fish and smoking the flesh of the sow, which was slaughtered after she'd finished suckling. But I'm restless for my story is not yet told, and again and again I find myself lost

*in the memories of those dangerous days following our return from Santiago.
Memories of betrayals and trials continue to haunt me even in the daylight
hours, but I know that despite my wickedness, Margery was wanton in her
behaviour too and I never felt safe with her.*

We set off with great vigour as soon as we disembarked at
Bristol. Margery was puffed up with pride, and I too was cheered
by our achievement. We'd completed the last of the three great
pilgrimages, which would have been a feat worthy of anyone
and even more so for two women of our age. Though we were
tired, we were in good health and refreshed by the ease of this
last journey.

The road took us north first, to Hailes Abbey, and Thomas
and Patrick proved kind travelling companions and were much
beguiled by Margery. She was so greatly pleased with herself,
and I heard her telling them many times of her great joy at
having fulfilled the vow she'd made to honour the memory of
her worshipful father. It was as if in speaking of him, she'd
thrown off her simple shift of sanctity and once again wore
the glorious gown of a grand gentlewoman. Thomas was even
more impressed and minded to provide hospitality for us along
the way, so we had no need to dig into the mean recesses of our
purses.

We spent two days at Hailes Abbey, an important foundation
of the White Monks. It nestled in verdant countryside
under the brow of a hill and was exceeding lofty, cool and
white, after the vibrant colours of the St James shrine. On
the second morning we waited in line with a multitude of
pilgrims until the blood of Christ was shown us in a jewelled
reliquary. As always, when a sacred relic is displayed, there
were gasps and sighs, and Margery, who'd been unusually

calm at Compostela, burst into shrill shrieks and screams.

At supper that evening, she spoke again of her pious thoughts and the honour of her family. Thomas stared at her like a mooncalf and Patrick gazed unceasingly, as if she were some angel come to earth. All this was gall and wormwood to me when I considered the iniquity of her father, so I left the table and went outside to the stables. Patrick came soon after to groom the beasts for our journey the following morning. He was a quiet man and we'd hardly spoken on our Compostela journey for he'd hung on every word Margery said. But now he wished to talk.

"Well mistress, you've travelled to many a holy place and walked perhaps on the very same paths as Our Lord and his heavenly mother. But mayhap it isn't needful to go so far afield when we have our own sacred treasures in this green and blessed land. And I trow you've never seen anything as miraculous as that phial of Christ's blood we were shown today, though you didn't say naught about it ..."

He narrowed his eyes and gave me an insolent stare.

"But Mistress Kempe, God bless her, she perceived it true the moment she set eyes on it, and was struck to her knees in awe." And I, completely forgetting myself in my hurt and bitterness, answered back:

"Well so far as I know it might have been the blood of a duck." He stared in amazement and turned away and though I said I was only jesting, he clammed up and spoke no more.

We left for Leicester at dawn and Margery urged us on, for Thomas talked of a special Mass at St Martin's church the following day, which she vowed to attend. As soon as we were lodged, she told me to launder her white garments and I resolved to spite her, irked by her incessant need to flaunt her purity. But for once heaven was on my side, the weather exceeding wet and her clothes didn't dry in time. So finally she set out for church with Thomas, dressed in her common pilgrim gown, though this still didn't stop her from making a great display, so he told me when they returned. He said the moment she saw the crucifix above the altar she'd howled like a trapped fox, disturbing the other worshippers and someone asked who she was and what ailed her.

It was evening when they came back and she retired to the upper chamber. I stayed with Thomas in the dark parlour and went to find a candle as he wrote to John to come and fetch us home. And just as I returned, a man rushed in, demanding I go with him to the Guildhall and speak with the Mayor. I was frightened, but he was rough with me and wouldn't listen to anything I said, and Thomas said not a word.

I was rushed off to meet the Mayor who was a small, mean-looking man. I was over-awed but he too would not let me speak.

"I hear tell you're the daughter of the late Mayor of Lynn and have come to Leicester to fulfil a vow. But all you've done is create much disturbance. You are a false strumpet, a Lollard and a heretic."

I tried to protest but was so afraid that my mouth dried up and I couldn't say anything. He continued shouting at me, then commanded the jailer to take me to prison until the steward could question me on the morrow. But the jailer, seeing my age and great fear, didn't put me in the common jail amongst the men and took me instead to his dwelling. I begged I might send a message to our inn, but he refused to do anything more for me. After that I said nothing but was sure Thomas would tell Margery and they'd come to find me and the mistake would be uncovered.

The jailer's wife put me in a closet with a small squint to the street outside and left me quite alone. I was most fearful in the night, remembering the careless words I'd spoken to Patrick and was sure he'd reported me, for a silent dog is always the first to bite. I cursed myself for my stupidity in speaking against a relic in these dangerous times, then reminded myself that though I'd said something foolish about the blood at Hailes, I had been mistaken for Margery, who had a very large mouth and was always preaching. And I wondered when she or Marshall would search me out and speak for me.

I didn't close my eyes once that night, first with waiting to be released when Margery came, but she did not, and then with rising anger as thoughts spun round my head and filled my belly up. When you're on your own, ill-will and the slights of others make you swell up like the bloated body of a dead animal. The dark hours were very long. At daybreak the jailer took me back to the Guildhall where Steward Stephen was waiting. He was exceeding ugly and his words rough, saying he'd heard I defamed the clergy, belittled the holy relics, preached and stirred up the people. Then grabbing my arm, he led me to a small chamber by the side of the hall.

I told him again I was not Margery, but he would not listen.

"Now, Mistress Kempe, I want to know from your own mouth whether your talk comes from God or the Devil," he demanded, "and if you don't tell me, I'll see you burn."

I was numb with terror. We were quite alone and he had that coarse look I knew too well. He came close, tugged at my tunic and pulled my wimple off. I felt quite undone and cried out. He was panting foully and held me tightly round my waist.

"Tell me whore, tell me this instance, confess you consort with the Devil," he whispered wetly in my ear, lifting up my tunic and pinning me against the wall.

I struggled and kicked, and at last I found voice to speak my pent-up anger.

"Let go of me," I screamed, "let me go and I'll tell you what you want to know if you leave me in peace. I'm not Margery Kempe, I'm just her maidservant."

He loosened his grasp and I continued quickly.

"She is indeed a woman who preaches and arouses the people. Question her and you'll discover where the Devil is at work. Call your clerks, let them guard me. Go to the inn where I was taken, and you'll know her by the white clothes she wears."

I've thought of this often since, not only of my wickedness but why he so suddenly released me. But though he'd no way of knowing whether I spoke the truth or not, I was so frightened, such a pathetic, pitiable creature that neither he nor anyone else could have believed I was capable of sermonizing to the rabble. I was indeed a paltry thing and so he saw me, and calling in his clerk he left me alone.

Sometime later I heard much noise and was ushered back into the hall. It was nigh on midday but full dark and gloomy, with heavy black clouds visible through the large arched window. Margery was already there in her white raiment just as I'd foretold and Thomas with her much reduced, like a startled hare, though neither saw me amongst all the people who had come to enjoy the spectacle, as townsfolk will. But Margery stood steady and serene like a noble hart, unaware of any possible peril.

Then everything happened very quickly. An arrow of lightning shot through the hall blinding us all, pursued by the drumming of thunder. As the booming faded, Steward Stephen brought me to Thomas's side and made us both swear that Margery was a woman of true faith, pure and chaste. Then a second flash of lightning cracked open the darkness, chased by further thunder rolls. We were all much dazzled and Thomas and I swore once again that she was a good woman of true belief.

Then the people clamoured we be released and so we were set free and pushed out into the storm. We hurried back to the inn but Thomas was dismayed by this turn of events, and packing his bags he called for Patrick and they bid me farewell. That they were fair-weather friends was not for me to judge when I considered my betrayal. I was now alone but had money enough for a few more days at the inn.

Margery did not return that afternoon, so I wrapped myself in my cloak and went into the street to hear what the people were saying.

"Did you ever see such a storm as that, terrifying it was, blinded and shook me all to pieces. I was afeared Doomsday had come ..."

"Fearsome indeed, a sign from the Almighty ..."

"An almighty omen to be sure, a warning of God's displeasure, a caution of some evil in our midst, those women, those heretics ..."

"Heretics? Are they Lollers, d'you think ..."

"Nay, nay, not so, not so. That Margery's a most saintly woman, she's been pilgriming to the Holy Land and did you see how radiant she looked when the lightning lit her up?"

"But what about those white clothes she wears? She's not a cloistered virgin, she's a married woman and they say she's borne scores of children, yet she wanders hither and thither, without her husband ..."

"Not entirely on her own though, I hear there's another

witchy woman who just stares at you and never says a word, and I hear she's been questioned too ..."

"Those clothes ... that makes me think of those women who came from over the seas some years ago, all wearing white and professing great holiness. "

"And, not one of them had a husband with her, just like them two ..."

"Yeah, yeah and wouldn't we all like to be like that? I'd gladly be rid of mine, free from his beatings and constant demands for sex ..."

"All those foreign women, adorned in white, claiming the right to live on their own, every one of them denying the sanctity of marriage, until our good King Richard, God rest his soul, issued a decree banning them from our lands ..."

"And right he was too, for it's not seemly for us folk to cast off our husbands - only a Loller would abjure the wedding vows ..."

" So, they are heretics then ..."

"Aye, they're a right worriment those Lollards, a threat to all us decent, thinking women. We don't want the likes of them around with old man Oldcastle still at large and folk travelling the land and taking messages for him ..."

"Nay, Mistress Margery's not one of those, she's a right honest woman, I heard her telling some of the Bible stories and she told them true and well ..."

"Mind you our Justices are sure to find her out if she and that other one, who pretends to be her maidservant, are Lollers. They're good at catching strangers ..."

"Well, we'll know soon enough when our Mayor questions her a few days hence and she'll not escape afore that, housed with the Steward's mother..."

At least I knew where she was but I feared for her and even

more for myself and stayed in our chamber, much terrified, until the day of her examination.

Two days later I followed the crowd to All Saints church where Margery was to be questioned and there was such a crush of people that many brought stools to stand on and get a better view. The Mayor was there with the Abbot and other clerics, all seated before the high altar and not a kind face among them. Margery was led in and made to swear she'd only speak the truth, and was set many questions about her understandings and beliefs. But the Mayor scowled and was not satisfied.

"I want to know why you wander about in white clothes," he demanded, "for I believe you've come here to lure our wives away."

She stared at him and then answered:

"I shan't waste my breath telling you why, you're not worthy to know it. But I'll gladly tell these worthy clerks by way of confession."

He stepped right up to her but the Abbot told him to stand off and beckoned to Margery. We watched as she spoke but could not hear a word. Then the Mayor was called to her side and after some talk he spoke out loudly to her.

"I won't let you go despite anything you say, until you get a letter from the Bishop of Lincoln, that I may be discharged of any responsibility for you."

And this she agreed to do, and the Abbot asked that she and the Mayor be friends and so they nodded to one another and she was given leave to go.

The crowd dispersed, and I joined her and we hurried back to the inn. I asked why she hadn't come to find me the night I was taken and she said God had promised her I would be safe.

But when I told her that he had given me no such assurance and how frightened I had been, she just berated me for my lack of faith and bid me pack our belongings and find a man to accompany us to Lincoln.

We had met Philip Repyngdon some years earlier, when Margery and John knelt before him and agreed to live chastely. He'd been generous to her then, giving her money to fund her white raiment. Now she welcomed the chance of meeting him again but he sent his clerk to speak with her instead. She asked for the letter giving her permission to travel freely, and he returned with it soon after. We lodged there that night but Repyngdon did not invite us to dine with him and Margery was surly and short, demanding I busy myself and hire another man to take us on to York.

"Margery, please let's go back to Lynn. These are dangerous times, you've already drawn too much attention to both of us and the people are saying everyone's being watched, especially women travelling on their own, and they're very suspicious of anyone wearing white. You've been tested once and proved yourself, surely that's enough, let us go back now ..."

"O you simpleton of little faith," she answered. "We now have permission to travel freely, and I need to go to York and thank those who've supported me."

"But York's even more dangerous then Leicester. I have Thomas's letter with me, we can stay here and send for John to bring us home ..."

"Well then, you stay here and I'll go on alone."

She wouldn't change her mind, so I found a man to guide us to York and we left on the morrow. It was now September and we'd been on the road some many months.

The anchoress in York did not receive Margery kindly and some of her friends shunned her too, for they'd heard of her arrest in Leicester. But she still heeded no warnings and the morning after we arrived, while she was at prayer in church, a priest came and pulled at her tunic.

"You wolf, what white cloth is this you wear?"

But before she could answer, some young choristers chatting nearby called out:

"Why Sir, don't you see, it's wool not wolf-skin, so she must be some silly sheep." And they ran off, skipping and bleating like a leap of spring lambs.

But she didn't desist from telling stories, both in church and among the womenfolk outside. There were many who liked to hear her talk, for she had been well schooled by Master Alan and other friends in Lynn and still had the ability to dazzle and outshine near everyone who heard her. Whenever I cautioned her not to preach, she wouldn't listen, and I followed behind her like a beaten dog, not so much to be invisible but to hide my guilt and shame. And those who gathered round her gave us hospitality, so at least we had food to eat and a safe place to sleep.

When she was not discoursing with friends she spent much time in the Minster at the St William shrine, where the coloured glass window with the miracle of the sleeping man saved from the falling stone was now in place. She worshipped there most days but was always pleased to cease her prayers and tell others of her own fabulous escape from the tumbling boulder. And once when she was doing so, a priest interrupted her.

"How long are you staying here woman?"

"Sir, I intend to stay fourteen days."

He continued to watch her especially when she was telling

tales, and when a fortnight had passed he questioned her again. And she was blunt with him, saying she hadn't said she'd stay for only fourteen days. He wasn't at all pleased to be outsmarted by her logic and commanded her to appear before him at the Chapterhouse.

Once again Margery was unperturbed, even by the multitude of people who had assembled, though they were mostly clerics and not a rowdy common crowd, and all wore a sombre face. First she was asked to tell why she'd come to York and she explained it was to worship at the Minster. Then they wanted to know whether she had a letter from her husband that she might pilgrimage.

"No I do not, but he gave me leave by word of his mouth, and Sirs why do you threaten me so, when you don't question other pilgrims?"

Some might have remarked that other pilgrims didn't dress in white and preach to the people, but instead they examined her on the articles of faith and ruled she should appear before Archbishop Bowet. Until then they ordered that we should be held in prison, but the common folk pleaded for us, and so it was agreed we'd lodge with a reputable couple from the town. And so for the next few days Margery held court in their home and seemed to have no fear of the coming ordeal except to fuss that I launder her white clothes yet again.

The people in York spoke well of Henry Bowet who had been campaigning against the Scots, while the King was fighting his wars over the seas.

"Aye, Bishop Bowet is fearless despite his great age, a most learned man with little love of heretics," one told me and she spoke too of his lavish hospitality, saying his household consumed eighty barrels of claret a year. Knowing how Margery judged those who feasted well, for she'd once been a great glutton herself, I feared she'd find occasion to scold his household and lose any sympathy he might have for her.

But I could not speak with her. She had become as silent as a cat watching at a mouse-hole and I wondered if she knew I'd betrayed her at Leicester. Then the summons came for her to appear before the Archbishop and she called me to help her dress. When we arrived at the Archbishop's palace at Cawood there was a mass of rowdy people in the street, jeering and chanting loudly, "Loller, Heretic, Heretic, Loller," and many swore we'd burn. Margery, in her usual way, called out laughing,

"I would be happy to be chopped in a thousand pieces and cooked in a pot for the sake of my Lord."

She added it was they who'd smoulder in hell for swearing so, which inflamed them further. They shook their fists in the air, booing and hissing, and came close, towering over us, tugging at our clothes and spinning us round and round. I held tightly on to Margery that I might not fall, then suddenly they ceased as two clerics came and led us into the chapel.

I was so dizzy I had to sit down but was pulled up when Bowet arrived, and then there was a dread silence. Margery was brought forward and everyone waited. He was indeed most ancient and thrust out his chin to see her better, staring at her a long while. Then suddenly he asked:

"Why are you wearing white? Are you a virgin?"

"No, my Lord," she answered. "I am a married women."

At that there were loud grumbles that it was a scandal she travelled without her man. But Bowet bid everyone hush and as before she was examined on her understanding of the faith and it seemed she answered well. Still the clerics were not satisfied, and called out again that she was evil and suspected of the

Lollard heresy.

"Well mistress, I've been told bad things about you and that you are a very wicked woman."

She responded swiftly:

"Sir, I also hear tell that you're a very wicked man, and if you are as wicked as they say, you'll never get to heaven unless you mend your ways."

Loud growls echoed through the chamber and there were many harsh protests, though I saw Bowet grimace much as an indulgent father will at a wayward child, and instead of upbraiding her he bid her swear an oath that we would leave his diocese immediately. But she replied she had to return to York to say farewell to her friends, then needed to go to Bridlington to speak with her confessor.

I was astonished by her brazen demands and even more so when Bowet said she might, so long as she swore not to teach the people.

"Nay, my Lord Bishop, I cannot and will not swear such an oath, for neither the Pope nor the Holy Church has ordained it is wrong to speak of God."

Now the yells and accusations were even louder and someone shouted:

"There, my Lord, you see she admits she preaches and ..."

"And Sir," called out another, "she told me the worst tale about a priest I ever heard."

"Nay good sirs," she interrupted. "I never once went into a pulpit, but only use stories and other good words from the Bible to bring the people closer to God, and no one will stop me from so doing, praise the Lord, until I am dead."

It seemed there was no boundary to her boldness and more cries of derision and scorn that she could be so impudent, but none of them had known Margery in her younger days when she was holding court in Lynn and would let nobody cross her in any way. I wondered how Bowet would answer her rudeness. But instead of rebuking her, he asked if she would tell him the hideous tale that had just been spoken of. She stood up and waited till all eyes were on her and began:

"My Lord Bishop and all you venerable clerics, listen to my story for I tell it for the good of your souls. It's about a particular priest who'd gotten lost in the forest and, seeking shelter for the night, came upon a magnificent pear tree wreathed in beautiful, bountiful blossoms. And as he stood marvelling at it, a great bear came by who was unruly and ugly to behold and, standing on his hind legs, shook the tree and devoured the flowers as they fell to the ground. Then, lifting his tail and turning his arse to the priest, he shat them into his face.

The priest was horrified and much disgusted and stumbled away in great alarm. Then he met a holy pilgrim and asked what the meaning might be. And the pilgrim told him that both he himself and his sacred vocation were that self-same tree with its pure white blossoms, gifts from our good Lord. But just as the bear had soiled his visage and blinded his eyes with shit, so he too befouled his ministry with feeble-mindedness, babbling the Mass, swearing and blaspheming with the brothers of his house, thinking only of ways of making money, of meat and drink and of the pretty maidens in his congregation."

Then she made the sign of the cross and continued.

"So mark you well, keep your thoughts pure, as sweet and fruitful as that beautiful white blossom and God save you all."

As they say it matters not whether the cat be black or white, so long as it catches mice. Margery had ensnared Bowet with her charm. He laughed heartily and said he liked her tale but still insisted she swear to leave his diocese, which she did. Then he asked who'd take us away. Many spoke up but he chose John, a melancholic old man and gave him money, though he grumbled at the amount, to lead us back to York, then on to Bridlington and finally home to Lynn. And so we travelled back to York where Margery's farewells were soon said for several of her friends were not so keen to be seen with her after her appearance before the Archbishop.

After quitting York we were another two days travelling to Bridlington and I was much fatigued, unable to influence Margery in any way, so pleased was she to have outfoxed the Archbishop. Once again she was headstrong, glorying in these trials and accusations and proclaiming proudly that everyone was against her except the moon and the seven stars. But Sleightholme received her kindly and we rested there for some days while she confessed to him, then he gave us money for the journey home. Old man John was well pleased when we arrived in Hull, for once we'd taken the ferry to cross the Humber we'd only be a few days journey from Lynn.

But he couldn't stop Margery from visiting the church. On our return we met some people going there to celebrate the installation of a new window that had been donated by the Trinity Guild. At the head of the procession several women had gathered round an older woman, the widow of one of the aldermen. She was weeping loudly and splendidly attired in black, and Margery went straight to her, scolding her for her luxury. The widow was shocked and her companions sneered and spat at her, before John tugged at her sleeve and pulled her away.

That night I heard uproar in the street outside, until the Watch came and ordered the mob away. John said the people were stirred up by the widow Margery had insulted, and the innkeeper wanted rid of us as soon as the curfew was lifted. He woke us before dawn and led us to Hessle, where a ferry was moored. Margery and John were just about to board, while I had stopped to lace up my boot, when four men appeared and surrounded them. Two were Grey Friars, the other two were wearing the livery of some great Lord. They grabbed hold of Margery and the friars held on to John.

"Our Master, the Duke of Bedford, has sent for you," said one. "You are held to be the greatest heretic in this part of the country and in London town."

"We've been seeking you in many places," said the other, "and now we have you and we shall have a hundred pounds for bringing you before him."

John struggled, protesting loudly.

"No good sirs, you are mistaken. I am Archbishop Bowet's man, and he's already examined her and paid me to lead her back to Lynn, and ..."

But Margery interrupted him, smiling cheerfully and said,

"With a good will, sirs, I'll go wherever you will lead me." Neither she nor John called out for me, so I turned my back and hid behind a cart.

Some people emerged out of the morning shadows and I stayed where I was, terrified of being taken too. As it grew lighter more townsfolk appeared, so I mingled amongst them, while Margery and John were led through the streets with the rest of us following after. As we passed women stood in their doorways, shaking their distaffs, banging pots and crying out:

"Give her the faggot, burn her, burn her ..."

"Loller, Loller ..."

"Burn the false heretic ..."

and pelted her with rubbish. Some men joined in the sport as well, taunting her, and calling out in a mocking chant.

"Woman, give up this life you lead and go,

and spin and card wool as other women do."

And all the time she smiled, and called back that her suffering was nothing compared to Christ's pain on the cross.

I stayed amongst the crowd and wrapped my cloak tightly round me with my hood on so that no one would recognise me. When we arrived back in Hull, Margery and John were put in a wagon and the people said they would be taken to Beverley, to Lord Bedford. He was the King's brother, the most powerful man in the kingdom while the King was away at his war. Archbishop Bowet held spiritual authority in Beverley, but the Duke was the master and charged to hunt down heretics, bring them to trial as traitors and to the fire. I knew I had to follow them, but was frightened of travelling on my own.

All around me people were shouting, denouncing Margery and saying Bedford was sure to burn her. But I'd no need to worry about getting to Beverley for the mob was headed that way too, impatient to see what would happen next, and I was easily hidden amongst the crowd. It was past noon when we arrived there, but most folk turned back, grumbling when they saw no faggots in the market square. I rushed to the Minster in the hope of news and had the good fortune to meet with John. He was startled and tried to pull away, but I was urgent with him and demanded he tell me where Margery was.

"Alas that I ever knew her and agreed to accompany you," he said scowling. "I've been taken and imprisoned, all because of her."

He turned away but I gripped his arm and wouldn't let him go.

"Aye, they imprisoned me too. The moment we arrived they marched your mistress off to the home of one of Lord Bedford's men whose wife will keep her safe till she's taken for trial tomorrow. I demanded she be treated well and was shown where she was lodged, since Bowet charged me to keep her safe. And they're sending out search parties for you too. At first they wouldn't let me go and locked me in the common jail, but finally they believed I was Bowet's man and released me."

"He'll be none too pleased by this turn of events, but I'm not minded to make any further fuss for I'm already tainted by being with you both. I know not whether your mistress be pious or heretic but I don't care, either way she's trouble. And though you never speak I warrant you're in league with her. I've told the Archbishop I want nothing more to do with you, and wash my hands of you both."

He added that Bedford was sure to burn me as well for my shamelessness. But I would not let him leave until he gave me directions where I might find Margery.

The dwelling was in a small courtyard a little distance from the Minster. A large crowd had gathered there and I wondered what new disturbance had occurred though was quickly answered. Margery was standing at a casement on the upper floor telling tales. Everyone was listening intently and I heard one of them say:

"'Tis a shame she has to burn. She's a powerful way of telling the Bible stories.

Aye, she tells them well, but doesn't it say in the good book that a woman shouldn't preach and it's those Lollers who claim anyone can speak of God. And I heard tell she's a friend of Oldcastle and is perhaps his daughter. Lord Bedford will be sure to condemn her, and we shall have a burning …"

It was starting to grow dark and the people began to move away, but now Margery had seen me and called out that she was hungry and thirsty.

The young woman next to me stepped forward just when I did, surprised to be called until we realised we shared the same name. And I saw she was crippled. I told her I had money for provisions so we left together and bought a pie and a flagon of ale and when we returned we didn't know how we might get them up to Margery. But she was a resourceful maiden and I followed her as she hobbled into an alleyway and found a ladder, and so together we hoisted the victuals up and Margery was fed. And as I've noticed before, one good deed is often repaid by another and this young maidservant, for that was her work, did me a service and ate with me at an inn for I'd had no food that day and then offered me a place to sleep in her mistress's hall.

I'd been fuddled with fury and fright all day long, revelling in the wrong I judged my mistress for, but quaking too with the memories of my own stupidity and grievous faults. So it was good to have some company and forget our plight for a while. At first she only wanted to hear about Margery but when I told her I too had been to the Holy Land, she begged me talk of my travels. I delighted in her interest and the chance to speak of my own adventures. And I was curious about her too.

"My good, sweet mistress, God bless her, has been widowed these five years. Her husband was a cloth merchant and she continues to mind his business, for she often assisted him in the past and knows the trade well. She's vowed never to marry again, though many would have her for her kindness, skill and wealth. But she values her independence and the freedom to be charitable to those she chooses. And as she has no children of her own, she treats everyone in her household as kin. We all help with her enterprise and," she whispered, "she's teaching me to read, that I might have a better future and learn how to manage for myself."

I marvelled at such charity and thought how much I'd have liked to have a younger sister to whom I might offer such kindness and courtesy, or a like-minded, amiable daughter who'd be grateful to learn from me. And when we'd finished our meal we went to her home and she made a place for me to sleep in her mistress's hall.

I awoke with the dawn light and for a moment felt myself back at the farm in the comfort of my childhood, safe in the knowledge that Nanna was there and I was loved and cared for. I looked around and was puzzled for I saw nothing familiar. Then the horror of the day before returned. I rose quickly, pulled on my boots and tried to creep away, but the latch was stiff. A figure emerged from the shadows while I struggled with it, and a woman dressed in black called out:

"Good morrow mistress, there's no need to rush away. I heard from my maid that she gave you shelter last night and know the burdens you and your mistress must face this day, though I warrant you are innocent and will be safe. But you must eat before you leave, and let me give you some advice. Observe how the doorframe holds fast though the door itself must move, in and out, open and closed. So keep your heart steady like a well-crafted doorframe and let what troubles come, come in, then let them go out again. And never forget, everything passes in time."

And she brought me a tankard of ale and some bread and cheese, bid me take my time and leave when I'd had my fill.

I went soon after to the dwelling where Margery was held and was let into her chamber to help her dress. She was exceeding calm and I marvelled at that this since near every voice in town spoke against her. I told her how I'd hidden amongst the crowd and followed her, what the gossips had said, and how no one spoke of Bedford's mercy. I reminded her that she would be tried in a secular court and there was no escape from treason. And I begged that she be meek and humble, for I knew if she were safe then I would be too. But she just laughed and said to trust in God.

Then Bedford's man came to take us away and I knew we were doomed.

⚜

The streets were crowded, the people staring and hissing, nudging each other and pointing at me. They tramped behind us booing and heckling until at last we arrived at a grey stone building, the door was unlocked, we were ushered inside and it was slammed shut and bolted so none of the rabble could follow. We were led through a cold, narrow passageway into a dark hall where Bowet was assembled with priests and clerics. I waited for Lord Bedford to appear but he did not, and Margery was brought before the Archbishop. He was clearly vexed.

"What woman, are you come back again, and your maidservant too? Are you intent on causing a nuisance though I treated you kindly and charitably before? Truly I would gladly be rid of you both."

Then he turned to the company and told them:

"I have already examined this woman and her faith and found no fault in her, so this is not a matter for Bedford's court. I paid to have them both taken out of the diocese in order to quieten the masses and now they've been brought before me again. So why is this? If anyone has new evidence against these women speak it now."

Nobody said a word and I was much heartened until I noticed two friars whispering together, then one stepped forward and the silence was shattered.

"My Lord, here's a friar who knows many new things against her and that other woman too."

And he pushed the other friar in front of Bowet while everyone turned to look at me, though I tried to hide and covered my face with my hands.

"My Lord, I heard from my brothers in Lynn that some years back these two women read in secret with known heretics, disparaged the holy men of the Church, and boasted they could weep and wail at will. And had it not been for the charity of my brothers, they would have been taken and burnt long ago."

Then Bedford's two servants who'd arrested Margery in Hessle joined in with more allegations and accusations.

"Aye they're Lollards for sure and have come here to stir up the people and bring rebellion. Everyone knows Mistress Kempe condemns marriage and will not be beholden to any man, not even her own good man whom she's sworn to cast off. Just look at the way she flaunts her purity as if she were still a maiden. And let's not forget that other woman who hid from us at Hessle so she could sneak away and spread messages around the countryside while we brought Margery into Beverley."

"And as for their stories about going to Jerusalem," said the second. "They're far too frail and feeble to have travelled over the seas, and everything else they say is a lie and a falsehood."

Bowet listened quietly and I watched his face, wondering whether he was still minded to excuse us. But while the young often have tempests or sunshine writ upon their brows, the elderly rarely let their thoughts be read upon their visages. Once again a pall of silence fell over us and no one moved. At last he turned to Margery.   .

"Woman, what do you say to this?"

And she, crossing herself, replied in earnest sincerity,

"My Lord, saving your reverence, all the words they say are lies."

Then he asked me the same and I did my best to still my trembling and nodded to him, and answered just as Margery had.

Bowet said nothing but bowed his head, fingering the cross that hung around his neck as if at prayer. He was still for some long time and I held my breath. Then, turning to the friar who had brought the accusations he told him firmly:

"Yet again all I hear is hearsay not heresy. As I said, I've found no wrong in Mistress Kempe save an excess of enthusiasm and I will not condemn her for that. As for the maidservant, this is the first time I've heard anything against her."

"The Duke of Bedford is determined to have them both," answered the friar, "and he shall judge where the treason is in them …"

But Bowet interrupted him.

"I see no cause to send them to the secular court, but despite my judgment I'll speak some more with you since you say you've known of them for many years. In the meanwhile they must be kept in some secure dwelling until I'm ready to question them again."

Once again we were comfortably lodged and Margery remained serene and merry, assuring me that God would protect her. But I feared the hellmouth was ajar and we would never be free. I dreaded this next encounter, recalling my meetings with Ralph's friends long ago and remembering that even Spryngolde had not trusted me. And I saw how different

Margery and I were. She was ever ready to tell all and everyone what the Lord said to her in visions and prayer, whether they believed her or not. She was like an open book. But I was secretive, and always fearful that my guilty secrets might be revealed, terrified someone might read my mind, look deep into my soul, see my doubts and disbelief and discover I was indeed a true heretic.

A few days later we were summoned to a private meeting in Bowet's chamber. There was no one in the streets but still I followed Margery in great fear. Apart from the Archbishop and his steward only the two friars and one of Bedford's retainers, who had spoken against us, were there. Bowet greeted us, then turned to one of them.

"You told me friar, you had specific charges to make against Mistress Kempe and her maidservant, so now I give you leave to question them, and if you satisfy me of their wrong-doing, I'll agree to hand them over to Bedford."

I was certain I'd be found out, but was mistaken, it was an entirely different question the friar put to us.

"It's said you two went to visit Lady Westmoreland, who is aunt to our Duke Bedford, and spoke with her daughter Lady Greystoke. So tell us now when was that and what was it you talked about?"

Both Margery and I answered at once. I wanted to tell them that John Kempe had been with us, we were there for only one night some four years hence, and I'd not met either lady. But the other friar interrupted me, demanding I come to the furthest part of the chamber and speak with him separately, though I doubt he heard a word I said as he paid scant attention and appeared more interested in Margery's account.

It seemed a great row was brewing. The friar was accusing

her of telling Lady Greystoke to leave her husband, adding that
was a treasonable offence and she would die for it. Margery
was as white as her vestments, but said she'd be happy to speak
with Lady Westmoreland again and seek a testimonial that
she'd suggested no such thing. The friar shouted back he could
wait while we were held in prison. I ran over to him in tears,
Margery continued to protest her innocence while the steward
intervened shouting out,

"Let's get rid of both of them, send them far away, back to
their menfolk. And if they ever come here again, I personally
will burn them both."

Bowet held up his hand as if to bless us, then shook his head
and muttered,

"Dear Lord I pray you, spare me from these women. I do not
know what I might do with them."

Margery was swift to seize the advantage and swore to leave
forthwith. She asked Bowet for a letter showing she'd vindicated
herself against her enemies and no heresy or treason had been
proved against her, and that his man be engaged once more to
guide us home. Bowet was quick to agree, dictated the letter
then and there, told us to wait and summoned John to escort us
back to Lynn. The old man looked none too pleased when he
arrived and Margery called out:

"Be you happy, it is full merry in Heaven,"
which he did not take kindly, turning a sullen face to her and
answering,

"Holy folk should not laugh."

Bowet told him to meet us early on the morrow, dismissed
him and bade us kneel to receive his blessing, which I did with
great gladness.

We stood up but then, just as the steward was leading us to

the door, the friar who'd questioned Margery stepped in front of me, blocking my way.

"Ah, now I see you, it was too dark before. I recognise you and remember too where I last saw you, some years ago, in Cheapside at the tanner's workshop where I went to enquire after Ralph from Lynn, a Lollard and an associate of Oldcastle. You rushed away mighty quick then, just as you did at Hessle, but now we have you."

He grasped my arm and Bedford's man came towards me and held the other.

"The friar knows you and condemns you. Let us now for the secular court."

They both dragged me towards the door.

Time stopped. My legs were ice. I could not move, yet the door was open and I on the threshold of death, eternal damnation and the fires of hell.

"I pray you, a little less haste," said Bowet, and his voice seemed to come from a great distance. "It's for me to decide whether she be heretic or not before you judge her traitor." And they pulled me towards him, their hands on my head, pushing me down to kneel before him once more.

"Woman, I will ask you just three questions and you must answer sincerely. If you do not, then both body and soul will be in peril of the fire. Tell me now, how do you understand the bread and wine at communion?"

I knew the Lollards judged worshipping the Eucharist as idolatry, but had learnt otherwise at the convent.

"It is the body and blood of our Lord Jesus," I said.

"Can a Bishop serve two masters?"

Was I then to help him out of his dilemma about spiritual and secular authority and the demands of Bedford's men, I

271

wondered, but knew what Margery would say.

"God is my King."

Someone scoffed that that was no good answer but Bowet hushed them.

"And now, finally, what do you understand by repentance?"

I was seized by sudden dread. Sister Margaret had sometimes encouraged me to seek within, to consider my faults and make amends, while Margery sought succour as often as she could in confessing to priests and begging for penance, and though I seldom saw an increase in charity when she returned from Mass, she was often full of joy. But I knew too there was much I would never confess to a priest as I expected no understanding, solace or absolution. I looked at Margery and her eyes were downcast.

"It is confessing to a priest," I whispered, "being contrite and doing penance."

Bowet put his hands on my shoulders and bid me stand up.

"You may go now my child, I see no heretic in you, just a simple faith."

"Simple," hissed Bedford's man. "Simple indeed. What of her consorting with Lollards, her secret reading, and hiding from us at Hessle?"

"And what does she say about visiting Cheapside and searching out the traitor Ralph who was later burnt for his part in the rebellion in St Giles Fields?"

The friar pushed me down again, Bowet said nothing and I started to weep. Then I heard someone behind me and Margery was kneeling by my side.

"My Lord Bishop, you have judged my servant rightly, God help her. She is indeed a simpleton and would have been a slut too like her mother before her, if I had not had my eye on her. Ralph was once a member of our household but I saw he grew impudent, impious and incontinent in both his beliefs and conduct. And she took too much delight in him so I dismissed him before she could fall into sin as her mother had done. Then sometime after, when I was visiting my Lord Arundel at Lambeth, she ran away to find him. I would have dismissed her then but had promised my father on his deathbed that I would look after her. And I will not break my vow."

"I commend you for your charity, dear lady," said Bowet wearily. "I now wish to hear no more of this. You are both dismissed and be sure to be ready to leave tomorrow at first light. And you gentlemen may stay and pray with me awhile."

He gestured to his steward to let us out.

We said nothing to each other on the way back. I packed our belongings while Margery knelt at prayer but before I blew out the candle she held my wrists.

"You know I did not lie, everything I said was true. And do not forget this. My father gave you a life with me, now I have saved you and settled my debt to you."

Our journey south was swift. We returned to the ferry crossing at the river Humber and though we were stopped and questioned, John showed them Bowet's letter and we were permitted to pass. Once we'd crossed over, he asked a couple who were London-bound if we might travel with them as far as Lynn. They agreed and so he was freed of his burden, and left us without a backward glance.

It was an easy journey with no disturbance from Margery, who would not talk to me. We stopped at Lincoln where I begged to rest. Our companions were happy to have her for company and I was grateful to be alone with my thoughts. I was still much shaken but resolved to let Margery glory in her own truth. I was beginning to understand that though we were bound together we were two, not one.

It was nearing the end of November, the wind harsh, the land barren, the skies a sullen grey. Soon the countryside grew familiar and then we came to West Lynn by the crossing of the Ouse; the spires of St Margaret's and Greyfriars Tower were visible beyond the masts and rigging of the vessels moored at the quays. Margery refused to cross over and booked a room at an inn, saying Bowet had told her to go immediately to London and seek a letter there to sanction her vow of chastity now that she had completed her three pilgrimages. So I took the ferry on my own and returned alone, meeting no one, for it was late afternoon and raining, the streets deserted. I had a message for John that he make haste to meet Margery.

He greeted me warmly, but was not pleased to be summoned to go travelling again and implored me to come. But Margery had made it plain she didn't want me. I was happy to be released from further service to her, and he gave me some coinage that I might eat while they were away. He promised to send word before their return, hoping it would be by Christmastide. He left reluctantly and I fretted for he looked despondent. He was not a man much capable of caring for himself, and I'd no doubt that in our absence spiteful neighbours had mocked him yet again as a coward and cuckold. And I think he still had blind hopes that Margery would be reconciled to him after all her sufferings.

At first I was content in Fincham Street, so weary was I after all our troubles. John had dismissed all the household since the failure of his enterprises, except for an old man who brought in wood and rushes and minded the livestock in the yard: some poultry, a goat and a scraggy cat with ragged ears, only one seeing eye and a terror of vermin. There was also a slovenly young wench who'd cooked and cleaned for him, but I told her I was sick, gave her money to buy some provisions and said I'd summon her if I had need of her again. I had the solar to myself though it was caked with dirt, and on the first day when I tried to light the hearth, a raven's nest fell down and nearly started a fire. Tired though I was I cleaned the dwelling first, then retreated to my bed under the covers. I slept long for several days and more, and dreamlessly.

One morning I awoke in alarm and realized for the first time in my life I was truly alone. The solitude and silence irked me, I missed the breath and smell of another living soul. I thought to bring the cat inside for comfort and tried to tempt it with a saucer of milk, but it was so wild and untrusting that I gave up chasing it. So I left the yard door open that the fowl might come in and cheer me with their clucking. I knew I'd have to go out into the town one day and give account of myself, and hoped the neighbours would treat me kindly. Yet I was so used to feeling invisible and flinched at the thought of being rejected.

I dithered and dallied for many days, unable to find the courage to show my face in town. It was as if I were a small child again, keen to explore yet overcome with shyness. Then came a Sunday, I knew it was so for I heard the church bells ringing the call to prayer several times. Then a peal rang out again as it started to grow dark and there was much clamour in the street and bangs on the door. I guessed some alarm had been raised and the old man came jabbering in, though I could make no sense of any word he said.

So finally I went out, where there was great rejoicing. News had come that Oldcastle had been arrested, tried by Lord

Bedford and was to burn the very next day in London. Such was the relief that he'd finally been caught, the fear of traitors and bloody disturbance diminished, that a special thanksgiving Mass was to be celebrated that evening. Everyone was full of joy and welcomed me. And since no one asked about Margery or our recent pilgrimage, though some knew she'd gone to London with John, I felt accepted. Nor did I hear any word that news of our arrests had yet reached Lynn, for now the only chatter of the people was the safety of the realm.

Soon the Christmas season came and various acquaintances I met that Sunday, asked me to help with their New Year festivities. I'd often done so in the past, and enjoyed preparing riddles and word games. Besides I had need of money for a message came from John saying Margery was not willing to leave London so soon. At the same time I thought of her children, and wished to send them word of my return and their parents' absence, together with some New Year gifts. Both William and Godfrey had left Lynn to ply their trade over the seas, keen perhaps to cut their ties from a disgraced grandfather and a mother whom many mocked. But I knew the girls would be pleased to have some news.

So, despite my misgivings I found work again, and had coins enough to send greetings to Margery's daughters, a coney muff for Isobel and a little gold ring for Mary. New Year came and I began to feel stronger and had enough occasional employment to buy food. Yet still there was no word from London.

Only one person ever knew what happened next and I hesitate to write it, but it belongs to my story. Soon after the New Year festivities and certainly some weeks before Candlemas I received a messenger. Mary sent a boy from Isobel's household, thanking me for their gifts, and asking if she might come to stay. Of course I was delighted, nor did she have need of asking since Fincham Street was her home. I hadn't seen her for several years and she was now, I reckoned, fourteen or fifteen. I wondered what would bring her back while her parents were away. The winter months were not the time to visit, for the cruel winds and damp sea air made Lynn unfriendly, but it was not my business to tell her no.

She came before the week was out with a valet from Isobel's household, who left immediately after. She'd grown to be a pretty young woman, plumper than I remembered, with more the look of her father than her mother except for her eyes, which had Margery's sparkle when she smiled, though that she did not much. She looked well and I wondered what service she required, but she said she just wanted to come back home for a while. And she proved easy to care for with a quiet modesty and undemanding nature. She'd also learnt some simple skills, and when I was out at work she'd have some small supper prepared on my return.

Yet I was puzzled for she watched me intently, as if always about to speak then saying nothing. She talked little of herself, but often asked about my journeying and I was much pleased, for it is seldom the way of youth to be interested in other people's lives and especially not the elderly. One evening when I returned from helping a neighbour, I found her sitting in the dark and called the old man to bring wood for the fire, then lit some candles and soon it was homely again.

"What ails you Mary, you're more than usually quiet?"

"Nay nothing, nothing truly. But I was thinking today, I've known you all my life and often think of you as more than mother, not only those wonderful tales you used to tell at bedtime, but something in the heart of me. Yet I know nothing about you or your kin, where you lived as a child, and why you joined our household."

For one long moment I was minded to tell her everything, the true story, that she was kin, but could not countenance the thought of causing her distress. Besides, though we were familiar and she always most courteous and kind, yet she was born into gentility and I was not.

"I grew up in the country on a farm, a good day's ride from here, maybe even more. My kin died many winters ago."

"Did you have any brothers or sisters?"

"Yes, two brothers, but not of my blood…"

"How come? Where were your parents?"

"Ah Mary, it's a sad and joyful story. I never knew my parents. They died of the plague when I was born, that is the sadness. But the joy is that though I was a motherless child, I had the good fortune to be taken in and cared for by country folk, and Nanna, my good, kind foster grand-dam …"

And suddenly I saw tears coursing down her cheeks. I took her hand, and she started sobbing piteously.

"Mary, dear heart, Mary …"

"I don't know what to do. I am with child and don't know what to do. I came here for shelter. You're the only person I can trust. No one knows. You must help me. Can you help me, will you care for my babe …?"

"Of course, Mary, of course."

I was shocked. She was so young. I took her in my arms and thought of my mother and wondered if Mistress Brunham had hugged her.

"Mary, can you tell me more? Will you talk of the father? Is there no hope for the two of you?

"No, no, there's no hope at all ..."

"Now listen child. I'd never judge you. But tell me, were you ill used? Isobel's husband comes from worthy family and he's bound to protect the honour of his kin."

"No, I wasn't badly treated, it was all my fault."

I knew too well that recourse to self-blame, but remained silent and let her continue.

"I was lonely in Isobel's household, in need of comfort, a mother's love. She is in many ways like my mother used to be, rejoicing in good food and company, in flattery and flirtation but with little natural affection. Late last summer she held a banquet and one of her guests, a casual acquaintance, a friend of a neighbour, sought me out and I fell for his charm and let him have his way, then heard he was married. It's most unlikely he'll ever visit again and I do not esteem him at all."

I raged at the neglect, that no one had taken proper care of her, that her mother had abandoned her, having more thought for the childhood of Jesus than her own dear children. We talked long into the night, I told her the dangers of too much innocence and how she should value her own loving nature and spend it wisely. And I promised I'd never betray her, would attend her labour and find foster parents for her babe.

I went to Sybile the next day and told her of Mary's situation, knowing she was no friend to gossip and would never disclose her plight. I knew I could manage the birth on my own but asked if she'd give Mary shelter, should Margery return before her time came. This she promised to do for unless she was called to be midwife, she did not welcome visits from neighbours and kept her door closed against prying eyes. The townsfolk still held her in awe for her skill in birthing and burying, and did not pester her lest she refuse to give them aid when they had need.

I'd heard talk of an old woman in town who gave herbs to those who wished to purge themselves of their unborn burdens, but Mary would never agree to this. So who might take her babe? When I lived in the convent infants were sometimes abandoned at the parlour door and farming folk often offered to stand as parents, for many had generous hearts. In Lynn foundlings were left on occasion at the Mary Magdalene hospital or taken secretly at night to the Grey Friars, for though they might rail against immorality they did not hold an innocent child should suffer for lack of a father. But it was a hazardous undertaking to abandon a babe even to the Church, as the Justices did not sanction such practices, especially in Lynn where sailors sought their pleasure at the stews or public baths, and were careless about what they left behind. Recalling my own good fortune, I wished this little one might have the same loving care that had been given me, that kindness of strangers. But I didn't know anyone who might shoulder this task.

Sybile surprised me.

"Have no fear. If Mary agrees, I'll adopt the babe myself. I've brought many into this world but never had the good fortune to bear one of my own. She shall have a loving home here with me and no one will inquire whose she is, for I warrant she'll be a girl-child. Her secret will be safe. And you too may have the care of her, for you've also been mother to many, and this little one will not be a complete stranger."

Before I could thank her she continued,

"Labour in childbirth is only one of the trials of motherhood. Bonds that should be forged sometimes fail. A mother may die and never enjoy the fruits of her pain. Another may have no natural affection and reject her offspring. But we shall not let this infant, Margery's grandchild and Brunham's kin, suffer from any such neglect, and so we two shall heal that wrong that was done many years ago."

And guiding me to the door, she bid me farewell before I could say a word.

I was much comforted, as was Mary. It was soon Lent but I'd stocked up that she might eat well during this time. Few required my help over these weeks so we spent those quiet days together. Then a message came from John that they would stay in London until after Easter, so I had no fear of their sudden return. When the time came it was an easy birth and, as Sybile predicted, a beautiful little girl, placid and content, the image of her mother.

Mary fed her babe for two weeks and then prepared to leave. Before she left I bound her breasts to cease the flow of milk. She threaded the ring I'd gifted her on a little gold chain, hung it round her daughter's neck and vowed she'd send for her and adopt her as her own when she married. I took the babe to Sybile and we named her Isolde as Mary had requested and we both marvelled at her, this motherless child who had two loving childless foster mothers.

Margery and John returned soon after Easter and though both seemed tired Margery had that determined look I knew well. She had procured what she'd wanted, a letter from the new Archbishop acknowledging her vow of chastity. She had sought it for many years and now she had it with his seal attached. As soon as she arrived she went straight to St Margaret's to give thanks for her safe return, bearing the deed in her hand that all might see and know it.

John, pleading weariness, stayed at home and I felt for him now any hope of winning Margery back was lost. She'd made it clear they could not live together, knowing that the gossips would nudge each other and say that although she made a show of chastity during the day, she'd clamber and romp in his bed at night as had been the delight of her youth. I wondered why she hadn't sought an enclosure by the church, become a hermit in an anchorhold as other pious women did, so she might be truly recluse. But it was not Margery's way to hide herself from the world.

So, in a short while we moved out of Fincham Street. I'd lived there for nearly twenty-five years though in recent times it had become less homely, once the children had left and we'd been much away. This would have been the ideal time to leave Margery, but I hesitated. She'd spent all her money on travelling and charity and was in debt again, and I doubted she would treat me generously. Besides she had not yet paid me for my service since our return from Rome.

I knew I'd find occasional work in the town and the money I didn't need for lodging and food while living with Margery, I could save for Mary's babe. That secret salted my bitterness and sweetened my spite. Serving Margery was no longer so demanding that I couldn't find time to visit little Isolde. And so we moved to a small tenement in Skinners Row near the Fynnes Lane crossing with both St Margaret's church and St James' chapel nearby. And John found lodging close by in Fullers Row.

When you grow old it's as if time changes and speeds up. Yet nothing much happened in those first few years after we moved, nothing except Margery's almost constant illness. Sometimes her head tortured her and when it did she screamed and said it was never so painful as Christ's crown of thorns. Oftentimes she had a bloody flux, and once I sent for her priest believing she was near death. The physics proposed many recipes, but this time she listened to me and took the potions I brought from Sybile. Nevertheless the trouble persisted for many months and in time she shrank so much she looked like one of those stick and straw men they put up in the corn fields to scare the birds away. Finally the attacks were less frequent, but then she complained of a wound in her chest, and told all who'd listen that it was nothing as grievous sore as the lance that had been thrust into Christ's side.

When she was not sick, Margery was out in the town, spreading her pious words, teaching not preaching as she assured everybody, often on her knees, sobbing loudly and meddling as usual. Several clerics came again to read from the holy books. But as always she divided people, just as I still felt so divided about her in my heart. She accepted the insults when they came and they often did, as if they were gifts from God, whether it was a chamber pot some enemy tipped over her, a priest who caused her to be banned from church, friars who forbad her attend their sermons, or the Devil's lewd temptations which continued to disgust her. At other times she gloried in the attention of those who loved and esteemed her.

Then something occurred which changed many people's hearts, and even left me much amazed. It was the winter season, two years after Margery's return from London and the day of the Tuesday market. I rose early that morning, a dawn of clear bright skies, to be the first to buy whatever produce was available. As I was returning with my baskets, walking down Stockfish Row, I saw smoke rising in the sky and people ahead of me running in all directions, and I heard much shouting. So I ran too.

Near the square thick dark clouds were billowing out from the Guildhall, and I saw a chain of people passing buckets of water from the river to douse the fire. Then a fierce wind started to blow and hungry flames flared up, and those with homesteads nearby rushed to save their goods from the burning sparks that had set their thatched roofs alight. Many ran screaming to St Margaret's. I followed and there was Margery near the altar urging Spryngolde to take the holy host towards the flames, assuring all that God would halt the fire.

Black smoke started to fill the church; there was the dread sound of heated stones and crackling wood, the great lantern tower caught fire and burning timbers fell down on the altar. Margery called out and told us all to get on our knees. Suddenly it grew dark, the wind roared and with it a great snowstorm came and in no time at all the fire ceased. Those in the church crowded round her, proclaiming it a great miracle and many believed it had come about through her prayers. It was indeed most wondrous, and many were in tears, thanking and praising her.

I don't know how this happened, and though I did overhear an old seaman muttering that such sudden winter storms had visited Lynn in the past, Margery did not brag and boast as she used to and many forgave her for the swagger and swank of her earlier years. Thereafter she continued to be busy with works of mercy, visiting the sick and those in need. And once a message came from a neighbour beseeching her to visit his wife who'd become crazed after the birth of her first babe, just as she had all those years ago. She spent many days at her bedside until the distraught mother was calm again, though I do not think for a moment the cause of her madness was the same as Margery's.

We'd no news of young John, whose birth had caused her such grief many years before, until sometime after we came back from Spain. Yet as they say an apple does not fall far from the tree and though I know he feared rejection, he also sought his mother's love. So at last he came back to Lynn from his apprenticeship overseas and dwelt with one of the merchants in town, though he was still often away doing trade along the Baltic coast.

At times he came to visit us, always wonderfully arrayed in the kinds of silk, satin and brocade his mother had once favoured, in all the latest fashions, and he had the same glad eye that revelled in attention as she. He was not yet wed and it was rumoured he was very free with the local wenches. Margery had little time for him, only telling him off for his loose manners, pestering him to give up trade and study for the priesthood instead, and once I heard her tell him:

"Now John, since you will not leave the world at my advice I charge you, at my blessing, at least to keep your body clean from women's company until you take a wife. And if you do not I pray God chastise and punish you for your lust."

I saw then his brazen stare, for no young man likes to be rebuked, least of all by his mother. Yet I also knew that beneath this boldness he would be smarting sore, since all that charm and bright display were just childish ploys to find favour in her eyes, for the mother who'd never shown him love. There lay the injury, for the more he tried to attract her, the more he felt rejected by her exhortations to chastity. But he was not minded to give up his pleasures and soon stopped visiting us, though once in a while I caught sight of him at the quays conducting business with the merchants or charming the damsels. Then I saw him no more until one day I heard he'd been dismissed from his master's service, because of some terrible disfigurement on his face, which oozed with boils and bloody pimples.

So once again there was meat for the gossips to chew on, fed no doubt by him, who let it be known that his mother had cursed him with a witch's spell. While some remembered the miracle of the fire and snowstorm, others still enjoyed the scandal of Margery's pomp and pride and now blamed her for her son's disorder. She told them all she did not care, that he'd never get better till he asked for her forgiveness. But I couldn't bear to see him suffer so and went to Sybile to seek some remedies, which I contrived to give him. Soon the pustules got better and he came to Margery asking for money to go on pilgrimage to Rome, to give thanks for his cure. And she, believing her prayers had brought this about, borrowed money and sent him off with her blessing. That alone was balm for his troubled soul.

For several years after this peace reigned in our town. I continued to serve Margery when she had need of me, but often had the freedom to assist Sybile and spend time with our little daughter. She was an amiable child and as soon as she could talk I started showing her the numbers and letters I'd enjoyed at her young age, and Sybile took her into the forest to gather herbs and simples. So the weeks and months passed quietly and I felt more at ease.

Now there was more warmth between my mistress and me. She struggled less to prove herself despite the enmity of others, even if at times she raged and railed against them privately. But as her health improved, she grew impatient, often fretting that there were no neighbours to share her visions with. This had always been her way, swinging between high hopes and deep despair, one moment held in the palm of God's hand as she so often told me, at other times trampled underfoot by the Devil. I always worried she'd cause disturbance again with her unstaid ways, until one day the thought came to me how to bring her back to steadfastness.

"Margery, Master Alan was speaking the other day of Bridget's book and how it was written down in Latin from her mother tongue. Other priests too have read us books about the lives of holy women, and told us those women dictated their books to their confessors. So why should we not write down our story?"

"Our story ... we?"

"Your story, Margery, yours. You can tell it and I shall write it. We can do it secretly, in English, then others can read it later for themselves. ... what think you of that?"

"Yes, tis true. Repyngdon did suggest it, as did Arundel when I spoke with him in his garden under the starlight, and he told me I should put down my holy thoughts just as I spoke them."

"And we can do so in the long evenings when you come back from church or after ministering to the sick ..."

So it was agreed and I purchased parchment and ink saying it was for John. It was slow work for though I knew the alphabet letters I struggled to form them into words, and private too since we feared accusations of heresy should anyone discover our labours. And when Margery insisted I be audience to her contemplations, she still had to listen when I told of my adventures, though we never wrote those down. She made it clear that it was her book and never even listened when I said my memories were different to hers. So it seemed I just wasn't there with her in the stories she told.

Yet nothing ever stays the same and change comes when we least expect it. It was some four or five years after our return from Compostela when one afternoon someone came banging on our door. We were both at home about our business of

Margery's book, and quickly hiding our endeavours, I went to see who called. It was a neighbour from Fullers Row and she was much distraught.

"Where's Margery? O Margery you must come quickly. John's fallen down the stairs and has many wounds about his person. He's badly cut, there's blood everywhere and he cannot stand. We've sent for the physicians and they're just now plugging several holes in his head. At first he couldn't utter a single word but now he can, and he's calling for you Margery and you must come."

John and Margery rarely saw each other since they lived apart, but she often told me God reminded her in her meditations of John's kindness. She hadn't forgotten him, and taking her cloak she hurried to his home. He was indeed gravely hurt, and even when his head began to heal there was some deeper affliction for he could hardly speak, was never able to make any sense, his limbs shaking and askew so he could only shuffle a few steps here and there, and could not even feed himself. More than that he was no longer able to answer the call of nature, and never went to the stool but pissed and soiled his garments whenever he willed.

For the first few weeks we took turns in minding him, but it was exhausting work with all the washing and feeding, and he so querulous and afraid, frightened of the dark as children often are, so that one of us always had to stay the night with him. As usual this was joy for those townsfolk who held malice in their hearts and were soon saying it was all Margery's fault he was ill, since she'd forsaken her Christian duty as wife to care for him, and they swore if he died she'd be to blame. So finally we had no choice but to bring him back to Skinners Row and look after him there.

Then one afternoon when I was alone with him, Sybile's man came with a message asking me to come. I sent him back saying I'd leave as soon as my mistress returned, thinking she had some new medicines for John. Within a short time he came again, insisting I make haste for Sybile had urgent need of me. I was suddenly much afraid because there was sickness in town and I hadn't seen little Isolde for several days. So I covered John with a blanket, put more logs on the fire and left him in his chair, though he whimpered and whined like a dog that has lost its master.

It was already darkening as I hurried to Sybile. There was little water in the fleet, the tide was on the ebb. Rain fell softly, the lanes were empty, all the folk safe and warm indoors. I heard footsteps ahead of me but saw no one in the gloom. A single candle burning in the casement guided me to Sybile's home, where a crow sat on the lintel. I sensed before I'd even knocked there was little joy awaiting, and when she let me in, tears in her eyes, I knew Death had come to call before me.

Isolde, our secret, winsome daughter, lay still and silent in her bed, as pure and innocent as the little angels in the Nativity painting in the Gesine chapel. As I stroked her cheek I found it was not yet cold, though there was no sign of any breath in her. She'd slipped away just before I came. But there was no anger in my sorrow that her little life had ebbed so soon, rather a great gratitude that I'd been able for so short a while to enjoy the care of her, the gift of this child, my own sweet kin.

I told Sybile I'd let Mary know. But first I needed time to mourn the little creature on my own and walked to the staithe beyond the Purfleet Bridge, where I'd stood the day my uncle sailed away, full of hope and later in despair. It was a still evening with a gentle drizzle. There was salt in the air and the smell of fish from the evening catch. Water lapped along the edge of the quays. I heard the Watch calling out the hour. Life and death come at their appointed time, but I knew I would never forget the smile and chatter of this little grandchild.

A few days later I paid a man to take a message to Mary and gave him the ring that she'd hung round Isolde's neck. I told him to tell her privately that I'd found it in some cloth I'd been sewing for a toddler's smock, but the child had died before I'd finished my work and I guessed the ring was hers. I knew she'd understand. A week later a message came back from Isobel. There had been tragedy in her household. Mary had fallen into the river as she was walking along the bank one evening and had drowned. She was already buried and much missed, mourned for her kindness and especially for the love she had for the children thereabouts. I did not think for a single moment this was an accident and felt a great and endless grief.

After that the weeks, months and years became increasing tiresome. Poor John Kempe changed not at all except to grow worse, needing endless attention, and was usually left in my charge. We had little time to work on Margery's book. I still assisted Sybile, but there was less joy in these visits though we often spoke of Mary and Isolde. Margery continued much as before, on her knees at prayer, with her priests, doing her good works or travelling to shrines here and there.

Once I accompanied her to Norwich where we saw a terrible sight. A woman, Margery Baxter she was called, bareheaded and bare-foot, clad only in a shift with a candle in her hand and a bundle of faggots on her back, was being jeered at by a crowd as they led her away to church. They said she was to be flogged for claiming human beings, who bore so much suffering, were the true cross and they alone should be worshipped. This was what Sawtre had preached many years before, and now I knew in truth, after all my woes, that this was my belief, and I agreed with her.

Then news came from young John. Since his return from Rome he'd set up business in Danzig, where he'd married a German maid who was now with child. He asked if he might come and visit when the babe was born and bring his family with him. Margery was much pleased that her eldest son had wed, but as for the news she'd now be grandmother, she did not seem to delight much in that. But I suppose it was memories of John's birth that troubled her.

This would be her first known grandchild since Isobel, her eldest daughter, had none of her own. I wondered at this, remembering how her mother's pregnancies had been as constant as the tides. Isobel suffered many miscarriages over the years and then, a year after Isolde and Mary died, she too died in childbirth. Yet whenever we were alone Margery never spoke of her children, and only asked I put down more of her revelations. We'd been working at her book for several years, but I was growing weary of it and mostly vexed because she still let me play no part in it. So I often told her my eyes were tired and could write no longer.

Young John sent word again some months later to say Magda had given birth to a little girl. They'd planned to take a ship and sail to Lynn, but a fierce gale had blown the day they left and they'd returned to harbour. The season of storms had come early, so he wrote they'd travel overland and sail from Calais, leaving the babe behind as she was too young for such a long journey.

I knew he'd be disappointed not to show his daughter to

Margery. All children want their parents to know they too can be parents. But John's need of his mother's love had not yet been fulfilled, for she never sent him messages. I'd hoped to see his child, but still was happy he was coming with his wife, since Skinners Row had become a gloomy place with no laughter, only the constant care of poor John Kempe.

They sailed into Lynn early one Saturday and I went straightway to the market to buy some festive food to welcome them, because we now kept a very meagre kitchen; Margery had stopped eating meat again and John could only take pottage. I brought back one of the lads to help, and soon the board was laid with hearty dishes, the fire lit and our home was warm and comfortable once more. Yet when young John sat down to eat, he looked wan, and after only one plate had to lie down. I wondered if the excitement of being back with his mother had overwhelmed him.

But the next day he was no better and though we sent for physicians, they could not say what ailed him. Sybile came and even she was puzzled. It seemed he was just wasting away. So now we had two invalids to nurse, and Magda and I were busy mopping brows and wiping dribble, washing sheets and cooking simple dishes, trying to feed our patients as if they were two little children.

John died one Friday evening, a month or so after his arrival in Lynn. Three weeks later his father, though that must still remain a mystery, also died. Two funerals in one month. Will I be unkind if I say Margery did not seem much distressed? Of course, John Kempe's death was in some ways a blessing, a relief, and perhaps her son's death was too, for she'd been tortured by guilt for nearly forty years. What distressed her more was the cruel gossip, for many hadn't forgotten how she had abandoned her husband and cursed her son. But I mourned them both, more than she seemed to do.

Magda might have been more saddened too, but for the delight she now found in Margery's company. Soon she was watching her as a sated cat will stare at a dish of cream. Margery had found a willing apprentice to the trials and joys of sainthood. The two of them were always on their knees, talking to the priests or doing charitable works. And suddenly I found myself like one of my mistress's cast-off garments, after all my years of service to her, no longer her handmaid in whom she might sometime confide, but just some serving wench.

8

Bishop's Lynn, Danzig, Aachen, Bishop's Lynn, 1431–July 1441

'I thanked God for his kindness'

Yesterday I went to Lynn, to St Margaret's, for the celebration of Margery's anniversary Mass. Since I left Skinners Row I seldom go to the town anymore, busy with writing my story and doing chores for Agnes. It seems I have more to do now than all those years ago when I was Margery's handmaid. Everything takes much longer, I'm often tired, my eyes are failing and my back hurts when I walk. Nor do I hear clearly so find it difficult to be with too many people. Though month by month there are fewer left to talk with. Death comes to gather us all.

Of all my acquaintances Sybile's death was the hardest to bear for we had shared much. But not everything.

After the Mass there was an anniversary feast, to which out of charity I'd been invited. I didn't want to go and tried to slip away at the end of the service, not that slipping away is easy at my age, despite the use of the stick which Hilda made for me from a sturdy branch of birch-wood. But the young priest with the beaming visage, whom I'd seen buying vellum some time before, came rushing over, gripped my arm and would not let me go. He was so excited that he no longer sang out his words but hurtled them at me, like an urgent sermon, with barely a pause for breath.

"God's greeting my good lady, how fare you … you're just the person I want to see … they tell me that you, God bless you, that you were Margery Kempe's maid and I've much to ask, much indeed … I've just made copy

294

of certain passages from her book, may all the saints protect her, and I need to speak with you, have much to ask you, and now I am speaking with you, thanks be to God."

He made the sign of the cross, gasped and started again.

"It's the prayer I want to talk about, the prayer she used to say every morning, where she beseeches God that she be given grace to withstand the temptations of her spiritual enemies, a long prayer, a holy prayer and it ends, it ends ..."

He crossed himself once more, took another breath and rattled on.

"It ends: 'And I thank you, Lord, for all those sins you have kept me from, which I have not done, and I thank you, Lord, for all the sorrow you have given me for those sins which I have done, and I thank you Lord for all those who have faith and trust, or shall have faith and trust, in me and my prayers until the world's end.' And did she teach it you, did you say it with her, God bless her, and what prayer did she say at the day's end before retiring?"

He gasped again and began with yet more questions, but by good fortune one of the monks came over to speak with him and I was excused an answer. I'd never heard that prayer before though it sounded just like Margery. I was there when she and Spryngolde worked on her book and noticed she often let him put down his own words, a generosity she never afforded me. And to my mind Spryngolde was much more eloquent than she, and especially he fashioned a marvellous fable out of our last pilgrimage though neither of them ever knew the most wondrous part of it.

After the deaths of her husband and oldest son the gossips gave Margery no peace, forever carping and chiding, telling each other that though she had fountains of tears for her holy thoughts she never shed any for her dead family, though how they knew for whom she wept I cannot tell. When news came that William and Geoffrey had both drowned in a shipwreck, we went straightway to church and I knelt there, mourning all those lost at sea. What she prayed for I do not know, but for sure her quest to be God's wife and handmaid was more important than any prayers for her family.

Her tears became more vehement as the years went by and she was reproached by many priests, who resented this disturbance to their carefully worded sermons. It had long been a matter of dispute between her supporters who spoke of those holy women who had been graced with the gift of tears, and those others who thought her a false hypocrite. Whether it was to silence them or quell her own sad thoughts, she had the notion to get her book completed and wished it be finished fast. And since I would do no more of it, she asked a young priest to be her scribe.

She gave him my work and fabricated a falsehood saying it had been written by one of her son's friends who'd now returned to Germany. He looked at it and complained he couldn't read a word. I wondered if he were feeble-minded and told him to sit nearer the casement that he might have more light. But he continued to baulk, saying the letters were all muddled, the words too cramped so I sent him away to purchase some spectacles. When he came back with them he said he could see the pitcher of ale on the sideboard quite clearly, but swore he still could make no sense of the writing, so I told Margery I'd read to him. But she would have none of that and thus the work was left. Perhaps he had need of more faith, but then again he may have been a milksop.

Maybe this is rancour on my part but there were several simple-minded priest cubs we met at this time. It is the way of youth to think they alone always know what is right and judge anyone who says differently to be wrong. I notice this folly especially in those young scholars studying for the priesthood, who mostly believe themselves much cleverer than the common folk on whom they look down, and never learn the value of common sense. Humility and learning seldom share the same board.

It was this same, seemingly unlettered priest who told us of a cleric he'd met, one newly arrived in Lynn, who offered to sell him a fine prayer-book but said he had need of the money first and would then bring it to his house. Though I cautioned him he wouldn't listen and, having handed over the coins, he saw neither man nor book again. There was another greenhorn who was duped into lending several marks to a travelling friar, who departed the following day and no one heard of him after. Once again I'd advised against this, and I have to say it is the folly of old age to gloat at so often being right, for of course we may all be wise after the event.

There were indeed many scribes who worked on Margery's book. The one I'd tried to write, the one that kept us occupied in the dull days after our travels, that one stayed with the young priest who couldn't read it. Later, when we returned from Germany, he came and said he could now read it and was ready to complete the work. So he copied it and left the one I'd written at Skinners Row, which I put in the bottom of my mistress's chest. And there it lay until I found it after her funeral. Some years after Margery asked Spryngolde to copy it once more with some additions, and he added many of his own words, a vindication and validation of her life. It talked of her pomp and pride, suffering and sickness, revilement and rejection, repentance and grace. Then he wrote how she was commanded to have her revelations put down so the people should praise the Lord. And she also asked him to compose another book of our last journey, and it was as if I had no part in that one either, that I did not go with her, that I was not there. But I'm glad I kept the first draft of Margery's book, as there were events in it from long ago I might have forgot, unlike the memories of our last pilgrimage, which remain as clear as this very moment now.

Memories, memories. Presently I find in my solitary reflections I often return to those days of my childhood, when it seemed the skies were always blue and every morning a sunshine promise of delight, of seeds and feathers dancing in the breeze asking to be caught, of flowers in the meadows waiting to be picked, fruit and berries hiding in the hedgerows and birdsong I'd never heard before. Sometimes there was a rainbow to wonder at, the fluttering of a butterfly's wings, an insect clinging to an underleaf, and sparkling raindrops dangling on the bare branches of a tree or captured in the tracery of a cobweb.

The bright yellowy fragrance of gorse, delicate white scent of hawthorn, bluebell promise of summer days, and the warm, friendly smell of just-laid eggs, of drying hay, newborn pigs and pups, all those come back to me with a startling freshness. And when the skies were full of clouds there might be pictures of wondrous beasts and curious visages to behold. Even on winter days I remember the joy I found in a sudden flurry of snowflakes or images carved in the slithers of ice, and at night there was the puzzling mystery of the stars and the waxing and waning of the moon.

And I marvel more and more at the long road I have travelled, especially that last journey over the seas, the most difficult and delightful of them all.

Magda and Margery continued to find much comfort in each other's company, twinned as they were in their spiritual endeavours. Mostly they stayed close together, but once when I was alone with Magda I asked her about the merchants from her town and if she'd ever heard the stories of the twins, the maiden who died in England and her brother who was lost at sea many winters after. Whether she'd not heard of those sad misadventures or thought it ill fortune to tell, I learnt nothing and still ached from not knowing more about my mother.

Some two years passed and I remained as if invisible, just minding the household. Then a foreigner came knocking at our door, one of Magda's relatives who brought messages from her parents, calling her back home to them and her babe, and she agreed to go. He said he'd booked passages on a vessel newly arrived at Ipswich that was bound for Danzig the following week.

Margery was much flustered to be losing her young companion. They went to St Margaret's together that Magda might make her confession before the hazards of the voyage and the priest asked who'd accompany her to the port, as he did not think it seemly that she go alone with the stranger. Margery persuaded him she should take her to Ipswich and bid farewell to her there. He agreed but insisted Reynald the hermit go with her, to bring her back to Lynn. Then she summoned me.

"Now, make haste, prepare my things for I'll leave on the morrow and take Magda to the vessel for her departure."

"But Margery you woke a few days past with pains in your feet and even now are quite lame and need a stick. Let me come with you so at least you'll have an arm to lean on and some comfort once you've said goodbye to Magda, rather than make a sad return on your own."

"No wench, I'll have Reynald with me. You stay here and look after the house."

But before cockcrow the next day she roused me urgently.

"God spoke to me last night and said it was his will I make another pilgrimage and now I'm determined to sail to Danzig, so I shall have need of you after all. Make haste, pack my white clothes and all the other necessaries, then go fast foot to Mark the mercer, take this ring, these buttons, brooches and buckles. Say I need the coinage this very moment but mind you do not tell him the true cause. Spryngolde must not know for I fear he will not countenance my journeying and I've no time to tell him of God's words. Tell Mark I need the monies to pay the passage for my son's widow and beg him give me all he has. And yes, yes, you may as well come too. And on your return summon Reynald and bid him bring the wagon at first light."

And I was overjoyed and any fear of the dangers ahead, for it was still winter, the weather foul and many storms at sea, all that counted for nothing when I thought that finally, after all these long years, I would travel to my mother's land.

We left the following morning and joined the Milky Way, the pilgrimage route to Walsingham. First we walked barefoot to the Slipper Chapel. It was small and dark, sweet smelling and crammed with jewels donated by grateful parents. I remembered how my Loller friends were wont to chant "Walsingham-Falsingham," but recalled too that worshipping at this holy shrine brought much comfort to distressed parents who'd come to beg for Mother Mary's intercession.

It was told of this place that in years gone by a noblewoman was instructed in a dream to build a likeness of the Virgin's home for the easement of motherhood, and this she did. We'd seen the true place in Nazareth though it was much dilapidated. Besides the rich votive offerings, there were many waxen images of babes hanging by the altar, in memory of those sickly infants who'd made recovery after their mothers prayed here. And I was sad thinking I'd not been able to do so for Isolde.

We journeyed then to Norwich for my mistress wished to speak with a Grey Friar and tell him of her vision. He said that it was true, and if it were God's will then she must go on pilgrimage and gave her his blessing. From there we went to the Ipswich quays where we found the ship waiting. Only then did Margery speak of her resolve, and dismissing Reynald she hobbled up the gangplank. Magda was surprised and said she'd no further need of her, but Margery insisted. And so we set sail on a bright spring day with a fair wind blowing. I remember this was on a Thursday, and I thanked God for his charity and was full of joy.

By the following morning we'd crossed over the sea and I saw the mud flats near Zierickzee, the place we'd sailed to some twenty years before on the start of our Jerusalem journey. The weather continued fair and we stayed near the coast all day, heading for Jutland, to navigate the passage into the East Sea. This was no pilgrim ship but a trading vessel so there was no praying on board, just a quiet calm as the sailors went about their business, and in the daylight hours we were able to stay on deck. But it was a calm that did not last, for on Saturday a strong wind began to blow, with high seas and a bitter cold and we were ordered below. The ship tossed and turned all night long, both Margery and Magda were sick and I much discomforted.

On Sunday, Palm Sunday as I recall, the winds blew even stronger with rain that fell in torrents. The captain shouted down that we'd been blown off course, the rudder broke, main sail rent and he would let the vessel go where the wind directed for he could not steer against the gale. Then he fastened the hatches and we were left in the hold in the freezing darkness. It was indeed most frightening and searing cold, with the pitch and roll and crashing of the waves, and seawater pouring down on us. Margery was in much terror. She no longer evoked God as the great helmsman and her prayers seemed uncertain and mumbled so I comforted her, for now it was I who felt assurance that none of us would perish.

So in time, as Spryngolde later recorded, God and all his saints defeated this devil of a storm and we were allowed on deck again as we made a slow progress, finding shelter between many islands, with towering snow-covered mountains beyond them. Then we came to an inlet and a harbour, Bergen it was called, and tied up on the quays alongside a row of wooden houses of many different colours, belonging to the Hansa merchants of this Norwegian town.

When we had leave to disembark, we went to church for the Easter celebrations. There I thanked God once more for his kindness, that after all my sufferings he had heard my pleas at last that I might visit my mother's country. We returned to our vessel once the damage was repaired and set sail with fair winds again for the rest of our voyage. It remained exceeding cold with ice on the rigging, but the crew lent us furs and I stayed warm on deck with a cape wrapped round me, while Magda and Margery sheltered below. We sailed for many days past the coast into the East Sea and along the flat, sandy stretches of this Baltic land. And I thought of my mother and how she must have seen all this but from the opposite direction when she left more than sixty years ago to come to Lynn.

We arrived at dawn and it was as if I were coming home. I'd woken early and knew we'd changed tack for the weather now blew from a different direction. I saw we were sailing in a wide bay with a lighthouse on a low spit of land, then we turned into the mouth of a river with reeds and marshland on either side. We followed the bend of the river, tacked again and there ahead of us stood a grim redbrick castle on an island, and behind was the waterfront where many cogs were moored with their great oak hulls and single, tall thick masts. There were noble stone houses along the quays, painted in gay and colourful hues and gently lit by the rising sun. Beyond them were the steeples and spires of many churches and a vast sky of icy blue.

A large crowd had gathered when we moored: townsfolk, merchants, porters, children, and a motley flock of brightly dressed wenches waiting to hail the sailors home. Magda's parents came to her with much relief that she had survived the storm, and welcomed us warmly, though they had not been expecting to play host to two old ladies. We stayed with them for several weeks recovering from the rigours of our voyage, though I was dismayed I could not play with John's childling, who did not know our language and seemed frightened of us.

When the merchants heard of our coming, they came to greet us for many of them had known John and others recalled those of Margery's kin who'd done business there in the past. Such ventures were much prized in the town, and so we were accepted into their fellowship and often invited to dine with them, as it was the custom of this town to honour strangers. Sometimes I asked privately if any knew of the twins who had died tragically over the seas many years ago; but I was no more successful than I'd been with Magda yet I no longer despaired, for time heals much and more than time as well.

When Margery was not feasting, she gloried in the attention and since no one knew of her sometime bragging she suffered no scorn. She spent most of her days visiting many of the neighbouring churches. Usually she went out with one of the household maids for she'd quarrelled with Magda, who now no longer relished hours on her knees but preferred to entertain her little daughter and enjoy the attentions of the lusty young man whom her parents wished her to marry. And I was allowed to go where I willed.

Mostly Margery sought solace in St Bridget's church where her bones had lain before being taken for burial in her own country. I found comfort at St Mary's, a spacious building of red brick with lofty ceilings and many curious chapels, and especially I enjoyed the image of St George saving the maiden and vanquishing the dragon. There was a guild of St George here too, for he was patron saint of all the merchants along the coast and their hall was in a building called Arthushof, which was richly decorated with cunning models of trading-vessels fashioned out of amber.

Then the time came for our return and Margery, who had become most fearful of the seas, was minded to travel over land and make further pilgrimages to other sacred places. But we had no fellowship to accompany us, it was a long, uncertain journey and no one wanted to be our guide because of the conflict raging thereabouts between the Teutonic Knights who ruled that place and the Hussites, who were said to hold some of the same beliefs as the Lollards in our country. And furthermore these Teutonic Knights tried to hinder our departure because of their disputes with some English traders but at last a Lynn merchant, on business there, heard of our plight and arranged a licence for us to leave.

He also introduced us to a man, Jann was his name, who said he'd take us first by boat to a safe port along the coast and then by land to Wilsnack and Aachen, where we might make pilgrimages, and so to Calais and back to England. He asked only that we pay all charges and expenses, and bid us be ready to depart the next day.

On that last night in Danzig I went to St Mary's church to bid farewell to the image of St George. And as I stood there, an ancient, bent old woman appeared out of the shadows, calling to me and holding out her hands for alms. She was dressed in rags and I know not whence she came for the church had been near empty when I came in, empty and dark with just a few candles lit and a solitary monk or nun praying here and there.

Her form was frail, but as she stretched out her hands I saw her palms were white and beautifully formed, the hands of a young gentlewoman. I gave her the pittance I had, which she hid within her sleeve. Then she reached out to hold my hands and, as she looked up at me with a radiant smile, I saw the same odd eyes as mine. Then she was gone.

Now Margery had told me of her visions countless times and I never knew whether they were true or no. No more did I know then, or now, if this young-old woman were really there or not. But I was much awed and thought it a true miracle for I knew, yet cannot tell how, that she knew me as a mother always knows her child. And as I stood there I came to understand that my doubts were nothing more than waves rising and falling on the sea, and so the Devil no longer had power over me. I thought too that all the wrongs that had been done me could hurt me no more.

For in truth, I realised I should no more expect a good and loving God than a safe and easy journey, but knew him to be a mighty King who sets us ordeals and quests such as Arthur's knights had to endure, that we might kill the dragon of our loneliness and fear, and win our peace and loving friend. I marvelled at this revelation and the gratitude it gifted me that I had at last found the grace of honest prayer. In all the travails and tribulations of my life and many pilgrimages, I had always come back safely. As for a mother, I no longer had need of one, since I'd met with so much kindness over the years, which I all too easily forgot. I'd seen the country of my mother's childhood and was now ready to go home.

It was indeed a small cog Jann procured for us and very low in the water with no covered cabin, just benches in the hull where we might sit and sleep. We followed the coast and the seas were calm, though Margery was full of fear and would not look at the water. But I felt secure as if in another world, musing on that wondrous encounter at St Mary's and watching with my mother's eyes as I said farewell to our country. In some few days we disembarked at Stralsund, and after a day's rest Jann urged us on to Wilsnack as he was much afraid of the war around this place.

So we set off and struggled to keep up with him since he would take no heed of our age and Margery was overcome with tears, not I think so much from holy thoughts as from despair. Every day we pleaded with him to slow down, but he would countenance no delay and told us soldiers would come and steal our silver and cut us into pieces if we ever lagged behind. Then one noontime as we were following a path through the forest, we were alarmed by the fervent clamour of fighting ahead, the thunder of horses' hooves, clash of steel, bellows and bugle blasts and Jann pulled us roughly into the undergrowth, pushing us down flat on the ground. And there we lay, silent and trembling, hidden by the burze.

I looked up and saw a horde of troopers pursued by soldiers on their steeds, swords unsheathed, hacking here and there, then I buried my head in the earth and covered my ears, not wanting to hear the groans of the wounded and triumphant yells of their attackers. In time the clamour ceased, the soldiers galloped away and we lay still a very long time until Jann bade us creep deeper into the forest and left us while he sought news. He returned as it grew dark and said the trouble had passed, but we had to spend that night in open country with no food and only a small fire for comfort.

He was now in even greater haste to quit the region and demanded we always walk in silence. A few days later when we stopped to eat in the shade Margery refused to take another step despite his protests, beseeching loudly that we rest awhile. He shouted at her and then suddenly a soldier who was fully armed came charging through the trees and stared down at us.

"Look," whispered Jann, as he hid behind us in great trepidation, "what do you say now?"

But she told him sharply:

"Trust in our Lord God and dread no man,"
and she greeted the youth, who bowed his head, bid us Godspeed and went quietly on his way.

We had no more frightening encounters after that but the way was long, the going hard, and every night Margery confided in me that she feared some man would come and rape her. This foolish, vain idea astonished me but she would not be comforted. We were always worried that Jann might leave us, and every day it was harder to keep up with him. One night soon after, when we were lodged in the meanest of hostelries with only damp straw for bedding and no warm water to bathe our blistered feet, Margery declared she wouldn't leave on the morrow. And she was right for a fearsome storm greeted us at dawn and tore through the heavens all day so even Jann dared not set out on the road. Though the innkeeper kept a miserable house we begged him find us a wagon, which he did. We left the following morning in lighter spirits for Wilsnack where there were more relics to behold much to Margery's delight, while I continued to delight in my own secret revelation.

At Wilsnack we hired another cart for the journey on to Aachen, where more marvellous relics were to be displayed, and as Margery spoke of them she started sobbing again. The more she wept the more I saw how much it bothered Jann. He said that it might be another five weeks or more on the road before we reached Calais and advised us to take a different route rather than waste time going to Aachen. Then she began scolding him for impiety as she had done all those years ago to our fellowship on our Jerusalem journey, and it was hard to keep the peace between them. Our travelling became exceedingly trying with their arguments especially as we had to let go of the wagon and were on foot again, and still a goodly distance from Aachen.

One afternoon when we very hot and weary, we stopped at a river to fill our water bottles and saw some of Jann's countrymen on pilgrimage like us on the other side. Two young men were swimming with just their braies on and the others were drinking and feasting, cooking on a fire and making merry with music and chatter. There was a young monk there with them too. They waved and called out to us as we crossed over the little bridge.

"God's greetings to you, good pilgrims, pray come and join us."

"God bless you friends," said another. "Come share our food and before you do please go to the monastery nearby and fetch us another pitcher of wine which the good monks make there, for we have a rare thirst for drink and joy."

Margery would have none of it and turned a sour face to them.

"No, I shall not, and you should all be ashamed of yourselves, making such sport and neglecting your pilgrim vows. Rather than make merry, think of the sufferings of our Lord. And though I might seek refreshment from a house of nuns, I would never enquire for wine from a house of monks. Their duty in life is to serve God and not to ..."

The monk took umbrage and rebuked her sharply.

"Fie on you Madam, I'll thank you not to preach my Christian duty, nor to pour such sanctimonious misery on all around you."

And she answered him back, quoting the Bible words:

"They that sow in tears shall reap in songs of joy,"

and other such sentiments, and the young men heckled us, calling us English devils with tails, then turned on Jann and accused him of aiding his country's foes. He answered them in their language and when they handed him a bottle he took a swig of it and then there was more chatter and finally much laughter.

Then he came over to us, emptied our coins from his purse and wished us a safe journey home. Margery scorned him for lack of loyalty and breaking his word, but he put our bags on the ground, said he no longer wished to guide us and, joining his new friends, they moved to a further place along the riverbank, abandoning us in this strange place. Now it seemed we were in even more danger and might be hunted down as enemies ourselves. It was near nightfall and we were much distressed and Margery was weeping copiously. I took her by the hand, led her to the monastery and begged the monks that we might shelter there that night, but as to finding a way out of our sorry plight I had no idea.

The next morning we met a group of pilgrims there, who were on their way to Aachen. By signs and broken words we were able to treat with them and they agreed we might join them, though we would never have travelled with such folk in England. They were rough, plain people who begged for food along the way, while we had money enough to dine and sup at inns. They slept at night under the stars, but we paid for a bed and a roof over our heads. Whenever we came to a river it was their custom to take off their garments, pick off each other's lice and wash themselves, then sit in their shifts until their laundry was dry. Margery was much disgusted, but it came to me I had forgot the ways of country folk so I bathed too and enjoyed the freedom of the water, the sun on my skin and the prospect of a clean tunic. When she complained of fleas and dirt, I told her to shed her clothes and go into the river, but it seemed she would rather itch and scratch than show her common human nakedness to the world.

At last we came to Aachen after many hard days walking and said goodbye to our companions. We spent nearly two weeks there, resting from our journey and waiting for the day when the precious relics were to be displayed. The town was busy with many pilgrims and I watched carefully, looking for comrades to accompany us to Calais and back to England. Then a lady arrived, a widow from London, with many maids and menservants, chaplains and squires, and Margery invited her to dine, hoping we might join them. But she left early the next morning without us. We waited another day in great despondence, until we met an elderly friar who'd lost everything to thieves and asked him to be our guide. He agreed and we set off at once at a gentle pace and whenever we needed to stop he was willing and kind to us.

After some time he took us to a hostelry where we rested, but just as we were having our refreshment, Margery saw the London widow again and swiftly dismissing the friar, insisted I take our bags and rushed after her. But it was a rash decision for when she spoke to the widow she had no welcome in her heart.

"What! Do you think to go with me? No, I'll not get involved with the two of you, so help me God," and calling to her company, she turned away. We were once again alone, without a guide.

We were of course misguided in thinking that fellow pilgrims in a foreign land would be full of Christian charity. Besides we were in a wretched condition, having made little preparation for this journey. I'd packed in haste and had taken my old pilgrim tunic but it was frayed and threadbare, nor had I been able to launder Margery's white garments for some long time, which were soiled and torn, and our boots were worn and broken. For certain we must have seemed truly crazed rushing from one pilgrim group to another, Margery weeping noisily and I, who so used to being invisible that I wondered if people saw me or only the shadow of a wraith. And no one would have expected two old ladies like us to be wandering alone along the road.

Margery sobbed piteously at this new predicament and I did my best to reassure her as we waited lost and in sad despair by the wayside. Then, just as it began to grow dark, we saw the old friar again and he welcomed us, though there was no longer room for us at the inn. So he led us through a wood where there was a small dwelling. And though they had no lodgings, the good people let us sleep in their barn and brought us milk and bread and bracken that we might lie on.

We left at dawn and it was another two weeks until we came to Calais, making a slow and weary journey up and down hills, across valleys and streams, then trudging through sand dunes with little to eat or drink, parched by the sun, and suffering further discomfort in mean lodgings every night. But when we finally arrived, frail and footsore, we were truly as gay as larks, cheered by the sound of English voices and the promise of a comfortable bed and clean water. And so we paid the friar for his service and found an inn close by the harbour.

We stayed in Calais for several days, worn out from our travels but happy to be so near home. A kindly woman let me use her tub and I washed and mended our clothes and took our boots to be newly cobbled, while Margery found acquaintances thereabouts, for the Lynn merchants often did trade in this town. We spoke together of the dangers we'd endured and she said that now our journeyings were at an end she was resolved, once home again, to ask Spryngolde to write the account of this her last pilgrimage. And then she thanked me for my service.

I was heartened by her kindness and that gave me courage to speak.

"I've served you Margery for many years and tried to be as sometime sister to you. I've accompanied you on all your travels and kept you safe. Now that you have the wish to tell this, your last story, the story of your pilgrimage not mine I think you'll no longer need my service. So I beg you pay me what you owe me once we're back in Lynn, that I may set up home and give shelter to two little girls. I also need money for my keep. It was our father's wish and you owe it to me."

She stared at me as if she'd never seen me before, and I waited for an answer but there was none. So, I continued:

"There's one more thing. Come what may, I'll never wash your clothes again. You chose to make this display of your virgin piety, so it's mete you launder them yourself."

She opened her mouth to say something but I stopped her.

"Never again, Margery."

And she was speechless, at last.

The widow from London was also in Calais, waiting for a vessel that was England-bound and though I cautioned her, Margery was determined to take the same ship as she. When she learnt which one it was, she bid me take our bags there, while she said prayers at Notre-Dame for our safe crossing. I waited for her to come on board, but she did not, nor did the widow and her company. I dared not leave as I'd stowed our belongings and paid for our passage.

Then another vessel in the harbour raised anchor and set sail, and I rushed to ask our captain whither it was bound. To Dover, he said, but he would not now be leaving until other passengers joined us. I wondered if either Margery or I had mistaken the name of the ship, then guessed that in her eagerness to travel with the widow she had forgot me and followed her instead. For one moment I felt betrayed. But then I remembered myself and felt pity for her, that she always needed to be seen and praised in exalted company. I was no longer pained by her malice and meanness and even forgave her for not once calling me by my proper name, only Missie or Matty and a few times, strangely, Marion as if she really did not know who I was.

I had come to peace at last and understood the devils she had to fight, for ever needing to be accepted, as if she were nothing unless she were accorded the worship she felt was her due as the honourable daughter of the oft times Mayor of Lynn. At the same time she craved to be acknowledged and admired as the meek and dutiful daughter of our Lord. Whereas I just did not want to be overlooked. But still I worried what I might do when we came to Dover, and hoped she'd be waiting there for me.

We did not leave until the following morning. A ship newly arrived in Calais brought reports of storms along the English coast and our captain decided to wait until the winds lessened. I remained on board and when we did set sail, the weather was fair and the white cliffs of Dover clearly visible, beckoning us home. It was an easy crossing and I was much cheered by an English couple from Calais, Nicholas, a tall weather-beaten bearded sea captain and Constance his tiny graceful wife. They were not young, some sixty winters old or more like me, travelling to Canterbury on pilgrimage and also to visit family.

I enquired of Margery as soon as we docked and a sailor recalled seeing an old woman, much distressed and on her own, who'd departed for Canterbury the day before. My new friends took me to the pilgrim's hostel and promised to help me search her out in Canterbury, but when we came there no one knew of Margery, and I was vexed since my friends had hurried to help me find her. But they were gentle and said they were grateful for my company since I was able to tell them all there was to see in the cathedral. And though it was familiar, I saw everything anew with my own true eyes and not through Margery's tales and tears. We were there two days and happily I met one of Margery's acquaintances who said she'd borrowed money from him to hire a man to take her to London. But I was still troubled, not knowing how I might now return to Lynn and Constance saw my distress and laid her arm on mine.

"Fear not, good soul, we'll take care of you, won't we Nicholas?"

"Of course we shall, dear heart. Now mistress, cast your cares

314

aside. On all my many voyages I've learnt just one thing, never to be a fair-weather sailor. Hard times will come and I've known many I can tell you that, but here I am, hale and hearty …"

And stroking his beard with one hand, he held Constance's hand with the other.

"… Yes, hale and hearty, though I've been becalmed for weeks on end, and I and all my crew near death from lack of sustenance, and at other times my barque's been torn by tempests and us near drowning. But here I am and I've learnt to share my troubles and those of others. Is that not so, my dear Constance?"

"Yes it is, dear Nicholas."

"So you shall come back to Dover with us and stay for a few days with my uncle Robert, and take some care of him so his wench can have a rest, and for your service we'll give you bed and board. Then we'll take a boat to Lynn for I am more accustomed to travel by sea than land. And once there you'll take us to the Nicholas church as we wish to see the new roof, which I hear tell is adorned with flying angels and each one playing a different instrument, and you will come with us. Is that not so, Constance?"

"Aye that is so Nicholas."

"And we have much to thank St Nicholas for, don't we my sweet heart?"

"Yes Nicholas, yes we do."

"You see mistress, whene'er I went about my business on the seas, Constance prayed to the good, kind Nicholas that he might keep me safe."

"That I did for true, prayed every day in front of the beautiful image you made of him, carved out of driftwood, prayed my man might come safely home."

"And of course, I did, didn't I Constance?

"That you did, Nicholas."

"And then on my return, before we'd even feasted we played music, the two of us, I on my pipe and tabor and she, my dearest Constance, with her lute, to entertain the saint and give thanks for his protection. So now you'll do us this favour, come back with us to Dover, then on to Lynn and give thanks in his chapel for all your safe journeyings, and at last you'll be comfortably home."

And so it was decided between the two of them, in their joy and love for each other and their simple, sincere beliefs. I rejoiced in their friendship as we returned to Dover.

Nicholas's uncle was lean and lanky, with a balding pate and deep-set sea-blue eyes. He was just fifteen years older than Nicholas whose own father William had been the oldest of many brothers and he, Robert, the youngest. They'd worked together in their youth as shipwrights in Lynn, helping to build trading vessels and repair those that had suffered damage on the seas. Though he was now infirm in body, his memory was as clear as seawater on the stillest of days, and he loved to gossip and tell stories. He too had travelled to the Holy Land so we had much to talk about.

So it was that I had another strange encounter, and am reminded of the mosaic artists I'd seen working at their craft at the Church of Gold in Venice. I'd watched them work one afternoon as they took the little coloured stone and glass pieces, and put them here and there as if they saw the invisible outlines of their pattern on the empty surface. It was only when they'd laid the final fragments that everything fell into place and the image became distinct. And that's how it was, as Robert and

I sat talking together, that the last mystery of my life became miraculously clear.

It was the morning before we were going to set sail for Lynn, warm again after several chilly days. I'd taken Robert to sit outside in the sun while Nicholas and Constance had gone to the market and I was content listening to his stories, and he was happy to hear mine. As I was recounting some adventure, he suddenly held my chin in both hands and tilted my face towards his.

"I hadn't noticed your eyes when we were inside but now I see them true. I've only seen such odd eyes once before and that was a strange and tragic tale."

Before I had even time to miss a heartbeat he began his story, and it was as if I was hearing something I'd known always and forever.

"It was very many summers ago near springtide as I recall, for it was still the season of gales. I was working with my brother William in our yard in Lynn, when a message came calling us to repair a ship we'd built that was urgently needed for trade. John Brunham it was who summoned us, a merchant of that town, and he needed it shipshape fast as it was commissioned for a voyage. He came most every day to oversee the work, impatient for it to be finished. And soon it was near done and he came to have account of the cost.

He returned the next day when there was just a day's work left and spoke privately to William, then sent him back home alone with a purse of money and asked me to finish on my own. He was in a rare rush and urged William to make haste. He seemed both happy and sad, joyous because his lady had just given birth to a little girl-child but I did not know the cause of his distress.

William said Brunham had asked him to take a message

to his wife, that she come back with him at once. I thought this strange for she'd not long given birth, but Alyson was a most obedient woman. Brunham told me to send for him the moment they returned and so I did. Then he came and he had a babe with him, a little girl, hidden in his cloak, an orphan whom he'd vowed to look after. He said he could find no wet-nurse and beseeched Alyson to do this service, promising he'd send more monies for her care. And in their kindness, and from the delight of having children of their own, my brother and his wife agreed to foster this motherless babe.

She was a mere mite of a thing, a tiny little creature. But though Alyson nursed her as her very own, she did not thrive and died within the year. And they said her fate could never have been certain for she was torn in two with one little blue eye looking into the distance seeking the heavens, the other brown eye focused here on earth."

And so the pattern was complete. Now I knew what Brunham meant when he told Margery to support two orphan girls in his memory, and I remembered too my sometime childhood happiness, chatting to my unseen sister, my Marion, sharing my fancies with her, as well as those moments of deep, dark sadness when I knew something had been broken and could never be mended. And in my sorrow all that time thinking I was alone, I knew now I was truly alone, but felt a heavy burden had been lifted from me. It was as if I had for years been living two lives and now had just this one, my very own.

Nicholas and Constance came back soon after and Robert entertained us with his tales. I was content to let them talk and smiled at his stories, but my inner smile came from the knowledge deep within me that, despite the death of this unknown sister, I'd been granted the gift of life. Who needs miracles and visions, penance and piety, God and the demons, Satan and the saints, when life itself is a miracle even with all its sorrows and joys?

The weather was fair and we left at dawn, making good headway with a steady wind and anchored at Lynn before nightfall. I was safely home.

Margery returned some weeks later but I was not worried as she'd sent word of her arrival in London. Reynald brought her back and bid her go straightway to Spryngolde who was angry she'd travelled over the seas without his permission. She was in truth, most upset by his unkind words, humbled herself and begged his pardon. But he imposed a heavy penance and forbade her attendance at any church in Lynn for several months.

So she had no opportunity to tell the townsfolk of her last pilgrimage and did not even talk to me about those weeks after we parted at Calais. It seemed I was to blame again for abandoning her, but I held my tongue, for she looked frail and soon took to her bed with an ague. She stayed there for many weeks until Spryngolde released her from her penance and she was forgiven and happy again. So finally I only heard her story when she and Spryngolde were working on her second book, and of course I was not in it, but it is true I was not with her after she'd sailed for Dover.

In this book she told that when she arrived after a stormy crossing, the widow brushed her off again, refusing to let her travel with her to London. So she went to a poor man's house, begged him to take her to Canterbury, borrowed money and came to London still in her pilgrim sackcloth, which is true too because our bags with her clean white garments were on board my ship. She was much ashamed to be seen so commonly dressed and hid from her friends until she had new clothes made.

Now here's a strange tale that she recounted in her book. She told how she was often invited to stay and dine with strangers and talked much of God's love, of her holy visions, sacred sentiments and many pilgrimages. She said she flattered no one, condemned all pompous fashions and behaviours and rebuked cursers, liars and other vicious people. All this she dictated to Spryngolde, and it was nothing new. But there was more. She also told that it happened once when she was with strangers who'd come to listen to her, she heard them whispering about a woman from Lynn who was wont to find fault with everyone, especially those folk who liked fine food, while she said she herself ate only the simplest, humblest pie. And some of the people there then joked about that false, pretending hypocrite who always left the coarse meats and helped herself to the most tasty food. They said she'd murmur to herself,

"False flesh you shall eat no good meat,"

"False flesh you would now eat red herring but shall not have your will."

"False flesh you shall eat no herring, but only eat the pike." And then she would give in to temptation and pile her platter high with the most delicious dishes. But she could not abide being teased and so revealed herself, then said she won them all over with her story-telling and wise words.

Hearing this part of her tale, a memory came back to me from long ago. It was after the time Margery came with Brunham to my home when we were children. Of course I did not know then who they were, or how our lives would be so tightly woven and tangled together. I envied her her fine clothes and hated her too since she would not play with me, but only found occasion to tease me because my hair was not braided and I wore no shoes.

After they left I was cross with everyone, tormented the cat, kicked the boys and settled into a stubborn sulk, and Nanna came to find me where I hid, wailing and complaining in the barn where a broody hen was sitting. She held me firmly in her arms, as she always did when she had something important to say, until I stopped fighting. I know now that those arms were the bonds of love and it was only from this seat of affection that she could feed me her wisdom. I recall her exact words and the rhyme she told me then, as is often the way when we grow old that the events of yesterday are forgot while those of years ago come back with startling freshness.

"Listen girling, stop your tears and hark to what I say. I'll tell you a rhyme my own grand-dam learnt me when I was but a child and now I'll teach it you. And it goes like this ...

'A pike of ancient pedigree
came from his rivulet to the sea,
and with no title to be vain
treated the sea-fish with disdain.
A herring then indignant said,
"What folly has thee hither led?
Thou mightest be something in thy stream
but here thou'll meet with no esteem."'

I knew well what pike was as we lived by a stream and my uncle had the right to take one pike for our dinner every month. We all enjoyed those pike days because it was much tastier than herring which we had on all the other fish days. But I had to ask what disdain and esteem meant, was puzzled that a pike might look down on a herring, and wondered why the herring scolded the pike and called it foolish, until Nanna explained that herrings were common and ordinary and lived in the sea where there were many other kinds of fish.

"The sea is much more water than you could ever imagine, greater in length and breadth than all the fields and everything that lies beyond our farm, the forest, heath and marsh. I only saw it once when I was a littl'un, as little as you are now, and I was much mazed by it for it went on and on and never seemed to end.

Now the herring we eat oftentimes swim in that very big sea and as there are hundreds and thousands of them, they don't think themselves as something special. But the pike only knows the shallow, weedy stretches of the stream where she lives, waiting for small fry that swim above her so she can snap them up for dinner. And because she's bigger than any fish she sees from the bottom of her stream, she believes she's a very exceptional fish, much more important than a common herring.

So remember this my dear sweet creature, we mustn't judge others as less than we are, as that pike does who believes she is grander than anyone else, for we're all of us quite ordinary just like herring."

And she coaxed me out of my huff as she held me tight and made me laugh when she ruffled my hair, gave it a sniff and said I was the tastiest, most scrumptious fish she had ever smelt and she was going to eat me up.

The second part of Margery's book doesn't say how long she spent in London, but it tells how she was scorned for sobbing in all the churches where she went to worship, and so she stumbled from one to another. Then she travelled to Syon Abbey, a new foundation of the nuns of St Bridget. I don't know how long she was there, but at last she met Reynald who brought her home.

After she recovered from her sickness and Spryngolde had

forgiven her, they became good friends again and he visited often, rewriting the first book about her life and travels to the Holy Land, then setting down the story of her German pilgrimage. She was much engaged with this and rarely went out, so when I was in the market, people often asked me if she were sick. They missed her, they said, though I think what they really missed was teasing her until they found someone else to taunt, though this poor soul was truly devoid of her wits.

There had for many years been an ancient, ugly fishwife who never left the docks. This mad old scold spent all the hours of the day wandering along the quays, and would have been at it all night too had the Watchman not always taken her to her hovel-home at sundown. She did indeed look much like a fish and never seemed to close her eyes, which were red and rheumy and ran with pus. She hobbled everywhere, I think she was near blind, and carried an old and broken oar to mark her stumbling way, using it like a broom to sweep the rubbish out of her path. She made this silent, busy progress for several years. Then one day, when I'd gone to purchase fish, I heard much tumult by the moorings where a noisy crowd had gathered and there she was, standing on a fish crate, sermonising in strange and strident tones.

"Harken to you all and everyone, listen to me, to me myself, to my worthy words, for the true truth has been revealed to me in reverend revelations by our good sovereign Lord and King. And you must pay holy heed to me and listen well, to secure the safety of your souls, and save your sorrowful selves."

The mob whistled and cackled, but she paid no notice and carried on.

"All those fishy fishes in the salty seas, the mackerel, haddock, plaice and merling, brill, butts, skate and sparling, flathe, garfish, turbot and sole, all those fishy fish have declared to me, so now I know it, like those disciplinary disciples, I now know I can separate the heavenly bad from the wickedly good."

There were more hisses, hoots and guffaws but this did not distract her.

"Aye, and I know you, know you all and who of you is truly bad. And I tell you this truly, and this is the true truth, that if you do not bow down before the Good Fish then the horny lecherous Leviathan will come out of the deep and drag you down, all you sinful sinners, into the hellish hellmouth of his lair."

The townsfolk sniggered and scoffed and pelted her with rotten eggs and old cabbages until one of the Grey Friars bid them desist and let her be. Poor old woman, she was indeed no holy fool, but simply crazed.

So the years passed quietly. Margery had many debts to repay and when I asked for my wages she put me off and said to be content that at least I had my keep. And I was grateful for that since these were very lean years, a time of failed harvests, worse than we'd ever known, and a return of the pestilence. In the fields sheep and cattle died of the murrain and in some parts of the country there was famine, though at least we were spared that as there was always fish to eat. And I no longer felt the need to leave Margery for she no longer had power over me. I was grateful too that both she and I had been able to tame our mad minds back to clarity.

Over the seas our war with France did not prosper, and I was told a strange tale, which the townsfolk heard from the returning soldiers. It was said that the French fortunes had suddenly turned after the intercession of a young peasant maid called Joan. She had from the age of twelve received many visions of saints who told her to be a good girl and go to church, and later they urged her to drive the English out of France. Although she remained a maiden she eschewed wearing white and instead cut her hair, dressed as a knight and rode into battle. She too, they said, had been afflicted by the gift of tears, but the French soldiers were greatly inspired by her and fought fiercely and so regained many of their territories, which had formerly been held by the English.

Then she was captured, tried by Lord Bedford who was at that time regent in France, condemned as a heretic and burnt at the stake, while still not yet twenty years old. This was the same Lord Bedford whose men arrested Margery all those years ago and called me heretic, and I too might have been burnt had not Archbishop Bowet exonerated me and let us go. And I marvel that both my mistress and this young maid were inspired by their visions but in such different fashions. And I thought God does indeed does work in mysterious ways.

When Margery's books were finished, Spryngolde took them away so that some of his friends might read them. She was now free to go out again but no longer quarrelled with our neighbours and her tears seemed to have dried up. She also had a new devotion and often went to the Holy Trinity chapel. Then one day an alderman came, bringing an invitation asking her to join their guild. She was much pleased and immediately had a new gown made for the occasion of her admittance feast, in the finest white cloth. She did indeed look radiant, despite her great age, as I accompanied her to the door of the new Trinity Guildhall. She must have comported herself well as she was invited again the following year though was by then too ill to attend. She died a few weeks later.

As I write this I smile, thinking even now as I'm coming to the end of my story, Margery still wants to have the last word.

Now I'm nearly finished I've been asking myself why I've been writing this. In the early days I thought it was to have my revenge and tell the true story. But recording my memories has helped me know myself a little better and I've learnt that truth has many faces, as I smiled and wept at what I felt and thought, and have come to understand that others think and feel in their own ways. So both Margery's book and mine are true, even if they tell different stories in part.

I remember my unease when first we left to go over the seas. I did not have the same lofty aspirations as Margery, who sought sanctity and perfection. I was more like those pilgrims who believed that if they made great sacrifices and endured much hardship, they could purge themselves of sin and win forgiveness. But then I learnt that was not my way. And though I hated the doubt and hardship I found a sometime unfamiliar courage to accept each new burden as it came and bear my grief with patience and fortitude.

I have come to understand that putting down my story was what I needed to do to make sense of my pilgrimage in life, to talk to someone who does not know me, who will not judge me, like you perhaps, a stranger, reading what I've written. In sharing my story with you, you may know me and I can make all my doubts, my good and evil intentions, my hopes and fears, real … then cast them out into the world like the stones in my shoe.

I'd thought at one time I might find the answer in books and for sure the Bible taught me much. But finally all that really counted was my own truth and the hard task of forgiving those who let me down. And I now know that I did not have a great dream like Margery but was always making my way, step by faltering step, on my own uncertain pilgrimage towards acceptance and joy. I also know that I am the same as Margery, despite our many differences, but have been seeking salvation on an untrodden path. And then I ask myself again and again, if perhaps our destinations were not somewhat the same after all.

9

Bishop's Lynn, July 29th 1443

'some safe harbour'

I woke early as I have for many years now. As the sands of my life diminish, so it is as if someone urges me to live every daylight moment and I'm thankful for that even though I miss the comfort of sleep, not that sleep is much comfort with all my aches and pains. And there is one more story I need to set down but have no more parchment so must go to Lynn and buy some.

The sky was streaked with red and violet as the sun rose this morning, more a winter sky than the heavenly blue of summer dawns. Seeing it I was reminded of the purple robe of Our Lord and laughed, thinking Margery would have been proud of me, seeing Jesus in everything. I watched the gathering of the rooks, their raucous, eerie antics, then busied myself with the household chores. I do them by myself since Agnes is dead and Hilda has married a young lad in the town.

It is now steamy hot and thunderous sultry and I'm slow about my work, unsteady on my feet, and know I must make haste to get to town before a storm comes and it grows dark. The shortest way is along the riverbank but if I'm quick I'll soon be back. But first I need to write down the dream, which woke me in the night. It was one of those dreams that seem to belong to a very different but familiar realm and the images were clear and bright. And I was not in it, yet it was as if I were observing it in the present time of that very moment.

Afterword

The main character in this book is almost entirely fictitious although the rest of it is based on fact. Margery Kempe was a real person. The Book of Margery Kempe was first transcribed by Margery's priest at her dictation in the 1430s, in Bishops Lynn. It was later copied some time before 1450, then both were lost and the copy was subsequently rediscovered in 1934 stuffed in the back of a cupboard. Prior to that nothing was known of Margery except for a few excerpts from her book, which had been included in a collection of sacred tracts printed in the early sixteenth century. From the content of these it was generally thought she was a mystic, but after the discovery of the complete text of her book came controversy. The jury is still out.

There are now numerous articles, books and websites about Margery Kempe. The book you hold here is not, however, another one. While she was undoubtedly on a spiritual quest as is clear from the many visions and meditations recorded in her book, she tells us very little about the external details of her life – and this was a woman who suffered a period of insanity after the birth of her first child followed by another thirteen pregnancies, who set up and subsequently failed at two businesses, who then got a separation from her husband and travelled to Jerusalem, Rome and Santiago in her forties and continued her pilgrimages to Danzig and Germany in her sixties. The absence of personal detail is disappointing because her book is often described as the first known autobiography of a woman written in English.

There is perhaps a good reason for this lacuna which is that the Margery who is portrayed in "her" book is largely the creation of her priestly scribe: his fiction of a sinful woman whose lust and arrogance are ultimately redeemed by never-ending confessions and repentance. At times we do hear her voice especially when she is argumentative or determined to get her own way, but the fervent and florid devotions, which she recounts in great detail, seem less idiosyncratic and rather more indicative of the extroverted emotional sensibility which was a collective aspect of late medieval popular religion. Nor can her meditations be compared to the introverted revelations of her more famous contemporary Julian of Norwich, whom she twice visited.

I have used most of the events and many of the actual conversations that are recorded in her book in my story although Margery is not the central character, much as I suspect she would have liked to be. I have chosen instead to write her maidservant's tale about whom nothing is known except that she existed. In Margery's book she quarrelled with this maidservant whilst on pilgrimage to Jerusalem and then again in Rome (this was not unusual, Margery quarrelled with everyone) after which she is not referred to again. She just disappears. But I think it most unlikely that a woman of Margery's background would not always have had a maidservant with her, and even if she is not mentioned it does not mean she was not there. In the Middle Ages a maidservant was often as much a companion as a servant and considered part of the family, sometimes sharing a bed with her mistress and acting as confidante. And while they may not have been of the same social class, Margery's maidservant is likely have been reasonably well born and have had some education.

What then does the Margery of The Book of Margery Kempe not tell us? She appears to have had scant self-knowledge or insight so there is very little about herself, her daily life, her numerous pregnancies and experience of childbirth. In fact only one of her children is ever mentioned. We read little about how she travelled to all those pilgrimage sites, or about sailing to the Holy Land and what it and the other countries she visited were like. There is no mention of the turbulent times in which she lived, the so-called 'Peasants Revolt,' the five kings who reigned during her lifetime (one was murdered, another deposed), the effects of the Black Death on the economy and social structure, the wars with France and burning of Joan of Arc, the rise of literacy or Wycliffe's English Bible and the subsequent movement known as Lollardy.

It would be surprising if none of these events had an impact on her life or coloured her experiences. So I asked her maidservant to tell the story and discovered she had a very different tale to tell. Numerous books were written in the Middle Ages about pilgrimage, many with useful tips about what to take, what to see, what to avoid and how to make the appropriate arrangements. Below are a few titles, which I found very informative since they all draw on contemporary accounts and filled some of the gaps in Margery's book:

H.F.M. Prescott, *Jerusalem Journey* (London 1954)

R.J Mitchell, *The Spring Voyage* (London 1964)

H. & M.-H. Davies, *Holy Days and Holidays; the Medieval Pilgrimage to Compostela* (London 1982)

Diana Webb, *Pilgrimage in Medieval England* (London 2000)

Jonathan Sumption, *Pilgrimage* (London 2002)

And for Margery's book see also:
Anthony Goodman's *Margery Kempe and her World* (Essex 2002)
Anthony Bale, *Margery Kempe: A Mixed Life* (Reaktion Books 2021)

In my dream I see a storm-torn vessel, mast broken, rigging loose, sails rent, hull split, the wood all rotten. It looks as if it must surely sink as it dips low in the water at the bow. I was reminded of all those perilous voyages, my fear of hellfire, shipwreck, the deaths of my uncle, Mary and Isolde, and all the hurt and damage I had suffered over the years. But then I see it has come to rest in some safe harbour and is perfectly still. And as I look, it slowly starts to change and soon becomes a beautiful galleon, cunningly crafted out of amber, like the one I saw some years ago hanging from the ceiling at the Arthushof in Danzig.

I remembered then an old man saying that golden amber is the tears of angels. And a strange thought came to me and I wondered why this now, and where my next pilgrimage will bring me.

So I will hasten to go, that you shall hear the last of my story on my return.